THE MAGIC OF THAT FIRST JOB

could be magical indeed, if you happen to have the talent for it. But exactly what kind of career might a sorcerer or enchantress end up with these days? Some of fantasy's most imaginative spell casters tackle that very question in such stories as:

"Audition"—When you're in corporate security, stopping profit-threatening breaches—whether mundane or magical—is what the job is all about. But this time the stakes were higher than he could imagine. . . .

"Back Door Magic"—Could you run a magic shop successfully when you were positive you had no magic of your own?

"Stocks and Bondage"—How could you avoid fulfilling a clause that had been magicked into your contract after you'd signed it?

"Chocolate Alchemy"—The chocolates she created were literally enchanting but even magic couldn't seem to keep the corporate wolves from her door. . . .

WIZARDS, INC.

More Journeys of the Imagination Brought to You by DAW Books:

UNDER COVER OF DARKNESS *Edited by Julie E. Czerneda and Jana Paniccia.* Fourteen all-original tales of the true powers that work behind the scenes—the covert masters of time, space and destiny. . . . From an unexpected ally who aids Lawrence in Arabia, to an assassin hired to target the one person he'd never want to kill, to a young woman who stumbles into an elfin war in the heart of London, to a man who steals time—here are unforgettable tales that will start you wondering whether someone is watching you from the shadows or changing your destiny at this very moment. . . .

IF I WERE AN EVIL OVERLORD *Edited by Martin H. Greenberg and Russell Davis.* The fourteen original tales in this volume run the gamut from humorous to serious, fantasy to science fiction. These are stories for anyone who has ever played the role of an Evil Overlord, or has defeated an Evil Overlord, or would like to become an Evil Overlord. After all, isn't it more fun to be the "bad guy"?

ARMY OF THE FANTASTIC *Edited by John Marco and John Helfers.* Thirteen original tales of battles fought by magical creatures in fantastical realms, and our own transformed world. . . . Includes stories by Jean Rabe, Rick Hautala, Fiona Patton, Tim Waggoner, Alan Dean Foster, Tanya Huff, Mickey Zucker Reichert, and more.

WIZARDS, INC.

Edited by Martin H. Greenberg
and Loren L. Coleman

DAW BOOKS, INC.
DONALD A. WOLLHEIM, FOUNDER
375 Hudson Street, New York, NY 10014

ELIZABETH R. WOLLHEIM
SHEILA E. GILBERT
PUBLISHERS
http://www.dawbooks.com

First Printing, November 2007
1   2   3   4   5   6   7   8   9

ACKNOWLEDGMENTS

CONTENTS

Foreward   1
Loren L. Coleman

Jamaica   3
Orson Scott Card

Audition   29
Steve Perry

Back Door Magic   47
Phaedra M. Weldon

Occupational Hazard   87
Mike Resnick

Ties That Bind   79
Annie Reed

Hostile Takeover   96
Nina Kiriki Hoffman

A Different Way into the Life   120
Jay Lake

Disaster Relief   139
    Kristine Kathryn Rusch

KidPro   163
    Laura Anne Gilman

Stocks and Bondage   177
    Esther M. Friesner

The Keeper of the Morals   200
    Dean Wesley Smith

Cosmic Balances Inc.   222
    Kristine Grayson

Theobroma   239
    Diane Duane

Chocolate Alchemy   266
    Lisa Silverthorne

No Rest for the Wicked   283
    Michael A. Stackpole

FOREWARD

by Loren L. Coleman

THERE are two types of people in the world . . .
You've heard this one, right? Often as the lead-
in to some generalization meant to pass as wisdom for
the ages (or at least for the next few moments). A
little armchair philosophy, if you please. I've been as
guilty of it as the next man, I'm sure. But stay with
me a moment longer.

I have a point to make this time.

Promise.

So: There are two types of people in the world.
Those who choose their profession, and those whose
profession chooses them.

It may not be Nietzsche, but I am fairly certain that
almost everyone reading this anthology can relate. In
fact, I'm sure you have a story of your own, and have
had many conversations on this topic. Because we
can't help talking about what we do for a living. What
it's like. How we got started. It's a great topic—a *safe*,
comfortable topic—for cocktail parties, among your
neighbors, and for people who are trapped in a stuck
elevator. One of the easiest questions you can ask a
person. *What do you do for a living?* I know I've been
put on the spot many times in my life.

I'm a student. *Good for you. What are you studying?*

1

What made you interested in that field? How soon until you graduate?

I'm in the Navy. *What ship are you on? What is it you do? What made you choose that branch? Did you look to see what the <insert other military service> had to offer?*

Right now, I'm a stay-at-home dad. *Oh, how old is your child? Boy? Girl? Do you have pictures? Umm, so what is it your wife does?*

I'm a writer. *Really? What is it you write? How many books have you published? How did you get into* that?

I'm a wizard . . .

Imagine the other people in *that* elevator. What questions would they have? And what kind of stories would the wizard be able to tell? It's a good hour or better until the fire department can get everyone out safely. Here's a captive audience, most of them caught up in the minutia of normal, everyday life. You've heard the lawyer and the carpenter already tell their tales. Why not break the ice and try (try very hard) to relate?

Which is what you will find in the following pages. Fifteen tales from that *other* person in the room. The *slightly off* one. The one whom you've wondered about, sure he or she had some fascinating story to tell. You were right. From the corporate "hired gun" to the small business owner to one of heaven's own CPAs (that would be Certified Piety Accountants)— come see how the *other side* answers their call to the daily grind. I'm sure you will be as fascinated by these tales as I. Because there are still two kinds of people in the world.

Those who want to believe in magic.

And those of us who already do.

Enjoy!

Jamaica

by Orson Scott Card

A P CHEMISTRY was a complete scam, and Jam
Fisher knew it. Riddle High School was the cess-
pool of the county school system. Somebody in the
superintendent's office came up with a completely logical solution: since statistics proved that high schools
with the highest enrollment in Advanced Placement
courses showed the highest rates of graduation and
college placement, they would make *all* the students
at Riddle High take AP courses.

How dumb do you have to be to believe something
like *that?* Dumb enough, apparently, to go to college,
get an Ed.D, and then work in the Riddle County
School System.

Jam was one of the few kids at Riddle who would
have taken AP Chemistry anyway. But now, instead
of studying with other kids who were serious about
learning something, he was stuck in a class with a
bunch of goof-offs, dumbasses, and idiots.

Which he knew wasn't fair. They weren't actually
dumb, they were simply out of their depth. *They* didn't
have a college-grad mom like Jam did, or have a small
shelf of books in the living room which were written
by relatives (but read by almost nobody).

Fair or not, the result was predictable. In order to
have a hope of teaching anybody anything, they were

dumbing down the curriculum, and so Jam would have to work twice as hard to educate himself in order to do decently on the AP tests. Mom would go ballistic if he didn't ace them all and come out of high school with a whole year of college credits. "If you don't have a full-ride scholarship, you'll be at Riddle Tech, and that means you'll be qualified—barely—for janitorial work."

And here he was on the first day of class in his junior year, listening to some overly chummy teacher making chemistry into a joke.

"What I have here," said Mr. Laudon, "is a philosopher's stone. Supposedly it could change any common metal into gold, back in the days of alchemy." He handed it to Amahl Piercey in the first row. "So before we go any further, I want every one of you to hold it—squeeze it, taste it, stick it up your nose, I don't care—"

"If I'm spose to taste it, I don't want it up Amahl's nose," said Ceena Robles. Which provoked laughter. Meanwhile, Amahl, not much of a clown, had merely squeezed it, shrugged, and passed it back.

The stone was passed hand to hand up and down the rows. Jam saw that it looked like amber—yellowy and translucent. But nobody seemed to notice anything special about it, till it got to Rhonda Jones. She yelped when she got it handed to her and dropped it on the floor. It rolled crookedly under another desk.

"It burned me!" she said.

Shocked you, you mean, thought Jam. *Amber builds up an electric charge. That's the trick Mr. Laudon must mean to play on us.*

But Jam kept his thoughts to himself. The last thing he needed was to have Laudon as an enemy. He'd done a year where he antagonized a teacher and it wasn't fun—or good for the grades.

"Pick it up," said Laudon. "No, not you, her. The one who dropped it."

"My name is Rhonda," she said, "and I'm not picking it up."

"Rhonda." Laudon scanned the roll sheet. "Jones. Yes, you *will* pick it up, and now, and squeeze it tightly."

Rhonda got that stubborn look and folded her arms across her chest.

And with a resigned feeling, Jam spoke up to take the heat off her. "Is this an experiment or something?" asked Jam.

Laudon glared at him. *Good start, Jam.* "I'm talking to Miz Jones here."

"I'm just wondering what's so important," said Jam. "It's not as if there's such a thing as a philosopher's stone. It's just amber that builds up an electric charge and shocked her when she got it."

"Oh, excuse me," said Laudon, looking at the roll. "Yep, I checked, and right here it says that *I'm* the teacher here. Who are *you?*"

"Jam Fisher."

"Jam? Oh, I see. That's a nickname for *Jamaica* Fisher. I've never heard of a *boy* named Jamaica."

Some titters from the class, but not many, because in the lower grades Jam had been through bloody fights with anybody who said Jamaica was a girl's name.

"And yet you have the evidence right there in your hands," said Jam. "Doesn't the roll have a little M or F by our names?"

"It's gallant of you, Mr. Fisher, to try to rescue Miz Jones, but she *will* pick up that stone."

Jam knew he was committing academic suicide, but there was something in him that would not tolerate a bully. He got up, strode forward. Laudon backed away a step, probably afraid Jam intended to hit him. But all Jam did was reach down under the desk where the stone had rolled and reach out to pick it up.

The next thing he was aware of was somebody slapping his face. It stung, and Jam lashed out to slap back. Only his hand barely moved. He was so weak he couldn't lift his arm more than an inch before it fell back to the floor, spent.

The floor? What was he doing, lying on his back on the floor?

"Open your eyes, Mr. Fisher," commanded Laudon. "I need to see if your pupils are dilated."

What is this, a drug test?

Jam *meant* to say it. But his mouth didn't move.

Another slap.

"Stop it!" he shouted.

Or, rather, whispered.

"Open your eyes."

With some fluttering, Jam finally complied.

"No concussion. No doubt your brain is in its original condition, despite having hit the floor. You—the two of you—help him stand up."

"No, thanks," murmured Jam.

But the two students delegated to help him were more afraid of Laudon's glare than Jam's protest.

"I'll throw up," Jam said. Or started to say. But the last part came out in a gush of lunch. By good fortune, it landed between desks, but it still got all over Jam's shoes, and the shoes and pantlegs of everyone near him.

"I think he needs to go to the nurse," said Rhonda.

"Need to lie down," Jam said. Whereupon he fainted again, which accomplished his stated objective.

He woke up the next time in the nurse's office. He heard her talking on the phone. "I can call an ambulance for him," the nurse was saying, "but school policy does not allow us to transport a sick or injured student in private vehicles. Yes, I know you wouldn't sue me, but I'm not worried about getting sued, I'm worried about losing my job. You don't have a job for a fired nurse, do you? Then let's not argue about the policy. Either I call an ambulance, or you come get him, Miz Fisher, or I keep him here to infect every other student who comes in here."

"I'm not sick," murmured Jam.

"Now he's saying he's not sick," said the nurse, "even though he still has puke on his shoes. Yes, ma'am, 'puke' is official nurse lingo for vomitus. We speak English nowadays, even in the best nursing schools."

"Tell her not to come. I'm okay," whispered Jam.

"He says for you not to come, he's okay. Weak as a baby, probably delirious, but by no means should you leave work to come get him."

Within twenty minutes, Mother was there.

So was Mr. Laudon. "Before you take him, I want it back," he said to Jam.

"Want what?" asked Mother. "Are you accusing my son of stealing?" Jam didn't even have to open his eyes to see his mother right up in Laudon's face.

"He picked up something of mine from the floor, and he still has it."

Jam noticed that Laudon didn't seem to want to tell Mother or the nurse that what he was looking for was a stone. "Search me," Jam whispered.

Mother immediately was stroking his head, cooing at him. "Oh, Jamaica, baby, don't you try to talk, I know you don't have it."

"He offered to let me search," said Mr. Laudon.

"So this boy of mine, this straight A student who comes home from school every day and takes care of his handicapped brother and prepares dinner for his mother, *this* is the boy you want to treat like a criminal?"

"I'm not saying he stole it," said Mr. Laudon, backing down—but not giving up, either. "He might not even know he has it."

"Search me," Jam insisted. "I don't want your philosopher's stone."

"What did he say?" said Mother.

"He's delirious," said Laudon. Jam could feel his hands now, patting his pockets.

Jam opened his hands to show they were empty.

"I'm so sorry," said Mr. Laudon. "I could have sworn he had it. It wasn't in the room when they carried him out."

"Then I suggest you take a good hard look at some *other* child," said Mother. "Jamaica, baby, can you sit up? Can you walk? Or shall I have Mr. I-Lost-My-Rock-So-Somebody-Must-Have-Stolen-It help you out to the car?"

Rather than have Laudon touch him again, Jam rolled to one side and found he could do it. He could even push himself into an upright position. He wasn't so weak anymore. But he wasn't strong, either. He leaned heavily on his mother as she helped him out to the car.

"What a great first day of school," he said.

"Tell me the truth now," said Mother. "Did somebody hit you?"

"Nobody hits me anymore, Mama," said Jam.

"Damn well better not. That teacher—what was that about?"

"He's an idiot," said Jam.

"Why is he an idiot who's already on your case on the first day of school? Answer me, or I'll tell the principal he touched you indecently when he was patting you down and that'll get his ass fired."

"Don't say 'ass,' Mama," said Jam.

"Ass ass ass," said Mother. "Who's the parent here, you or me?"

It was an old ritual, and Jam finished it. "Must be me, 'cause it sure ain't you."

"Now get in that car, baby."

By the time they got home, Jam was recovered enough that he didn't have to lean on anybody. "Maybe you should take me back to school, Mama, I feel a lot better."

"So does that mean you were faking it before?" asked Mother. "What's so bad that you want to get out of it and jeopardize your whole future by skipping school, not to mention jeopardizing my job by making me leave all in a rush to take you home?"

"If I could've talked, I would have told the nurse not to call you."

"Answer my question, Jamaica."

"Mama, he was passing around a stupid stone, talking about alchemy as the forerunner of chemistry, and claiming it was a philosopher's stone. Only it picked up a static charge and zapped Rhonda Jones's hand and she dropped it, and Mr. Laudon was having a hissy fit, trying to *make* her pick it up even though she had already touched it and what's the point *anyway*, he was just going to tell us that alchemy doesn't work but chemistry does, so why should we all touch the stupid rock?"

"Let me guess. You saw injustice being done, so you had to put your face right in it."

"I just bent over to pick up the stone, and I must have passed out because I woke up on the floor."

"You didn't pick it up?"

"No, Mama. *You* accusing me of stealing now?"

"No, I'm accusing you of having something seriously wrong with your health and having visions of getting called out of work next time because you turned out to have a faulty valve in your heart or something, and you keeled over dead on a basketball court."

"The only way I'll ever get on a basketball court is if I'm already dead and they're using me for a freethrow line."

"I got too many hopes pinned on you, you poor boy. If only—I should have killed him instead of marrying him."

"Don't go off on Daddy now, Mama."

"Don't you call him Daddy. He's nothing to you or to me."

"Then don't bring him up whenever anything goes wrong."

"He's the reason *everything* goes wrong. He's the reason I have to work like a slave every day. He's the reason you have to earn a scholarship to get to college. He's the reason your poor brother is in that house on his bed for the rest of his life, your brother who once had such . . . so much . . ."

And then, of course, she cried, and refused to let him comfort her until he made her let him hug her, and then it was *him* helping her into the house, making her lie down, bringing her a damp washcloth to put on her forehead so she could calm down and get control of herself so she could get back to work.

He closed the blinds and closed the door as he left her room. Only then did he go into the living room where Gan's bed was, in front of the television, which he didn't really watch, even though it was on all day. The neighbor lady who supposedly looked in on him several times a day would set the channel and leave it.

"How you doin', Gan?" said Jam, sitting down on the bed beside his brother. "Anything good on? Watch Dr. Phil? I already got myself in trouble with a teacher—chemistry teacher, and a complete idiot, of course—and then I passed out and smacked my head on the floor and threw up. You should have been there."

Then, even though Gan didn't say anything or even make a sound, Jam knew that he needed his diaper changed. It was one of the weird things that Jam had been able to do since he was nine, and Gan got brain-damaged—Jam knew what Gan wanted. He learned not to bother telling Mother or anyone else—they just thought it was cute that "Jamaica thinks he knows what Ghana wants, isn't that sweet? Always looking out for his brother." Jam simply did whatever it was Gan needed done. It was simpler. And it gave Jam a reputation among the neighborhood women as the best son and brother on God's green earth, when he was no such thing. It's just that he knew what Gan wanted and nobody else did, and nobody would believe him, so what *else* was there to do?

Jam got a clean diaper from the box and brought the wipes and pulled down his brother's sheet. He pulled loose the tabs and then rolled his brother over. And this was the other weird thing that had started when Jam began taking care of his brother: his skin never actually touched the diaper or anything in it. It was like his fingers hovered in the air just a micron away, so close that you couldn't fit a hair between, and he could pick things up and move them as surely as if he had an iron grip on them. But there was never any friction. Never any contact.

All that Mother noticed was that Jam was tidy and never soiled his hands. She still made him wash. Once, defiant, Jam had gone through the whole handwashing ritual without ever letting the soap or water actually touch his skin. But it took real effort to repel the water, not like fending off solid objects. So he didn't bother pretending, when washing was so easy. Didn't bother defying anybody, either. Except when somebody was being a bully. If he'd stood up to Daddy, got between him and Gan, maybe things would have been different. Daddy never hit Jam, it was only Gan he lit into, even at his angriest.

The diaper was a real stinker, but it made no difference to Jam. It didn't soil his hands, and he had stopped minding the smell years ago. Dealing with anybody else's poop would make him sick, but it was Gan's, so it was just a thing that needed doing. Jam cleaned off his butt—it took three wipes—and then folded the diaper into a wad and dumped it into the garbage can with the anti-odor bag in it.

Then he opened the clean diaper, slipped it into position, and rolled Gan back onto it. Now that everything was clean again, he didn't bother fending—his hand touched the bare skin of his brother's hip. He was about to fasten the diaper closed when suddenly Gan's hand flashed out and gripped Jam's wrist.

For a moment all Jam felt was the shock of being grabbed. But then he was flooded with emotion. Gan *grabbed* him. Gan *moved*. Was it a reflex? Or did it mean Gan was getting better?

Jam tried to pry Gan's hand from his wrist, but he couldn't—his grip was like iron. "Come on, Gan, I can't fasten the diaper if you—"

"Show me," said Gan.

Jam looked at his face, looked close. Had Gan really said it? Or was it in his mind, the way Jam always knew what Gan wanted? Gan's eyes were still closed. He looked completely unchanged. Except for the grip on Jam's wrist, which grew tighter.

"Show you what?"

"The stone," said Gan.

A shudder ran through Jam's body. He hadn't told Gan anything about the stone. "I don't *have* it."

"Yes, you do," said Gan.

"Gan, let me go get Mama. She has to know you're talking."

"No, don't tell her," said Gan. "Open your hand."

Jam opened the hand that Gan was gripping.

"Other hand."

Jam's right hand was still holding the tab on the diaper, preparing to fasten it. So he finished the action, closing one side of the diaper, and then opened his hand.

Right in the middle of his palm, half buried in the skin, was the stone. And it was shining.

"Power in the stone," said Gan.

"Is it the stone that healed you?"

"I'm not healed," said Gan.

Then, as Jam watched, the stone receded into his palm and the skin closed over it as if it had never been opened.

"It wasn't there before, Gan. How will I know when it's there?"

"It's always there. If you know how to see."

"How'd I get it? I never touched it. How'd it get inside me like that?"

"Your chem teacher. He serves the enemy who trapped me like this. He gathers power for him and stores it in the stone. Steals it from the children. When he has to tell his master that he lost it . . ." Gan smiled, a mirthless, mechanical smile, as if he were controlling his body from the outside, making himself smile by pulling on his own cheeks. "He'll want it back."

"Well, *yeah,*" said Jam.

"Don't touch him," said Gan. "Don't let him touch you."

"Who's his master?"

"If he ever finds out you're involved in this, Jam, you'll end up like me. Or dead."

"So it wasn't Daddy?"

"Daddy hit me, yes, like he hit me a hundred times before. Do you think I'd ever let *him* hurt me? No, my enemy struck me at the same moment. And Daddy got blamed for it." Then, as if he could read Jam's thoughts, he added, "Don't go feeling sorry for Daddy. He *meant* to hurt me every time."

"Is it the stone that's letting you talk?"

"The power stored up in the stone. When you stop touching me, I'll be trapped again."

"Then I'll never let go. Can you get up and walk?"

"I'd use up everything in that stone within an hour."

"What's going on, Gan? Who's your enemy? Are you in a gang?"

Gan's body trembled with grim laughter. "A gang? You could say that. Yes, a gang. The gangs that secretly rule the world. The turf wars that are invisible to people who have no nose for magic. Sorcerers with deep power. This is the price I pay for being uppity."

"Isn't there anybody who can help you?"

"There's nobody we can trust. You never know who is a servant of the Emperor."

"There's no emperor in America."

"In the *real* world, there's no America. Only the wizards and their toys and playthings in the natural world. What's a president or an army or money compared to someone who controls the laws of physics at their root? Now let go of me, before we use up the stone. We'll need its power."

"Are you under a spell? Like in a book?" But there was no answer, for Gan had let go, and now skin was not touching skin. Gan lay there as he had for all these years, slack-faced, inert, unable to move or speak or even show that he recognized you. But he *was* inside that body, just as Jam had always believed, just as Mother pretended to believe but didn't anymore. Gan was alive and he had spoken and . . .

Jam sank to the floor beside Gan's bed and cried.

Mama came into the room. Jam stopped himself from crying, but it was too late, she had seen.

"Oh, baby," she said, "are you really sick? Or is there something wrong at school?"

"Gan," said Jam. And then she thought she understood, and sat beside him on the floor, and cried with him for her great strong son Ghana, who had once been her friend and protector, and now lay on a bed in her living room like a corpse in a coffin, so her life was one long, endless funeral. Jam understood now, and longed to tell her what was really going on. But Gan had told him not to, and so he didn't. He just wept with his mother until they were worn out with weeping.

Then she went to work, and Jam went outside and watered the tomatoes and sprayed them for the fungus that wiped them out last year. They'd already had so many tomatoes this year, what with Jam spraying them every two weeks, that they'd been sharing with half the neighborhood. And Jam and Mother were so sick of tomatoes that they were giving them *all* away now. But Jam couldn't stop watering and spraying them. It was as if having too many tomatoes this year made up for having almost none the last.

Jam thought about what Gan had told him. An emperor. Wizards. Gan involved in a war—a revolution?—and nobody knew it. How futile it was that Jam had worked so hard last year to learn the name and capital and location of every nation in the world—only to find that they don't even matter. He wondered what the map would look like if the cartographers knew who really ran things.

And yet the government still took taxes and controlled the cops and the army—that was power, it wasn't *nothing*. Did the wizards meddle in the wars of ordinary people? Fiddle with the laws that Congress or the city council passed? Mess with zoning laws? Or bigger stuff, like the weather. Could they stop global warming if they felt like it? Or had they caused it?

Or merely caused people to believe it was happening? What was real, now that a small part of the secret world had been revealed?

I have a stone in my hand.

Mr. Laudon showed up so soon after school let out that Jam suspected he dismissed class early. Or maybe his last period was free. Anyway, if he knocked on the door, Jam didn't hear it. The first he knew Laudon was there was when he saw him standing near the gate to the front yard, watching as Jam picked the ready beans off the tall vines. Jam was carrying the picked beans in his shirt, holding the bottom of it out like a basket.

Jam couldn't think of a thing to say. So he said, "Want some tomatoes?"

Laudon looked at the beans in his shirt. "That what you call a tomato?"

"No, we just got plenty of tomatoes. We ain't sick of beans yet."

He could see Laudon wince at "ain't." Laudon was the kind of teacher who would never catch on that whenever he wanted to, Jam spoke in the same educated accents and careful grammar as his mother. The kind of teacher who thought there was something morally wrong with speaking in the vernacular.

"I came for the stone," said Laudon.

Jam rolled up the front of his shirt to hold the beans, then pulled it off over his head and set it on the back lawn. He pried off his shoes. Pulled off his socks. Pulled off his pants and tossed them to Laudon. Wearing only his jockeys, he said, "You want to sniff these, too, Mr. Laudon? That what you came over for?"

Laudon glared—but he went through the pockets of the pants. "This proves nothing. You've been home long enough to hide it anywhere."

As if I'd let it out of my sight, now that I know what it can do. "What's so important about this stone, Mr. Laudon?"

"It's an antique."

"A genuine philosopher's stone."

"A stone that people in the Middle Ages genuinely believed to be one."

"That's such a lie," said Jam.

"Watch what you say to me."

"You're in my backyard, watching me strip my clothes off. I'll say what I want, or you'll be explaining to the cops what you're doing here."

Laudon threw the pants back at him. "I didn't ask you to take your clothes off."

"There were a lot of kids in that room, Mr. Laudon. I'm the one who was unconscious, remember? Why not search among the ones who were awake? What about Rhonda Jones? She's the one who dropped it. Whatever's in that stone, it bothered her, didn't it? Maybe she took it."

"You know she didn't," said Laudon. "You think I don't know how to track the stone? Where it is, and who has it?"

"And yet you checked the pockets of my pants."

Laudon glared. "Maybe I should go ask your brother."

"Go ahead," said Jam. But inside, he was wondering: Was Laudon the enemy who did this to Gan? Would he harm Gan, lying there helpless in bed?"

Laudon smirked. "You haven't given it to him, I know that much. You don't know how."

Jam wondered what would happen if he touched Laudon. Not *hit* him, just touched him. Would Laudon get a jolt of power the way Gan did? Or would Jam have power over Laudon? How did this stuff work?

"You've got the fire in your eyes," said Laudon. "Ambition. You're wondering if you can use the power in the stone. The answer is, you can't. It's a collector. A battery of magic. Only someone with power can draw on it. And that's not you."

He said "you" with such contempt that it made Jam angry. He bent over and plunged both hands into the muddy soil around the tomatoes. But he did it while fending, so that when he pulled his hands out, they were clean—not a speck of dirt or mud clung to them. He showed his hands to Laudon and then walked toward him. "Does this look like 'no power' to you?"

"You can fend?" asked Laudon, glancing around. "Then why did you let me. . . ?" He clamped his mouth shut.

Why did I let him in here? Interesting. So the fending he did was supposed to work farther than just a micron's depth of air surrounding his body. Jam had never tried to push things farther away than that. He tried to do it, to use the fending to push outward.

It was like when he decided to try to wiggle his ears. He had already noticed that when he grinned, his ears went up. So he stood in front of the mirror, grinning and then letting his face go slack, trying to feel the muscles that moved his ears. Then he worked at moving only those muscles, worked for days on it, and pretty soon he could do it—move either ear up and down, without stirring a muscle on the front of his face.

This was the same thing, in a way—not a muscle, but he did know how to fend a little. Now he isolated the feeling, the thing he did to make the fending happen, and pushed it outward from himself. At first he had to move his arms a little, but quickly he realized that this had nothing to do with it.

His shirt, twisted up on the ground with the beans inside, began to roll away from him. The garden hose snaked across the grass. Laudon took a step back. "You don't know what you're doing here, Jam. Don't attract the attention of powers you don't understand."

"You're the one who doesn't understand," said Jam. "You said the stone was nothing but a collector, but that's not true. That's what *you* are, gathering whatever magical power your students have. Rhonda had a lot of it, didn't she? But you don't know what I have."

"I know you fainted when you touched it."

"I never touched it," said Jam.

"And I know it's here. Somewhere close."

Jam gathered his fending power and made a thrust toward Laudon.

Laudon staggered back. He looked frightened. Now Jam was sure that Laudon himself was no wizard. He tried to bully Jam only as long as he thought Jam was powerless, just a kid who stole something. Now that he knew Jam had some power—apparently more than Jam himself had guessed—it was a different story. Laudon was frightened.

"The Emperor will hear of this."

"As if you ever met the Emperor," said Jam contemptuously. "All you're good for is gathering power for somebody 'else. And *not* the Emperor."

"A servant of the Emperor," said Laudon. "The same thing."

"Unless it isn't. Didn't you take history? Don't you know how this works? How do you know the one you serve, the one you've been gathering power for, how do you know he's really loyal to the Emperor? How do you know he isn't gathering power to try to challenge him?" Jam gave Laudon another shove, which knocked him off his feet this time.

This is cool, thought Jam.

He flung the hose at Laudon now, and it went after him like a flying snake, hitting him, splashing him with the dregs of water left in the hose.

"I'll report this!"

"What can you do to me that's worse than was already done? My brother's lying in there like a *vegetable,* and you think I'm worried about the treasonous wizard you serve?"

"He's not treasonous!" But Laudon looked worried now—about a lot more than a garden hose or a few grass stains on his butt. "You don't know who you're messing with!"

Which was true enough. Jam had no idea who the Emperor was, or who Laudon's master was, or anything but this: He had a stone inside his skin, and now when he touched Gan, his brother came to life under his hand.

He also knew that when he made wild accusations about Laudon's master, he got more anxious and fearful. So maybe there was some truth to it.

I shouldn't mess with this, thought Jam. *I'm out of my depth. Whatever Laudon's afraid of, I should be afraid of it too.*

Or maybe not. Maybe I shouldn't let fear decide what I'm going to do. Gan never showed fear of *anything.*

Then again, Gan ended up as a vegetable for all these years, trapped inside a body that couldn't do anything. *What might happen to me?*

What will happen to me—and Gan, and Mother—if I don't do anything?

"Who is your master?" demanded Jam.

Laudon rolled his eyes. "As if I'd tell you."

"I'll ask Gan."

"Yes, yes, go ahead," said Laudon, taunting him now. "If he *knew,* do you think he would have let down his guard? You don't know anything, little boy."

"I know that *you* don't know anything, either. In fact, you know less than nothing, because the things you think you know are wrong."

"It's the madness of power on you, boy. You think you're the first? You realize you've got something that nobody else has, you realize you've got your hands on something powerful, and suddenly you think you're omnipotent. But go look at your brother. See what you think about *his* omnipotence!"

"No, I don't think I'm powerful," said Jam. "Just more powerful than *you.*"

"But not more powerful than the one I serve. Never more powerful than that. And every word you say, every push you make with that fending power of yours will only draw attention to you. Attention you truly *do not want.*"

"But I do want it," said Jam. "I want the Emperor to come here! I want the Emperor to judge between us!"

Where had that idea come from?

Gan? Was it Gan, telling him what to say?

"You tell the Emperor who your master is, and how he trapped Gan, and how he's using you to gather power."

"It's for the Emperor, I told you, *all* the power I've gathered."

"Then let the Emperor come, and I'll give the stone to him!"

"So you do have it."

Jam rolled his eyes. "Duh."

"That's all I needed to hear," said Laudon. He stood up. Started walking toward Jam.

Jam fended him. Laudon didn't even pause. "I can feel your little pushes, boy," he said. "That made it easy to pretend you had power over me. But you don't. You're like a baby with a squirt gun." Laudon reached out and took Jam by the throat. "Where is it? Not in your head—though that wouldn't stop me. I'd have your head. It belongs to my master just like everything else does."

"Nothing belongs to your master!" cried Jam. "It all belongs to the Emperor!" Or at least it would if this magic society worked like feudalism.

"Do you think the Emperor cares what happens to you?" Laudon ran a finger down Jam's neck and chest until it rested directly over his heart. "Which arm?" he asked. Then his finger traced out and down to Jam's right hand. "I'll have that back now, thanks."

"No, you won't," said Jam. He rammed his knee into Laudon's groin.

"Owie owie," said Laudon sarcastically.

"I should have known," said Jam. "You gave your balls to your master along with everything else."

"Open your hand."

"Open it yourself."

"Right down to the bone if I have to," said Laudon. Then he pulled a sharp piece of obsidian from his pocket and prepared to slice Jam's palm open.

So all his bravado had come to nothing. And yet there *was* a power that could save him—or destroy him—but what else could he call upon? He had only just learned that there *was* an emperor, and yet somehow he knew all about him. No, he knew nothing about him but his true title—and the only other thing that mattered. That Jam could trust him.

He pulled away from Laudon and fended him with all his might. "I call upon the Emperor of the Air, to come and judge between you and me!"

His fending was more powerful than Jam had dared to hope—Laudon flew away from him clear to the fence and fell into the cucumbers.

"Oh, master!" cried Laudon, reaching out his arms beseechingly.

Oh. It wasn't Jam's power that had thrown Laudon so far. Jam had called on an outside power, but it wasn't the Emperor who had come.

Jam turned to see Mother standing in the back door. "Why did you come back here!" she demanded of Laudon.

"He has it," Laudon said. "I told you he had it."

"I would have known," she said. "Do you think he could have it, and I not know?"

"He admitted it! And he can fend. He has power."

"He has no power," said Mother. "Do you think I can't tend my own house?"

Jam's mind reeled. Was it possible that his own mother was his enemy?

"No, baby," said Mother. "This man is a fool. He has no business here."

"You know about all this," said Jam. "About the stone, and collecting power, and Gan being enchanted."

"I only know that my boy is standing in the backyard in his underwear while a high school teacher is lying in the cucumbers," said Mother. "That's enough for me to call the cops."

Laudon chimed in. "He already called somebody."

"Do you think *he'd* waste his time?"

"Are you still loyal to him?" demanded Laudon. "I haven't been helping you commit treason, have I?"

"Shut up, Laudon," said Mother. "Nobody wants to hear what you have to say."

Jam turned to see how Laudon would react, but saw instead that Laudon had no mouth. Just a smooth expanse of skin from nose to jaw.

Mother reached out her arms to Jam. "Come on inside, baby."

"He was going to cut me with this," said Jam, holding up the obsidian blade.

She held out her hand for it. "That's too dangerous for you to play with it."

"Dangerous for me, Mama? Or you?"

"Come inside."

"Are you the one who locked Gan inside his body? Are you the one that made him a vegetable?"

"A talky vegetable, judging from your attitude right now. Jamaica, don't make me cross with you. We're too close for such a spat between us."

"You haven't denied it yet."

"Oh, how television of you. No, darling, I didn't hurt Gan. But if I *had* hurt him, would I tell you? So why bother asking a question that has only one possible answer, whether it's true or not?"

"Has it all been an act? All your tears for Gan?"

"An act? Gan is my son! Gan owns my heart. Do you think I could do this to him?"

"I don't know," said Jam. "I don't know anything. Nobody's who I thought they were. Nothing's what it seemed like up to now."

"My love for you is real."

"Are you Laudon's master?"

"Jam, I'm not anybody's master."

"You've got Gan on a bed where he can't do anything, not even speak."

"And that is the greatest tragedy of my life," said Mother, starting to cry. "Are you going to find a way to blame me for that?"

Arms closed around Jam from behind. "I've got him now, Master," said Laudon.

Jam fended him viciously, and abruptly he was free. He glanced over his shoulder and saw Laudon sprawled on the grass.

"Oh, very nice," said Mother. "Is that how I taught you to treat company?"

"What I want to know is, does Father have any of this power? Are we all magicians?"

"You're not, and your father isn't, and Gan *was*, but now he's not," said Mother.

"But if you have so much power, Mother, why don't you *heal* Gan?"

"*Heal* him? He chooses to be the way he is."

"Chooses!"

"He was not a dutiful son," said Mother.

"And what about me?" said Jam.

"There has never been a better boy than you."

"Unless I refuse to give you the stone."

Her face grew sad. "Ah, Jamaica, baby, are you going to be difficult, too?"

"Was that what happened to Daddy? He got 'difficult'?"

"Your father is an animal who doesn't deserve to be around children. Or anybody, for that matter. Now come here and open your hand to me."

"It doesn't show," said Jam.

"Then open your hand, so I can see for myself that I can't see it."

Jam walked to her, his hand open.

"Don't try to deceive me, Jamaica," said Mother. "Where is it?"

"This is the hand it's in," said Jam.

"No, it's not," said Mother. Then she pressed her ear against Jam's chest. "Oh, Jamaica, baby," she said. "Why did you have to do that?"

"Do what?"

"Swallow it."

"But I didn't."

"I'm going to get it from you," said Mother. "One way or another." She reached out a hand toward Laudon. In a moment, the obsidian knife was in her grasp and she was singing something so softly that Jam couldn't catch a single word of it.

She reached out with the obsidian blade toward

Jam's bare chest. "It always hides in the heart," she said. "I'll have it now."

"Are you going to kill me, now, Mother?" asked Jam.

"It's not my fault," she said. "You could give it to me freely, though—then I wouldn't have to cut."

"I don't control the thing," said Jam.

"No," said Mother sadly. "I didn't think so."

The obsidian flashed forward, and she drew it down sharply.

But there wasn't a mark on Jam's skin.

"Don't try to outmagic *me*," she said. "Your father tried it, and look where he is."

"He's better off than Gan."

"Because he's not so dangerous to me. I trusted Gan before he turned against me. Now stop fending."

"It's a reflex," said Jam. "I can't help it."

"That's all right," said Mother. "I can get inside your fending."

"Not if I don't let you."

"You're part of me, Jam. You belong to me, like Gan."

"As you told me growing up, if I can't take care of my toys, I'm not entitled to have them."

"You're not my toy. You're my son. If you serve me loyally, then I'll be good to you. Haven't I always been till now?"

"Till now I didn't know what you did to Gan."

"I must have that stone!" she said. "It's mine!"

"That's all I needed to hear."

Mother and Jam both turned to see who had spoken—the voice certainly wasn't Laudon's.

In the middle of the backyard, standing on the lawn, was a slim, young-looking man with flashing eyes.

"Who are you?" asked Jam.

"I'm the one you called," said the Emperor of the Air. "Now your mother has admitted that the stone is for her."

"For me to give to *you*," she said, sinking to her knees.

"What would *I* do with it?" he asked.

"Why, how *else* do you get your vast powers?

"Virtue," said The Emperor of the Air. "You hid your deeds for years, but you should have known you couldn't hide forever."

"I could have, if this boy hadn't—"

"She's not really your mother," the Emperor of the Air said to Jam. "No more than Gan is your brother. She took you, as she took Gan, because you had the power. She tried to use Gan's power as a wizard, but he rebelled and she punished him. You're the substitute. She stole you when Gan was confined to bed."

"She's not my mother?"

The Emperor of the Air waved his hand, and suddenly the dam inside Jam's mind broke, and he was flooded with memory. Of another family. Another home. "Oh, God," he cried, thinking now of his real father and mother, of his sisters. "Do they think I'm dead?"

"That was not right," said Mother—no, *not* Mother—she was Mrs. Fisher now. "We were so close."

"Not so close you weren't willing to tear his heart out to get at the stone. But you wouldn't have found it," said the Emperor of the Air. "Because you never knew what he was—and is."

"What is he?" demanded Mother.

"His whole body is a philosopher's stone. He gathers power from everyone he touches. The stone flew to him the way magnets do. It went inside him because it was of the same substance. You can't get it out of him. And that knife of yours can never cut him."

"Why are you doing this to me?" she cried out from her heart.

"What am I doing to you?" asked the Emperor of the Air.

"Punishing me!"

"No, my love," said the Emperor. "You only *feel* punished because you know you deserve it." He held out a hand to Jam.

Wordlessly, Jam took his hand, and together they passed Mrs. Fisher by, entering the house without even glancing at her.

The Emperor led Jam to Gan's bed. "Touch the lad, would you, Jamaica?"

Jam leaned down and touched Gan.

Gan's eyes opened at once. "My lord," he said to the Emperor of the Air.

"My good servant," said the Emperor. "I've missed you."

"I called out to you."

"But you were weak, and I didn't hear your voice, among so many. Only when your brother called did I hear—his voice is very loud."

Jam wasn't sure if he was being teased or not.

"Take me home," said Gan.

"Ask your brother to heal you."

Jam shook his head. "I can't heal anybody."

"Well, technically, that's true. But if you let your brother draw on the power stored up inside you, he can heal himself."

"Whatever I have," said Jam, "belongs to him, if he needs it."

"That's a good brother," said the Emperor.

Jam felt the tingle, the flow, like something liquid and cold flowing through his arm and out into Gan's body. And in a few moments he was out of breath, as if he had been running for half an hour.

"Enough," said the Emperor. "I told you to heal yourself, not make yourself immortal."

Gan sat up, swung his legs off the bed, rose to his feet, and put his arm around Jam's shoulders. "I had no idea you had so much strength in you."

"He's been collecting it his whole life," said the Emperor of the Air. "Everyone he meets, every tree and blade of grass, every animal, any living thing he has ever encountered gave a portion of their power to him. Not all—not like that trivial stone—but a portion. And then it grew inside him, nurtured by his patience and wisdom and kindness."

Patience? Wisdom? Kindness? Had anyone every accused Jam of such things before?

Gan hugged Jam. "We can go home now," he said. "I to the Emperor's house, and you to your true family. But you're always my brother, Jamaica."

Jam hugged him back. And with that, Gan was gone. Vanished. "I sent him home," the Emperor explained. "He has a wife and children who have needed him for long years now."

"What about Mother? I mean Mrs. Fisher? What she did to Gan. To *me*. Taking away even my memories of my family!"

The Emperor nodded gravely, then gestured toward Gan's bed.

Mrs. Fisher lay there, helpless, her eyes open.

"I'm kinder to her than she was to Gan," said the Emperor. "Gan did no wrong, yet she took from him everything but life. I've left her eyes and ears to her, and her mouth. She can talk."

Then Mr. Laudon stood beside the bed. "And *that* will be Laudon's punishment, won't it, dear lad? To take care of her as Jam once cared for Gan—only you get to hear what she has to say." The Emperor turned to Jam. "Tell me, Jamaica. Am I just? Is this equitable?"

"It's poetic," said Jam.

"Then I have achieved even beyond my aspirations. Go home now, Jam, and be a great wizard. Live with kindness, as you have done up to now, and the power that flows to you will be well-used. You have my trust. Do I have your loyalty?"

Jam sank to his knees. "You had it before you asked."

"Then I give you these lands, to be lord where once this poor thing ruled."

"But I don't want to rule over anybody."

"The less you rule, the happier your people will be. Assume your duties only when they demand it. Feel free to continue high school, though not at Riddle High, alas. Now go home."

And at that moment the house disappeared, and Jam found himself on the sidewalk in front of the home where, in fact, he had lived for the first twelve years of his life. He remembered now, how he met Mrs. Fisher. She came to the house as a pollster, asking his parents questions about the presidential election. But when Jam came into the room, she rose to her feet and reached for his hand and at that moment he was changed. He remembered growing up with *her* as his mother, and being Gan's brother, and the tragic incident where "Father" knocked him down and damaged his brain. None of it true. Nothing. She stole his life.

But the Emperor of the Air had given it back, and more besides.

The door to the house opened. His real mother stood there, her face full of astonishment. "Michael!" she cried out. "Oh, praise God! Praise him! You're here! You came home!"

She ran to him, and he to her, and they embraced on the front lawn. As she wept and kissed him and called out to everyone in the neighborhood that her son was home, he came back, Jam—no, Michael—murmured his thanks to the Emperor of the Air.

AUDITION

by Steve Perry

IT was January, and raining in Seattle—there's a big surprise—and my boss, Jenkins, the corporate VP for Operations, was extremely unhappy.

I stood in front of his desk on an Iranian carpet that cost more than my car and condo combined and listened to him rant. I already knew the gist: The warehouse at the mill in Port Angeles had caught fire and burned to the ground early this morning; more, it had done so in a pouring rain, with the local fire department pumping a pond full of water on it not two minutes after it started. *And* the flames had been shot through here and there with a beautiful blue-green color, which meant that unless somebody had been sprinkling the fire with copper dust and going on about "The colors, man, the colors!" the arsonist had gotten past armed guards and expensive magical wards and done it with some kind of unknown spellduggery.

As assistant to the Head of Security, it was, of course, my fault. I was the man on the ground, the hands-on guy, and I could feel my job going up in flames, too. Maybe I could pull it out—I'd always been able to spot bad guys pretty well. A shame my luck at spotting bad *girls* was not so good—which is why my love life was currently as wet as the local weather.

I couldn't even keep a cat for more than a few days before it got bored and left. Story of my life . . .

Perkins rolled on: "You have any *idea* of what this is going to do to our stock?"

Actually, I did. I didn't know squat about the stock market, and what I knew about the workings of magic I could stuff in my ear, with room left over for my finger, but I knew that when three warehouses belonging to a major paper company all caught fire in the space of a week and wound up piles of cinders, that it was bad for the corporate bottom line. Insurance would cover the structures, but not the nosedive the stock was already taking. And I was pretty sure I knew why it was happening.

"Sir," I said, interrupting his tirade, "who's courting us? Is there a corporate raider who'd benefit from a drop in our stock's value?"

"Why do you ask?"

I swallowed my smile. Jenkins was vice president of one of the largest paper companies in the country, he made more than a million bucks a year, and yet he didn't seem to know the first rule of investigation when it came to such things: *Follow the money.* Then again, he wasn't entirely stupid, and if I needed this to take care of business . . .

"Three serious ones: Schmidt, the German. Parkrose, in the U.K. Sutarko, in Java."

I nodded. "Okay, so one of them is behind it. Who are their wizards?"

"Schmidt uses Amalgamated European, Parkrose's companies are with Merlin, Inc., I don't know about Sutarko, he's new. Some rich guy out of Jakarta wants to be a player."

I pulled my cell phone. I didn't know dick about magic, but I knew who to ask.

Jenkins raised an eyebrow.

"I'm calling our research guy," I said. "We need an Indonesian."

"How do you figure that?"

"Our magicians should be able to stop anything

Amalgamated or Merlin can throw at us. They didn't. Got to be something else."

The guy I wanted was Javanese, named VerMeer, which didn't sound very Indonesian to me. He had a small office in a strip mall just outside North Seattle, and the most noticeable thing in it was a huge gun safe against the wall behind his desk. Steel-trap-mind investigator that I am, I figured that out by the logo painted on it: Freedom Gun Safes.

VerMeer was a short and brown-skinned man, with white hair, who had to be pushing eighty. He chewed on the stem of a briar pipe which was not lit, but left the faint aroma of a fragrant and spicy tobacco in the air. This was good—I had a leather pouch of expensive pipe tobacco in my jacket pocket. Research had told me that was a traditional offering when approaching an *empu*, which is what the old man was. All I knew was that the word supposedly meant "mastersmith," which didn't help much.

I produced the pouch, approached his desk, offered a short bow like the research guy had told me, and said, "A small gift for you, Guru."

The old man smiled, showing surprisingly white teeth for a man who smoked.

"Ah, always a pleasure to meet a young man who bothers to learn the old ways." He took the pouch, opened it, and sniffed at the contents. "Javanese blend. Very thoughtful." He pocketed the pouch. "How may I aid you, Mr. Preston?"

I laid it out for him. He fiddled with the pipe, nodded, and when I was done, said, "You are beset with *hantu*. Ghosts."

I shook my head. "We have a full-service contract with WoA, and that includes a guaranteed-rider against poltergeists, lost spirits, or phantasms."

"Wizards of America is a fine old house, but their expertise is with *Western* ghosts. *Hantu*, *djinn*, and the like do not manifest in the same way."

"You're saying our wards won't keep these out?"

VerMeer shrugged. "Self-evident, is it not?"

Had me there. I wasn't the kind of guy who would look at a passing bumblebee and aver by all the rules of aerodynamics that it was impossible for the bug to fly when it obviously could. "What can we do?"

The old man arose and approached the safe. It was not locked, and the big door swung open silently to reveal rows and rows of what looked like elaborate, ornately sheathed knives. He removed one of them and brought it back to the desk. He pulled the blade clear of the scabbard. The handle was planed wood and looked vaguely like the stock of a flintlock dueling pistol, or maybe a stylized carving of an old man bent over with a fever. The steel was black with streaks of bright silver, in odd-looking whorls and patterns. The blade was also wavy, an asymmetrical guard making it wide at the base, narrowing to a point. It appeared to be sharp on both edges and a bit more than a foot long, not counting the handle. Nasty-looking.

I had a passing familiarity with weapons, and though I was not any kind of knife expert, I knew what this was. Me, I preferred guns. Twenty cents' worth of copper-jacketed lead was a powerful deterrent to all kinds of bad ju-ju. Guy started some wicked-sounding incantation? A bullet was a great conversation stopper, and you didn't have to get close to do it. In theory. I hadn't had to shoot anybody on the job yet.

"A kriss?" I said.

He smiled. "We pronounce it '*keris*,' but yes. A magic dagger. The patterns you see are nickel, created during the forging. The black color comes from soaking the steel in a mixture of arsenic and lime juice and allowing the metal to cure in the hot sun. The nickel does not take the color, as you see."

I nodded.

"Each pattern—they are called *pamor*—has a particular kind of power. In Indonesia, it was long the tradition that young men—and sometimes women— got their first *keris* from their father or an uncle, at about age twelve. The pattern they receive is determined by who they are and what they will do in life, and the magic is shaped by many things—the *pamor*, the number of *luk*, or waves, the length, the time it was made, the season, and so on. Some *pamor* are reserved for royalty or warriors, being too powerful for ordinary folk. There are hundreds of such—some are for physicians, to aid in healing. Some are for merchants, to insure profits. Some are more dubious, like the patterns traditionally used by executioners.

"Good and evil, Mr. Preston, just as most magic."

"I'm still with you."

"This blade has a *pamor* called *lar gangsir*, 'wings of the cricket,' and this particular specimen is designed to prevent fire. It will protect any building it inhabits from *hantu* who try to burn it."

"We have a dozen mills and associated warehouses in the Pacific Northwest," I said.

He shrugged. "Not a problem. *Empu*—bladesmiths— have been making *kerises* for more than a thousand years. I have more than enough of them to supply your needs."

Well. That would solve the problem of our buildings burning down. But a guy in my job had to look farther along the road.

The old man beat me to it. "But, of course, *hantu* are not limited to starting fires, they can be instructed to make other mischief. They are but tools. You must find the *tukang sihir*—the mage—who is behind the ghosts, and stop him."

I nodded. "And how do I do that?"

He turned back toward the gun safe. "I have just the thing."

Which is how I came to find myself late the next night outside Sekiu, Washington, far out on the Olympic Peninsula, wet and getting wetter, in the brush among the fir trees next to the mill. Sekiu is not the middle of nowhere—it's way past that. The locals liked to say that the sun—on those rare occasions when it actually showed its face around here—came up be-

tween Sekiu and town. The rain was a steady drum-
ming pour; the ground seemed to undulate in patches,
where the slugs covered it and crawled; and then there
was the odor . . .

There's no real way to describe the stench of a
working paper mill unless you've smelled it. Garbage
rotting in the summer sun, mixed with the stink of an
overfilled outhouse, with a touch of fresh vomit, that
might come close. The rain kept the smoke near the
ground, which didn't make it better.

Despite my Gortex windbreaker and pants, I was
wet, cold, breathing a vile stench, and waiting for a
Javanese ghost to show up and cause trouble. I needed
to consider getting into another line of work. Real
estate, maybe. Something inside.

Tucked into my belt was a wooden scabbard, the
main length of which was covered with a silver
oversheath bearing etched floral designs. In the sheath
proper, which had a mouth carved into a boatlike
sweeping curve, was a *keris* with five waves in the
blade, and, a *pamor* called *buntel mayit*, which meant
either "complicated," "twisted-tree bark," or "death-
shroud," depending on which of the myriad Indonesian languages you used to translate it.

What it looked like was stripes on a regimental tie,
silver threads angled cross the steel. The *keris* had,
according to VerMeer, extremely powerful magic, but
it was not a talisman just anyone could handle. If you
were not strong enough, it could turn on you. Such a
weapon was, according to legend, wicked and full of
enough magic to sneak out of its sheath while its
owner slept, and to fly about on the night wind looking for victims whose blood it could drink.

How would you deal with that if you were out walking on a Seattle street one night? Big black knife come
zipping out of the dark all by itself and slashing at
you? That would get my attention pretty damn quick.

How peachy. Just what I needed. A magic knife
that might choose to bite my hand off instead of helping me defeat an evil magician.

Even selling insurance was starting to sound good about now.

It was nearly midnight, and the rain showed no signs of slacking, when the *keris* rattled in the sheath. Scared the crap out of me, even though the old man had told me to expect that if danger approached. That was how a good *keris* warned its owner of trouble, he'd said. Passing tigers, dragons, ghosts, all like that, the dagger would rattle and give you a heads-up.

It reminded me of the first cell phone I'd owned. I'd set the thing to vibrate instead of ringing and tucked it into my shirt pocket, then forgot about it. First time somebody called me, I felt this heavy buzzing in my chest and thought I was having a heart attack.

But this wasn't somebody phoning to offer a deal on my long-distance service. I touched the handle of the dagger lightly, and the *keris* stopped rattling. I left it in the sheath—it wasn't necessary to draw it, Ver-Meer had told me. One didn't use a *keris* like a knife; it was the talismanic properties that mattered, and they worked just as well with it tucked into your belt as if you were waving it around. You might damage it using it like a knife. So he had said.

I felt a chill, even through the cold rain, and caught sight of a faint glow to my left. It took only a moment to see that there was—well, okay—a *ghostly* figure moving through the Doug fir and undergrowth toward the mill. It was hard to see clearly, it shimmered with a pulsing blue-green phosphorescence that kept the form within it indistinct. I got the impression of a young and well-built man wearing a sarong and a white shirt, but that was more of a feeling than a clear picture. Definitely not the clothes of a Western spook.

I took a deep breath as the *hantu* approached, then stepped out in front of it.

"Hi, there," I said. "Terrible night for a walk, hey? Why don't you just, you know, go home and leave my mill alone?"

The shimmering figure stopped, and I got the distinct impression of a frown.

VerMeer had told me that the *keris* I carried was sufficiently powerful to stop any ordinary ghost. That had bothered me a bit.

And what happens if I run into a ghost who isn't ordinary?

Unlikely, he had said. Ghosts powerful enough to get past your *keris* won't be doing the bidding of any but the most powerful of mages. A ghost that strong would be . . . a problem. Certainly dangerous.

Which means that if it doesn't stop, I'm in deep shit?

Well, yes, you could put it that way.

Great.

But the ghost I was facing had stopped, and while I got the feeling it wanted to keep going, it couldn't. After a few tense moments, it turned and started to glide away.

I was greatly relieved when the spook backed off.

Here was the tricky part. Stopping the ghost wasn't all that I was after. I needed to catch whoever was sending it, unless I wanted to spend the rest of my career hiding in the bushes waiting for more *hantu* to show up. So I had to follow it. And not be seen doing it.

It was hard going, in the dark, the rain, the woods. The *hantu* didn't seem fazed by the obstacles. On the other hand, I was slipping in the mud, getting slapped by wet branches, and now and then banging into a tree I didn't see until it was too late.

Maybe even being a 7-Eleven clerk or a cook at Mickey D's was better than this. Not as if I had a wife or a girlfriend to support. There was something to be said for minimum wage. You didn't have to chase ghosts to get it. You want fries with that, sir?

The ghost headed for a logging road that led to the highway, and the state highway was the only way leading away from the mill. If I could find who'd sent it, I could call and have company security or the local sheriff set up roadblocks, we could catch the guy, and end of problem.

At the logging road, the ghost stopped moving. I gained on it, and when I was maybe twenty yards away, it vanished—*pop!*—like a soap bubble. It got very dark.

I kept lurching forward. I had a flashlight and now was the time to use it. A diver's light, and waterproof, which was good, because my jacket was soaked and so was the light.

I put my other hand under my jacket and onto the butt of my revolver, a stainless-steel, K-frame Smith & Wesson .357 Magnum. I might not be able to stop a tank with it, but ninety-six out of a hundred people I might shoot would fall down if I hit them solidly. That was comforting, in a macho kind of way.

Ten yards away, the bright beam found my quarry.

A woman. She was short, black-haired, dark, and gorgeous, wearing a green T-shirt, blue jeans, and running shoes. No jacket. Maybe thirty, about my age, and apparently waterproof because she was completely dry and the falling rain didn't seem to be hitting her at all.

Really gorgeous in that tight T-shirt and tight jeans. Heart-skip-a-beat beautiful. Despite the situation, lust threatened to rear its ugly head. Why was I always attracted to the bad girls?

She smiled into the light. "Ah!" she said. She glanced at my belt, where I had the *keris*. She closed her eyes. "*Buntel mayit?* I wouldn't have thought that to look at you." She sighed. "The old man doesn't give up easily."

"Listen, honey," I said, "I just sent your *hantu* packing, and this game is over. You can't get away. Our people will set up roadblocks and stop every car. Why don't you just come along quietly?"

She laughed, a bright, happy sound. "Oh, please. Where did he find you?" She paused. She looked at me, turned her head to one side, like a curious puppy. She looked familiar, though I knew I'd never seen her before. You don't forget a face like that.

"You have a name?" she said.

"Will Preston." I'm not sure why I told her. Well, no, that's not true. I told her because she was a beautiful woman, and she asked. That didn't happen a lot to me.

"I am Malina," she said. "Interesting to meet you, Mr. Preston. Can I call you Will?"

I shrugged. *You* can call me anything you want, honey—but before I could say it, she vanished. Just like the ghost. There was a *pop!* and she disappeared.

So much for roadblocks.

At VerMeer's office, I got to the part where she vanished, and he smiled. "She didn't actually vanish," he said, "merely turned invisible."

"Oh, right, that's totally different. Not such a big deal, just turning *invisible*."

My sarcasm, heavy as it was, was lost on him. He shrugged. "Not so much, no."

"Yeah, well, she apparently knows you. Said something about the old man not giving up easily."

He smiled. "Oh, yes, I know her well. Malina's mother was a powerful mage. She's retired now, and living on an island she owns in the archipelago. Malina's grandfather is still alive, an *empu* who has made a few knives of passing note, though he was never as strong as either Malina or her mother."

"Nice to be in the family biz, I guess. How do I find her?"

Another smile. "You don't need to worry about that—she'll find you."

"Really? More attacks on the mills?"

"Not exactly. You see, when you stopped her *hantu*, you challenged her power. In traditional Javanese magic circles, such challenges must be answered."

"Whoa, whoa—hold on a second! You didn't say anything about that when you gave me the *keris*!"

"Didn't I? I'm old, I forget things. Sorry."

"You forget things? Sorry? What am I supposed to do if she shows up with blood in her eye? I'm not a wizard, I'm a corporate geek who has a magic dagger you gave me with a mind of its own that might choose to be on *her* side!"

"I doubt that. You have hidden reserves, Mr. Preston, I can feel them. With the power of your *keris*, you can protect yourself from what Malina can send against you. Most of it."

"*Most* of it? Crap! How about 'any' of it? I don't know jack about how to make the *keris* work!"

"I can show you. It's not that hard."

"No, thanks. I think maybe I might retire from security. Go find a job selling popcorn in a theater or something. Watch a lot of free movies."

"It's too late for that, Mr. Preston. Malina will come to try you. She can find you no matter where you hide. Without the *keris*, your chances of surviving are, um, not good."

Oh, wonderful, just fucking *wonderful!*

The old man didn't seem concerned. He smiled and took a moment to light his pipe. A fragrant cloud of bluish smoke rose into the air around his face. "Ah. Really good tobacco you brought."

I stared.

"Shall we get started?"

The tricks VerMeer showed me weren't that hard to learn. After a couple days of practice, I could turn invisible, hop twenty feet into the air and land safely, and, in theory, ward off ghosts and minor *djinn*. I could resist fire and water and wind to a degree, for a short time, and my *tenaga dalam*, or inner power, was apparently very strong—for a white man. As long as I remained calm and didn't get too excited, I should be able to control the power of the *keris' pamor*.

And if I got too excited?

That, the old man said, would be . . . bad.

It just kept getting better and better.

I went about my business, and for the next week, there were no fires at any of our warehouses or mills, nothing unusual at all. I found out that turning invisible had its uses, and that the women's locker room at the Gold's Gym where I worked out was definitely worth touring without anybody noticing you. Yeah, I know, I shouldn't have, but nobody knew, so no harm, no foul . . .

My personal stock went up with my corporate superiors, there was talk of a raise, and I began to hope that maybe it was all a done deal, and I'd never see the lovely Malina again.

On the one hand, being fond of my life, such as it was, that was good. On the other hand, she was the best-looking woman I had ever met, and I wouldn't mind another peek at her. I mean, she didn't really *feel* like a bad girl. Of course, my track record in that area left much to be desired. In this case, I could be dead wrong.

So I was jogging in the park near my condo just after dark a week later, to celebrate the brief cessation of the rain—twenty-one hours at that point—when I felt a presence.

I had the *keris* with me. Since VerMeer and I talked, I always had it with me. When I took a bath, it perched on the edge of the tub. I slept with it under my pillow. I also had my revolver, which tended to drag at the sweatpants drawstring a lot, but which I was willing to live with to have it handy.

"Evening, Will," Malina said.

She sounded close, but I couldn't see her. I had, however, a solution for that. I put my left hand on the *keris* and uttered a syllable the old man had taught me.

The air shimmered ten feet away to my left and the lovely Malina appeared suddenly. This time, she wore tight spandex shorts, a sports bra, and running shoes. She was built like the captain of the women's soccer team. Damn.

"My," she said. "You learned a trick."

I couldn't help myself. I said, "Don't you get cold?"

"Nope," she said.

She was one of those people who looked better with

fewer clothes, and that said something. I wondered what she looked like in the altogether-naked state.

"You're staring, Will."

"Sorry. I couldn't begin to tell you how . . . good you look."

"Why, thank you. But I still have to try you, you know."

"Be okay by me if we skip that part," I said.

"I would, but it's the custom. Sorry."

"Me, too."

She waved her hands in an intricate little pattern and a trio of *hantu* appeared behind her.

"If they touch you, you join them," she said.

Not a thought to inspire calmness. I fought to keep my breath slow.

The three ghosts spread out and started toward me.

My grip on the handle of the *keris* was maybe a little on the tight side, but that was just how it was going to be. I recalled the chant VerMeer had taught me, and how to concentrate on my inner power to focus it.

The nearest ghost was four feet away and reaching for me when I spoke the words of the spell.

Three *pops!* and they vanished.

"Hey," Malina said, "that's pretty good. You aren't a ringer, are you? Somebody the old man has been working with for a long time?"

"No, ma'am, I just met him a week ago. He showed me some stuff."

"I'm impressed. Not a lot of men could focus that spell with only that much training. Especially white guys."

"What say we call it a draw?" I said. "Or you can call it a victory, whatever. I'm easy."

"You want me to leave?"

"Not really. I'd love to have you around—I just don't want you to turn me into a pile of smoking ash or anything."

"If you are able to joke about it, you must not be too worried."

"I'm a natural clown," I said. "Believe me, I'm worried."

She laughed, and despite the fact she might be about to kill me, I enjoyed the sound. "I like you, Will. Let's see how you do against my *djinn*."

I didn't much care for the sound of that.

She made a few more motions with her hands, said something I couldn't quite understand, and there was a sound like a big waterfall. The air wavered, and a seven-foot-tall man appeared in front of me. He was not only tall, but built like a power lifter, huge, three-fifty, four hundred pounds, easy. Save for a turban on his head, he was naked. He could get the job as power forward for the Lakers tomorrow, and if he didn't feel like round ball, he could go into the pornographic movie biz—because if he were a clock, his, uh, *pendulum* would dangle past his knees.

As I stared at him, pretty much awestruck, and maybe a little envious, he closed his right hand into a loose fist and snapped it in my direction as if tossing a Frisbee.

A fireball shot from his fingers and right at my face.

I closed my eyes. I might have said something to the effect of him having an incestuous relationship with his female parent.

I felt the heat splash against my head, but it dissipated in an instant. I opened my eyes. I was alive. Not even warm.

"Fireproof!" she said. "I don't suppose it will do any good to try water or wind?"

"I hope not," I said. "Those are supposed to be covered."

"Even VerMeer couldn't have given you that if you didn't have some juice. Well, all right, then. Hand-to-hand. You and Larry."

"The *djinn's* name is Larry?"

She shrugged. "What can I say? He had it when I got him. Go, Larry."

He was slow, but he would get to me soon enough.

I pulled my gun, pointed it at the onrushing center of mass, and cranked off six shots double-action as fast as I could pull the trigger. I'm guessing three-quarters, maybe a second was all it took. All six rounds hit him the chest, pretty good shooting, given the circumstances. I didn't even hear the reports.

Larry grinned and just kept coming.

I jinked to my right, and resisted the urge to throw the gun at him. If bullets didn't work, bouncing the revolver off his body wasn't going to do shit, either. I dropped the piece.

I managed to get just outside Larry's reach. Well, mostly so. He got a couple of fingertips on my shoulder, and it was like being hit by a crowbar. I was spun away like a human top as Larry skidded to a stop on the still-wet ground and came around for another pass.

I blurted out the word for the jumping spell just as he extended both hands to crush my skull. I leaped up for all I was worth, and sailed over Larry. Too high. I was still in the air and just starting back down when he got turned around, and moved to stand under me. I was screwed—the jumping spell only worked if you had something to push against. Once he got those paws on me, I was going to be a giant wishbone.

Frantic, I jerked the *keris* loose from the sheath as I fell. Yeah, it was a magic talisman and all and I might damage it, but it was also a dagger, and it wasn't as if I had a whole lot of options here—

I came down. Larry—how weird was that, to be killed by a *djinn* named Larry?—grabbed at me, caught me by the thighs with hands that felt like steel pliers. I was about to have a fatal charlie horse. I scrunched down and stabbed at the top of his turban with the *keris*. Probably it would only piss him off, but how much deader could he make me?

Larry hissed, a truck tire blowing a valve stem, and let me go. Then he . . . deflated, like a stabbed beach ball. He sagged and spread out on the ground into a lumpy blanket.

Holy shit!

Malina shook her head. "Want something done, do it yourself."

As I fell on what was left of Larry and rolled up, Malina pulled a *keris* of her own and leaped at me, knife raised to stab.

I managed to get my empty hand up in time to snag her wrist. I grabbed and held on, and brought my own dagger around. She caught my wrist, and while she was passing strong, I knew I could force my blade down enough to skewer her.

We were face-to-face. Well, her face was at my chest-level, but she was looking up into my eyes.

Something passed between us. Not heat, exactly, but some kind of energy.

I should stab her, I thought. But the truth was, I didn't really want to stab her. At least not with the *keris* I held. What I wanted to do—what I did—was bend down and kiss her.

Best kiss of my life. Something about a beautiful woman magician trying to kill you that maybe gave it that little extra spice. Her lips—I can't even begin to describe how it felt. It was perfect.

I let go of my *keris*. I needed that hand to hug her. And I needed the other one for that, too, so I let go of her wrist. If she wanted to use her blade at that point, so be it. I would die a happy man. That's how good the kiss was.

But she didn't drive that black steel into my throat. She let go of her knife and hugged me back.

After what seemed like a long time, we broke the embrace and looked at each other. I was in love. I would follow this woman into hell if that's where she wanted to go. Shoot, I'd run ahead and hold the gate for her.

"See?" came a familiar voice from behind me. "I told you I'd find the right one."

I turned. VerMeer?

"What are you doing here? Who are you talking to?" I managed.

"To my granddaughter," he said.

Granddaughter?

Yeah. Of course. That's why she looked familiar. I could see it now.

I thought, *What the fuck is going on here?*

I said, "What the fuck is going on here?"

Malina and VerMeer both laughed.

As we walked back toward my condo, I said, "So, let me see if I have it straight." I looked at the old man. "You have been looking for a husband for your granddaughter."

"Correct."

"And this whole deal with the warehouses being burned was just to get us to meet?"

"Well, not entirely. Malina is a mage, and she is working for a corporate raider out of Jakarta. The son of an old friend of mine who hired her because I asked him to."

"You are a devious man, Grandfather," Malina said. She had her arm around my waist and if truth be known, I wasn't all that upset with VerMeer, given that arm and how it felt.

"And you knew she would be coming here to torch the warehouses."

"Yes. And that you would be the one sent to deal with it."

"How did you know about me?"

"Oh, I've been keeping my eye on you for some time. I felt your *tenaga dalam* one day, and went to find you. So few white men have much inner power. I would have preferred a Javanese man, of course, but Malina is, alas, an American to the core."

He looked at her. "She insisted that if she had to be married, it would be to an American. And, of course, her mother and I could not allow her to wed a man without sufficient power to hold his own with her."

"Oh, of course." I looked at her. "Did you know any of this?"

"Well, I knew he was looking. He sent a couple of other candidates."

"What happened to them?"

She shrugged. "They were . . . inept."

I thought about that for a second. Talk about a tough audition.

"Are you angry?" Malina said.

I grinned. "Not even a little."

VerMeer said, "You see? Next time, you'll believe me when I tell you something, yes?"

"Yes, Grandfather."

"And you, you will be joining the—what did you call it?—the 'family biz.' You might be an American, but you aren't going to waste your talent working for a corporation."

"No, Grandfather," I said.

What the hell. I had been thinking about changing jobs anyway, right?

BACK DOOR MAGIC

by Phaedra M. Weldon

THE fire spark blew her a raspberry before vanishing in a black puff of sooty smoke.

Brenda blinked a few times in the abrupt darkness before grabbing up the flashlight perched handle up on the table. *Since when did elementals have a sense of humor?*

The evening shadows elongated at that moment, stretching their hollow limbs into the crevices of the store's tall shelves. A row of authentic skulls, nestled among a neglected Halloween decoration of dried autumn leaves and miniature pumpkins, all illuminated by the streetlight outside, peered down at her from the top shelf near the cash register.

I never asked Granny to whom those belonged— maybe those are the skulls of hapless idiots like myself who thought they could make money at magic.

They starved to death.

Maybe this wasn't such a bad thing—sitting here in the dark. At least she couldn't see the deed of sale spread out on the table in front of her. She didn't really need to see it to know what it said. The deadline to pay the back taxes and overdue mortgage on the shop was Friday, less than four days away.

With renewed anger (masquerading as determination), Brenda attempted again to conjure another fire spark. Nothing answered her call. Empty space and the faint smell of sulfur.

Could it get any worse?

Granny Pollsocks had lit fire with a snap of her fingers—sometimes with only a glare. One look from her violet eyes, and all the fire sparks in the room jumped to do her bidding. Of the six grandchildren, Granny had declared Brenda to be the one gifted to carry on the tradition of magic in the family. None of the others had been interested—or really *believed* in it.

And before Granny died, Brenda had shown *some* aptitude for a few spells and potions. Flash powders were a sore subject. She'd managed to blind a store full of patrons one summer afternoon by accident. Granny had made sure Brenda practiced upstairs after that.

But then she died, and left "Back Door Magic" to Brenda. Books, supplies, scrolls, amulets, bills, and debt included. The steady customers, the ones who'd depended on Granny for years came to Brenda at first, hoping she had even the slightest peep of the talent Granny had had. But after six months—the customers dwindled away.

The money dried up. And no matter how hard Brenda tried—she couldn't turn lead into gold.

Just yesterday they'd turned off the power. And now she shivered in the November evening, unable to light a simple candle. She couldn't find the matches— but Granny had never needed them.

She heard the familiar backfire of her mother's car outside the door, pulling up along the curve in the street outside the shop. Detective Jackie Grafton always parked on the street, in a no-parking zone. Married wealthy, widowed wealthy once, never sick, never injured, always in a good mood. Of course, the widowed wealthy had come after Brenda's father had died, with husband number two.

Another noise came just as Brenda stood. She stopped and pivoted slowly on her worn sneakers. Most of the shop was dark and scary.

Just the way Granny liked it.

Well, I don't like it that way. And that noise sounded like it came from the stairwell.

Four steps that led to a back door that opened to a brick wall.

Brenda figured Mom could get in on her own—she had a key. She switched on the flashlight and took several cautious steps to the back of the room, closer to the stairs. "Hello? Is there someone down there?" Her voice echoed in the empty shop.

She aimed the beam down the stairwell—

—and a pair of green eyes looked back up at her, eyes filled with pain.

It was a man!

The front door opened. "Brenda? You in here? Oh, gawd—where are the lights, child? There're enough candles in here—hell—light up one of those seven-day candles."

Brenda turned at the sound of her mother behind her, and then turned back to the stairwell and shined the light back down again.

The heels of her mother's boots clacked noisily behind her as Jackie neared. "What're you doing? You see something down there? Rats?"

Brenda blinked. She thought she'd seen a man in trouble.

A man with beautiful green eyes.

Her mother sighed. "Never could figure out why that door was there. Never made sense." She turned. "Let's get some light in here. I think there are matches behind the cash register."

Brenda barely noticed her mother's retreat, the clacking of the heels, the faint odor of White Shoulders perfume drifting about the air like an errant ghost. Her mind, her flashlight's beam, and her gaze focused again on the empty stairwell. Five steps down. To a door that went—nowhere.

She knew that. But Granny Pollsocks never let her get too close to it—and even through these six months alone Brenda hadn't bothered to go down the stairs. Too dingy. Too grungy.

Too . . . *weird*.

With a frown she turned and looked at the register counter. Her mother had found the matches and had several different candles lit—one of them a warming candle of red-and-orange-swirled wax. "Why did Granny keep that door?" Brenda moved to the register, switched off the flashlight, and set it handle up on the table beside a frog-kissing stone, guaranteed to turn black the moment a toad—disguised as a gorgeous man or woman—delivered their pick-up line.

Brenda hated them. They always stayed black for her.

Jackie lifted her gaze from the warming candle and shrugged. Her red hair was streaked with white—mostly by choice. She wore her usual boot-cut pants and tailored, thigh-length coat jacket. And, as she'd been doing for several days now, clutched at her left side. "For years I thought it was the door to the basement. So I went down there and opened it."

"You saw the wall."

She nodded. "Brick wall. Granny laughed at me," Jackie made a face as if she smelled something bad. "Come to think of it, she called it her back door."

Brenda glanced to her left at the front glass with the words Back Door Magic painted backward on the inside. "You mean like her shop name?"

But her mother didn't know, and didn't care. "Nonsense. All of this place. Now—you got those papers signed? You know I have to give you marks for trying to keep this place afloat, Brennie. But to think you could do magic like Granny?" She gave a snort. "Disappointing. You just don't have it, girl. Neither did I. I'm afraid the magic died with Granny."

With lowered shoulders, Brenda shook her head. She didn't want to believe the words her mother spoke—and yet each letter, each syllable burned a mark into her skin and dug deeper into her subconscious, weakening her own belief that maybe—just maybe—she was a magical creature after all. "No—I have till Friday, Mom. And I'd rather just hang on to things until then."

"You're just prolonging the inevitable, Brenda." Jackie's hands rested on her hips, and the flickering candles lined up along the counter beside the register cast shadows that only enhanced the no-nonsense look on her face. "The shop's going to be sold. And then you can go back to college. You're not too old to be taught some sort of trade or skill. We might even make enough money to where you won't have to work—just find a rich man and marry him."

That didn't feel right. It never felt right when her mom mentioned selling the shop. But Brenda wasn't sure if it was the selling part, or the money part. She suspected if she jumped the broomstick now and sold before the deadline that she'd somehow be missing—*something*.

But what?

She glanced back at the door. Where had that man gone?

"Well, I'm off, then. Got a date tonight—a nice Irish man. Sexy accent. Dark hair and blue eyes." She moved from behind the counter, and Brenda was sure if the register actually had money in it, Jackie would have taken it. "You'll be all right? Need groceries? Though," she looked her daughter up and down. "You could stand to lose a pound or two."

Brenda stared at the floor.

"Well, that's good. Okay—I'm gone. You just go ahead and sign those papers, Brenda, and we'll both be well in the green." She waved and clacked back to the front of the store where she disappeared behind the door.

Brenda took in a deep breath, clutched at the counter with both hands, and then exhaled.

"Yes, quite an exhausting woman, isn't she? Thought she'd never leave."

Brenda gave a slight squeal and spun around, shoving the edge of the counter into the small of her back—closer to her kidney.

The green eyes were standing in front of her. They belonged to a nice long face, with a perfectly shaped nose and full lips. Pale skin. Very wiry in jeans and an oversized green sweater.

His hair was shoulder length, a mass of reddish brown curls.

"Oh, sorry, I'm not in the habit of startling my saviors," he said, and she heard the accent that time. English—Surrey? Maybe a little bit of Liverpool? Soft and melodic. "I'm sorry—it's just that I'm in the middle of a very—" He looked down at his right side, where Brenda saw a red stain spreading over the fibers of his sweater beneath his long-fingered hand. He looked back at her. "Uhm . . . a very tetchy situation."

His eyes glazed over, and he nearly fell. Brenda went out to him and moved under his left shoulder, the side that wasn't bleeding. "What happened?" She hated the flat, nasal sounding voice she had in comparison to his. "Were you shot?"

"Yes, and no," he said and stumbled with her as she guided him to the table she'd been sitting at earlier. With a grunt, Brenda eased him into the chair and then pushed the papers away.

She frowned at the wound. He didn't look too good. Very pale.

Bone pale.

"What can I do?"

His eyes opened then, and though she saw intelligence there, she also saw the pain she'd seen before at the stairwell. "Do? Why, my dear Brenda, you can heal me."

Heal? Me? "*Heal* you?" She shook her head and took a step back. "I'm sorry, mister—" Did he say his name? "*Mister*, but I'm not a healer. I'm supposed to be a magician, but I'm really not any good at that, either."

With a nod the stranger smiled. It was a very nice smile, and would have lit up his whole face if it wasn't for the shadow of pain she saw just beneath the surface. "Actually, you're a lot better than you think." He winced. "And though confidence is something you do lack the skills in, I'm afraid I don't have the luxury of time right now to teach it to you, so," he bent over for few seconds.

"Oh, damn," Brenda ran her fingers through her hair. "Look, what's your name. I can't call you 'hey you' all the time."

"Edward," he managed to say in the middle of another wince. "Edward Darlington. Yes, yes. That will do this time. Now, speaking of time, we don't have much. The door is locked and the outside looks vacant. So, grab the wormwood, the St. John's root, and some of the Dragon's Blood Rede from that shelf over the necromancer tomes."

She blinked at him. "Edward—I didn't understand—"

"Brenda," he smiled again. "Just let your hands guide you. Please hurry—I'm not going to be conscious much longer."

Let my hands guide me? Geez! She turned and ran to the designated shelf. Luckily, Granny had things labeled, and she was able to gather the bottles of each of the items Edward asked for. She set them on the table in front of him.

"Good, good," he said. He was sitting funny in the chair. "Now—you need a small amount of mandrake oil—and I mean small. Maybe a dab and that's it. Too much, and I'm dead anyway."

She found it on a different shelf and grabbed it— then paused as her gaze rested on a large green marble mortar and pestle, a small grater, and a white-handled knife. Letting her hands guide her, she put the smaller items inside the mortar, dumped in two more ingredients, and carried the whole thing to the table.

He watched her and smiled. "See? You know what you're doing, Brenda. You just need confidence."

She set all the things out on the deed of sale and then looked at him. "Now what?"

"Now what?" His eyelids drooped and leaned at

an odd angle, nearly out of his chair. "Now—I lose consciousness. Brenda . . ." He tried to catch himself with both hands, but the blood on his right hand slipped on the table. "It's up to you . . ."

And he crumpled to the floor in a heap. Brenda tried to catch him—but he'd fallen too fast. With a sigh she pushed and pulled him, getting him onto his back.

"Edward?" She tried jerking his shoulder back and forth. "You have to tell me what to do. Edward?"

But he was unconscious, his breath sounding ragged and harsh.

Biting her lip, Brenda moved to his right side and pulled the sweater away from the wound.

As a detective's daughter, Brenda had seen all kinds of wounds. Gunshot, knife, and even lead pipe. But this—

This wasn't right. This looked like he'd been bitten by something big.

A bear?

Oh, no, Brenda'that's just stupid. But it really did look like huge teeth marks. His skin was slick with blood that pooled on the dingy tile floor.

How am I supposed to heal this? This man needs an ambulance. She stood with that thought and took a single step to the counter where her purse lay tucked inside the lower shelf—and then remembered she'd left her phone at her mother's.

Edward moaned.

She turned to the table and the collection of things sitting about the mortar and pestle. *He'd said it was up to me. Me. Me how?* She'd never been taught any sort of healing magic from Granny. A quick search through her memory didn't unearth anything about Granny ever using healing.

In fact—Brenda had never gone to Granny for healing. She always went to a regular doctor.

Let your hands guide you.

Yeah. Right. Fire sparks were sticking their noses up at her, but she was supposed to save a dying man?

Brenda looked down at Edward. She knew her mother would yell at her right now, and be on the phone to the hospital. But he had believed in her. And his encouraging words had helped.

A little.

After taking a deep breath, she closed her eyes and did what he told her—let her hands guide her. She'd known to get the mortar. And somehow in her mind's eye she could see the potion. Saw it in a pot—over a flame.

She grabbed up the block of Dragon's Blood and then used the grater on one side. Brenda never opened her eyes—but she saw in her mind what needed to be done—much like a paint-by-numbers canvas. She knew what went in first, and second, like what colors went last. And she knew how much.

Once the St. John's root was properly ground, Brenda took the mortar to the side room where Granny Pollsocks hung herbs, hex and bless charms and amulets, and microwaved the occasional quick bowl of soup.

She grabbed some bottled water out of the small office fridge and poured in enough to make half a cup of broth. Six turns deosil, six turns widdershins, and then six turns deosil. Clockwise, counterclockwise, clockwise.

Brenda shoved the entire mortar inside the small white appliance and turned it on to medium for one minute.

It never dawned on her to question how a microwave worked with no electricity.

When the first bubbles came to the surface, she jerked the door open, grabbed a towel, and lifted the mortar out of the microwave, poured the contents into a clean, green ceramic mug with the face of the Green Man on the side, and hurried back to Edward.

With no thought about what she was doing, Brenda grabbed a large, fat kabuki brush from a side shelf of glass pens and cartography books, dipped it into the steaming mess and began painting the wound with it.

Edward's eyes came open. Deep pools of emerald agony.

He screamed. Brenda screamed.

The flesh beneath her potion curled, smoked, and then wove together the cuts and tears of flesh into a garish, puckered line.

Light came into her bedroom from the dingy window facing Abercorn Street. Brenda blinked slowly and noticed the oak next door still had its leaves. Orange, yellow, red, and brown. And as she watched, several of those leaves came off in the gentle wind and spiraled around her window.

She took in a deep breath.

And smelled bacon.

Bacon?

And she heard voices downstairs as well.

Och—was Jackie in?

Brenda stretched as she moved about her room, pulling on her socks, her jeans, shuffling into the bathroom to brush her teeth—and it was at that moment, staring at her reflection in the mirror, that she remembered puckered flesh.

Smoke.

Green eyes.

Edward.

After choking on toothpaste, she rinsed and ran downstairs—

—and stopped just inside the shop.

People. There were people inside. Customers, taking a look at things and then actually picking them up! Carrying them to the counter—and handing out cash to—*Edward*.

She shuffled forward, pausing once to avoid walking into two gossiping little Goth girls. Edward was grinning, his color radiant, and his smile—intoxicating.

When the paying customers were gone, he turned that smile on Brenda. "Hullo, sleepyhead. You made it up. Cup o' tea?" He arched his eyebrows. "Or I've made bacon and biscuits—real English biscuits, though." He frowned. "So I'm not sure they're what you're accustomed to."

It was at that moment she caught the fluid movement of a brown feather duster cleaning off the bookshelves behind the counter. She blinked. There wasn't anybody actually *holding* the duster—it was just cleaning things itself.

With a slow pivot in her house slippers Brenda saw several other things moving on their own about the room. Window cleaner and rag moved in perfect counterclockwise circles on the front window. A second duster moved with precision over the rows of skulls, which now looked as if they were grinning at her, happy to be given some attention.

And in the corner a broom swept several tumbling little mouselike things about. They twittered and chattered—reminding Brenda of finches. She moved closer and narrowed her eyes down at them.

"Dust bunnies," Edward said beside her. "Nasty little buggers. They're all over this room. Hiding in the cracks and crevices." He said crevice with an "a" sound, much like cre-vace.

She looked up at him. His eyes sparkled as he handed her a white mug. "Tea?"

"We have tea?" Brenda looked at the amber liquid inside. "And bacon?"

"Well, you have an assortment of things—" He winced. "I'm not sure they'd all qualify for tea—and the bacon came from your neighbor, two doors down. He needed a poultice but didn't have his wallet with him. Oddly enough, his wife returned with a pound of bacon." The grin returned. "Interesting, isn't it? But I did find some commercial bags in that little workroom in the corner."

She took the tea. It did smell normal. She sipped it. Mmmm. And it tasted normal. Nice and sweet. "Honey?"

"Well, I'm not sure our relationship calls for terms of endearment yet—seeing as how we just met and— oh." He beamed again as comprehension dawned.

"Sorry. Yes. I used honey. Don't have much use for sugar—toddles about with the magical lines." He put a hand to his side—the damaged one. "Oh, and nice job you did. Hurt like all rot, but look," he held up his sweater and showed her a nearly perfect, smooth side.

Pale. But smooth.

She also noticed how nicely lean and muscled he was.

Edward pulled his shirt back down and motioned for her to follow him to the counter. As she moved forward, she noticed the shop was empty, save for the repeated, precise movements of the cleaning objects.

"Now, I hope you don't mind, but as a thank you for helping me out last night, I decided to put my own skills to work for you. I've got all the appliances working—including the bathroom," he frowned. "And I don't mean to sound tetchy, but you might want to use some cleaner now and again in there. It was disgusting."

Brenda was watching him, listening to him, but wasn't sure how to respond. Finally, her brain caught up with her and she said, "I—*I* healed you? That potion healed you?"

Edward stopped at the counter and took the cup from her shaking hand and set it on the counter. "Yes, yes. Didn't you look when I showed you? Do you want to see again?" He grabbed at his sweater.

"No, no," Brenda raised her hands. "It's just that— I suck."

His excited smile transformed into a confused frown. Edward pulled up his sweater, exposing the healing scar again. "You sucked out the poison?"

"No—I didn't suck it."

"Well, I hope not—" He lowered the sweater and arched his eyebrows at her. "You'd get one hell of a negative headache."

"I sprinkled the—*negative* headache?"

"Right—nasty thing, that. Buggers up the whole positive aura. Pretty much clogs the magic pipes," he frowned again. "Didn't I say that already? Oh, no—that was sugar wasn't it?"

Brenda blinked.

"But—anyway—you knew what to do. You always knew what to do. It just took something like last night to give you that kick in the backside. Well, so to speak."

"Edward," she held out her hands, palms down. "What the hell are you talking about? And where the hell did you come from? And what," she pointed to his side. "What thing bit you that badly?"

"Doubt."

Pause. Blink. "What?"

"You asked me what bit me? Doubt. Now that's a corrupt piece of thought, doubt is. It's the single worst thing to come out of Pandora's Box. Loads of people thought famine and disease were the tops—but no—doubt was the worst. I mean, when you really think about it, if you didn't have doubt, hope might have a fighting chance. Hope is so strong and pure—and it was the last thing in the box, did you know that? And if you had hope, you'd know that positive thinking and confidence can win against famine and disease, but there's always that—"

"Edward!"

He cocked his head to the side. "Are you all right? You're looking at little flushed, Brenda."

She put her hands to the sides of her head. "Edward—where did you come from?" She was thinking since the bite question wasn't getting her anywhere, maybe this question would.

"Back door."

Eh? "Edward, there isn't a back door. Not a real one."

He glanced in the direction of the stairwell. "It's over there. Down those steps. Nice door."

"It opens up into a wall."

He gave her a lopsided grin and leaned in close. "Yeah—for those who don't believe in magic."

Brenda glared at him, and then looked at the stairway. With a sigh she stalked to the stairs, took them two at a time, put her hand on the doorknob, and yanked it open.

Brick wall.

With a growl she slammed it shut and looked up at Edward. "See? Brick. Wall. No back door."

"It's because you have doubt, Brenda. And as long as you doubt who and what you are, then you'll never get it open."

"Oh, this is stupid," Brenda stomped up the stairs. Edward stepped back, and continued to step back as she pushed him back to the shelf with the grinning skulls. The duster cleaning the books moved away, and she could hear the chitter of dust bunnies. "I can't do magic, Edward."

He winced. "Please, Brenda. Don't say that. Please don't say that."

"I suck at it, Edward. I can't do half of what you're doing," she pointed to the duster and the moving broom. "I can't even tease a fire spark."

"Why would you want to tease one? They'll start a real fire if you bend them round the twist, you know."

"Edward."

"Brenda," he smiled, and a small bit of her ire vanished. "Not all wizards and witches can do the same thing. If they were all the same, there would be fewer of you. Granny Pollsocks—she was best at what?"

"Well, curses, really. Getting rid of them. And amulets. Tokens."

He held up a long, think index finger. "Right. But she couldn't mix potions—just look at her shelves. At her stores of things. Even you had to have noticed how out of shape everything was."

Brenda took a step back. "Yeah . . ."

"I'm here to tell you that your strength is in potions. You can heal, Brenda."

"Heal?"

He nodded. And there was an excitement around him that buzzed and sparkled. "Yes. You can heal. I came to you because I knew you'd heal me. You have the gift. You knew what to do with those items. I didn't. Anyone can bake a cake, Brenda. But you—you can make it into a Bavarian crème masterpiece with chocolate sprinkles." He nodded. "Eh?"

She took another step back. Something in what he said rang true—she'd always known how to treat injuries to her pets, to her mother on really bad cases, and even to her friends. Skinned knees always healed with no pain around Brenda. She'd even considered going into medical school before Granny chose her to inherit the shop.

"Are you saying that if I change a little of what Granny did—make it my own—I can make this place work?"

He nodded. "And I'll help. It's what I'm here for."

It was right then she knew that Edward wasn't really what he appeared to be—a youngish Englishman with shaggy hair and a rather melodic voice. No—he was more, much more. "Edward—what are you?"

He put a hand on each of her shoulders, and Brenda could feel the heat from his skin through her clothing. "I'm here for you, Brenda." He frowned. "Don't you know?" His smile returned with a radiance to block out the sun. "I'm your familiar."

Edward seemed to know what he was doing—in a sort of ordered chaos. He moved about with a catlike grace, and yet still managed to break a few things. It was like grace, charm, and newborn enthusiasm all rolled up in a very neat and somewhat gangly package. Together—with the aid of the magically touched broom and dusters—they cleaned out the corners, the cabinets, and the shelves.

Tuesday and Wednesday passed with the ever-present ding of the cash register—even as the two of them tidied up. Men and women, old and young, familiar and new, all of them came back to the shop and asked for remedies.

Aches, pains, cuts, bruises, colds.

And it seemed that Brenda could look into their eyes, into each of them, and know if the remedy was for them personally, or for a friend or loved one. She knew what to do. Brenda had always known what to do.

Late in the evening on Wednesday, and after a rousingly well done day at selling and doling out advice, Brenda settled at the table with one of Edward's cups of tea—apparently the man kept a kettle warm all day.

And without a hot plate.

He stood at the register, tallying up the day and announcing that—as of five—they had two thirds of the money needed to satisfy the creditors. "Ah—so bank that, you scoundrels. One more day and you should be caught up."

"How?"

He frowned at her as he bagged the money. "How what?"

"How is that possible? I mean, as of two days ago, no one would come in here. Suddenly they're all in out of the woodwork. Did you do something?"

"Well, yeah," and his grin widened. "I sort of spread the word. Offered many of them a back door. Did a bit of advertising. Sort of my job—it's what I do to help you."

"Back door?"

He put the money into a box on the counter and put his hands on the counter, palms down. "Back door—it's what I tried to tell you on Monday. Hrm. Or was it Tuesday. Oh, can't remember. But you have to look at the analogy. A back door means what?"

Going with the first thought in her head Brenda said, "A way out."

He held his right hand in the air. "Exactly. And that's what Granny did for them. Gave her customers a back door. It's hope, Brenda. There's always hope. And my back door was you. I could have curled up in the nothing and simply ceased to exist—and allowed your doubt to become stronger and stronger. But I couldn't. Because I have hope."

A back door. A way out. Hope that there's something better on the other side. Alarmingly, it all made sense.

"Edward—why are you a familiar?"

Waiting until he had the money safely locked in the iron-and-steel safe Granny Pollsocks kept in the broom closet, Edward joined her at the table, a cup of tea abruptly in his hands. "Why? Why are you a witch? Or why does the moon go round the sun? That's sort of rhetorical, isn't it?"

"No, no," she shook her head. "I mean, familiars are usually small creatures—like cats or toads or some such thing. Usually not grown—men."

The left side of his mouth twitched and turned up. "Familiars are a part of lore and myth, just like witches and wizards. And how many of the old books got those facts right?" He winked. "If I believed them, you should be some scary old hag with a wart at the end of your nose, sitting about and eating children for breakfast."

She smiled. Ah—point taken.

"Don't give in to doubt, Brenda." Edward sipped his tea. "Believe in yourself."

The front door burst open. Both of them turned to watch Detective Jackie Grafton come in, her boots stomping on the newly cleaned and shiny tiled floor. She wore her usual black pants suit and a tan trench coat. Her eyes were wide as she took in the shop, staring at the improvements, at the working lights.

"What have you done?" Jackie's voice boomed out.

Brenda actually shrank in size in her chair.

"Well, hello," Edward stood up and walked up to Jackie, his hand extended. "You must be Brenda's mother. So charmed to meet you."

Jackie narrowed her eyes at him. "Who are you? What are you doing here?"

"I'm Brenda's new employee. Edward Darlington."

He glanced down at his still extended hand. When it was obvious she wasn't going to shake it, he clasped his hands behind his back. "Care for a cup of tea?"

She moved past him to Brenda and loomed over her. "What is this nonsense about not selling the shop? I got a call from Mr. Bitterman—he was all happy and gushy that you'd nearly paid up your bill? And you'd given him a sachet that completely cleaned out the cat-pee from his house?"

Brenda tried not to laugh—but she did smirk. "Yes, Mom. I did that. But I told you I didn't want to sell— that was your idea."

"Oh? And you think you can keep this place working with two days of good luck?" She snorted. "Oh, please, Brenda. Just give it all up. You'll never be as magical as Granny. None of us were."

Just then one of the dusters swished out from behind a bookshelf and started its controlled and precise sweep of each shelf. The broom came from behind the counter, chasing dust bunnies across the floor— though they were much smaller than before.

Brenda liked the look of disbelief in her mother's eyes. It was a look that rarely sat at home there. "I'm afraid you're not quite right on that, Mom." She knew Edward wanted to answer her in the same manner, but she felt it was better if it all came from her.

"Oh?" She glanced at the broom and duster again. "Parlor tricks. That's all. You can't do magic."

"Maybe not magic the way Granny could, Mom. But I can. I can heal. I can give advice. And I can even make a great cup of tea." She held up her cup. "Would you like some?"

There was something else happening here, and she didn't realize what until she looked at Edward. She knew it when she looked at his eyes. She knew it when her knees didn't knock. She knew it when her palms didn't sweat.

She was nervous around her mother—but she wasn't doubtful.

"No. I don't like tea. Well, you're doomed to fail

at this idea as well, Brenda. I'd hoped to spare you from that harsh reality. But those same people who turned on you when you failed them before will turn on you when you fail them again."

Brenda stood then and Edward moved a little closer. He held a candle in his hand. A thick, white candle. He handed it to her. "I won't fail, Mom."

"Yes, you will, child. I don't have magic. You don't have magic."

"I have back door magic, Mom." And she looked at the candle wick and snapped her fingers.

No fire sparks appeared. No wisps. Not even a tinge of smoke issued from the candle. A single spark, and the flame ignited and burned a tall, strong blue. Brenda knew it wasn't magic—she didn't know how to conjure fire without a fire spark. But she'd thought of the door, and she'd thought of Edward's faith in her, and she'd thought about the faith she had in herself.

And hope.

She'd seen the back door in her mind.

Jackie's expression was resigned. She adjusted the purse on her shoulders, straightened her coat, and went back to the door. She opened it and then turned to face the two of them. "I won't be back, Brenda. I tried to help you. But it's all in your hands now. Yours," she narrowed her eyes at Edward. "And his."

And with that she slammed the door.

Neither of them said a word until Edward moved closer and pinched out the flame. "You thirsty? I'm thirsty. But not for tea. I know this splendid pub over in Yorkshire—and they have the worst meat pasties— but a fine dart board. Care to come?"

"Yorkshire?" Brenda blinked at him. "As in England?"

"Well, of course."

"Edward, how are we going to get to—"

"Back door," he nodded to the stairwell. "And we'd better get a move on."

She grabbed her coat as she followed him down the

stairs to the door. It looked different somehow. More alive. Vivid colors that seemed to swirl and move all around.

"Ready?"

Brenda put her arm in his. "I could kiss you for being here for me."

"Ah—one rule for familiar to witch or wizard," he looked down at her. "No fraternizing. Can't be mixing it all up." And with that, he smiled and gave her a soft but firm kiss on the lips.

"Edward?"

And he opened the back door.

OCCUPATIONAL HAZARD

by Mike Resnick

I HAVE just given 75-to-1 against Lowborn Prince, who has not finished in the money since G. Washington chopped down the cherry tree, and I am wondering what kind of idiot puts five bills on this refugee from the glue factory when Benny Fifth Street walks up to me and whispers as follows:

"I saw you take that bet. Lay it off."

"What are you talking about?" I say. "Booking five hundred dollars on Lowborn Prince is as close as a bookie can come to stealing."

"Lay it off," he repeats.

"Why?" I ask.

He looks around to make sure no one is listening. "I just got word: The hex is in."

"Not to worry," I assure him. "I paid my hex protection to Big-Hearted Milton not two hours ago."

"You don't understand," says Benny Fifth Street. "Don't you know who made that bet?"

"Some little wimp I never saw before."

"He's a runner for Sam the Goniff!" he says. "And you know the Goniff. He's never bet on a fair race in his life."

The horses are approaching the starting gate. It's too late to lay the bet off, so I just make the Sign of

67

the Pentagon and cross my fingers and hope Benny is wrong.

The bell rings, the gate opens, and Lowborn Prince fires out of there like he's Seattle Slew, or maybe Man o' War. Before they've gone a quarter of a mile, he's twenty lengths in front, and I can see that Flyboy Billy Tuesday has still got him under wraps. He keeps that lead to the head of the stretch. Then Billy taps him twice with the whip and he takes off, coming home forty-five lengths in front. By the time Billy has slowed him down and brought him back to the Winner's Circle, the race is official and the prices have been posted, and Lowborn Prince pays $153.40 for a two-dollar bet. But I didn't book a two-dollar bet. I pull out my pocket abacus and dope out what I owe the Goniff, and it comes to $38,870, and I know that I have to pay it or the Goniff will send some of his muscle, like Two Ton Boris or, worse still, Seldom Seen Seymour, to extract it one pint of blood at a time.

I hunt up Big-Hearted Milton, who is sitting at his usual seat in the clubhouse bar. As he sees me coming he pulls a dozen hundred dollar bills out of his pocket and thrusts them at me.

"Here's your money back," he says. "I didn't deliver, so I won't keep it."

"That's fine, Milton. Now give me another thirty-seven grand, and we'll call it square."

"That was never part of the deal," he says with dignity.

"Neither was letting a hex get by you."

"I *tried* to find you and give it back when I heard what was coming down," says Milton. "It's not my fault you were ducking out of sight because the cops were making the rounds."

"You *knew* Lowborn Prince was going to win?" I demand.

"I knew the hex was in. I didn't know who was going to win, because I didn't know who the Goniff was putting his money on. There were three other long shots in the race. It could have been any of them."

"What went wrong?" I ask. "You've broken lots of hexes for me."

"Yeah, but they were from normal, run-of-the-mill mages. Not this time."

"Who the hell does the Goniff have hexing for him?" I ask.

"You ever hear of Dead End Dugan?" says Milton.

"Dugan?" I repeat, frowning. "When did he get out?"

"Not *out*," Milton corrects me. "*Up*. They buried him in Yonkers, and that was supposed to be the end of it."

"So?"

"So he's a zombie now, and my magic isn't strong enough to counteract his."

"Look, Milton," I say, "this is serious. If I take one more beating like this, I'm out of business, and probably out of fingers and other even more vital parts as well. What am I going to do?"

"You need a real expert to go up against him."

"A voodoo priest, maybe?" I ask.

"Yeah, that might do it," says Milton.

I gather Benny Fifth Street and Gently Gently Dawkins and tell them we're leaving the track early, that we've got to find a voodoo priest before I can go back to work. Benny immediately suggests we buy plane tickets to Voodooland, but I explain that there isn't any such place, and Gently Gently says that he's got a friend up in Harlem who belongs to some weird cult and for all he knows it's a voodoo cult, and I tell him to offer his friend anything but make sure he brings his voodoo priest to my place, and I'll be waiting there until I hear from him.

So I go home, and I send Benny out to bring back some healthy food like blintzes and chopped liver and maybe a couple of knishes, and then there is nothing to do but sit around and watch the sports results on

my new 20-inch crystal ball. The big news of the day
is Lowborn Prince, and it is so painful to watch that
I almost can't eat my blintzes, even though I have
loaded them up with sour cream and cinnamon sugar,
but at the last minute I decide I have to practice a
little self-denial so I only pour one container of straw-
berries on them, and I spread the chopped liver over
little poker-chip-sized pieces of low-cal rye bread.

Finally, at about eleven o'clock, there's a knock on
the door, and it's Gently Gently Dawkins. He walks
in and tosses his hat onto a table.

"So where is he?" I demand.

"He's on his way up the stairs," said Gently Gently.
"He's an old guy. He don't climb as fast as I do."

"And you left him alone?" I yell.

"Believe me, no one's going to bother him," says
Gently Gently and, just as the words leave his mouth,
in hobbles this stooped-over, bald, wrinkled, old black
guy, and I would say he was dressed in rags but Ezek-
ial the Rag Merchant would take offense.

"*This?*" I say. "*This* is what you spent all day looking for?"

"I'm pleased to meet you, too," says the old guy.

I turn to him. "You're really a voodoo priest?"

He shakes his head. "Do I *look* like an amateur?"

"Don't ask me what you look like and maybe we
won't come to blows," I say. "If you aren't a voodoo
priest, just what the hell are you and why are you
here?"

"I'm here because this nice man—" he gestures
toward Gently Gently Dawkins, "—put the word out
that he was looking for someone who could neutralize
a zombie's hex." He smiles and taps his chest with an
emaciated thumb. "You're looking at him."

"Okay, you're not a voodoo priest," I say. "What
are you?"

"The answer to your prayers," he replies. "Also, I
happen to be the only *mundumugu* in New York."

"What's a *mundumugu*?"

"You might call me a witch doctor."

"I might also call you a crazy old man who's wasting my time," I say.

He makes a tiny gesture in the air with his left hand, and suddenly I can't move a muscle.

"Oh, ye of little faith," he says with a sigh. "I ought to leave right now, but Dead End Dugan is giving a bad name to both hexes and corpses. My name is Mtepwa." He extends his hand, and somehow I extend mine, even though I am not trying to. "And you are Harry the Book. I am almost pleased to meet you."

He snaps his fingers, and suddenly I can move again.

"I hope you didn't take offense, Mr. Mtepwa, sir," I say. "It's been a bad day."

"I understand," says Mtepwa. "But tomorrow will be better."

"It will?"

"It will, or my name isn't Cool Jumbo Cool."

"But your name *isn't* Cool Jumbo Cool," I point out.

"Details, details," he says with a shrug.

"Uh, I hate to seem forward," I say, "but what is this gonna cost me?"

"I haven't decided yet," he says. "But whatever it is, I promise you'll be pleased with the price."

The fourth race at Belmont is coming up, and I'm getting really nervous. Bilgewater, who couldn't beat my mother around the track, even if she was carrying 130 pounds on her back and running with blinkers, is 120-to-1, and this time the Goniff doesn't even use a runner, he comes up and makes the bet himself: $1,800 on Bilgewater.

"That's a big bet," I note. "I'll probably have to lay some of it off."

"You can if you can," he says, and I realize that the word is out that Dead End Dugan has hexed the race and there is no way that any other bookie will take part of the bet. "I hear you've got a new boy working for you," continues the Goniff.

"Boy isn't exactly the word I'd use," I reply unhappily.

"I just want to do you a favor, Harry," he says.
"Don't waste your money on another mage. I guarantee you that nothing in the field can beat Bilgewater.
There's simply no way."

He utters a nasty laugh and walks off to his private
box, and Mtepwa approaches me.

"That was Sam the Goniff?" he asks.

"That was him."

He looks after the Goniff, and nods his head. "I
knew someone who looked just like him—a long
time ago."

"Maybe it was just the Goniff when he was
younger," I say.

"I doubt it," says Mtepwa. "This was before Columbus discovered America."

I wonder just how gullible he thinks I am, but we
have more important things to discuss, and I tell him
that the Goniff has admitted that Dead End Dugan
has hexed the race and that nothing in the field can
beat Bilgewater.

"Well," he says with a shrug, "if they can't, they
can't."

"What?" I scream, and then lower my voice when
everyone starts staring. "I thought you were here to
put Dugan in his place!"

"You have undertakers to do that," answers
Mtepwa. "I'm here to make sure that his hex doesn't
work."

"But if no one in the field can beat Bilgewater . . . " I
begin, but then there's a cheer from the crowd and I
realize that the race has started and I turn to watch
it, and I immediately wish I hadn't turned, because
Bilgewater is already leading by ten lengths and as far
as I can tell he hasn't drawn a deep breath.

I look at the rest of the field. Most of them are
lathered with sweat, half of them are lame, and the
rest spend more time watching the birds in the infield
than the horses ahead of them.

"I should never have listened to Milton!" I mutter.

"Voodoo priest my ass! I need a .550 Nitro Express and a telescopic site."

"Be quiet," says Mtepwa. "I must concentrate."

I don't know why, but I do what he says. Bilgewater enters the far turn fifteen in front, and Flyboy Billy Tuesday hasn't touched him with the whip yet, and then Mtepwa mumbles a little something that sounds like it's right out of *King Solomon's Mines*, and suddenly there is a big black-maned lion on the track, and he launches himself at Bilgewater, and the horse goes down and Billy Tuesday goes flying through the air and winds up in an infield pond, and the whole field circles around the lion, who is busy munching on the tastier parts of Bilgewater, and then the race is over and Benny Fifth Street and Gently Gently Dawkins are thumping Mtepwa on the back so hard I'm afraid they're going to damage him, and I shove them away.

The stewards post an Inquiry sign, and a moment later they announce that the lion has been disqualified and placed last, and the result is now official. And two minutes after that, the Goniff comes storming up to me, blood in his eye.

"I don't know how you did it," he says, and he's so hot I am surprised steam isn't shooting out of his nose and ears, "but it had better never happen again!"

"Don't bet on bad horses, and it won't," I say cockily, because as far as I know this is the first bet the Goniff has lost since he was five years old (and no one ever saw the winner again).

"You listen to me, Harry the Book!" he says, shoving twenty large into my hand. "Kid Testosterone is fighting Terrible Tommy Tulsa at the Garden tomorrow night. I'm putting this on him to win by a knockout. If you pull anything funny, if you mess with my boy Dead End Dugan again, you won't be alive to gloat about it. Do I make myself clear?"

He turns on his heel and stalks off before I can answer, which is just as well because I have no idea what to say.

"Who is Kid Testosterone?" asks Mtepwa.

"It is possible that he is the worst fighter who ever lived," I say. "At the very least, he is the worst fighter still licensed to get his brains beat out. He has fought 47 times, and has been knocked out 46 times. His greatest triumph was when he lost a unanimous decision to Glass Jaw Malone eleven years ago."

"I see," said Mtepwa.

"So what are we going to do?" I say. "The Goniff never backs down on a threat. If the Kid doesn't win, I won't be alive the next morning."

"No problem," says Mtepwa.

"No problem for *you*, Mtepwa," I say. "But what about *me?*"

"I've got 28 hours to figure it out," he says. "And I wish you'd start calling me Cool Jumbo Cool. Mtepwa just doesn't seem right in this venue."

"Just get the Goniff and his zombie off my case once and for all, and I'll call you anything you want," I promise.

"Every occupation has its hazards," he says. "You shouldn't let this upset you."

"I don't mind being upset," I tell him. "It's being dismembered that bothers me."

I am just as upset when we show up at the Garden the next night. Mtepwa has gone into some kind of African swami trance, and only comes out of it an hour before the fight. I ask him what he was doing, and he says he was napping, that he's a 683-year-old man and he's had a lot of excitement and he needs his sleep.

"Did you solve our problem?" I ask.

"Well, actually, it's *your* problem," he explains. "Nobody's going to bother me no matter how the fight comes out."

"All right, did you solve *my* problem?" I say.

"I'm working on it."

"Well, work faster!" I snap. "If the Kid wins, I'm broke, and if he loses, I'm dead!"

"Fascinating problem," he said. "Rather like Fermat's Unfinished Theorem. Of course, if he'd simply paid me the five cattle and the virgin, I'd have shown him how to solve it."

"Will you please concentrate on Harry the Book's Unfinished Theorem?" I say pleadingly.

Before he can answer, I sense a presence hovering over me, and I turn and there is Sam the Goniff, smoking one of his five-dollar cigars, and with him is a guy who smells kind of funny and whose eyes seem to be staring sightlessly off into the distance and who has a lot of dirt under his fingernails, and I know that this is Dead End Dugan.

"Hi, Harry," says the Goniff. "I'm glad to see you're a fight fan. I'd hate to think that I'd have to go looking for you after the Kid knocks out Terrible Tommy."

"I'll be right here," I say pugnaciously, but that is only because I know that hiding from the Goniff is like hiding from the IRS, only harder.

"I'll count on it," he says, and heads off to his ringside seat with Dugan, and I notice that Seldom Seen Seymour is already there waiting for him, just in case he needs a little help collecting after the fight.

"Have you come up with anything yet?" I ask Mtepwa.

"Yes," he says.

"What is it?" I ask eagerly.

"I've come up with a sinus problem, I think," he answers. "Too much cigar smoke in here."

"What about Kid Testosterone?" I demand. "If he loses, I die!"

"Then he can't lose, can he?" says Mtepwa.

"But if he wins, I'm not only broke, but I haven't got enough cash to cover the Goniff's bet, and Seldom Seen Seymour will take me apart piece by piece."

"Then he can't win, can he?" says Mtepwa.

"I've got it!" I say. "You're going to shoot him before the fight starts!"

Mtepwa just gives me a pitying look, and turns to

concentrate on the ring, where they are carrying out
what's left of the Missouri Masher, and then Kid Testosterone and Terrible Tommy Tulsa enter the ring,
and the ref is giving them their instructions, such as
no biting or kicking or low blows, and because this is
New York, he also tells them no kissing, and then
they go to their corners, and the bell rings and they
come out and Tommy swings a haymaker that will
knock the Kid's head into the fourth row, but somehow his timing is off and he misses, and the Kid delivers a pair of punches that couldn't smash an empty
wineglass, but suddenly Tommy's nose is bleeding, and
he blinks his eyes like he can't believe that the fight
is thirty seconds old and the Kid is still standing.

But the Kid is still on his feet at the end of the
round, and it later turns out that one of the three
judges actually gives him the round, and another calls
it even, and that is the way the fight goes for three
rounds, but I am not watching the fight, I am watching
Sam the Goniff, and between the third and fourth
round he somehow gets the Kid's attention and holds
his fist out with his thumb down and I know he has
just signaled the Kid to end it in the fourth round.

I am not the only one who has seen it. Mtepwa is
staring right at the Goniff, and he just smiles, and I
know he's got something up his sleeve besides his arm,
but I don't know what.

The bell rings and the fighters come out for the
fourth round. Terrible Tommy connects first, a blow
to the solar plexus that should double the Kid over in
pain, but instead Tommy screams and pulls his hand
back like he's just broken it punching a concrete wall,
and then they circle around until the Kid's back is to
me, and suddenly Mtewpa starts mumbling again, and
the Kid throws his money punch, and I look, figuring
this is the end and Terrible Tommy is going down for
the count, but it's *not* Terrible Tommy, it's the Goniff,
and he takes the punch on the point of his chin and
goes reeling around the ring, and the Kid starts pum-

meling him, and it occurs to me that the Kid looks a lot more like Rocky Marciano and a lot less like Kid Testosterone.

Every time he delivers what looks like a knockout blow, Mtepwa starts mumbling again, and no matter how much punishment the Goniff takes he stays on his feet. Finally, the Kid winds up and knocks him through the ropes and he falls to the floor right in front of me.

"Is there something you'd like to say to me before you climb back into the ring?" I ask pleasantly.

"I ain't climbing back in there!" he mutters through bleeding lips.

"Yes, you are," says Mtepwa, and against his will the Goniff gets to his feet and turns to face the ring.

"All right, all right!" he says. "I cancel the bet!"

"You don't even have to cancel," says Mtepwa before I can stop him. "Just promise you'll never bet with Harry again, or use Dead End Dugan to hex a sporting event."

"I promise," says the Goniff.

The instant the words are out of his mouth he collapses, the referee declares Kid Testosterone the winner, and the Goniff is carted off to the hospital.

"Thanks for nothing!" I say to Mtepwa. "We didn't cancel, so I still have to pay off! The bet was that the Kid would knock Terrible Tommy out, and he did!"

"The evening's not over yet," he replies, and indeed it isn't, because the Kid fails a urine test, which doesn't surprise anyone given that he made it all the way to the fourth round, and the fight is declared a draw—not a noncontest where I would have to return the Goniff's money, but a draw, where everyone who bet on either fighter loses and only those who bet there'd be a draw win.

And that's the story.

Well, not quite all of it. I'm not a bookie anymore. I took on a full partner—Cool Jumbo Cool, who even-

tually decided that *this* was the payment he wanted—
and these days we head a pretty successful betting
syndicate.

Jumbo's really gotten into the swing of things; he
likes this milieu. Tonight he's hexed the big game between the Montana Buttes and the Georgia Geldings.
I gave Benny Fifth Street a promotion, and we've even
got a couple of new runners. In fact, I have to close
now. It's time to pass my money to Dead End Dugan
and the Goniff and tell them where to lay our bets.

TIES THAT BIND

by Annie Reed

THE first hint of trouble came from Gris in Research and Development.

"We're having a bit of a problem getting the enchantments to stick to the new cuffs," he said to me in an early morning phone call.

I've never done mornings well, but when you're the wizard in charge of the largest magical enhancements company in the city, and a woman in a man's profession to boot, whether you do mornings well or not doesn't matter one damn bit.

I leaned back in my leather chair and gazed out my tenth-floor office window at the overcast sky. The streets below were still wet from last night's rain. I could almost smell the wet asphalt. It would probably rain again today. I pinched the bridge of my nose against an impending headache that wasn't all sinuses.

"Is it the alloy or the spell?" I asked Gris.

"Can't tell yet," he said. "We're still testing. Just thought you should know, Nell. Considering."

Yeah. Considering.

My company had a contract with the city to supply enhanced weapons and restraints to the police department. Research and Development had been testing redesigned handcuffs. Lighter weight with an easy snap-close lock, the new handcuffs were supposed to

79

address problems the cops had with the old handcuff design. Personally, I thought any set of handcuffs that could keep a changeling in its true shape or prevent a wizard from casting a spell to escape custody were good enough, but my father built this company by supplying our customers with whatever they wanted. And what the customer I had a meeting with later today wanted was new and better handcuffs.

"Keep me informed," I said, and I hung up the phone.

I unlocked the bottom drawer in my desk and took out the thick, three-ring binder I kept there under lock and key. To the uninitiated, the binder looked like nothing more than what a high school student might carry around in a backpack. But instead of notes on Shakespeare, calculus, and the culture of ancient Rome, this notebook was chock-full of page after page of spells and instructions written in a tiny, crabbed hand, all neatly separated into categories by brightly-colored index tabs. My father had been anal in the extreme. This was his spellbook. What he'd built this company with.

And what he'd handed over to his only daughter when he died.

I glanced at my watch. Eight-fifteen. I had a little less than two hours before my meeting with the city's purchasing director. If the problem was in the enchantment, the answer should be in the spellbook. I might not be powerful enough to cast the spell myself, but that didn't mean I couldn't spot a problem with the enchantment.

I opened the binder and started to read.

Templeton Rae showed up for our meeting ten minutes early. Not surprising. Templeton was a born pencil pusher. He probably dreamed about numbers in neat, orderly columns that always balanced and never dipped over into the red. Tall and gaunt-looking with a movie villain mustache, Templeton handled the city's multimillion-dollar purchasing contracts as if every penny the city spent came from his own pocket.

I met him in the ninth-floor conference room. Outside of my office, this corner conference room had the best view in the building. If the sky hadn't started pouring rain an hour ago, we could have seen the snow-tipped peaks of the mountain range to the east from one set of floor-to-ceiling windows and across the bay to the exclusive homes on Marlette Island out the other. The view today wasn't quite as impressive. Still, it never hurt to treat Templeton Rae to the best.

He didn't shake my hand when I came into the conference room, not a good sign. Still, I smiled my warmest smile and asked him about his family.

"Fine, they're all fine, but let's get to the point," he said as we sat down—on opposite sides of the conference table. "I've received a bid for lightweight, enchanted handcuffs that's quite a bit lower than yours."

I tried to keep my face impassive even though my heart rate went through the roof. Our contracts with the city for the various enhanced items we produce comprised more than half of my company's annual revenue. If we lost the handcuff contract, that would just be the start of a long, slow slide into downsizing and maybe even bankruptcy.

"I didn't know you put the job out to bid," I said.

"We put every job out to bid."

"After you sign the contract?"

Templeton had the good grace to look uncomfortable. "This bid did come in quite late. I wouldn't have looked at it if the numbers weren't significantly lower."

"How much lower?"

"Significantly."

I only had so much I could cut off my bottom line, and Templeton knew it. He was fishing, trying to see how low I would go.

"We've got a signed contract," I said. "It's a little late to renegotiate this deal, don't you think?"

Templeton did what I like to think of as a mental shrug. He leaned back in his chair just the slightest, and the tension in his face loosened a fraction. If he'd been a less-seasoned negotiator, he might have actually twitched his shoulders, but he didn't.

"It's never too late to renegotiate, you know that, Nell," he said. "Besides . . . the delivery date's in a week, and your people haven't spoken to anyone in Receiving about when to expect shipment. That's not like you. It makes people on my end nervous."

It made *him* nervous, we both knew that. What I didn't know was that no one had been in touch with the city about the shipment, and that made *me* nervous.

Templeton was right. This wasn't how my company operated. I wondered exactly how long Gris had known about the problem with the enchantments, and why he waited until this morning to tell me. What exactly was he hiding? If we couldn't deliver the cuffs on time, that gave the city a reason to back out of the deal.

This was all too coincidental. Never trust a coincidence, my father used to say. And Templeton showing up the same morning Gris told me he had a problem with the cuffs was a damn big coincidence.

Whether I wanted to believe it or not, the conclusion was inevitable. I had a spy.

Gris Mellion was my father's oldest friend. They'd gone to school together, raised hell—almost literally—together, and been inseparable until graduation, when they went their separate ways—my father to start a family and this business, Gris to travel the world and continue learning how to be the best wizard he could be.

Unfortunately for Gris, the best wizard he could be wasn't all that great. Sure, he could learn incantations and he had great ideas. He just couldn't put his ideas to practical use. My father could.

When Gris came back from his travels with a dozen sketchbooks filled with vague ideas, a leather-bound spellbook less than half the size of my father's binder, and no money in his pocket, my father gave Gris a job as head of Research and Development. Together again, the two of them clicked. With Gris's ideas and my father's practical know-how, they invented most of the magical weapons the police department used every day.

After my father died, I inherited his share of the patents for those weapons and the income generated from licenses for their use. I kept Gris on, made sure he had assistants with the same practical know-how my father had, and I wrote a hefty bonus structure into his employment contract commensurate with the income his inventions brought the company. Gris had as much riding on this contract with the city as I did.

After my meeting with Templeton Rae, I rode the elevator down to the sixth-floor lab that Research and Development called home. I found Gris swearing at the top of his lungs at a vaguely handcuff-shaped wad of green goo.

Gris barely looked up when I stopped on the other side of the pristine white workbench in his office.

"Let me guess," I said, nodding at the green goo. "That's the alloy that won't behave?"

Gris looked every bit like a fairytale wizard. Long white beard, long white hair, gnarled knuckles, wire-rimmed spectacles perched on the end of a prominent nose. Gris wasn't really all that old, not for a wizard, but according to my mother, the things Gris and my father did in their young and stupid days took a toll on both of them. Although my mother never said, I got the feeling the things that made Gris look old before his time were the same things that took my father's life.

"Damn stuff," Gris said.

He waved his hand over the goo, muttered an incantation, and with a whiff of ozone the stuff blinked out of existence.

"Back to Minerology," Gris said in response to my stare.

I had a strict rule—the company recycled whenever possible. Gris hadn't really zapped the goo off the face of the earth, although he probably wanted to. Instead, he'd reduced the stuff to its component minerals to be used in something a little more practical. Like a paper clip.

"Figure out what's wrong yet?" I asked.

Gris wiped his mouth with the back of his hand. "I'm using the same enchantment we've been using on handcuffs since the day we invented the things. The enchantment works." He pointed to a length of silver chain, the links barely larger than the ones in the necklace I wore. "Try wrapping that around your wrists," he said.

I held my wrists together and Gris looped the chain around them. As soon as the chain wrapped around once, it started to emanate a faint green glow—the binding enchantment was working. I shouldn't be able to use any magic as long as the chain was wrapped around me.

I tried a simple incantation to transport a cup of tea from my office to the table in front of me. Nothing. I tried moving my wrists, but the chain held tight. I tried breaking the chain, it was flimsy enough. No go. The chain might as well have been made of titanium.

"So it's not the enchantment," I said as Gris unwrapped the chain and the enchantment went dormant. I had a thin cut on the back of my right hand where I had tried to get free. It stung like a paper cut. I rubbed at it to make the sting go away.

"And it's not the cuffs," Gris said.

He reached into a cardboard box on the table behind him and took out a pair of the redesigned handcuffs. The cuffs were noticeably thinner than the last generation we produced for the city. They felt just as sturdy when Gris snapped one cuff around my left wrist. Unfortunately, it took only a minor incantation on my part to unlock the cuff. It wouldn't keep any magic user restrained for more than half a heartbeat.

"But we put the two together . . ."

Gris held his hand over the cuffs and murmured the spell for the enchantment. The handcuffs took on a green glow for a moment like they were supposed to, and then the cuffs seemed to absorb the glow—again, like they were supposed to. But as the last of the glow faded, the metal handcuffs seemed to shiver, and the cuffs simply melted. Another mess of green goo.

Great. Just great. "And you didn't tell me about this earlier because . . ."

Gris shot a long-suffering look over my shoulder. I turned around to see a stack of cardboard boxes a good six feet high against the side wall of Gris's office. The sides of the boxes bowed out, damp and disgusting looking, and now that I was turned in their direction, I could smell the same whiff of ozone I'd smelled when Gris made the goo disappear.

"We didn't have this problem until yesterday," Gris said. "I enchanted these cuffs last week, Shipping packed them up, had them inventoried and invoiced, ready to go. I got a call yesterday afternoon from Eleanor wanting to know who the practical joker was so she could roast his head on a spit."

Eleanor, the manager in Shipping, was a dwarf with a head for details and a quick temper. Nobody, including me, liked a call from a pissed-off Eleanor.

"And the cuffs were fine last week," I said.

Gris nodded. "We overproduced on the cuffs, so I tried the enchantments again last night and this morning. This time . . ." He sighed. "Well, you saw what happened. The Production Department's working overtime re-creating the cuffs, but without the enchantment, we might as well melt them down into keychains for all the good they'll do."

"Who knows the enchantment besides you?"

"No one," Gris said.

"You have it written down anywhere?"

"No." And he sounded upset that I asked.

The magic-inhibiting enchantment was my company's biggest trade secret. My father had stumbled on the spell while he was playing around with another spell—one that was supposed to inhibit the growth of weeds, of all things. The enchantment worked by interrupting a magic user's connection with the natural world. As long as whatever held the enchantment was latched in a complete circle around a magic user—like handcuffs, or the chain Gris had wrapped around my wrist—the spell was complete and the magic user's connection to the source of their magic was interrupted.

The spell was written down in my father's binder. Gris had memorized the spell after my father died so that he could perform the incantations. Gris was the only person I trusted with the spell, and he'd promised me he would never tell another living soul. If someone knew the spell, not only could they use it to make their own enchanted weapons—like the bidder Templeton Rae told me about—but they could, in theory, add an enchanted mineral to the alloy for the cuffs that would render the spell inert.

"And I suppose you've checked the formula for the alloy, made sure nothing's in the mix that would cause the green goop effect."

Gris shook his head. "I've gone over it, Minerology's gone over it. There's nothing in the cuffs that should be causing this."

Nothing should, but something was. If it wasn't Gris and it wasn't something in the cuffs, that meant I had a magic user, and a pretty powerful one at that, interfering with the incantation at a level far beyond what I could detect.

I needed help.

It was time to talk to my father.

Fortune-tellers were a dime a dozen in the city. Some were legitimate, most were bogus. My mother was the real thing.

When I was little, my mother would annoy me no end by grounding me for things I hadn't done yet. Oh, I'd thought about doing them, even worked out schemes in my mind for ways I could trick my parents, but it wasn't until I was nine years old that I realized my mother was a precog.

After my father died, I spent a good deal of time being angry with my mother for her apparent lack of grief over her husband's death. She only laughed at me and told me the world was a far bigger place than I could see. One night she brought a crystal ball to my house, made me sit with her at my dining room table, and showed me what she meant.

I canceled my afternoon appointments, made sure my father's spellbook was locked up nice and tight, with a second level of security spells just in case, and took the ferry to my mother's house on Marlette Island.

"I need to talk to Dad," I said when she answered the door.

She raised an eyebrow, but I must have looked harried enough she didn't grill me. She took my soggy raincoat, made me a cup of tea—decaf—and led me into what she called her parlor. The room was circular, lined with floor-to-ceiling bookshelves loaded with decades worth of books—fiction; no spellbooks for my mother—and French doors that overlooked her gardens. The gardener, a wood elf with long, flowing, brunette hair, was at work in the rain planting spring seedlings. The scene looked peaceful. Sometimes I wished I could be like that—impervious to the weather and the bottom line, just living in touch with nature. Unfortunately, my abilities were more in tune with the business world.

My mother sat in a deeply-padded wingback chair. Her crystal ball rested on a small round table next to her. I sat in another wingback chair, this one not as well-used or as well-padded, the hot cup of tea cradled in my hands.

"I don't suppose you want to tell me what this is all about," my mother said.

"We're having a problem with one of Dad's spells," I said. I didn't want to tell her all of my suspicions. While I knew my mother was the real deal, I didn't want to influence her in any way. When she contacted my father, I wanted to know I was really talking to him.

My mother sat back in her chair and closed her eyes. She didn't need to touch the crystal ball, unlike the charlatans who hovered over their tables and wailed and fluttered their fingers over crystal that remained stubbornly clear. No, my mother just closed her eyes and concentrated. I suppose it helped that my father had been—and still was—the one true love of her life. It gave her a connection to him that no one else had. Even me.

I sat still and quiet, held my tea but didn't drink any of it. I watched the gardener walk on top of the muddy ground, his boots clean, no footprints in his wake. He seemed to commune with each seedling he put in the ground. It could have been my imagination, but I almost sensed the conversations they were having.

The air in the parlor suddenly seemed heavy, and the light had an odd quality, as if someone had layered more clouds in between the earth and the sun. My heart started beating faster. I had an odd taste in my mouth, something metallic and unpleasant. In the garden the wood elf stopped in the middle of putting a seedling in the ground, his head tilted as if he were listening to something only he could hear.

I glanced at the crystal ball and gasped. The inside was roiling with dark clouds shot through with bolts of lightning.

That had never happened before.

A loud, ugly laugh echoed in the room. My mother's head lolled sideways, her mouth open and slack.

"Oh, Nelly, Nelly, who have you come looking for?"

The voice coming out of my mother's mouth was just as ugly as the laugh. It made my skin crawl.

"Who are you?" I asked.

"Don't you recognize your dear old dad?"

This was not my father.

"Who are you?" I asked again.

I felt power crackle around the room. I started to say an incantation to create a layer of protection around my mother.

"I wouldn't do that if I were you."

I watched as my mother's face took on a blue tinge, and I realized she wasn't breathing.

"Stop that!" I shouted.

I must have dropped my teacup. I dimly heard it shatter on the hardwood floor. It was enough to break my concentration, and the spell I had started to cast drifted away from me. Color returned to my mother's cheeks.

"You've been a bad, bad girl, playing with things beyond your comprehension. I've put a stop to that."

What?

"Who *are* you?"

The air coalesced in front of me. Mist formed into shape, and shape took on substance.

My father's face. The thing in the room with us wore my father's face.

The French doors burst open, and the wood elf practically flew into the room on a gust of wind and rain. He shouted something in a language I didn't understand and threw a handful of greenery at the misty shape of my father's face. The mist exploded in a barrage of light and sound. I screamed and clamped my hands over my ears, shut my eyes, but I could still see my father's face.

Only it wasn't his face as I remembered it. This face was evil and hateful, the eyes full of vengeful fury, the mouth filled with sharpened teeth. It was the stuff of nightmares.

When I opened my eyes, the presence was gone. The wood elf crouched on the floor with my mother cradled in his arms.

I crawled over to her, touched her face. Her skin was cold and clammy, her breaths shallow, but at least she was breathing.

"Mom?"

It took a minute before her eyelids fluttered open. I watched as realization hit her, and she began to cry.

In an odd reversal of parenting roles, I fixed my mother a strong cup of tea. The wood elf, who introduced himself as Diray Gant, brought a blanket to wrap around my mother's shoulders as she sat huddled at the kitchen table, then he brought in a potted geranium from the garden to put on the table next to her. She tried to smile at him, but her eyes were too haunted for the smile to work. He sat down next to her and held her hand, and I realized he was probably more than just her gardener.

"What was that?" I asked after I got a cup of tea for myself.

My mother shared a look with Diray. He nodded almost imperceptibly.

"I need to tell you something about your father. Your father and Gris, actually," she said. "You've known all your life that your father dabbled in things he probably shouldn't have."

My father's "wild days" were legendary. But apparently not everything had made it into legend.

"There's a dark side to the magical world," my mother said. "I don't have to tell you that. You work with the police, and the police deal with it every day. The criminals they arrest, the ones they use your cuffs to restrain—that's just the tip of that side of the magical realm. Your father was a curious man. Both of them were. He and Gris. So sure of themselves. Young and cocky, they thought they could just go on a little vacation and none of what they did would touch them."

She took a sip of tea. I didn't want mine anymore. A sick little ball of dread had started to squeeze my insides into a tight knot.

"Of course, it did touch them," my mother said. "It took Gris's youth, and eventually it took your father's life. I believe deep down inside he knew it would, which is why he spent so much time and energy developing things to contain the evil he'd tasted." She looked at me, her eyes moist and sad. "He didn't want it to touch you, to touch us."

It made sense. Most of the patents my father and Gris had registered were for devices that contained magic. The story about how he developed the incantation as an accident was just that—a story, no more real that the fiction my mother loved to read. He'd been looking for the right spell all along.

I took a deep breath. "So that was my father?"

My mother shook her head. "No. No, that wasn't your father. It was just using him. Hitching a ride on his memory to frighten you away."

"It?"

"You don't want to know more than that. Trust me on this, Nell."

I saw the fear in my mother's eyes. I believed her.

So whatever it was, it was using my father to get to me. To get to us.

Using him.

To get to all of us? Including Gris?

If it had touched my father, had it touched Gris?

What if Gris had been saying the wrong incantation all along and didn't even know it?

I put my tea down on the table and got up.

"I have to go." I kissed my mother on her forehead. "Take care of her," I said to Diray.

"I will," he said. His voice was melodious and soothing. He looked at me with his gray eyes. "Take care of yourself as well."

I hoped I'd be able to do that. First I had to save my father's oldest friend, and with any luck, I'd be able to save my company along the way.

By the time I got back to the office, the workday was over. The nine-to-five employees were gone, but I knew I'd find Gris still hard at work in his lab. First I wanted to stop by my office. There was a section in my father's spellbook I needed to read.

When I inherited the spellbook, it had taken me

months to read through all my father's notes. The last section, separated from the rest by a red tab, contained only a few pages of lined paper. The pages were blank. I asked my mother about it, but she simply said that section was for spells my father hadn't invented yet. On the ferry ride back across the bay, I had started to wonder if that section wasn't blank after all, only hidden. Before today I had no reason to doubt my mother's explanation. I knew a spell for revealing hidden text. If that section held what I thought it did—my father's notes on what he learned of dark magic—I might need them.

I threw my damp raincoat across the back of one of the visitor chairs in front of my desk. I didn't care where the water dripped. I dug my desk keys out of my purse and sat down in my chair before I even realized something was wrong.

My desk drawer had been jimmied open, the security spells shattered.

My father's spellbook was missing.

Gris!

I ran to the elevator, punched the button for the sixth floor with a trembling finger. The elevator barely seemed to move, yet before I was ready, the doors opened on the lab.

The stench was overpowering. The smell of ozone from the green goo was magnified a thousandfold. All the lights in the lab were blazing bright. A sound like thunder crackled through overheated air.

I found Gris in his office. My father's spellbook lay open to the red-tabbed section on Gris's worktable. Words crawled across the page as Gris stood over the book, hands extended, sweat running down his face. The wispy ends of his hair and beard seemed to float on unseen currents of air.

"Gris!"

He flinched when I called out his name. I realized he'd been muttering something under his breath. He glanced up at me, his eyes wide and wild.

"It's our fault, Nell," he said. "I had a dream this

afternoon. A vision. I realized what happened to the spell. Who our 'competitor' was." He laughed, not a sane sound. It sent shivers down my spine. "We've seen him before. Your father and I. I know how to fix it."

Gris had never been the best wizard. Even I knew what he was attempting was beyond his ability.

"Gris, stop. Please stop."

The air grew heavy and the flourescent lights dimmed. Lightning began to crackle along the edges of my vision.

"I can beat this," Gris said. "I have to, don't you see? I'm all that stands in its way."

Mist swirled around us and began to coalesce.

I darted forward and grabbed the spellbook from Gris. The writing disappeared as soon as I took it from him.

Dammit. I had no time, no time left at all.

I cast the revealing spell as quickly as I could. The air became thick and hard to breathe. I held the spellbook in one hand as words re-formed on the blank paper. I scanned the pages until I found the incantation I knew had to be there.

"No!" Gris shouted. "It will know you, too, don't you see? *It will know you!*"

I looked up in time to see the mist form into the shape that wore my father's face. The horrible thing smiled at me.

"Go back to hell," I said, and I began to cast the spell that would carry out my words.

The thing screamed. All the windows in the sixth floor blew out with the force of its fury.

I felt something wrap slimy tendrils around my neck and squeeze. Blood pounded in my ears and the unpleasant taste of metal filled my mouth, but still I murmured the words of the incantation.

"No! You can't have her!"

My vision was beginning to darken, but I still could see well enough to watch Gris rush the thing out of the corner of my eye.

And then I saw something I will never forget.

I saw my father.

Not the thing wearing my father's face, but my father—ghostly and indistinct, but *there*.

Gris must have seen him, too. He reached for my father with one hand and for me with the other. Power surged through me like lightning.

The tendrils around my neck loosened. My throat was raw, my voice nearly gone.

"Finish it, sweetheart," I heard my father say.

I did.

And the room exploded in light even as I drifted into darkness.

We delivered the redesigned handcuffs to the city two days early. It took Production three days of working around the clock to reproduce the hardware. I didn't sleep for the two days it took me to cast the enchantments on each box of cuffs.

I called Templeton Rae myself to tell him we were fulfilling our contract. Templeton actually seemed relieved.

"I hope you'll give us an opportunity to bid on the next available contract," I said. My voice was still a little hoarse. If Templeton noticed, he didn't mention it. Maybe he thought I was getting a cold.

"The city always welcomes your bids," he said. "You're known for the quality and integrity of your work."

I wondered again if someone in our company was leaking information to Templeton. At this point I didn't care. Let them leak what happened on the sixth floor. Maybe it would give Templeton second thoughts about dealing with the wrong manufacturer.

I leaned back in my desk chair and stared out at the city, and wondered if it was all worth it.

My father's spellbook was back in my bottom drawer. Gris had survived, but he wouldn't be coming back to work. He had a permanent tremor in his hands, and I saw the fear in his eyes when I visited

him in the hospital. Gris, whose mind had been failing
for years, had finally gone against something too big
for him, and he knew it. He'd found his limits. I'd
make sure he was taken care of for the rest of his life.

My mother said my father was truly gone now. She
seemed diminished somehow, even though she still
had Diray and the house and her garden. And me.
She still had me, although I was diminished, too.

Gris had been right. The thing I'd banished knew
me now. It knew the taste of my magic, just as I knew
its taste, too. That was the final ingredient in the enchantment spell for the cuffs—the taste of the magic
it was meant to contain.

My father and Gris had been the only wizards I
knew who could cast that particular spell. I'd tried
over the years, but I'd never been successful. Until
now. And I knew why. The real containment spell was
in the red-tabbed section of my father's spellbook. The
spell I thought Gris had been using all these years—
the one I'd thought I wasn't powerful enough to cast—
was a decoy. I'd been powerful enough to cast the
real enchantment all along. I just had to take a walk
on the dark side before I could use it. I had truly
become my father's daughter.

I turned the key to lock up the spellbook. I thought
about my father as a young man dabbling in things
he couldn't begin to understand. I thought about the
criminals who didn't understand any better than my
father, but who gave their lives over to dark magic
willingly for a little money or power. Was I any different? I thought about the work my company did, the
lives we saved. Was it worth the dark owning a piece
of my soul?

Ask me in fifty years or so, but I have a feeling the
answer will be yes. Right now I just need a drink.
Anything to make the damn taste of that thing in the
mist go away.

HOSTILE TAKEOVER

by Nina Kiriki Hoffman

I'M a thirty-year-old woman who lives at home with her mother. When guys do this, I suspect it's because they can't find a woman their age who will cook and do laundry and pick up after them the way their moms do. When a woman does it, the only legitimate excuse is that Mother is feeble and needs help.

My mother refuses to be feeble. I could cast a spell on her to make her feeble, but she has a rule: no witchcraft in the house. This is why I have to have an outside office to craft the spells I sell on my Web site. I have broken Mom's no-magic-in-the-house rule a couple of times, but she really means it when she says she'll kick me out if I do it again without permission.

I tell people I still live with my mom because she needs my rent checks. I make twice as much money with my spell business as she does at her florist job. The checks meant something to Mom while Dad was defaulting on the alimony, but now that he wants to get back together with her, he's paying regularly, so my expressed reason for living with Mom is a lie.

What I really crave is living with someone who understands me. This is a big secret. Not my biggest one, but one of the top ten. My twin sister and I became witches the same day, and for a while we grew into

our power together. We were close before we turned
into witches, but afterward, we were so tight I had
trouble loosening up enough to find a boyfriend.
Tasha and I went to the same teacher and learned the
same lessons. We practiced our arts on each other . . .
until I took a turn toward the dark side, and she refused to follow. She got all mystical instead, dedicated
herself to the powers of Air, and left me so she could
pursue her new faith. Now she travels the world practicing weird rituals that don't get her anything but
good will. I can see that being a bankable asset, but
only if you spend it sometimes, which Tasha never
does.

Mom's the only one in town who understands me.
So she's stuck with me, whether she likes me or not.

As part of my business practice, I hung out at the
student union building at the local university. My regular spell customers knew to find me there, and I
hooked up with new ones all the time. The right con-
versational opening gave people all the excuse they
needed to complain. Once I knew their problems, I
knew which spell to sell them.

The S.U.B. was a rambling building. There was a
bowling alley/video arcade in the basement, a food
court on the second story, offices for university clubs
and special interest groups scattered throughout, potted plants, meeting rooms, and snarls of conversa-
tional furniture everywhere. I could lurk there with
impunity.

A boy witch bumped into me in the food court. I
was waiting to buy a gyro, and he was heading toward
a girl. In addition to sideswiping me and not apologiz-
ing, he totally dinged my witch radar. I'd encountered
other witches here and there on campus, but never
somebody else with such powerful vibes.

"Hey," I said, giving New Witch Boy the up-down.

He brushed past me without answering. I wasn't the
most beautiful woman in the world unless I worked

at it, but I had style. Short, dark hair in a clean cut, and single-color tailored clothes. I passed for college age all the time. Was this guy gay?

I wandered after him, not so much offended as intrigued. Maybe he didn't have witch radar and didn't recognize me for what I was. I'd met a number of powerful people, and power made its home in them in different places; I no longer expected anyone else's power to match mine.

"Shelley," he said, catching up to a girl who was hurrying away. I was disappointed. She had that blonde cheerleader look—long, washed-out hair, big blue eyes, lush lips, and big pushy breasts—so beloved in teen-centric TV and too often in real life.

"Not *now*, Gareth," she said. Her voice incorporated acid. "My boyfriend's watching." She swung away, bobbing gently in front, and Gareth stood, his mouth half open in either idiocy or preparation for a remark that never made it past his teeth.

I stopped beside him. "If you're that interested in her, why don't you enchant her?"

His mouth closed and he stared at me with angry amber eyes.

"Hey, hey, I was just asking," I said.

"Get away from me," he said.

"Sheesh, you don't have to be nasty."

"Did my mother send you here to pester me?"

"No, but I'd like to meet her."

He blinked. "What?"

"If she's the type of mother who sends girls to torment her sons, she might be my kind of fun."

"Who *are* you?"

"My name's Terry Dane. Can I buy you a cup of coffee?"

"Terry Dane? Do you run that spell Web site?"

I smiled. "You've heard of me!"

He looked madder than ever. "What the hell do you think you're doing?"

I shrugged. "Making a living?"

"With those watered-down imitation spells? More like wholesale fraud."

"Come on. Have you tried them?"

"I bought the spell for studying harder. It hardly helped at all."

"Did you dissolve it in hot water?"

"What?"

"You have to use hot water to make it truly active —the hotter the better."

"Oh—I thought—"

"I include instructions with the spells for a reason. It's not my fault if you ignore them. I'm feeling generous today, so I'll give you a replacement for the last one you messed up, but this is a one-time deal." I shrugged out of my backpack and rummaged through my sample case. The spells I carried with me were stronger than the mass-produced ones I made for mail order, on the principle of intermittent conditioning, and the desired-recapture-of-the-first-time syndrome. If your first hit was really effective, you kept thinking the next one would work just as well. Every once in a while I sent out the stronger versions through the mail to keep my regular customers coming back. "Here." I held out the little gray-paper-wrapped cube that was the "increased study skills" spell. "Hot water. Tea or coffee works."

He hesitated.

"Don't use it until you're cramming for something. The effect is temporary unless you reinforce it with actual studying on a regular basis. Wait until the night before the exam; it only helps you retain things for forty-eight hours, and that's an outside estimate. Why do you need something like this, anyway?"

"What do you mean?"

"Oh, come on. You're a witch. You could make your own."

He grabbed the spell and strode away without a backward look.

"So, no coffee?" I yelled.

About fifteen people turned to look at me. Usually I kept a low profile, but at the moment I was past caring. Had I just wasted a free spell on a guy who was going to ignore me?

"Hey, Terry? You got an attract spell on you?" asked Seth, a short guy with bad teeth and too many green pieces of clothing. One of my best customers. I'd slipped him a free "see yourself as others see you and figure out how to fix your obvious errors" spell once, the permanent version, because it increased the effectiveness of all the other spells I sold him. He had learned to smile with his lips closed, but he couldn't seem to overcome his penchant for green. "There's a girl I want to impress right over there."

"Sure," I said, instead of, "Another one? What happened to the last six girls you used an impress-her spell on?" The spells had to have worked, or why was he coming back for more? Maybe it was a case of wanting something until you actually had it, or maybe the short-term effect had kicked in. If you didn't actually interest the person you attracted after two or three exposures, the spell would wear off and the relationship was over. I fished out the red-wrapped spell Seth wanted—one of my best sellers—and he handed me fifty bucks.

"Thanks." He ran off. I wondered if I should use an attract spell myself and pursue Gareth, but he'd already vanished.

The next time I saw Gareth was in the supermarket by the produce section.

Ding! Ding! Witch in the vicinity! I turned from the mountain of Minneolas I was casing and saw Gareth squeezing an avocado. I decided to stalk him, since the straightforward approach hadn't worked.

He put three avocados in a plastic bag and turned to hand the bag to a woman. Ding! Okay, that was why two dings the first time, and maybe why he could ignore me so easily—he already had a companion witch.

"Gareth, I said *four*," she said.

A testy companion witch. Twice his age.

Two girls rushed up, stair-steps, wavy brown hair, with the same tawny eyes Gareth had. "Look, Mom! Stephanie found the brown sugar!" said the taller girl, and the other one said, "Lacey got the flour!"

"Good job, girls," said the woman, smiling down at them, an edge of enchantment in her expression. For sure the kids felt loved. Cheap trick. I had that one in my repertoire, but it was so easy I rarely used it. Maybe I should try it on Gareth. He was probably used to it; and would fall faster than someone never exposed.

A slender young woman, her brown-gold hair in short curls, arrived and set a bag of raisins carefully in the cart, offering the mother witch a tight smile.

"Thank you, Rae," said the mother, her voice not so supple and graceful this time.

"What else do you need?" asked Rae.

Mom witch consulted her shopping list. "Chocolate chips."

"Why didn't you tell me before? Those were in the same aisle," said Rae. She frowned and marched away.

"Mommy, what else can we find?"

"Bread, girls," said the mother to the two girls, who jumped up and down. "Look by the back wall." She gestured toward the store bakery, and the two raced off, giggling. She held out the bag with three avocados to Gareth without a word, and he went back to the produce aisle.

I edged over to him, reached for an onion. "Okay, I get why you're allergic to witches," I muttered, "but I'm not your mother."

He jerked and dropped three avocados on the floor, started an avocado avalanche. I snapped my fingers and stopped them all from tumbling, sorted them back into a stable pile. "You've got to work on your people-sensing skills," I said. "I didn't actually sneak up on you. You could have seen me in your peripheral vision."

"Are you following me?" He stood, picked up the three fugitive avocados, and placed them carefully with the others.

"Maybe."

"Get away from me."

"Am I totally unattractive to you?" That came out more plaintive than I liked. I didn't let Helpless Me out to play in public. This guy was demoralizing me, and I should probably move away from him. Instead, I said, "I can change."

"Why are you even interested in me? I'm not sending out signals, am I?" His eyes widened. "Did I put a spell on you?"

"Simmer down. I'm just short of witch company at the moment, and you're the first likely candidate I've sensed in a while."

"I'll be interested in you if you can teach me how to stop being a witch," he whispered, just as his mother swooped down on us.

"Didn't you find another avocado yet? What's taking so long?"

"Hey, Mom. This is Terry, my new girlfriend." Whoa! I was promoted! He went on, "Terry, my mother, Sally Mathis."

She stiffened immediately, worked hard, and came up with a smile. "Nice to meet you. You won't distract him from his homework too much, will you?"

"Is schoolwork a problem for Gareth?" I asked. Did she or didn't she realize I was a witch? Maybe she was one of those instinctive practitioners who had never explored the range of powers available to her. In which case, Gareth might be completely untrained. I could turn him into whatever I wanted.

I grabbed a perfectly ripe avocado and handed it to Gareth.

"He lacks concentration," said Gareth's mother. She was being pretty bitchy about her son to someone she didn't even know.

"I can help him concentrate," I said, in my best cat-purr voice.

"Wonderful," said Sally with a sour frown. "It's a thrill and a half to meet you."

"Likewise, I'm sure."

Gareth put the avocado I'd chosen in the bag with the others and handed it to his mother. "We're going for coffee."

"But—" said Sally.

I linked arms with Gareth, smiled at his mother, and led him away. I left my half-filled basket on top of a pyramid of cans of corned beef hash.

Outside, we headed for the nearest Starbucks. We both ordered the house blend, and I paid, since I'd offered to before. We settled at one of the tiny round tables, and I hunched toward him. "So what's your new agenda?" I asked. "It's quite a distance from 'get away from me' to girlfriend."

He hooked both hands behind his neck and pulled his head down like someone getting ready to be searched by cops. "I thought you could help me figure out how not to be a witch."

"Why would you want that? Are you totally not getting what a blast this is?"

He looked up. "She wanted the girls to get the power, but they didn't. She's scared of me having it."

"Are you still living at home?" I asked.

He nodded.

"Well, there's your first mistake. Get away from her." Like I could talk. My own mom was completely ready for me to move out. I was the one who wouldn't go.

"But I don't know how to— Dad's out of the picture. He hasn't paid child support in three years. There's four of us, and— She just barely managed my college tuition, even though I have scholarships. She can't afford to pay for a dorm room for me, and I—"

Couldn't he work his way through school? I guessed it depended on his skill set. "How old are you, anyway?"

"Seventeen."

"Oh." He couldn't even vote yet. But if he'd graduated high school early and gotten scholarships, why did he need spells to help him study? "How do you use your witchcraft on a day-to-day basis?"

"I don't."

"Not at all?"

"Not on purpose," he said, and flushed.

"How about your mom? What does she do with hers?"

"Woman things," he muttered, his gaze on the tabletop.

"What the hell does that mean?"

"She won't tell me. She does it at home in a room with the door closed. All I know is there's stinky incense involved, and words I can't hear through the door. The craft has passed from mother to daughter in our family for generations. She hates that I got it instead of the girls."

"Gareth," I said, exasperated. Then I thought, No, he knows from rough women. I better be gentle or I'll lose him.

I started over. "Okay, listen. I can't unwitch you— I don't know how—but I can teach you how to make it work for you."

"With those stupid spells you sell? I don't know much, but I can tell they don't work very well."

"They don't have to work well to sell well. I don't want to upset the social balance by giving anyone giant advantages in any of the areas I service. That might lead to scrutiny I don't want. I can teach you how to be a much better witch, but you have to agree to help me. If I train you in the business, you can make enough money to get your own place. What do you say?"

He stared at his coffee cup so long I thought he wasn't going to answer, but at last he said, "Okay."

First, I took Gareth home with me. I figured he should know what a mom was supposed to be like.

"It's mac and cheese again, Terry," Mom called from the kitchen at the back of the house as I ushered

Gareth in through the front door, "unless you have other ideas."

"I have a guest, Mom." We passed through the living room and the hall into the kitchen, the heart of the house, where Mom and I spent all our together time after she got off work. The patina of a million cooked meals covered the kitchen ceiling in a yellow haze. The center of the room was a round table, often stacked with newspapers and mail, with just enough room for us to set our plates and silverware down. Sometimes we cleared the debris off, but it didn't take long to build up again. The kitchen colors weren't very inspiring, beige and brown, with a yellow fridge, all geared toward comfort and convenience. A cheese-and-boiling-pasta scent greeted us.

Mom stirred a pot on the stovetop, her silvering brown hair coming down from its neat coils around her head to drift in long, limp tendrils around her face. She was flushed from the stove's heat and still wearing the white shirt, black pants, and black suspenders she wore at the florist shop. It was a weird uniform that made her look more like a waiter than a flower shop girl, but they liked that at Flowers While You Wait. "Gareth, this is my mom, Rebecca Dane. Mom, this is Gareth Mathis."

"Hi, Gareth! I hope you like mac and cheese. Terry, could you throw together a salad?"

"Sure." I checked the fridge and remembered why I'd gone to the supermarket in the first place. Produce! We were out. I sighed. "Well, I guess not, Mom. I forgot to shop."

"Frozen broccoli, then." She nodded toward the microwave. I got out the broccoli.

"Gareth, would you like something to drink?" Mom asked.

"That'd be great." He looked lost, standing in our kitchen, his hands clasped in front of his chest as though he were begging or praying, his brown-blond hair squiffed by the wind.

"Help yourself to whatever's in the fridge. Cups are in the cupboard over there."

Gareth poured himself some orange juice.

Mom asked, "Where'd you two meet?"

"At the supermarket," I said. "Gareth's a witch, but he hasn't had any training. I thought I'd get him started." I filled a glass with water and took a seat at the table.

"Really?" Mom put the lid on the mac and cheese and came to the table.

Gareth had gone red again. "Terry," he said, his voice squeaking in a surprising way.

"What?"

"Maybe he didn't want me to know he's a witch," Mom said. "It's okay, Gareth. I don't tell anybody these kinds of things. I appreciate Terry being up front about it, too. It's when she's keeping secrets that I get upset. Have a seat."

"Are you a witch, too?" he asked as he settled in a chair beside me.

"No, not at all," said Mom.

He turned to me. "So where'd you learn?"

"I had a teacher for about six years after I turned into a witch." I could take him to meet my mentor, but then I'd lose my chance to train him up to be my new twin and business partner. Besides, my mentor no longer let me cross her threshold. She was pretty strict about not dabbling in the dark arts.

"But you still live at home," he said. "And you think I should move out?"

"His mom makes him feel bad about what he is," I told my mom. "She's scared of him."

"Oh, honey," said my mom. She put her hands on Gareth's, squeezed. "So sorry you have to deal with that."

"Did Terry put a spell on you to make you say that?"

"Nope. No magic in the house," said Mom.

"He doesn't even know how to check for spells," I said. "I've got my work cut out for me."

"For once, I might actually approve of what you're doing," said my mother.

"So can I start his training here?"

Mom frowned, tapped her index finger on her mouth a couple times, and then nodded. "As long as it's just matter stuff, not spellcasting on people. For the dark stuff you have to take him somewhere else. Okay?"

"All right."

We had dinner, and afterward, Mom sat at the table with coffee and a crossword puzzle while I explained basic principles of magic to Gareth. Mom loves hearing this kind of stuff. It gives her insight not only into me but into my traveling twin, who blows home every once in a while. (I mean it about blowing, too. She brings the wind with her before she remembers to tell it to go outside and play.)

I said, "You have to perceive things to be able to affect them—or, at least, it helps. Do you ever sense things other people don't?"

"I don't know. How could I tell?"

"I knew you were a witch, and that your mom was, too. I learned it through my witch senses. Do you ever get strong feelings about people or things?"

His eyes narrowed, and he glanced past me, as though looking at something out a window, though he stared toward a wall. "I used to when I was little, but not for a long time. My mom's dresser set. Her brush. It's old. It felt like it might be able to—but she wouldn't let me touch it, after that time she found me waving it around."

"Hmm," I said. "Good news, probably. You have the senses. They're just asleep. Once we wake them up, you'll be able to do things. I'll try a spell to open your witch eyes. Wait here a sec. I have to get my kit." I ran upstairs, grabbed my traveling witch kit, and dashed back to the kitchen. I cleared newspapers off the table. "Mom, is this okay?"

"Does it hurt anybody?"

"Not physically. I don't know about the psychic consequences. It should show Gareth what he does and doesn't see."

"Gareth, are you ready for this?" Mom asked.

He laughed, with scorn in it. "Hey, I've seen her work before. I don't expect anything to happen."

Mom slanted a look at me. I smiled back at her. "Go ahead," she said.

I assembled dust of ages, scent of spring gone, sound of three high notes on a piano, and a trace of vanished sunrise. Power pooled in my palms as I bracketed my ingredients with my outstretched fingers. "Show us what he could see, and why he doesn't," I whispered, not a spell I'd ever said before. I wasn't sure if it would work. It didn't even rhyme.

The ingredients flared, mixed, and vanished, leaving a twist of smoke behind. The world shifted around us. Everything in the kitchen glowed with colored light, and streams or strings stretched between people and furniture, appliances, floor, ceiling, walls. Some pulsed, beads of light sliding along the strings between things intimately connected; some shimmered in time to the hum from the refrigerator.

In the midst of all this weaving, an overlay that didn't obscure the physical forms of things— translucent as it was pervasive—something hovered above Gareth's head. A miniature thicket of rose bushes, and trapped inside, a pair of eyes, their irises deep, shifting gray/golden/dark and shadow. The bushes had cleared from in front of them, so that they peered out, as if from a cage. They looked this way and that. Whatever they looked at deepened and in- tensified. They looked at me, and I felt warmth against my face as though I leaned toward a fire.

"What is this?" Gareth cried, and his extra eyes looked at Mom. She had been turning and gaping at the room, trying to take in everything at once, but now the power of the eyes' gaze focused her into con- centrated Mom. She was taller, with a crescent moon in her hair—wrong symbol, I thought; Mom was hardly a virgin goddess—and a veil of golden haze surrounded her.

"What did you do?" Gareth asked, turning on me,

and again I felt the warmth of his regard. I held out my hands, studied what the eyes made of me. I was cloaked in shadow so dark it made me look like a silhouette, but flashes of color rippled through my new outer skin.

"Why are you closed most of the time?" I asked.

"What are you talking about?" Gareth demanded. "What's with all these visions? Did you spike my orange juice?"

The eyes blinked, a shuttering of images—all the color left the world, then returned as the lids rose. The eyes rolled up until mostly white showed.

"Someone put a spell on you to blind you." I reached out, my hand a black spider against the green and red and dark glow of vines and flowers. "Do you want to be free?"

"Make it stop," Gareth said.

"I'm not talking to you," I muttered. With my shadowy hand, I touched the roses caging his vision, pressed this stem and that. A thorn bit my finger and I sucked in breath. Itching tingle spread from the puncture. The eyes stared at me. The shadow cloaking my outstretched hand faded as the itching tingle spread from my finger to my palm, and up my arm. My powers leached away as the shadow faded, revealing nothing but normal flesh, blood, and shirt.

Damned spell! Could it kill my witchness? I never thought anything could. In trying to save Gareth, was I dooming myself to being normal?

Before my darkness left me entirely, I murmured power words and picked more carefully through the roses, looking for help. The thorns sprouted and pricked my hands again. Weakness spread through me. Both my arms were bland.

Near the base of one of the vines, I found an aphid like a small hard bump, then another. I rested fingertips on their backs. "Small things, strengthen; change the balance. Shift the spell, let loose the sight. Sip the sap and wreck the roses; give me back my stolen might," I murmured, putting the remnants of my power into it. The aphids listened and grew strong, sucked the lifeblood out of the rose spell until it withered and fell away. They nestled in my palms, gleaming soft, fuzzy green, the size of kiwi fruits, full of the power they'd sucked from the spell.

Gareth groaned. "Stop it, Terry! Whatever you did, make it stop!"

I exchanged a glance with the eyes. They blinked again, then the lids closed, slowly, and all the extra color faded from the room.

"All right," Mom said, "what was that, Terry? Did you break a rule?"

"I just did what I said. We saw what Gareth would see if he used his witch senses."

"What, all that?" he said. "That was crazy."

"You have to get used to it." I sat in a chair at the table and rubbed one of the aphids against my cheek. So soft. It made a small, vibrating sound like a purr. I was exhausted, and a little worried: the rose had poisoned my power. My defenses were weak, now; if anything with power came at me, I could be badly hurt, though not destroyed, because of my secret protection. I needed to find a spell to restore me.

Chances were the rose spell had also poisoned Gareth's powers somehow, maybe paralyzed them. Now that it was gone, maybe he could get some joy out of his power. Maybe he'd be grateful. I hoped so. I wanted to use him in many different ways. "That's where you begin with your powers," I said. "See what you can see. Then decide how you want it to change, and work toward that."

"What does this have to do with those spells you sell?"

"I decide what the spells will do. I infuse them with power and direction. Once I craft the spells, other people can use them."

"You hypnotized me," Gareth said.

I sighed and rested my hands on the table, palms up, with the aphids in them. I wasn't sure what to do with my new friends. They solved the problem for me, sank into my palms. A flush of unfamiliar power flowed through my veins, mixed with the power the roses had sucked out of me, now come home.

I leaned back and closed my eyes, felt this foreign power move through me. It was a slivery power, like bamboo under fingernails, a power with hate in it, and strength, edged with elegance and beauty. "Tell me who you belonged to," I whispered, and learned about Gareth's mother, forced by her mother and grandmother to use her power when all she had wanted was to be normal. They put a geas on her to pass her power to her daughters, but none of her daughters had been born gifted. A boy with gifts was an abomination. When she discovered Gareth's gifts, she locked them in a hedge of roses and put them to sleep. This was a power she had to renew constantly, as his witch eyes struggled to open.

And in the meantime, with that geas on her, continually unsatisfied, she twisted up in some truly unpleasant directions.

I accepted the foreign power as part of my arsenal. Strange to meet power darker than my own. Everyone I knew in the witch community thought I was the bad guy, the unnatural one who forced people into things against their will. I was as capable as Gareth's mother of mistreating other people.

I would take joy in foiling her.

Gareth shook my shoulder. "Terry?" he said. "Terry—it's happening again."

"What is?" I asked.

"The world looks screwy!"

I straightened and rubbed my palms together as a final thank you to the aphids. I felt not only restored after the rose's poison but augmented.

I glanced around. The room seemed normal. I studied Gareth, and realized his aura had awareness in it now. He looked all around, panicked.

"Your witch eyes are open now, Gareth. You can close them if you don't like it, but you can also open them whenever you want. What you see, you can change."

"Can I change you? You look like the Grim Reaper."

"Really? Skull and all?"

He stared at my face. "Mostly it's the dark cloak. I guess I can see your face. Are you smiling at me?"

"I am, Gareth."

"How come your mom has a moon on her head?"

"I don't understand that myself. It's not there when I look at her. Have you figured out how to close your eyes yet?"

He glanced around, looking hunted again. Mom got to her feet, shaky, and went to the coffeemaker for a refill. She had some experience with weird witch effects—most of them from my sister, who was allowed to witch around the house, since she didn't hurt anyone. Mom hadn't had enough exposure to be relaxed about it, though.

"I can't—oh," said Gareth. "Oh, it's all gone again. Okay, good."

"Terry. Explanations?" asked Mom. She dumped extra sugar in her coffee and drank.

"Gareth's mom put a spell on him to close up his powers. Did you see the roses?"

"I did. Thanks, by the way, for making me part of the equation."

I couldn't tell if she was being sarcastic, but, even though I hadn't planned for her to see everything, I was glad she had. It meant she knew more about Gareth's problem. "She planted those to keep his powers asleep. She tends them constantly to make sure he's crippled. My spell messed hers up. Now his powers are awake, but he doesn't know how to use them. Can Gareth live with us, Mom? If he goes home, his mother might shut him down again."

Mom's frown was ferocious, but I knew she'd cave. She had the softest heart of anybody I knew.

"I have rules," Mom said, the start of her consent.

Gareth moved into the guest room. We went back to his house the next morning, when his mother was at work and his sisters had gone to school, to retrieve his belongings.

The house had no witch vibes. It looked like a TV sit-com house, not distinctive, not identical.

His room was a sad excuse for a boy's room. There were red roses winding in the wallpaper, and no pictures of cars, airplanes, metal bands, or things blowing up. His clothes were all neatly folded or hung on hangers—no dirty laundry on the floor or draped over the desk chair. I was more of a boy than Gareth was.

I'd brought a duffel bag for him. He put everything in it very neatly, then stuffed his backpack with a bunch of books.

On our way to the front door, I said, "So where's the room your mom uses for her rituals?"

Gareth looked over his shoulder toward a doorway I hadn't noticed before—and that disturbed me, because now that I knew where to look, the witch vibes coming from it were incredibly strong. "We're not allowed to even open the door," he said, as I grabbed the doorknob. A stinging jolt shot through my hand, the same poison Gareth's roses had carried. I jerked back, shaking my hand. Weight in my other hand made me look: I saw one of the aphids, shrunk to the size of a marble, rising from my palm. As soon as it separated from my skin, I held it near the doorknob; it leaped the gap, fastened to the protect spell, and fed.

"What is that?" Gareth whispered.

"This is what freed you yesterday." I hadn't realized they could manifest again, but I was thrilled. Spell-suckers! A staggering number of household applications occurred to me. "I found them feeding on your mother's power-suppression spell, and helped them eat faster. They broke the spell for you. I wonder if they're yours?" The aphid on the doorknob was as big as a cantaloupe. My right hand, still tingling from the spell jolt, unhosted the second aphid, and I set it to join the first.

When they were both the size of fuzzy, pale-green watermelons, the tiny scritching sound of their feeding stopped, and they dropped from the doorknob. I caught one, and Gareth caught the other. "Do you want the power?" I asked.

"What?"

I cradled my aphid in both hands, and it deflated, feeding me spell power again, exquisite hate and strength, a hot syrup both burning and sweet. "Put it down if you don't want the power." My voice was hoarse as my body adjusted to this influx. I was lucky to have had a taste the day before, otherwise I could see this killing me, as poisonous as it was—or it could have killed me if I hadn't had my special protection. What if someone random touched the doorknob?

I directed the power flow into a fireproof box in my mind. I could store this power and dilute it for personal use later.

The aphid vanished into my palm again.

"It's stuck! Ouch! It burns!" Gareth tried to shake the aphid off his hand, but it clung, a gelatinous mass, and shrank. He keened, a high, mindless wail.

He didn't have the defenses to handle this. I grabbed his hands as the aphid vanished under his skin and followed floods of power along dried riverbeds inside him, places where his witch power ought to flow. I couldn't stop the rush of hot new power, but I could soften it by adding power of my own, cold power I rarely tapped. He gasped over and over, and I saw that his mother's power didn't poison him, either. He had been living with the restriction spell inside him long enough to acclimate to it.

The power rushed through all his channels and reached the river's source, burst through a wall, and uncapped the spring inside. I had to let go of him then, he burned so hot.

He screamed. I covered my ears with my hands and waited it out.

Finally, he collapsed, twitching, on the floor.

I went to the kitchen to get a glass of water. I wasn't

sure that was the right prescription, but I figured it couldn't hurt.

When I rejoined Gareth, he sat up and took the glass from me, and my shoulders, tight as corsets, loosened. I hadn't been sure there was anything left of his mind.

"I feel sick," he whispered.

"I know." He could talk! I relaxed even more. "Do you need anything I can get you?"

"An explanation?"

I laughed, relieved he could ask. I rose and grasped the doorknob. It didn't bite this time. I turned it and pushed on the door, but the door rattled: it was locked. Mechanical protection in addition to magical. I knew a lot of unlock spells, though, and the first one I tried worked. "Let's see what we earned." I hauled Gareth to his feet. He staggered, straightened, wiped sweat from his forehead with the back of his hand.

I let go of the doorknob and stepped back, giving him the choice. He studied me, then gripped the knob and turned it.

First thing out of the room was a smell, cold and rotten, like a cave where corpses were stored. The door opened inward. Gareth pushed it and let it swing. The floor inside was painted a light-sucking, tarry black.

"God," he said. "I'm glad I never saw this before. I couldn't sleep in the same house with this again."

His mother's altar took up the whole far wall, a black freize with niches in it where tentacled god-statues lurked, some veiled with dark lace, others staring, visible and revolting. On the flat stone bench below, a large brass bowl held ashy remains of burned things and a scattering of small charred bones. A red glass goblet was half-full of dark liquid. A scorched dagger lay between the goblet and the bowl. A carved ebony box stood on the bench, too.

One of the god-statues waved three tentacles at me. I'd had dealings with him before. For a dark god, he had a great sense of humor. I wiggle-waved back.

"Let's go," Gareth said.

"Wait. Look in there with your witch eyes. See if there's anything you need to take."

"What?"

"Look."

Along the side walls of the room—any windows had been covered over—there were shelves full of magical aids and ingredients, and a small library of hide-bound books. Gareth stepped over the threshold into the room. A shudder went through him as he stood in the heart of his mother's power. "What am I looking for?" he asked.

"Something that belongs to you."

"I've never seen any of this stuff before."

I shrugged. He examined the shelves without touching anything. I wouldn't have touched, either. Everything looked dusty or dirty, even the ingredients I recognized.

After a tour of the room, Gareth stopped at the altar. He held his hand above the dagger, the bowl, the goblet, and finally the box. He lifted the box's latch and swung the lid up. Soft light glowed from inside. "Oh," he cried. His hand hovered, then dipped in. He lifted a fist and pressed whatever he held against his breastbone. When his hand lowered, there was nothing in it, and nothing on his shirt, either. He turned toward me. His face was alive with confused excitement.

The front door slammed open. "Who are you, and what are you doing in my house?" cried Gareth's mother. She saw the open door to her secret room, and shrieked.

"I'm the girlfriend," I said.

She stalked forward, her anger growing with every step, until her shadow towered above her, filled with lightning strikes in random directions.

"How dare you open that door?" she screamed, and then, when she saw that Gareth was in the room, she went silent, which was worse than the screams, though less ear-torturing.

At last she stepped forward, muttering words that hurt my ears. She slammed her left palm into my chest, sending a power-jolt through me that would have knocked me on my ass if I hadn't just processed a lot of her power. I was still humming with stolen strength, though, and her own power inside me shielded me from the new assault. She flicked her hand toward Gareth. A bolt of blue lightning shot out, sizzled through his shirt, scorched his chest. He staggered, straightened, planted his feet, and faced her.

"Okay," he said.

She gasped.

"I got your eviction notice, Mom. I'm moving in with Terry."

"What?" She stepped toward him. She laid her hand on his chest. "You—what?" Her voice was a whisper now.

"Good-bye." He pushed past her, and her hand slid off of him.

She ran to the bench and opened the ebony box, gasped again.

By that time we had grabbed Gareth's things and were headed for the front door.

Mom made cocoa in the kitchen for us after Gareth had stowed his duffle and backpack in the guest room.

"He'll be able to pay rent and utilities," I said. "I'm hiring him as my assistant, so he should make plenty of money." Too bad his mother was so shortsighted. She hadn't known what a valuable asset she had. He was mine, now. Her mistake.

"Sure, sure," said Mom.

"I better protect you, Mom. His mother's really scary. She might come after us."

"Great," Mom grumbled.

"Are you okay with me spelling you a shield against her? She almost killed us."

"Terry!" Mom reached across the table and grabbed both my hands, clutched them tight. "Don't do dangerous things! How many times do I have to tell you?"

"I had to rescue him, Mom. You would have, if you saw what it was like at his house."

She softened. She reached for Gareth's hand. He ducked her, then stilled and endured her touch.

"All right," my mother said. "Protect me, Terry."

Strange, almost scary happiness shot through me. Mom didn't trust me with magic; she knew my track record. She was giving me a new and precious chance.

I so didn't want to mess this up.

"Open your witch eyes," I told Gareth, "and watch what I'm going to do. This isn't a spell I sell anywhere."

I conjured magical armor for my mother, and she sat still for it.

After we washed dishes and cleaned the kitchen for the night, I followed Mom into her bedroom, leaving Gareth to settle himself in his new space.

"Lots of changes," Mom said.

"Yeah. Thanks so much, Mom." I sat on the bed. "Sorry I had to spring this on you without warning."

"Do you actually like the boy, Terry?"

"I don't know yet. He's got a lot of garbage to get through before he'll be useful."

She ruffled my hair. "There's my girl. I wondered where you went, honey. You've been way too nice all day."

I laughed.

Mom went to her closet. "I suppose you want to play with the pretties." She pulled her jewelry box from behind a stack of shoeboxes on a shelf. Not a very secret hiding place. I had warded our house against burglars, though. She could have left the box in plain sight and it would have been safe.

I opened the box, touched the charm bracelet Mom's grandmother had left her, the pearls my father gave her on their twelfth wedding anniversary, the malachite earrings she had given to her mother, taken back after her mother died. Buried under a tangle of chains, pendants, and bracelets, some of them gifts my twin Tasha and I had given her for various birthdays and Christmases, I found my heart.

I gave Mom my heart for her forty-fifth birthday. I made it into a really ugly brooch, red enameled and gaudy, with rhinestones. It was heavy and awkward to wear. If she ever pinned it to anything, it would drag down the material.

She treasured it the way she treasured everything my twin and I ever gave her, but she never wore it, which was just as well.

I knew Mom would never break my heart the way Gareth's mother had treated his. She wouldn't use my heart as a tool to supplement her own desires. As long as I kept my heart safe and separate from my body, I could not be mortally wounded, though I could be hurt—a lot. Now that Gareth had reclaimed his heart, he would be vulnerable to kinds of assaults he had been immune to before. I could make that work for me.

I held my heart in my hand just long enough to warm it, then hid it among the rocks and metal in Mom's jewelry box. I closed the box and handed it to my mother. She tucked it away.

She kissed my cheek goodnight.

A DIFFERENT WAY INTO THE LIFE

by Jay Lake

Sunday the 15th, evening

The exhausted wizard cupped her hand around the dog end of a hand-rolled cigarette and tried to get one last drag out of the wretched thing. Cold, wet wind snatched the trail of sweet smoke into the evening air.

"Bugger it," she snarled and flipped the butt with a practiced snap of her fingers. It spun away on the breeze, trailing a tiny spray of extremely short-lived Heisenbergian butterflies. Diamond dust wings glittered in the shadows before exploding into lacy clouds of ash.

The street glistened with damp. The air smelled rotten wet. It wasn't quite raining, one of those Northwest evenings where the sea had come down out of the sky to soak the world without ever quite precipitating into identifiable rain. Chilly, too. Amid the joys of Portland weather, she had toiled through another long damned day of badgering everyone on the street—krusties, transients, janitors, taco wagon drivers, professional bus riders, you name it. Anybody from the subeconomy or the underclass she'd found, she'd talked to.

Nothing to show for it.

Nada.

She pulled a crumpled photo from the pocket of her Gore-Tex coat. Portland in winter was no place for substandard clothing, and no one in their right mind used magic just to keep warm. That would be like setting your house on fire so you could have light to read by. The picture hadn't changed in the hours she'd spent showing it to people, looking for a spark of recognition or, even better, the dull glow of a lie. A girl, Cauc, midteens, pale brown hair falling over one eye, a smile that could buy her way through life if she used it right. Sunlight in the background over one shoulder, image cropped in tight to the right of her face.

"Have you seen her?"

"¿Usted ha visto a esta muchacha?"

Even Cantonese a few times, though she'd had to cheat to reach inside that language. Sparks flared when she did that, trees in sidewalk planters creaked, and once in a convenience store, two wine bottles had exploded.

Magic sucked.

She took the number 19 bus home and tried to figure a different way into the life of Maisie Potter. The easy way wasn't working too well.

Monday the 16th, morning

The wizard sat in her cubicle, looking blankly at spreadsheets. Melançon stuck his head around the corner, already talking before he could even see what she might be doing. "I need your end of the Buchanan proposal before noon Wednesday."

He wasn't a bad egg, for a vice president. There was some quintessential quality of assholery which seemed to be a prerequisite for promotion in corporate America. Melançon mostly kept it under control. He had rich guy habits—skeet shooting, overpriced clothes and cars—but he was okay.

She smiled at him, still worn out from her weekend of working the streets. "That's mostly up to Jason, boss man. I'm just doing the competitive analysis on

that one. Besides, I've got the Varicorp and United
Metathemics bids going, too, on tight deadline."
Deadlines he'd given her. It was a very short to-do
list, but very wide. Everything was top priority.

"You'll get it done." He smiled back, capped teeth
bleached to appliancelike perfection. "You always find
the time somehow."

Steal it, the wizard thought with a trace of worn-
out bitterness. All the work she'd put into her trade,
and what she did was steal time and look for the lost.
There weren't three other people here at Gierloff,
Williamson, and Closson with magical skills. Bartelme
in accounting, who was a wizard with numbers—saints
and madmen, she hated that phrase!—and that intern
who worked with the copywriters. The kid didn't know
it, though, completely raw. Had the glow, but no more
focus than an old CRT.

That was it. Them and her. In her little cube.

The walls were that horrid carpet fabric used in low-
end cubes everywhere. Most of her colleagues had
covered theirs with birthday cards, fuzzy scans of un-
funny cartoons, photos of vacations to Crater Lake or
Disneyland, and mountains of stupid plastic toys. Not
the wizard. She had her pouch of tobacco and rolling
papers—no smoking in the building, not here in green
Oregon—and the little skull from one of *them* that
she kept inside a Japanese paper box, but that was it.

Well, there were office supplies, files and whatnot,
but those came with the cube, not with her.

It was difficult to focus on the Buchanan response.
GWC had files on all major direct and indirect competitors, but she still had to go through each proposal,
looking for nuances. Was there an offshore angle?
What about mom-and-pops cutting into the business
with lowball pricing? Did they know who was running
the sales effort on the competitive side?

That was why GWC put up with her. Paid her in
cash, even, which was damned near illegal these days.
The wizard never wrote her name down on anything,

anywhere. She was, as they said, unbanked. Undegreed. Uneverything, really.

But she could reach out and see what the other guys were doing. No one could figure out the insides of a deal like her. No one without her talents, at any rate.

"Time to set the house on fire," she whispered, and took the tiny skull from the Japanese paper box.

Monday the 16th, evening

That evening was a little warmer than the weekend had been. After taking the bus home to eat and rest a while, she chose to walk back downtown, taking the Hawthorne Bridge. It was an old lift bridge, one of the first of its kind, she'd read, recently restored to a sort of industrial age beauty. The name had magical associations, of course, reaching back to Joseph of Arimathea. It was old, built in 1910, named after the director of Oregon's first mental hospital. Iron over running water, ancient Grail mysteries, and twentieth-century lost souls—it was a miracle the bridge didn't lift itself up out of the riverbed and dance under a gibbous moon.

The buses from her part of town, the near Southeast, generally ran over the Ross Island Bridge. It should have been a double crossroads—the bridge carried US-26 over I-5 and over OR-99E—which would have been very powerful indeed. Instead, the designers had gone to great lengths to ensure that neither crossroads actually met, instead extending the spans well onto the bluffs set back from the Willamette River on each side. The result was a monstrosity, a sort of giant magical trap, impairing the energies of the river below, which was already sluggish from the dam at Oregon City. To make matters worse, Ross Island itself had been gutted, the heart literally torn out by a gravel pit.

The wizard idly wondered as she walked how much of the effort at the distorted bridge design and the destruction of the island was aimed at the widow Re-

becca Ross, who'd once farmed there. One of Portland's founding witches, perhaps.

She paused as the Hawthorne Bridge passed over
from water to land. Sniffed. The air smelled crisp, almost hot, as if the doors had been opened on vast yet
distant ovens. Downtown was different tonight. The
cluster of high-rises by the river gleamed as their lights
fought back against the encroachment of darkness.
Red beacons blinked at their tops, warding the structures from sky-borne evil and incidentally warning off
aircraft. The streets gleamed this evening as well, with
a dusk dewfall beneath a sky clear enough to see stars
even against the city's glare.

The energies had shifted substantially from the day
before. Perhaps the change of bridges had been sufficient. The wizard promised herself she'd keep away
from the Ross Island Bridge for a while, and look into
the history of Portland's other bridges as well. Had
the office of the city's bridge engineer been in a state
of magical warfare for the last century?

She sat on a bench in Tom McCall Park, right along
the waterfront, and rolled another cigarette. Her right
hand was stiff, so she used it to hold the thing while
pinching and forming with her left. The tobacco was
a particular strain of white burley which came from a
grower in the King's Valley area who, much like the
wizard herself, worked on a cash basis only. Tobacco
was just a form of nightshade, after all, and carried
many of that poison's magical associations. Hers was
harvested by the dark of the moon and cured over a
fire of smoldering rose petals.

The smoke didn't give her a buzz. Rather, the cigarettes opened the doors of her mind. Different doors
than the little skull on her desk. Or rather, different
keys to the same lock.

Use the skull, see the world of numbers, businesses
sliding like icebergs on the ocean of commerce, individual executives and salespeople sailing dreamlike
through the air as small black clouds. Dreadfully mun-

dane, but it kept beans on her table and shoes on her feet.

She rolled her cigarettes in papers torn from old blackletter books of English statutes written in law French. She generally stole them from libraries and antique dealers. Lighting one of them let her focus in on the world of energies, what some called spirits. These ranged from the sad and simple thoughts of trees to the great, slow, vengeful musings of the rivers wounded by dams and bridges and sewer outflows.

People, as well, of course.

Like Maisie Potter. Living or dead, she would have energy. If Maisie had spoken to someone, been somewhere, walked, eaten, shat, or died, the wizard should have been able to see her.

Yesterday the city had fought her, the energies twisting wrong. In retrospect, she supposed she couldn't have found a penny in the street under those conditions. Today, she'd approached from a different portal, walking the span laid down in honor of Joseph of Arimathea's hawthorn bush at Wearyall Hill.

The wizard puffed her smoke into the gathering gloom. It sparkled a moment, then hissed away to the north.

She shivered. The smoke had moved against the wind.

"You're out there, aren't you?"

The wind gave her no answer, only direction. The wizard walked north, following the sparks. Behind her, the grass around the bench crinkled in a new circle of dark, dehydrated rot.

Monday the 16th, morning

The Buchanan proposal had been choppier than she expected. The numbers sea was in a froth, much as it had been back when Enron was gaming the California power crisis. The wizard sometimes wondered why more of her kind didn't play Wall Street the way the energy traders had.

Or maybe they did, and their efforts were mutually canceling.

Her home iceberg, GWC, radiated stability even amid the rough weather. That was Bartelme in Accounting keeping the company steady. The wizard gave him a sort of mental nod. Unremarked, no doubt. Bartelme had long ago made it clear he had no use for her.

Wizards were an unstable lot at best. Asperger's syndrome, if not full-blown autism, seemed to be almost *de rigeur* for her kind of powers. She had no illusions about herself—someone who refused to ever divulge her personal name bore no claim to normalcy whatsoever. Bartelme's indifference to her was as natural as breathing, for him.

The wizard's curse was that she *did* care about other people.

She set that thought aside. It belonged to the other part of life, the part that was currently wondering where Maisie Potter was. This part of her life was important now. Give Melançon his sales information. Every time GWC closed one of her deals, she got a thousand dollars in old, mixed-denomination bills. Above and beyond her weekly payouts.

She knew she showed up on the books as contract research. Her cube was listed as "Miscellaneous, Visitor/Contractor." She was nothing but a ripple that sometimes tossed up critical nuggets of fuel for the engine of commerce that employed her.

The wizard skimmed low over the rough seas, following the threads back to the iceberg that was Buchanan Sales and Services. It was much bigger than GWC. A glowering dark gray fog shrouded the upper shoulders of the berg. That would be their competitors. Though it was a strange presence, more of a mantle than the little cloud of an account executive sniffing around the deal.

When silver lightning crackled, she realized the competition was using a wizard, too. Someone much bigger and rougher than her.

She kept her distance, orbiting Buchanan and watching the fog. Shapes moved within. Rats, perhaps, gnawing at Buchanan. Definitely rougher than her. The wizard preferred finesse, a light touch, the magical equivalent of peering through windows. The competition was actively invading their sales prospect, turning Buchanan into a target. A resource to be exploited.

A big boy then, from the East Coast. Possibly Chicago or Los Angeles. One of the really high-end consultancies, the kind that had attorneys on the sales staff and quiet men in dark cars to do the street work. Most people didn't operate this way. Couldn't afford to spend the magical power, couldn't effectively manage the consequences if caught by the temporal world legal systems or press.

Melançon was not going to be happy.

The wizard backed away. She thought maybe she'd follow the cloud's track across the sea of numbers, give Melançon a name to work with at least.

Competitive analysis, her skinny brown ass.

Monday the 16th, evening
Just before she passed under the Morrison Bridge, the wizard stopped. The east bank of the Willamette was a glare of streetlights, Interstate, and warehouses, but she peered across the slow, muddy water anyway. She relit the hand roll and took a deep drag. When she released it, the smoke rose silver into the moonlight.

Nothing was pulling now.

Morrison was a strange bridge, too. It didn't really connect to Morrison Street at either end. The street was interrupted, energies of transit simply grounding off into the Willamette and the open air. A lie, this bridge. If you looked at the waterfront retaining walls in daylight, you could see the scars of the old Morrison Bridge, which had united the east and west extensions of the street.

More magical truncation? Or just the exigencies of traffic engineering in a city so inconveniently bisected

by a major river? North-flowing at that, in violation
of the southward trend of water in the United States.

She should pay more attention to geography, the
wizard thought. A *lot* more attention. She'd never focused on places in her magical work. Businesses,
which were of course abstractions, and people. She
resolved to take up the study, once some of her time
came back to her.

The wizard looked carefully at the bridge. Much less
decorative than the Hawthorne Bridge. Not so unnatural
as the Ross Island Bridge with its broken crossroads and
rape of the namesake island. No, Morrison was low, with
two squat piers holding the counterweights required to
lift the center span. Unremarkable concrete structures,
save for the control towers clinging to them on the south
side, where she also stood.

Carefully the wizard extracted the photograph of
Maisie Potter. She held it out at arm's length in the
reflected streetlight and stared at both the image and
the bridge beyond. The faint curl of smoke from her
cigarette wreathed Maisie and glittered once more.

"You under that bridge, girl?"

She took the stairs leading up from the park's espla-
nade to the bridge deck passing over. The wizard
needed to find the middle of the bridge, look out
across the water, see what the night could tell her.

Monday the 16th, morning

The dark cloud was unquestionably the cause of the
chop in the sea of numbers. The wizard followed it
some goodly distance, past icebergs, longships, little
islands with steaming hills, silver-backed beasts rolling
just beneath the surface of this strange ocean of
metaphor.

Time and distance were artifacts of the observer
here. Arguably, this was true in the temporal world,
too, but she couldn't take shortcuts through either of
those dimensions without expending considerable effort and creating noticeable side effects. In here the
transition was only a matter of will and word.

She expended the will and mouthed the word.

Immediately, the wizard was at the base of a black glass tower rising up out of the twisting sea of numbers. It seemed to plunge directly into the depths, while the upper reaches vanished into the sky. Not a tower, then, but perhaps a line drawn perpendicular to the plane of this inner world.

That took more power than the wizard had ever seen. Even the great banks in New York and London and Hong Kong, massive and stable as they were, had bounds and limits to them. Islands, or bergs the size of islands, but finite. This was a dagger stabbing through both sea and sky, faced with a million windows in which she could see a million workers toiling over a million desks.

A name. She needed a name to take back to Melançon.

The wizard circled, looking for a way in. She kept her distance. Simply coming up next to one of those infinite windows struck her as a supremely bad idea. Her lower back tingled at the thought. Clouds seemed to roil around various levels of the tower, close cousins to the one which even now gnawed at the Buchanan berg. Rats or worse lurked within those dark fogs. She wanted nothing to do with them.

Finally, the wizard had to conclude that there was no obvious entrance. No spiritual equivalent of a building sign, either. Just this overproud tower filled with people.

Where had they gotten all those people, anyway?

Ordinarily she would have thought this illusion, as everything was here in the sea of numbers, essentially, but there was too much solidity. The thing practically vibrated.

They couldn't be real. Everything here was a metaphor. How could this not be a metaphor?

People as a metaphor for what, she wondered, closing in slowly on the tower despite her fears.

The wizard noticed something odd. No matter how much she moved toward the tower, it remained the same apparent distance away. She circled, trying to get closer and closer, setting aside her caution, but there was no "closer."

Finally, she closed her eyes and extended her hand. (The wizard believed firmly in keeping her own body shape at all times—it created far less confusion for her.) She reached right into where she would have sworn the building stood, until her fingers closed around something narrow, cold, and sharp.

Stifling a shriek, the wizard pulled her hand back. There was a bloody line scored on the palm.

The clouds filled with rats moved quickly toward her. The wizard abandoned her mission and fled into the roiling darkness, low over the troubled waves of the numbers sea. She needed to be far enough away from the tower—Blade? Wire?—to release her hold on this world without being followed home by agents of that terrible entity.

Monday the 16th, evening

Out on the Morrison Bridge, the wizard flexed her stiff right hand. The scar was bright there, though she had never been cut in the temporal world. Not on the palm, anyway.

She stood on a sort of balcony, a place for pedestrians and bicyclists to wait while the bridge was being raised and lowered. She leaned over the railing and tried to see the pier beneath her. Where was Maisie Potter?

Another question occurred to the wizard in that moment, standing over open water on a bridge with a false name.

Who was Maisie Potter?

Her hand throbbed at that thought, her head aching in near-harmony. Right in the center, where the third eye would be if she had one.

She tugged the photo from her pocket. No Gore-Tex tonight. Instead the wizard wore a fleece zip-up over an old wool sweater and two oxford shirts. Layers, always with the layers. Keep warm and confuse others. She studied the picture of Maisie Potter once more.

"Why am I looking for you, girl?" she asked the night.

Maisie had a pretty smile, the wizard thought with a twinge in her gut. But why should she care? The wizard was still a virgin. It wasn't a requirement of her craft, but sex was messy and powerful and took too much away from what she could do. Should do. Needed to do.

She knew for a fact how overwhelming sex was, and she had the ache in her groin to prove it.

Who had given her this photograph?

She had been downtown the day before, looking in the rain, working against hard opposition from the energies of the city. Sunday, that was.

What about Saturday, the day before that?

The wizard tried to focus her memory. Nothing came clear. Hunting Maisie, maybe, in the warren of post-industrial streets on the east bank of the Willamette.

A problem, then. She wasn't born yesterday. She had a mother. Must have had a mother. A face, the wizard thought. What did her mother's face look like?

A name, then. Her own. Her mother's. The name of someone or something not connected to work. The only name she knew outside the walls of Gierloff, Williamson, and Closson was Maisie Potter.

Shaking from cold and fear, she rolled another cigarette, then lit it from a matchbook with a Matisse painting on the cover. She knew who Matisse was. For the land's sake, she wasn't ignorant! The wizard puffed on the cigarette and tried to let go of the birds of her fear.

They fluttered close, but they left her chest.

Was *she* Maisie Potter?

No. That couldn't be true. She would have noticed her own face in the mirror. Besides, the wizard told herself with a look at her hands, she was far too old to be the girl in the photograph. And rather the wrong color, too. Coffee-with-cream, the wizard thought of herself as being, though she drank neither. A pleasant enough skin tone, belonging to all races and none.

The walkway beneath her feet thrummed. The drawbridge pier was surely full of machinery, counterweights, the apparatus required to lift one hundred forty feet of span to the vertical for the passage of ships.

How could Maisie Potter be down there in the machine-darkness? Surrounded by iron-as-steel, and oil-the-blood-of-the-earth.

How could a million people fit inside the blade of a sword plunging from dark heaven to the darker heart of the sea of numbers?

Memories were beginning to break up in the wizard's head, to reassemble, finding new configurations.

Anger, too.

Someone was *using* her.

That made the wizard very angry indeed. With will and word, she set about cutting across time and space.

Monday the 16th, morning

Her face slammed into the work surface of her cube, narrowly missing the Macintosh keyboard. The wizard sat up groaning and rubbed her forehead. There would be a goose egg later, right in the center.

She stared at her hand. The skin of the palm was an angry, raw red. She'd grabbed something ugly, then. She'd grabbed a *building*.

That didn't make any sense.

The wizard felt a sense of anger coalescing inside her. She didn't understand where it was coming from, but she knew enough to let it gather, to see where the impulse would lead. There were different ways into everything. A wizard had to be ready for locks that turned the wrong way, doors that opened against their own hinges.

What pulled the sky and sea together, she thought? Nothing, they just were each what they were. What kept them apart? Again, nothing. It was all a matter of perspective, and perhaps the density of the water in the air.

The secret of knowledge was little more than a matter of perspective, then. Knowing where to stand and how to look.

She glanced up to see Melançon frowning at her.

"How's the Buchanan proposal coming?"

The wizard had never quite noticed the way her boss's eyebrows met when he was concentrating on something unpleasant. On her.

The small of her back tingled. That meant trouble was at hand.

"Big competitor," she said, sticking to the narrow truth. "Someone who's actually working the deal from inside Buchanan."

"Interesting." He made his frown go away, but the wizard could see that was an act of will. "You've sussed out who the players are, right?"

"No . . ." Careful, she thought, feeling the heat blooming within her. "They've got some pretty heavy coverage. Nothing for me to read."

"Come on, you can read anything."

You can find anything, he'd said once, his voice echoing from behind a locked door in the palace of her memory even as he handed her a photograph of a pretty girl. *Just keep looking.*

"Just keep working."

"I . . ." Careful, careful. "I think I'm going to lunch."

He made a show of looking at his watch in surprise. "Barely ten in the morning. You should try eating breakfast more often."

"Right." She forced a laugh. "I'll have more on the Buchanan competitor this afternoon."

He walked away, looking over his shoulder.

The wizard followed the thread of her anger. She knew she was at the other end of the burning strand, but where and how? There were many ways to do this, many reasons, but her other self had sent only anger, not a situation report.

She stood to leave her cube and found Bartelme squatting on a stool just outside.

"Back to work, missy," he said with a brown-toothed leer.

"No," said the wizard. With will and word, she set about cutting across time and space.

Monday the 16th, night

The wizard dropped about six inches to a filthy concrete balcony in a large room. She scanned quickly, hands up to ward off any attack. The space was huge but claustrophobic, filled with enormous machines barely visible in the light of a few distant bulbs. The ceiling groaned and popped and hissed.

She had to be inside the Morrison Bridge, in one of the piers with the draw equipment.

She snapped her fingers, and a cigarette butt spun out into the dark well of the pier. It flared, leaving a trail of brilliant butterflies, which in turn burst to glowing ash.

Nothing out there but weights and wheels and gears. Like the inside of a massive engine. But iron, so much iron it even gave her a headache. And grease, too, immense amounts of blood-of-the-earth spread here.

All squatting on the bed of the river outside these concrete walls, another insult to its free-flowing energy.

"Maisie!" she said.

The wizard was rapidly coming into possession of more and more of her memories. Melançon, offering her a job by letter hand-couriered to her little southeast Portland sublet. Arguments over where and how she should apply her skills. He had given her the Japanese paper box for her little skull, the bones themselves coming from a mossy grave in the Garden Beneath, a relic of the Bright Days.

What had the paper been? The wizard was horrified. She'd put one of *their* skulls inside paper, where anything could have been printed or written.

Melançon must have already begun to snare her

then, in a web of cash and inattention cast by that bastard Bartelme.

The wizard found her way down a ladder to the metal floor that gave service access to the great counterweights. This was a place of power, where *they* would have been nothing but cries on the wind in the presence of so much iron amid running water.

It wasn't that the world needed the Bright Days again. *They* had been terrible masters, cruel as cats, vicious as badgers, indifferent as the sweet songbirds in *their* apple trees. But *they* had given magic to humans. The first keys to the wizard's doors. *Their* path had been a different way into the life of the world.

Why was she thinking so much of *them* now? Not simply the memory cascade in her head, either.

The wizard rolled a fresh cigarette. Even in the shadows the word "maleficum" caught her eye on the torn page. Another one for the fire, she told herself. Good enough.

She lit the hand roll, took a deep drag, let the smoke open her own doors.

The picture. Maisie Potter.

The wizard took it out of her pocket once more.

The photo glowed.

"Maisie." She looked at the bright background over the girl's shoulder. *Where* had this been taken?

Truth dawned on the wizard. The Garden Beneath. Maisie Potter had been smiling somewhere Under the Hill when some wizard or fool had brought a camera past the stone doors.

And armed with that proof, Melançon had set the wizard to looking for the way back to the Garden.

Maisie. Not far from Maeve. Also known as Queen Mab, mistress over all of *them*. The mead-queen of the Garden Beneath, feeding blood to her lords and servants. Her own, in drops, mixed with that of children stolen from the temporal world. Potter for the Potter's field, no doubt, the traditional cemetery of the poor where the nameless dead returned from beneath the earth were buried.

Melançon wanted to bring *their* madness back into the everyday light.

That must have been the shaft she had found plunging into the numbers sea. The sword of *them*, reaching out from the Garden Beneath, needing only someone to open the door.

"Not by all the fires in Gehenna," said the wizard. She wedged the photo of Mab in the teeth of one of the great gears that drove the lift span of the Morrison Bridge, took another drag on her cigarette, then used the glowing tip to set fire to the photo. It flared, then burned sputtering bright as if made of magnesium.

That was good enough for the wizard. The next time the bridge lifted, the ashes would be ground between tons of cold iron, then fall beneath the grating of the floor to rot amid grease and leaked-in river water.

Now she had to deal with Melançon. And Bartelme, too, most likely. The wizard discovered she had neither the will nor the word to step across space and time now. That had been exhausted, and it would be some hours before she could find that part of herself again.

So instead she climbed, up the ladder to the balcony, then up the iron stairs to the door at the top. There she was defeated by steel locks on the outside, with a spell laid upon them. Though the wizard worked an hour or more, she could not budge the door by strength or spirit. Here in the room of iron and blood-of-the-earth, she could not call out for help. This pier was as much a magical trap as the Ross Island Bridge, only this one was folded in around her.

Eventually she curled up by the door and slept. There was nothing to do but wait, and she might as well be rested when the door next opened.

Tuesday the 17th, morning

The wizard awoke to a deep groaning rattle. The bridge was going up. She looked across the space at the lift machinery, counterweights descending down the depth of the pier, and realized that the far end would be exposed to air as the deck members lifted.

Moving as quickly as she dared, the wizard slid down the stairs and the subsequent ladder to the grating that served as a floor. She was all too conscious of the massive weights shifting just by her head as she passed them, but still she sprinted to the inspection ladder bolted to the opposite wall. The wizard scrambled up that ladder as the bridge reached its lift angle.

The interlocking hinges of the bridge deck and the lifting arms towered above her. She could be crushed here as easily as the ashes of Maisie's photo beneath her feet. The wizard scrambled up the exposed edge of the stonework and looked down.

The Willamette was perhaps seventy feet below here, dark brown in the early morning light. A small boat, certainly not what the span had been lifted for, bobbed in the water.

Melançon and Bartelme stood in the boat. Melançon waved cheerfully at her, then lifted a rifle.

Lacking any other choice, the wizard leaped into the open air, dropping toward them.

The fall, as such things do, seemed to stretch time like taffy. Much ran through her head as she plunged. The will and the word were back, but it would do her no good to send herself away. She needed to stop these two, now.

Melançon smiled, his perfect teeth gleaming, as he pulled the trigger. A skeet shooter, she remembered. The wizard was much bigger than any clay pigeon.

She summoned the will and the word and sent the bullet away from her. Though it had been aimed true at the wizard, the round cut across time and space to plow into Bartelme's ribs from the left side. The shock sent him tumbling with a shriek into the Willamette where the water now boiled from the pull of her magic.

The wizard burned the last of her will and word to land smack on top of Melançon, neat as jumping off

a ladder. She then used a very old-fashioned and de-
cidedly nonmagical elbow to break his perfect teeth.
His weapon had gone flying into the river when she
hit him, so the wizard settled for striking Melançon's
temple hard against the side of the boat, twice, before
she slipped into the warm river and let the water carry
her away.

Tuesday the 17th, night

The wizard sat in a coffeehouse in Southeast and
listened with half an ear to the news. She hadn't been
able to get back in to Gierloff, Williamson, and Closson to retrieve her skull. Security had turned her away
with a shake of the head, doubtless sometime before
Melançon's disappearance was known. The wizard was
willing to let that little problem slide. She wasn't so
sure she wanted to be near one of *them* anyway, not
at this point. Not even *their* bones.

Now the television was talking about the murder-
suicide of a local businessman and one of his employees. The coroner's office had reported a silver bullet
was used. The newsblonde made a werewolf joke.

The wizard stepped out into the evening dark, taking in the scent of the air and wondering what she
should do next. She never had enough money, but she
never quite ran out either.

Somehow, another job seemed out of the question.

The wizard lit a cigarette and walked into the shadows, confident she would find a different way.

DISASTER RELIEF

by Kristine Kathryn Rusch

WINSTON'S unusual sense of charity began late on Christmas night 2004. He and Ruby, his familiar, were watching television in the living room, Winston slouched on his couch, Ruby curled at his side. She had her tail wrapped around her small body, and her yellow eyes focused on the roaring fire.

They had exchanged a few gifts—he had made her a cat-sized box bed out of sandalwood, and she had given him half a dozen mice in various states of decay. He'd known what it had cost her to give them up— she'd probably been saving them for that proverbial rainy day—so he'd thanked her and placed them in a drawer to deal with later. He knew better than to give them back. He'd tried that with the dead rabbit on his birthday, and had hurt her feelings so badly that she hadn't talked with him for nearly a week.

He was surfing, looking for something, anything, a *Christmas Story*, the horrible live-action version of the *Grinch*, when he saw the *Breaking News* icon at the bottom of CNN's crawl.

"Change it," Ruby muttered. "It's probably some new tape from Osama Bin Idiot out to ruin the holiday."

She'd been calling him that since the presidential election. She didn't understand why someone didn't wrap their front paws around his throat and kick out his stomach with their back paws. At least she hadn't offered to get a familiar friend to sway his magical companion toward the dark side of magic to take care of the problem, like she had after 9/11. Then she had claimed she was taking the human approach to the problem, but Winston could see she was as broken up by the coverage as he had been.

He should have changed the channel; he realized that later. The moment he saw the Breaking News icon, the holiday really and truly was over even before he heard the word "tsunami" and heard that tens of thousands of people were feared dead.

Ruby shuddered against him as the initial video footage sent through some unbroken Internet connection showed a huge wall of water sweeping a beach, overcoming a pool, and slamming into a hotel. She buried her face in her paws and pretended to sleep, but after a few moments, she asked that he mute the volume.

He did, for both of their sakes.

And he resisted the urge to go to the window, to look at the ocean several yards below the stone wall of his tiny house, and to make sure that the waves he saw were small ones, familiar ones, the ones that always appeared this late in the season on a moonlit night.

Instead, he'd sent what little money he had to the Red Cross, mostly by the same internet that had given him the early pictures and ruined his Christmas. And when he and Ruby had gone to the shop on Monday the 27th, the first time they'd been there since the spending spree the tourists had indulged in on the 24th, she had insisted he stop the car at the beachside hotels, particularly the tall exclusive resort hotel that vaguely resembled the one demolished in Thailand. Ruby had wanted to get out of the car, to make sure the pool was still there, to look at the distance between the ocean's edge and the patio on the hotel's lower level, but Winston wouldn't let her.

He was as shaken by the images that came out of Southeast Asia as she was, only he didn't admit it verbally. He just stocked the cliffside house with cans of Fancy Feast and bags of Friskies. He bought enough bottled water to last four months, and he found all kinds of dehydrated food for campers and some Meals Ready to Eat from a military supply store on the web. That, and bandages, and first aid kits, and emergency flashlights, and candles, and blankets, and everything else he could think of.

Because, he realized after weeks of watching that footage, when the tsunami hit the Oregon Coast, Seavy Village would be as cut off as Banda Aceh. It took three weeks for rescue teams to reach some of the most remote villages. He figured any tsunami here would be triggered by an earthquake that would level Portland and maybe even Seattle; by the time people thought of Seavy Village and Newport and Tillamook and all the other coastal towns, the residents would be on their own for a very long time.

His house would survive even the biggest tsunami. The cliff face he was on was made of lava rock, and the house was way above the historic tsunami line. But his store wouldn't survive a tsunami, so he made Ruby practice the run that they'd have to make to the Church of St. Peter at the top of the hill. He'd instructed Ruby to jump on his shoulder, and he would use what little magic he had to glue her there, so that she wouldn't get trampled or hurt or swept away.

He found himself thinking of disaster and destruction much more than he wanted to. He would look at the ocean as an enemy, not as his beloved home, and then he would imagine trying to survive here with his very little magic, his beautiful familiar, and no rescue in sight.

By the time Hurricane Katrina formed in the south Atlantic, he had stopped watching television and listening to news on the radio. He huddled in his little shop, playing classical music on the Bose system he'd indulged in, and mixing spells in the back.

The spells were for his mail order business. He made a small living selling tiny spells—an aphrodisiac here, a love potion there (nothing powerful, just enough to send little waves of attraction), a protection spell or a spell that gave the user just a little bit of courage. He couldn't do much; he was never a great mage. But that didn't matter. Most people didn't want a lot of magic; they just wanted a bit of hope.

It wasn't until he went to the nearby grocery store for his favorite sandwich (turkey on rye with avocado for him; tuna on white with cheese for Ruby) that he realized Katrina had gone from another hurricane disaster to a nightmare on the scale of the tsunami.

He wasn't going to tell Ruby, but she knew. She could tell just from his face. She made him turn on the radio, and when they got home, she pushed the remote for CNN all by herself. When she didn't like that coverage, she went to MSNBC and Fox and the BBC, then back again, staring at the water as it pooled in that famous city as if it were coming for her.

One night during that awful week—he couldn't remember which one; they all seemed to blur—when he sat at his computer to give more money to the Red Cross (and some in Ruby's name to the Humane Society), Ruby jumped on his lap.

"What about Boyce?" she asked before Winston could punch the send button, completing his first transaction.

"Boyce?" Winston asked, feeling confused. Boyce Theriot was a colleague of his. They exchanged ingredients, shared recipes for some smaller spells, and occasionally helped each other with tough clients.

Boyce Theriot lived in New Orleans.

Winston couldn't believe he had forgotten that. He had relied on that fact so many times. Boyce had gotten him ingredients that no one else could, at least not in the states, because of New Orleans' voodoo culture.

"I'm sure he's all right," Winston said, not wanting to think about it.

Ruby put a paw on his hand, guiding it away from

the mouse and that click that would send a few hundred dollars into the ether.

"Would we be?" she asked, nodding toward the screen. "If it happened here?"

"Ruby, I've explained this. We don't have levees, and we're not in a hurricane zone—"

"I'm not stupid," she said in that tone she used when she was completely serious. She knew that the Pacific coast had its horrible storms—every winter they seemed to suffer what the Atlantic would call a Category 1 Hurricane—and it was only a matter of time before something bigger hit. But the Pacific coast seemed geared for wind and heavy rain. It was the tsunami, the earthquake, the threat of total annihilation, like that which had happened in Southeast Asia, that worried him the most.

"I know," he said, and slid his hand away from her very tiny, but very insistent paw. "I didn't mean to say you were stupid. I—"

"If something happens here," she said, "like the tsunami or the earthquake or if one of the volcanoes blows, would we be all right?"

She hadn't asked him this before. She had watched him buy the extra food and the bandages, watched him stockpile the blankets and the kerosene stoves, and hadn't said a word.

He'd been relieved about that. He didn't want to lie to Ruby, not that he ever had.

He wasn't sure he could lie to her, and keep her as his familiar.

"I don't know," he said. And that was truthful. He didn't know. The other correct, truthful answer would have been *it depends*.

"You don't know why?" She climbed off his lap and sat on the small square of desk right in front of the keyboard, careful not to touch the computer in any way. She was good about that, good about most things, really, except when she wanted his attention.

"Because," he said, "if we're here in the house, we should be okay, and I have a plan for the store. But if we're on the other side of town, or at the river crossing, which is below sea level, we might not make it home. We might not be all right at all."

"And," she said as if she were the one making the point all along, "your magic can't help us. You can't teleport like some. You can't fly. You can't—"

"I know what I can and cannot do, Ruby," he snapped. Then his face heated. He didn't like yelling at her. But her litany sounded too much like all of his instructors. They had finally decided that he was the most inept of all mages, the kind who had such a minor talent that they were barely better than the nonmagical. His skills were tiny, his knowledge of the magical world just about as small. Part of the problem, his mentor Gerry Bellier had said, was that Winston didn't even understand magic on the larger scale. It didn't make sense to him, like calculus wouldn't make sense to a three year old.

Only a three year old could grow into the mental skills that would enable him to understand calculus. Bellier implied that Winston would never understand the larger magicks. And so far, he was right.

"Boyce is more talented than I am," Winston said.

"But he runs a shop," Ruby said.

"A lot of mages do," Winston said. "It's a front."

"It's not his front," Ruby said. "It's his life. He's told you that."

"He's in the French Quarter," Winston said. "It didn't flood. He'll be all right."

She turned, slammed a paw on the return key, and somehow did not complete his Red Cross transaction. Then she hit the mouse with her tail, and suddenly they were in one of his favorite programs, Google Earth, flying over the entire country.

"Zoom in," she said.

He didn't ask where. He knew what she wanted to show him. So he found New Orleans, and on the old satellite pictures, taken before the disaster, the town looked like it always had.

His heart constricted.

"Type in his address," she said.

He did, and the program showed him the street, at the far end of the French Quarter, not too far from downtown.

"Now type in Charity Hospital," she said.

He did, and then closed his eyes. Boyce's shop wasn't that far from Charity. In fact, it seemed closer to downtown than the French Quarter proper. Had Boyce lied on his Web site, just to attract more business? Or were there some peculiarities that Winston didn't know about New Orleans, about the way it counted its neighborhoods, about the way it labeled its subcultures?

"Seems to me," Ruby said, "that little shop of his is filled with water. Where does he live?"

Winston didn't know. He'd known Boyce for nearly thirty years, and yet they hadn't spent time together since they were young apprentices in San Francisco. He'd never seen Boyce's home, and Boyce had never seen his.

They had become business acquaintances and nothing more.

"Maybe I don't understand all this human money stuff and everything," Ruby said, "but it seems to me if he earned a comparable income to yours in that city, he wouldn't be living in the Garden District. He'd be living somewhere that's also underwater. You think he's lying on his roof somewhere, waiting to be rescued?"

Winston winced. He didn't want to think about it. He wanted to go back to the previous screen and finish his donation to the Red Cross.

"Do you?"

"I could do a locate," Winston said feebly.

"And then what?" Ruby asked. "You can't just teleport him here."

"I know my weaknesses," Winston snapped. "Stop reminding me."

"Stop acting like someone with no magic at all. You have a friend here. Help him."

Winston stared at her. The sentiment was amazingly uncatlike. Cats did not help others in need.

Winston frowned. "Why do you care?"

She raised her chin. The whiskers on the end of it twitched, but the ones on her nose did not. The look she gave him was regal, and it implied that he was the stupid one in the room, not her.

"It could be us," she said. "We might be on our roof one day. We could be stranded here. I would hope someone would care enough to find us. I would hope that someone would care enough to help."

The thought was alien to him. He never expected help. He had had such a difficult childhood that when he became a mage, he didn't even expect help from a familiar. That had gotten him into trouble in his early years. An aphrodisiac he'd designed had gone bad because he hadn't had a familiar. His client nearly died, and he fled San Francisco with the police on his heels. They thought he was dealing drugs, and by his refusal to use a familiar, he probably had been. Magic made herbs special. Herbs without magic were simply cheap ways of getting high.

"You never thought of getting help, did you?" Ruby sighed.

"We're going to be on our own, Ruby," he said.

"Well, Boyce shouldn't be. No one should be. Jeez." She exhaled a mouthful of tuna breath so strong it almost knocked him over. Then she jumped on his thighs hard enough to give him bruises.

She left the computer and went back to her fireplace, sitting with her back to him, just to make sure he got the message.

What would he do if he located Boyce? Tell the authorities where to find him? They were already overburdened. He wasn't going to go to New Orleans. He wasn't the kind of man who went into a disaster zone, and for all her tough talk, Ruby wasn't the kind of cat who went there, either.

She barely liked to leave the house, tolerating the

ride to the shop only because she saw it as part of her turf as well.

Her anger radiated out toward him. He could feel it as if it were his own. Later, if he learned that Boyce had died and he could have done something to prevent the death, he would feel guilty. So guilty, in fact, that it might cripple him, just like that incident in San Francisco had.

"All right," he said. "We're going to do a locate. For whatever good that'll do."

Ruby's ears flattened, but she didn't turn around. She didn't believe him.

He got up and went to the small closet where he kept his personal supplies. He got a few herbs, mixed a tiny potion, and dipped his fingers in it. Then he recited the spell in English, because his Latin was atrocious, and leaned back.

A puff of smoke appeared between him and Ruby. In it, he saw a high school cafeteria filled with hundreds of cots. Aid workers passed out cards or certificates or some kind of identification—he couldn't tell—to the left of the vision; to the right, a guard stood at the door, watching people as they went in and out.

Winston didn't see Boyce, not that he was sure he'd recognize him even if he were there. In the last thirty years, their only interaction had been on the phone. And, it seemed, everyone in that cafeteria had the same Southern accent—long, slow, and charmingly musical.

"I don't see him," Winston said, and the moment he spoke the words, a man sat up. He wore a raunchy T-shirt one size too small and a pair of blue jeans a size too big. His hair was thin and pulled back into a ponytail. But his eyes were the same. They were almost silver and they accented his café au lait skin, making him seem exotic and magical at the same time.

He looked through the smoke at Winston. Then he tilted his head. "Who don't you see?" he asked.

Ruby trotted to Winston's side. Winston leaned forward. "Boyce?"

"Winston? Winston Karpathian, is that really you?"

Everyone around Boyce was staring at him as if he'd gone crazy. It would seem that way, too, if they had no magic. They wouldn't be able to see inside the smoke hole at the opening he had created in their corner of the universe.

"It's me," Winston said. "Where are you?"

"I dunno. Some podunk town that has more references to Jesus on its billboards than the churches in New Orleans do." He sounded lost.

"Hey, buddy." The man next to Boyce touched his shoulder. "You all right?"

"Tell me the name," Winston said. "We'll get you out of there."

"Who're you? God?" Boyce asked. Winston had never heard such hopelessness in a man's voice before.

"Hell, no," said the man next to him, obviously thinking Boyce was talking to him. "I'm just trying to help."

"I can wire you some money," Winston said. "Call me, and we'll figure it out."

"Call you. You have a phone number?"

"What the hell?" the man next to Boyce stood up, vaguely offended. "Lemme get some help here."

Winston felt his own cheeks heat. Of course Boyce wouldn't have his phone number. That was in Boyce's shop, probably like everything else.

"Yeah," Winston said. He recited the number and added, "You can call collect."

Then the smoke ring faded. Ruby leaned against Winston, her little body tense. "That's a human shelter, huh?"

Winston nodded. A lot of the details hadn't registered for him until now: How many people had just curled up on their cots, staring at nothing; How no one really talked, except the aid workers; How the kids played listlessly in the corner.

He shuddered, and Ruby leaned harder, as if he could make things better.

And then his phone rang.

* * *

The next few days became a blur. The $200 he was going to send to the Red Cross, and the $50 he was going to send to the Humane Society (which Ruby protested—she felt he should still send that money) went to a plane ticket that got Boyce Theriot out of northern Louisiana and to Portland, Oregon. Winston had to charge another $50 on his credit card—the one he kept for emergencies—to get one of those airport limos to pick Boyce up, because Winston couldn't do it.

His only car was a Gremlin, bought because he liked the magical name, and he'd had it almost as long as he lived in Oregon. He found the problem that made it belch blue smoke, but he knew the undercarriage was so rusted that one day it would simply fall off.

While he waited for the limo to show up, he cleaned the guest room. He hadn't had a guest since he moved into the cliff house decades ago, and the bed had gotten buried beneath books and blankets and trinkets he'd found. The job was larger than he expected, and he even had to use a cleaning spell—something he hadn't done in a decade—to get the dust out of the mattress. He went to the Factory Outlet store and bought fresh sheets, a new comforter, and towels. Ruby wanted to keep the new stuff for them, and let Boyce use the older things from Winston's bed, but that felt wrong to him.

Now that he had resigned himself to company, he wanted to do a good turn by him.

The limo arrived late Friday night. Winston watched through the front window as people piled out. In the glow of the streetlights against the dark sky, it almost looked like an art film version of those clown cars he'd seen as a child. More and more people got out until he thought the entire vehicle would collapse from their loss.

Ruby sat on the back of the couch, looking more like a cat than a familiar. She watched from a position that guaranteed she could see the people, but they couldn't see her. And she could run for the bedroom at a moment's notice.

Winston left her inside. He went onto his front stoop, watching as the tallest, thinnest of the group took a receipt from the limo driver. The air smelled clean and sharp; the wind was strong off the ocean, usually something he loved.

But he felt nervous now, as if he had plunged into a world he hadn't quite expected.

The limo drove off, leaving five people in the street. Only five. It had seemed like so many more.

"Winston?" The tall, thin man came toward him, and he realized it was Boyce. He hadn't remembered Boyce being tall or thin, but now that he saw Boyce walk, he knew that this was his old friend. How could anyone forget that walk, which was half sashay, half swagger?

Winston stepped off the porch and plastered a smile on his face. He hoped he wasn't shaking. "Boyce," he said, extending his hand.

"I hope y'all don't mind, but I gathered a few more of us. When I realized we could do a locate, I did, and then they did, and well, we can be our own little magical shelter, right?"

Our own little magical shelter was, at the moment, Winston's home. But he didn't say anything. He couldn't turn these people away. He knew they had less than he had.

"There's not a lot of room," he said. "But we'll make do."

Then he realized that everyone—except Boyce— was carrying an animal. Of course. Familiars. He felt his heart sink just a little. How would Ruby react to a French poodle, two other cats, and a Chihuahua?

He wanted to warn her (in fact, he wanted to remind her that Chihuahuas weren't food) but he couldn't. He just hoped she figured this out. He opened his front door, and let the crowd inside.

They squeezed in. In addition to himself and Boyce,

there were two more men and two women. Everyone looked a little lost. They all wore mismatched clothing, and their hair seemed in need of a comb. The animals clung to their mages.

Ruby still sat on the back of the couch, her yellow eyes wide. She looked at Winston as if demanding an explanation.

"I only have one extra bedroom," he said, "but it has a king bed."

As if that made a difference. As if five people could fit comfortably on that bed.

"If y'all don't mind, we can just pile up some blankets in the front room," one of the women said.

"Nonsense, Nurleen," one of the men said. "You women can have the bedroom and we men can stay out front."

Winston swallowed hard. He hated crowds. He didn't much like people, and he suddenly felt trapped here, in his own home. "We'll settle rooms in a minute," he said. "Let's do introductions first."

Introductions. He started by going over to Ruby and putting a hand on her back. She jumped. Then she crawled into his arms, just like the other familiars were doing. She watched as the introductions went around.

Nurleen Bremmer of Gulfport, Mississippi. She was heavyset and dark-haired, wearing a Metallica T-shirt and sweatpants that looked like they'd seen better days. Her home disintegrated around her and she was lucky enough to grab Princess, her white-and-gold cat (and familiar) before everything vanished in a haze of wind, rain, and water.

Wendi Phillips of Biloxi, Mississippi. She had red hair so bright it would've made Lucille Ball proud, and her French poodle looked dyed to match. Wendi wore her own clothes—she managed to fit some outfits and underwear in her purse, she later informed everyone—but that was all she had.

Palmer Kent of New Orleans stood beside Boyce,

and looked smaller for it. Kent wasn't much bigger than a child, and the Chihuahua he had with him—named after the Rock—didn't help much.

And Savion DeChutney, from Moss Point, Mississippi, who didn't say much because he looked like he might burst into tears at any moment. He was dark, with ritual scarring that made him seem scary, but his cat—Noel—spoke for him half the time because he was so honored to be taken in by someone who understood him.

Then Boyce sighed. "Y'all know me. To stop you from asking, the hurricane got Riddell. One of my bookshelves fell over as the house started to go, and he was crushed . . ."

Boyce didn't finish. Riddell was both his dog and his familiar. One of those small little decorative dogs—since Winston had never met him, he hadn't paid much attention to the breed—but he knew the dog probably hadn't been much bigger than Ruby.

Ruby shuddered and looked at Winston's bookshelves as if they were the enemy. Maybe they were. All he knew was that he would have to comfort her later.

"We sure are honored, Winston, that you took the time and trouble to give up your home like this," Boyce said. "To be among like-minded people, I can't tell you . . ."

Winston smiled at them, unsure what to do next. He hadn't planned to give up his home, just to provide a haven. "I've got some stew on the stove," he said, thankful that he'd planned a large meal instead of something for two. "Let's eat and get to know each other."

The stories made him sad. Wendi had a beauty shop in Biloxi—not the hairdressing kind, but the kind that with a bit of magic dust and a lot of pep made people feel like they had some worth. The shop was gone now. Nurleen taught sleight-of-hand to tourists, then did a full fledged David Copperfield-type of show in one of the casinos. From there, she used a bit of magic to see someone who was sad in the audience, someone she could help with a touch or a small wish. Nothing big, just enough to keep her hand in the practice.

Savion was a supplier—that was how Boyce knew him—specializing in difficult-to-find ingredients for hard-to-make spells. His warehouse had collapsed in the wind when the hurricane had come aground, the items scattered.

"No insurance," he'd said, head down, dipping the French bread Winston had baked in his soup. "I mean, how do you tell adjusters that eye of newt actually has a value?"

And Boyce, who hadn't gone to his shop after the loss of his familiar. He couldn't face it—partly because he knew that part of New Orleans was under water. Instead, he used what little magic he could to get himself out of the city, and then, drained and spent and worried about casting spells without his familiar, he hitched a ride to the nearest shelter, which took him to the high school where Winston had caught up with him.

Everyone was tired, sad, and lost, but grateful. Grateful to have a place to go, grateful to have something else to think about. The animals were quiet. They all eyed Ruby, knowing this was her turf, and she glared back at them, establishing herself as dominant.

But Winston wasn't sure how long that would last. She pretended to be tough, but she was soft at heart. He could feel her trembling as she sat on his lap, watching their guests.

When he finally took her into his bedroom that night—he wasn't willing to give up this little bit of personal space—she climbed onto the bed and closed her eyes.

"I'm sorry," she said. "I didn't know it would be like this."

She was so stressed she wasn't flirting with him. She wasn't acting tough. She seemed exhausted.

He lay down beside her and she crawled on his chest. She didn't purr.

"They can't stay," she said. "There's too much conflicting magic. I can't keep track of it."

"I know." He could feel it, too, and that seemed odd to him. Usually, he couldn't feel much magic at all.

She put her head on her paws, and stared at him. "What are we going to do?"

He sighed. He had saved some money. It was his emergency fund—enough for surgery if Ruby got ill or a repair to his house that he couldn't handle magically. He'd been trying to save for a new car, but he'd had trouble with that. The disasters across the country had tapped him—he gave money away instead of putting it in the bank.

He hadn't thought of the downside of his charity. He preferred to keep it—like everything else in his life—at arms' length. But now there were five people in his house, four of whom he'd never met before, and one he hadn't seen in thirty years.

Five people, and he could barely stand having two people in his store at the same time.

He shuddered.

"Big Boy?" Ruby whispered. "What're we gonna do?"

"I guess," he said, "we need to find a house."

Houses weren't hard to find in Seavy Village. It was a coastal resort town, filled with second homes, which the locals called weekenders. Most of those places were empty and half of them were for sale. Many that weren't were designated as vacation rentals.

It didn't take Winston long to find one big enough for the group. When he told the real estate agent who handled the rentals what it was for, she perked up.

"I'm sure we can get you a break on the rent," she said. "Maybe even get some local charity groups to kick in. You want me to check?"

He hadn't expected help from anyone else, seeing

this as entirely his problem which he brought on himself in a moment of selflessness. He mumbled something like that, and the agent grinned.

"We've all been hoping we can help the evacuees. Most of them just didn't come to Oregon or the coast. Everyone's been wanting to do something, though. Those images from the Gulf . . ." She shuddered. "It could just as easily be here, you know. We get bad storms and tidal surges and—"

"I know," he said, waving a hand. Her conversation was too close to the ones he'd had with Ruby. He didn't want to think about what-ifs. Thinking about what-ifs had brought him here, doing his good deed.

"Well," the real estate agent said with a smile. "Let me just see what I can do. No way should you handle this on your own."

And she stepped in. He felt relief which also made him feel guilty. Finally, a competent person handling the problem. Someone other than him.

By the end of the day, he had a fully furnished vacation rental with six bedrooms and three bathrooms, along with some donated clothes, food for the animals, and some cash for the evacuees. The reporter from the paper came to photograph them moving in, and asked for everyone's story. All of the mages looked confused when asked, and finally, the real estate agent had said that maybe the interviews should be done at a less traumatic time.

Still, the story ran the next day—*Gulf Coast Evacuees Find Home In Seavy Village*—and pictures of the mages, their "pets" and their meager belongings graced every single newspaper box in town.

Police Officer Scott Park, the only nonmagical person who know what Winston really did for a living, stopped into the store that afternoon. Winston was hiding in the back, hoping to have a little privacy. He'd hated the sound of the bell, worried that he'd have to be charming to a new customer, and was relieved to see that Park had come alone.

"Quite the good deed you did," Park said. Ruby

was rubbing her head against his hand. He'd helped save her life once, but she'd adored him even before that. She had been the one—by talking with him—to convince him that magic was real.

"Didn't mean to have it publicized," Winston said.

Park shrugged. "They say there's no such thing as bad publicity."

Winston nodded, but he couldn't meet Park's eyes. "They're all friends of yours?"

"No," Winston said. "Just Boyce. He helped you and me with a case once, remember?"

"Yeah," Park said. "How come they can't just conjure repairs?"

The question made Winston bristle, even though Park hadn't meant to be rude. Winston ran a hand over the glass case that separated him from the rest of the store.

"I guess I'm not the only one with small magic," he said.

"You'd think that people with larger magic would make it all go away," Park said.

Winston raised his head. He hadn't thought of that. If he had the ability, he would have done it. He wondered if there was something in the magical rules that prevented it, something about calling attention to one's self.

But he couldn't think of anything. Helping a neighbor or a friend with a serious problem was usually considered white magic (depending on the spell), and white magic was fine.

"Guess not everyone's as good-hearted as you," Park said, scratching Ruby at the base of her tail. She was purring so loudly that she could probably be heard on the street.

"I'm not good-hearted," Winston said.

Park grinned. "That's a matter of opinion, my friend."

Maybe it was. But a good-hearted man didn't force the people he'd invited into his home to move out the very next day. A good-hearted man didn't feel relief when the people he helped closed the door behind them. A good-hearted man didn't secretly hope he'd never see them again.

But of course he did. He was their contact in Seavy Village, and they came to him with questions. He was surprised at how much he knew.

When Nurleen asked who to contact at the local casino about performing her magical act, Winston told her. When Savion remembered that he had had a supplier in Portland who might need his services, Winston had the phone number. When Wendi wanted to know the name of a spa that might like a hairdresser who knew how to make her clients feel special, Winston knew the best place to go.

Winston even knew of a magic store for sale farther up the coast that seemed to suit Palmer Kent just fine. The owner wanted to get out of the area, and would take small payments, so long as they were guaranteed.

Winston didn't guarantee them—he didn't want that kind of financial burden—but Scott Park knew a banker who could (and did) arrange it all.

By the end of the first week, the group had a place to live, and four of them had work. Savion was heading to Portland in a few days, and Palmer was moving north. The women were so busy they barely spent time in the house.

That only left Boyce.

Boyce, who seemed lost without his familiar, Riddell.

Boyce, who had decided to spend his afternoons helping Winston in the shop.

Winston couldn't say no, even though he wanted to. He couldn't tell Boyce to leave him alone. Boyce had lost everything: his home, his business and, until he got a new familiar, his magic.

On his third day in the store, Boyce decided that Winston needed to redecorate.

Winston had kept the store the same since he

opened it, decades ago. The front was filled with tour-
isty impulse buys—toys, fake magic tricks, pinwheels.
He had a few real antiques in the window, mostly
bottles that looked like I-Dream-of-Jeannie bottles,
and some harmless potions to one side.

The back, where he did most of his work, was
blocked by a beaded curtain. In between the back and
the front, he had a glass cabinet with his cash register
on top, and some valuable stones inside.

Boyce had walked around the place, studying it as if
he would get quizzed on it. When he noticed Winston
watching, he said, "Y'all need some color over on the
north wall. And some carpeting starting just past the
door there, with maybe a raised up area for people to
sit. A red curtain might be nice instead of those beads.
And some new product. I mean, really, what do tourists need with antique bottles? I ask you."

Winston hadn't answered. He'd let Boyce talk and
draw up plans.

Ruby exhausted herself following Boyce everywhere, watching him make little drawings, glaring as
he rearranged the existing merchandise. Her tail
twitched every time she looked at him, and after a
few days of this, her ears flattened, too. She slept hard
every night because she couldn't nap; she was too
afraid he might actually start implementing his plans.

Winston knew Boyce didn't have the money to
make the changes, and Winston wasn't about to lend
him any. Winston liked his store the way it was. When
Boyce finally left, Winston would put the merchandise
back where it came from. But Winston didn't know
when Boyce would leave.

They weren't talking about it. Boyce wasn't even
searching for a new familiar.

Boyce did wait on the customers for him. Winston
had a few local customers now that the newspaper
articles had run. People were charmed to meet Boyce,
and they bought small things to justify their presence
in the store.

Winston mostly remained in the back, wishing he

had Boyce's skill with people. Customers laughed and joked, told stories and exchanged information. No one had ever seemed so relaxed in Winston's place before.

He hated it.

He hated it all.

And he felt mean, petty, and small for each little resentment. Boyce had lost his life, and now Winston felt as though he was losing everything he valued in his, one tiny bit at a time.

That thought made him feel even smaller, and he tried to banish it. But it grew, like a blackness across his vision. He was growing afraid to mix new spells, afraid his resentment would color the magic.

Finally, Ruby brought him a section of the local paper that someone had left near the front door.

She tapped an ad at the very edge of the back page. *Seavy Village Eighteenth Annual Dog Show.*

Contestants from all over the country compete for these prizes . . .

Winston frowned at it. "You're not a dog."

She rolled her eyes.

"You don't even like them."

"For Boyce," she whispered.

"You don't get familiars at dog shows," Winston said. "They're for showing off dogs that are already owned."

If Ruby could have put her paws on her hips like an angry woman, she would have. Instead, she settled for her glare and a quick twitch of the tail.

"I know how to find familiars," she said. "He needs to go."

So Winston contacted the convention center and signed up as a vendor. He made a few dog treats, some calming potions, and charmed a few collars. Then he sent Boyce to man the table, and hoped that would be enough.

Boyce didn't come back for two days, and when he did, he had a hollow ragged look around the eyes.

"Did you know?" he asked as he came through the

shop's door, carrying a box filled with the remaining merchandise, "how many animals got abandoned in the storms?"

Winston did know because Ruby followed the statistics. She wanted some kind of guarantee that she wouldn't get lost if a tsunami hit the coast. He continually promised her he'd do his best, but they both knew that might not be enough.

"They've got shelters in California taking some of the overload," Boyce said as he put the cash and credit card slips on the counter. He'd sold almost everything he brought. "They were doing a fundraiser at the show."

Winston stared at the money. Boyce had earned more in one appearance than Winston had earned all fall.

"Would you think it rude of me to volunteer down there? I know you got me this lovely home and all, but I'm rootless, Winston. And Miss Ruby here doesn't like me. I never did get on with cats."

"Pfff," Ruby said from a corner of the counter. "Like that's the problem."

Boyce glanced at her, started to say something, and then stopped. "I was just thinking that I could be useful, and much as I like helping you, you don't really need me. We both know that."

Winston swallowed. He didn't want to nod, didn't want to insult Boyce.

"I can hitch a ride with one of the volunteers. I have a bit of that money your locals gave me. The girls'd keep the house, if you don't mind a little friendly competition—"

Winston didn't see the women as any kind of competition at all. They were in different parts of the business.

"—and maybe I'd come back," Boyce said.

"You're not obligated," Winston said. "I just wanted to help."

Boyce grinned at him, then took his hands. "I know. And you have. You have no idea how much."

Not a lot. That was how Winston summed it up later. He hadn't helped much at all. He had given the five a destination, true enough, but he hadn't sacrificed more than a few days of his time and a few hundred dollars of his money. In the end, almost everything they'd received had come from the town, not from him.

And what bothered him the most was how much he had resented it. How much he wished for them to leave, for his quiet life to return.

Now that it was back, he felt only relief. And guilt for enjoying the silence. He'd tried to do something outside his nature. Somehow he had thought it would make him feel better. Instead, it left him feeling shaken.

He took some of Boyce's advice. He put a light blue paint on the north wall, and took on consignment some paintings of wizards and fantasy dragons from a local artist. He took some of the scarves he'd brought with him from San Francisco thirty years ago and draped them on the shelves, adding even more color.

He didn't change the beads, though, nor did he add a rug, which he thought would be a disaster in this wet climate. And he didn't add a sitting area. He didn't want the customers to stay any longer than they had to.

Ruby hated all the changes, until she realized that they brought in more customers, and more customers meant more pets for her. She preened at them, acted like a cat, and got a lot of attention. She even got her own write-up in the local paper as the most popular store cat in Seavy Village.

Her new-found fame didn't alleviate her fears, but Winston realized nothing would. Just as nothing would change the odd feelings he'd had since the first of the year.

Finally, at Christmas, he realized he was living each day as if a disaster was about to happen, worrying that he had done things wrong when he'd only done what he could. Instead, he needed to look at each day as a blessing, each moment he had with Ruby in his quiet house in his quiet town as a gift—one that could vanish at any moment, yes, but one that he needed to value just the same.

On December 26th, a year after the tsunami that started his strange journey, he got a phone call. Boyce was back in New Orleans, helping clean up the city.

He had a new familiar, a puppy born to one of the rescue dogs who'd made it to California.

"She's green," he said, "but she's enthusiastic. And she's polite. Kinda reminds me of Ruby."

Winston had almost laughed out loud at that. Ruby was never polite. And then he remembered: She had been polite in those days after the storm. She had been polite and considerate and frightened, just as he had been.

He congratulated Boyce, told his friend he admired his courage, and wished him the best. Then he hung up the phone and found his own familiar, huddled next to the fireplace.

She had stopped watching the television sometime in October, and he was grateful. Instead, she watched the flames. He picked her up, and held her close, feeling her little heart beat against his.

"It's okay," he said softly. "We're safe."

"For now," she whispered.

"For now," he agreed. Then he smiled at her.

"You got small dreams, Big Boy," she said.

He nodded. He liked his small dreams. And his small house. And his small life.

He liked it all, and he would enjoy it as much as he could, for as long as he could.

Ruby sighed and snuggled into his arms. He sank down onto the rug in front of the fireplace and watched the flames, relishing the moment.

Moments—that was all they had. But, he was beginning to realize, moments were more than enough.

KIDPRO

by Laura Anne Gilman

*I categorically reject the accusations. Not everyone can
get into KidPro. Heck, not everyone wants to. We encourage that. We only want the ones who are determined. The ones with the fire in their belly, you know?
The ones everyone looks at and says, "I always knew
he was going somewhere."*

*We're not a school, despite what you may have
heard, although we do insist that our Kids continue
their education both during their earning years and afterward. Nor are we a corporation-employer—our clients don't work for us, we work for them. And the
small sum of money we take in from their efforts is
nothing to the amount they are able to earn.*

And everyone's happy.

(Excerpt from interview with Arthur Miklos, founder
of KidPro)

THE morning had started badly, with a pint of
blood, peeing into a cup, and the usual round of
shots. The SEC should have had better things to do
than monitor his hormone levels.

But even that was better than what he faced this
afternoon.

They were in Richard's office; he was at the desk,

163

David leaning on the credenza behind him, scanning
the rows of disks and files like a nervous tick.

"You really don't care?"

"It's not such a big deal. I don't know why everyone
makes it into such a big deal."

David made a rude gesture with one hand. "Oh,
yeah, right. Like you wouldn't care if nobody came."

Richard shrugged, not even responding to David's
gesture. He was more intent on the news feed in front
of him than the conversation. Political discussions
were continuing over the disarmament, but there was
a bunch of chatter on other channels about troop
movements and an increase in medical supplies being
requested. His eyes flicked back and forth, then up
once to check the time.

"Richard?"

The KidPro building was never silent; too many
people working in too many time zones around the
globe defeated even the very best soundproofing. But
there was a distinct silence after David's plaintive
query.

"Oh, for . . . So I'm officially, legally, whoopee,
thirteen instead of twelve. So what? I still can't do
anything. I can't even," and he gestured at the screen
in disgust, "pick up a stock when I want to. It's always
tell us this and tell us that, and then they get to make
the call. It's my brain, my magic, so why can't I make
the deal?"

David rolled his eyes with the air of someone getting into an argument for the hundredth time and still
not satisfied with the answer. "Because we can't.
We're still minors."

"Exactly!" Richard slammed his hands down flat on
the desk with self-satisfying aggression. "Minors. And
I'll still be a minor tomorrow, and the day after that
and the year after that. All the way until I'm fifteen.
And they want me to be happy about that?" He made
a rude noise, and went back to studying the screen.
He could glance at the data in the rapid-scroll, and it
made perfect sense to him. More, it was a complete

picture: thus, so this, which meant that X would occur
if someone did Y. Adults could see it—but *he* could
make it so, just by focusing on, and tinkering the tini-
est bit with the Flow. The Wall Street Wizards, the
press called them. The reason why KidPro paid him,
and David, and Molly, and all the others nice packets
of money, to make it the hottest trading firm on or
off the Street

And why the government passed law after law hob-
bling them—'for their own protection'—so that they
weren't allowed to make any decisions on their own.
Every move they made, every ripple in the datastream
they influenced, had to be done though an adult;
someone who had no ability to do what they did, but
was legally allowed to just because their voice had
broken, or their period had started, and their magic—
the thing that made them special—was gone with it.

"It's not . . . you're not happy here?"

Happy? Richard shrugged. He was happy enough,
when they let him do what he was here to do. But
every six months he—like the others—had to be
poked and prodded by the clinic, give blood and mar-
row samples until he felt like a vampire's favorite
take-away. All because of those stupid laws.

"But . . ." David circled around to his original topic.
"But it's your birthday!"

"Cake and soda, and a lot of adults standing around
to make sure we all have fun. No big deal." He'd
rather be working, anyway. Hands and brain deep in
the Flow, feeling the hum of it surround him; tweaking
and redirecting and focusing the data stream by rede-
fining the possibilities . . .

The laws called it para-manipulation. The press
called it Wizardry. Richard just called it magic, and it
was all he wanted to do. Had since he was seven, and
the testers had come to his school and called his parents and showed him how, if he closed his eyes and let
his daydreams focus, he could help change the world.

Rumor had it that you didn't even really need the
feed to be running by the time you hit thirteen and

had enough hours in the system, but the one time he had tried to reach for the Flow without it, all he'd gotten for his trouble was a killer migraine, an IV drip in his neck, and a scowling, so-disappointed-in-you lecture from the Old Man.

Maybe he'd try again, once he really truly was thirteen.

Specialists defined para-manipulation as the ability to dip into the communal universe and redirect its intent. Scientists claimed it was all smoke and mirrors, except the random physicist like Osborne, who claimed it was an actual manifestation of one of Einstein's minor and long-discarded side theories about time and energy or something like that. Lots of jokes about "Real Mutants" and mental powers, and elf-struck changelings, but all it took was finding a financially viable use for it, and the tag "Wall Street Wizards" got stuck on all of them.

Richard preferred being a Kid, himself. Better perks.

"Well, there will be presents, won't there?" David said, like that was the end-all and be-all of the day.

Richard came back from his memories and looked at the boy by his side. Another Kid, a fellow, if newer, employee of KidPro. He was supposed to be mentoring David, showing him the ropes. His first mentoring job: a position of real trust and experience.

Whoopie.

"Presents? Bo-ring. Nobody'll get me anything that's not on the Approved list. I asked my folks for an Air Rover. I mean, it's not like we can't afford it, with what I pulled down last year."

"And?" David's snub nose practically quivered.

"And nothing. The Old Man won't let them. I might hurt myself. 'And then where would we all be?'" he said, mimicking the Old Man's tone, if not the room-filling basso. "Like, nothing we ever do has a risk. I swear, this place is so warded, I don't think anyone's gotten so much as a bruise in the past year."

It was all about their protection, valued and valuable as they were. KidPro sold itself as the safest place in the world for Kids; in three decades, there had been only four attempted kidnappings, and not one of them had succeeded. What they didn't say, when talking parents into giving up their darlings until puberty, was that the threat from boredom was greater than any physical harm.

For some of the Kids, anyway.

"Yeah, but that's in the lab. You're talking about going Outside."

Richard held back a sigh. David hadn't been Outside since he came to KidPro. He didn't want to go—Outside people were different, limited. They didn't see things the way he did, couldn't predict, precog, or predispose the Flow. It scared him, the way looking into the abyss never had. Richard was crazy, his expression clearly said, to want to go out there, even with an Air Rover.

"I don't want to *live* there," he said in disgust, and pushed his chair back and propped his loafer-clad feet up on the desk, in direct contradiction of the rules. Pressed khaki pants caught the afternoon sunlight, coming in from the office window, and held it within their tasteful folds. "I just want to . . ." He adjusted the cuffs of his shirt, and sighed.

What *did* he want, that wasn't here, in front of him? There was something brewing in the Flow, he could feel it, just under his nerve endings. Somewhere, someone was about to do something that was going to Impact. He wanted to be in the guts of it, sliding Possibility in his fingers, rushing down the Flow, chasing the shimmer, using the things only he knew, only he could do, to make the Flow do what he wanted it to do. . . .

But he'd been in the clinic just this morning, and you weren't allowed to Flow for a full twelve hours after that. He was locked out, except as a monitor.

And none of this was new: it had been going on for as long as he'd been with KidPro, and some days it felt as if that were his entire life. Twelve hours, twice a year, held against the other 364 days they let him do what he was meant to do . . .

"Yeah, and so like this is a new tick? I don't care." He snapped his fingers to show how little he cared, creating a tiny spark of flame between neatly trimmed nails, to David's clear envy and dismay. You weren't supposed to externalize magic, or do anything to make it clear you were a Wizard, even though everyone always knew, just looking at you. Wizards were different. Wizards *shimmered*.

"Never mind. Let's go; cake beats what they're serving in the caff anyway, and maybe someone'll have some gossip about what really happened to Mr. Bressen."

David didn't understand. David was only eleven; he had only been part of the System for a couple of years. He'd learn, the same way Richard had: you only got so long at the top, so long in the sunshine. And then it was all gray all the rest of the way.

But for now, anyway, there was no point putting off the inevitable. He was going to be another year older, party or no. Might as well make nice with it.

They logged off the main newsfeed system, but it didn't really matter: you never unhooked, not entirely. Not even when you were locked out. They were all integrated into the system the day they came to Kid-Pro, their blood and flesh worked into the fiber and wires in a complicated working that could never be severed, only wither away, once you hit the point of diminishing magics. That was so if one of their specializations should ping, no matter where they were, they'd be able to get back to work immediately. That was how they all wanted it.

You didn't get to KidPro unless you really, really wanted it.

The Main Conference Room was a huge space, lit with sunlight coming through the oversized picture windows. Twenty stories about ground level, there was nothing to obstruct the view except an occasional cloud. The floor was a rich brown marble, with just enough texture to it so that soles didn't slip, and the furniture was all solid brown leather and textured bamboo wood. Arthur Miklos had designed the room to serve a dual purpose: to impress the parents of his Kids with the money KidPro had at its disposal, and to give the Kids a place to see firsthand the rewards of what they were earning. Not that their own quarters weren't state-of-the-art, with almost every comfort a preteen could wish for, but this was an *adult* space. You didn't get to have your birthday celebration here until you were thirteen.

Now he stood in the doorway which connected the conference room with the service lifts, keeping an eye on the preparations. It was the least he could do. Richard was a good Kid; he'd been with the organization since he was nine, and in all those years his talent had kept growing, until Arthur honestly considered him the finest Pro in the entire company. It was a true pity that none of the treatments the Lab was working on had been able to maintain the gifts indefinitely. You could maintain them only so long, on the brink of puberty, and then unfortunate questions started being asked. Not by the families—oh, rarely them—but the government, occasionally, and their overseer committees, and certainly the SEC, who had no sense of humor at all about such things, and even less sense of adventure or curiosity.

What he wouldn't give, for one single Kid to retain his gifts into legal maturity. . . .

"Sir?" Golda was waiting, with the air of someone who has been there for a while, and will stand a while longer, as needed. He nodded to her, to indicate that she should go ahead.

"Sir, there's been a tremor on the Merger Flow. We've had three Kids pick it up, two of them modulating the tech stocks."

Interesting. "Anything more than that?"

"No, sir. We felt you should be informed, considering the recent fluctuations in the European markets."

"Yes, of course. Have someone . . . Jora, I think, have her take a dip into the M&A Flow, see what she can come up with. If it's a company we're heavily invested in, let things go accordingly. If we're not, see how much we can quietly buy up."

Golda nodded, relaying all of that to her assistants down in the offices below them, using a submike and fibers rather than the so-called Flow the Kids swam in. A pity, again. The Flow was instantaneous, if not faster; even the best tech could only react within physical world limitations.

Most of what they were doing was totally on the up-and-up, as current regs were written. Nothing was, technically, illegal. Some of it might have raised a few eyebrows, but that was what it took, to get to the size of KidPro and to stay there, year after year.

Golda had been a Kid, once, one of the few who had what it took to make the transition without breaking. She understood what the business was about.

"Keep me informed. Now, where is the birthday boy?" Arthur spotted Richard the moment he came in the door, and went across the room to greet him. "Welcome, my boy."

"Sir."

They shook hands, firm grip of almost-equals, a proud uncle and a promising nephew. It would have been a Press-worthy moment, had any Press been there to capture it. But Arthur was firm on that point: Kids were kept out of the limelight. If they wanted, as adults, to continue in the financial markets, then they could become media darlings. For now, while they were in his care, he kept them out of sight. It was for their own good; it was only a few decades ago that the Flow had been first documented and regulated, and there was still a lot of anger left about the Second Depression.

Not that magic had caused that—exactly. The realization that a bunch of seventh-graders, playing with their abilities, had manipulated the collapse of the oil industry as a game . . . well, the sector had been heading in that direction anyway, he believed, and most of the details had been hushed up quickly, in the aftermath.

But there was no point in being careless. When people lost money, they got angry, and when they got angry, they occasionally did stupid things: often stupidly *violent* things.

"Bit of excitement happening downstairs," he said in passing, after letting go of the boy's hand.

"The Merger Flow?"

Of course Richard would have felt it.

"Any ideas?" It was his birthday, so he would have been in the clinic, and therefore barred from connecting—safer, that way, until the treatments had a chance to disperse into his system—but his brain still functioned quite well, as did his instincts.

"No, sir, but then, I'm not a tech specialist."

No, his strength was in military supplies. An interesting specialization, that, and one that had equally interesting sidelines in the domestic markets. He had been a fine, fine addition to KidPro, and Arthur would be sorry to see him go, once the treatments became impossible to continue.

"Indeed. Well, if you think of anything which might be relevant, come to me immediately. Now, go, greet your friends. Enjoy your birthday. The office will still be there in the morning."

The room was pretty shimmer, Richard had to admit. Last year, and all the parties before, had been in the rec room, down in the living levels. Wide screen displays and a totally shim sound system, and whatever food you wanted, on your day. Plus the usual cake and stuff. Not bad, but after a few years it was all same-old, same-old.

There was a cake here, but it was a sleek, chocolate-frosted thing, one layer and dense. A grown-up's cake, to go in a grown-up room.

Everyone knew what having your birthday party in the conference room meant.

"Richard! Happy birthday!"

"You don't look a day over eleven!"

"Happy birthday, old man!"

"Shim party, Rich, totally shim."

The greetings went on and on; fellow Kids, and Execs and a couple of Teachers who were willing to come back after the workday was over—not all the Teachers were bad, and Mrs. Hutch was pretty cool, actually. Instead of waiting for the presents to be officially opened, like everyone else, she gave him a small leather kit that contained a set of miniature tools; she'd remembered how annoyed he was at having to wait for someone to come and fix something, when he was perfectly capable of rewiring the basics.

"Shhh, don't tell," she said, passing it like a bribe, hand-to-hand. It wasn't contraband, exactly . . . but it wasn't something he'd have been able to buy for himself, either. One more thing they were restricted from, For Their Own Good.

It wasn't just the government, either. KidPro regs discouraged them from using their hands for anything, like chipping a nail or getting a callus might somehow injure what they did with their brains. Idiot Execs. None of them had been Kids, ever.

The party went on, the room getting more and more crowded as people came, and only a few of them left. Richard kept a portion of his attention, as always, on the Old Man. He kept checking in with his ExecSec, Goldie, or Golda or something. The twitch in the Flow was happening, Richard could tell. Something was going down, and he was out of it.

Frustrating. Not even because he'd be cut out of the inevitable bonus, because there was only so much you could do with money, anyway. But to not be in on the Flow-ride, to miss out on what might be the big Redirect of the week . . . that *burned*.

Besides, if he focused on the stuff that was going on here, he could pretend that he wasn't thinking about other things.

He didn't look at his watch. He didn't look at the

door. But every minute that ticked off he felt in his skin, every time the door slid open and closed, he scanned the newcomers without turning his head.

He was being an idiot. They would come. They always came.

Maybe they had gone to the rec room, first, and gotten misdirected up here.

Maybe they were stuck in traffic, or there was a tie-up at the Tunnel, or . . .

They would come. They always came. Sometimes alone, sometimes with Michael, sullen because he wasn't a Kid, but they always came.

They didn't come.

The cake was thick and fudgy inside, and took two hands to cut, even with a sharp, warm knife. There were no candles, no singing, just a round of applause as the first slice was dropped onto a plate, and someone took the knife from his hand and gave him a fork instead. There was a table of presents, off to the side, mostly wrapped in demure green-and-blue papers, with the occasional glimmer of opticwrap. Small boxes, filled with things off his wish list: discs, mostly, music and readers. Maybe an earring or two, since he got his ear pierced last month, on a whim. Old-fashioned, but satisfying, the tiny prick of blood welling on his lobe, and the onyx sitting heavy in the flesh.

"Open the presents!"

"Nah, tell us what they are without opening them!"

Everyone laughed, although it was an old joke. If only being a Kid meant you could see through cardboard and paper as easily as that. A wizard should be able to see through things, shouldn't he? Magic should work on things as well as possibilities; if he could manipulate events, why couldn't he manipulate people, too?

"Here. To start you off." Teacher Wollin was standing next to him, a package the size of his palm offered, wrapped in plain brown paper.

It was a crystal cube. That was all. Richard looked

at it, then up at the Teacher, the youngest, newest on staff, barely out of credentialing himself.

"It's a resonator. To help you sleep."

Richard frowned. He'd only recently started having trouble falling asleep; were they monitoring him in his rooms, too? It wasn't impossible, but why?

"It's normal," Wollin said, as though reading his mind—impossible, he wasn't a Kid! "Being a teenager, you start needing more sleep and getting less. Push this, at night, or whenever you want to take a nap, and it will help."

"White noise? Hypnoscents?"

Wollin shook his head, but a smile looked like it was lurking under his normal, Teacher-serious expression. Richard started to bridle—he hated anyone laughing at him—but all Wollin said was: "It purrs."

"Purrs?" The word was enough to distract Richard for a moment, and he stared at the cube.

"You'll see. You'll know, soon enough."

That started the deluge of boxes, everyone taking turns handing him their best wishes individually. They were all nice gifts. Expensive gifts. Appropriate gifts. Richard made the equally-appropriate responses, and carefully placed the wrappings into the dispenser provided.

Jora and Tom, both Tech-Kids, gave him a fibrowand, allegedly designed to stimulate his skills and focus his magic no matter how much static there might be in the Flow. They knew about his experiments offfeed, and had suggested, quietly, that this might help.

He should have been invigorated, enthused. He should have been glorying in the fact that this one afternoon, he was the Man of the Moment, the guest of honor.

Instead, he felt slow, sluggish. His skin, normally humming with the feel of the Flow passing over and around them all the time, the possibilities only a Kid could feel, was cold and dry. That never used to happen to him, ever. Sometimes, recently, after a clinic visit. But it never lasted this long. Never took hold this strong.

The party was over. They hadn't come.

"Richard?"

The Old Man was standing behind him, looking out the window over his shoulder. The Old Man was tall, bulky. He dwarfed everyone else in his shadow, even when a growth spurt put Richard up to his chin, almost.

"I got a call. Your brother, he had to take a special test, for school. They thought they would be able to make it, but . . ."

"It doesn't matter."

"No. It doesn't. I have a special gift for you, though. One they'd hoped to be able to give you in person."

Richard turned, tried to look interested.

"There." And the Old Man gestured with his hand, at one of the thinvue screens. It displayed the garage, down under the building. Clean and well-lit, like everything else at KidPro, the garage was color-coded: blue for Execs, yellow for Teachers, and green for Kids. The space was green, barely—next slot over was blue. But the slot was green, which meant that the object inside it was for a Kid.

For him.

"Shim! Mine?"

"Yours." The Old Man sounded damned pleased with himself. "You've earned it. We had to do some finagling, to be sure, and you'll have to promise on your brainpan that you won't do anything stupid with it, but it's yours, free and clear. You can go anywhere you want."

Richard stared at the display, then nodded once, slowly.

"Thank you."

"You're welcome, son."

The Old Man waited a moment, then one of his minions came up and started speaking to him, quietly, without any obvious urgency, but everything they did here was urgent, one way or another.

The Air Rover gleamed the way only a brand new motor could; even dust was hesitant to land on it. The revs made it shiver as it floated several feet above the concrete floor, the leather-and-chrome sets pulsing as though anxious to be unleashed and on the road, ripping past everything slower like they were standing still. Richard could almost feel the warm air hitting his facc, the rumble of the engine in his bones.

None of it matched the Flow. None of it would ever match the Flow.

Driving age was seventeen, Outside. Even with special dispensation, fifteen, minimum, with an adult companion.

He shouldn't have been allowed an Air Rover. He shouldn't even have thought to ask for one. And they should never, ever have given him one, even with "finagling."

You've earned it. You can go anywhere you want.
Earned it.

His money, supporting his folks, his brother . . . until suddenly, maybe he wasn't going to be supporting them any longer and they didn't have to pretend, any longer.

His magic, making money for KidPro . . . until their treatments—oh, he knew about the treatments, everyone knew, but you never thought about them at all, not if you knew what was good for you—didn't work, and you were about to not be a good little earner for them anymore, and they could stop protecting you.

You can go anywhere you want.

"Yeah," Richard said, looking out the window at the roads flowing far below them. Empty roads, empty destinations. "I can go anywhere, now."

He wondered if he was actually as old and empty as he felt, right now.

STOCKS AND BONDAGE

by Esther M. Friesner

"AND that's where the witch works," said Rose-berry the elf, nodding toward the closed office door. "As you'll find out soon enough, poor thing," he added, dropping his voice to a whisper so low that Kurlian the dwarf had to poke him in the side with his pickax and ask him to repeat it.

Roseberry shook his head emphatically. "Nuh-uh. She might hear me. I'm an elf, not an idiot."

"Who said you were an idiot?" the dwarf protested.

"Puh-leeez." Roseberry rolled his eyes. "You dwarves are *born* clutching a volume of Dumb Elf Jokes."

"Well, you won't hear any such jokes from me," Kurlian said. "You're my colleague now; I'd never insult you. I *want* to work here."

Roseberry viewed the dwarf with a critical eye, as if measuring him for a uniform. From long red cap to long white beard, from the simple cut of his brown homespun tunic to the elaborately gemmed design of the gold belt girdling it, Kurlian Bluechip was all dwarf and a yard wide. About a yard tall, too.

Roseberry himself was a run-of-the-mill elf, un-speakably beautiful, tall and willowy and graceful. When he drifted down the woodland paths, his wake was littered with the corpses of suicidal spiders who'd

despaired over how poorly their webs measured up to
the delicacy of his flossy golden hair. As an elf, it was
Roseberry's archetypal obligation to scorn all dwarves
as gold-mad mud-grubbers, but now he just couldn't
bring himself to do so.

He wants *to work here!* he thought. *Poor little toad
doesn't know what he's in for. She'll have him for
breakfast. I might as well fill him in. It'll only postpone
the inevitable, but I'll sleep with a clear conscience.*

Wordlessly, Roseberry indicated that the dwarf
should follow him. Kurlian frowned, but dutifully
obeyed. After all, Roseberry was his guide, thus assigned by the Inhuman Resources Director. Dwarves
knew how to follow the leader. The small burrowing
folk were famous throughout the Seelie realm for
being excellent team players. (The elves said this was
just a nice way of saying no dwarf could think for
himself if his mineshaft depended on it.)

The dwarf's short legs were hard put to keep pace
with Roseberry's long stride, and the office corridors
seemed to go on forever. Kurlian's initial interviewer
at Under-the-Hill Enterprises, Inc., had taken great
pains to point out that the metaphysical plant of the
company was not merely multistory and multinational
but also multidimensional. It was logical that the main
office be large enough to touch base on all of the
world-planes served by U.H.E.: Logical, and damned
hard on the feet. Kurlian wished that the elf would
ditch the whole dark-doings-afoot *shtick* and cut to
the mother lode.

Just when the dwarf felt ready to collapse, Roseberry reached a particular portal in a particular corridor and hustled Kurlian inside. He slipped in after,
locking the door behind them.

"Dark in here," the dwarf remarked.

Roseberry snapped his fingers and half a dozen pixies housed in glass globes on the walls revved up their
auras, casting a vivid green glow over the room.

"Yeah, that's better."

"If you like working inside a radioactive lettuce,"

Roseberry said dryly. "Why we can't have electric lights like the rest of the world . . . sod tradition anyway." He crossed to a tall, blue-spotted mushroom which took up most of the little chamber, hoisted his rump onto the slightly shorter fungus beside it, and told Kurlian, "Pull up a Portabella and make yourself to home."

The dwarf noted that every article of furniture in the room was either a mushroom, a toadstool, or some other sort of saprophyte. Selecting an overstuffed puffball, he settled himself carefully. "Nice digs."

"Thanks," Roseberry replied without enthusiasm. "When I get hungry, I just set fire to the place, throw in a steak, and extinguish the whole mess with gravy. Office *aux champignons*, mmmm-*mh*!"

"Will my office be like this?" Kurlian asked, stroking the surface of the puffball chair lightly and watching with growing dismay as it began to disintegrate under his blunt fingers.

"What office?" Roseberry returned. "You're the new guy; you'll be lucky if you get a cubicle of your own."

"I wouldn't mind sharing."

"As if you'll have a choice! Like it or not, you'll *share*; I guarantee it."

"But I just said that I wouldn't mi — Wait a minute. What *kind* of sharing?" The elf's odd manner put Kurlian on guard. Dwarves weren't the sharpest chisels on the workbench, but they were not half as thick-skulled as they looked.

Roseberry leaned back on his fungus and lowered his eyelids. "It's not my place to say. Not outright. I can drop ominous and premonitory hints, or I can pose meaningful-but-cryptic riddles. Your choice."

Poor Kurlian's stomach began to crimp in upon itself, a phenomenon unheard-of in dwarvish circles. It took a tramload of anxiety to upset a digestive organ that could extract nutrients from shale, lignite, and—in a lean year—radishes. "Ominous hints, please."

"Really? Too bad. I had a really nifty riddle all

lined up: *What makes a dwarf bounce but never jump for joy?*"

"Bounce?" Kurlian echoed.

"You know, from thumping the mattress when you have to bed the witch. All right, your first hint is—"

"Bed the witch?" Kurlian's horrifed bellow made the puffball crumble. He hit the floor with a clang.

"Wow, and I didn't even finish giving you the first hint." Roseberry's admiration was genuine. "You're *good.*"

"Bed the witch . . ." Kurlian repeated, shaking his head slowly. "Oh, no, no, impossible. It must be a joke."

"It's a joke that's in your contract."

"It is *not!*" Kurlian protested as he hauled himself back onto his feet. "I *read* my contract before I signed it. There was no mention at all about—"

"That," said the elf enigmatically, "was then." He pressed a spot on his desktop, and a golden basin rose from the depths of the speckled mushroom. Shadows swirled over the elf's face as his gazed into it, chanting: "O great and whimsical procurer of all otherworldly knowledge, vouchsafe unto me a vision of the full text of the U.H.E. standard employment agreement."

The bowl seethed and bubbled, then gave a loud burp. Roseberry smiled. "There we are: Paragraph nine, section seven-A, dependent clause four. See for yourself."

"Don't have to." The dwarf growled. "Got my own copy right here." He pulled a tightly rolled parchment from the leather pouch at his side and unfurled it triumphantly for the elf's inspection. "That's the very clause, right there in crimson and ecru. It says that attendance at the company picnic is mandatory."

Roseberry regarded the proffered document and lifted one elegant eyebrow. "Does it?"

Something in his manner made Kurlian blanch and hastily run his finger down the margin. A choking sound rose to his lips. "It's—it's *changed*! My contract's *changed*!"

Roseberry sighed. "*All* U.H.E. contracts change after we sign them."

"But how—?"

"Remember the part where I told you she's a *witch?*" The elf shrugged. "*Duh.*"

Kurlian reeled backward, ramming the wall and joggling the pixies in their lightglobes. They squealed like a batch of mice in a cocktail shaker. "This is terrible," he gasped. "This is awful! This is—"

"—legally binding," the elf said. "No use making a fuss." He gently shepherded the dwarf onto another toadstool. "Get it over with quickly, that's the best way."

"I read a U.H.E. recruitment ad in one of our finest underground papers." Kurlian spoke in a dazed and wobbly voice. "An ad for mining engineers, top pay, good benefits. I want to get married, but my darling Gurfrieda's got a bride-price that's higher than the Scurvy Mountains. It looked soooo tempting!"

"Of course it did," the elf said. "Bait is. Though to be honest, you're the first in centuries to swallow it. Word's gotten out. None of the Seelie folk *ever* work for U.H.E. willingly. Usually our liege lords compel us, giving the witch our employment in exchange for settlement of their Accounts Outstanding. I'm surprised you didn't know."

"You miss a lot of gossip when you're digging mines," Kurlian said.

"Well, no use crying over spilled nectar. You signed the contract, you comply with the terms. You've only got to do it once, and the witch leaves you alone afterward. It's called paying your dues. Or sexual harassment, if you talk to the Mortals."

"There's not enough gold under a dragon's butt to pay *these* dues." The dwarf still had the stunned look of a man who has had a full-grown basilisk fall on his head. "Not even under the butt of the Red Dragon of J'thork, and that is one big-ass dragon!"

"Not anymore," said Roseberry. "He developed an eating disorder after his turn with the witch."

"His . . . turn . . . with . . ." Kurlian was aghast. "But dragons are a protected species!"

"Once you sign the witch's contract, there's nothing in all the worlds to protect you." Roseberry was grim as the grave.

"How can one creature command such power?"

"Easy. She's the best C.E.O. this company ever had, her ideas are a bottomless goldmine, and she keeps the stockholders happy. In all the realms—Seelie, Unseelie or Mortal—there is no greater magic than the bottom line."

"Oh, yeah? Well, I've got a bottom line of my own: I *quit*!" Kurlin thumped the handle of his pickax on the floor for emphasis and sprang to his feet. "I quit *right now*, and you can tell the witch that she'll be getting a stern letter from the Dwarvish Regulatory Commission!" He stalked to the door of Roseberry's office and flung it open with an extravagant gesture.

"Goin' somewhere?" asked the hall goblin blocking the way. He was a big one, ten feet tall if an inch, every inch covered with scales, warts, slime, and well-aged roadkill. He smiled tuskily.

The dwarf was no coward. Shifting his pickax to battle-ready mode, he glared at the hall goblin and gritted, "Who are you?"

The goblin's grin got wider. "The welcome wagon."

From behind Kurlian, Roseberry greeted the monster on his doorsill. "H'lo, Nutmeg. Come on in. How's everything up in Security?"

"Can't complain," the goblin replied. "They whip us when we do." He stepped into the elf's office, chivvying Kurlian back inside and shutting the door after himself.

"Take an early lunch today, did you?"

"How can you tell?"

"You've got a scrap of vice president stuck in your teeth."

" 'Ta." The goblin took a coil of rope from his belt and used it for dental floss. A thighbone, a bit of scalp, and a briefcase came flying out from between his fangs. Kurlian gaped at the carnal detritus and dropped his pickax.

"I'm not going anywhere, am I?" he asked.

"Not until you fulfill that clause," Nutmeg replied, all hail-fellow-well-et.

"*You* know about that?" The dwarf gave the goblin a hard stare.

"Everyone who works here knows," the goblin said. "Mostly 'cuz everyone who works here's had to fulfill it."

"Even you?"

"Yeah, even— Hey! What's *that* supposed to mean?" Nutmeg scowled.

"The witch is rather comprehensive in her amatory tastes," Roseberry said.

"Voracious, more like." The goblin shuddered, which nearly undid poor Kurlian. If the witch's intimate attentions were enough to make a *goblin* shake—!

"Now, now, Nutmeg, you're scaring the new guy." Roseberry acted as if they'd been discussing nothing more outlandish than the weather. "You survived it, I survived it, everyone survived it—"

"Not Yimiyimi," said Nutmeg. "Killed *him*, right enough."

"Wh— who's that?" Kurlian's hands opened and closed spasmodically, as if seeking the pickax he'd long since let fall.

"Yimiyimi?" Roseberry waved the goblin's scarifying testimony away on the interoffice breeze. "Well, of course it killed *him*. He was a pixie, no bigger than a gerbil's sneeze. Basic physics should tell you that he was never going to survive an encounter with—"

" 'Taint so," Nutmeg maintained. "Size don't matter with *her*. Witches is *awful* flexible."

"A pity Yimiyimi wasn't," said Roseberry.

"I am liking this less and less," Kurlian said, reclaiming his weapon from the floor. "*Much* less and less. I don't care if the goblin eats me—or *tries* to—" (Here he flourished his pickax belligerently, to let Nut-

meg know just how indigestible he could make himself.) "—I want out, I want it now, and no one's going
to stop me!"

"No one has to," said the elf. "Ever hear of a cap-
tivity clause?"

"A what?"

"Opposite of an escape clause. Its power binds you
to these premises until the witch herself releases you."

"Which she don't till you fulfill that *other* clause,"
the goblin said. Again he shuddered.

"You mean I'm trapped until—?" The dwarf looked
from elf to goblin and from goblin to elf for some
reprieve.

"Yup." Nutmeg nodded. "Y'can *try* busting out if
you like, but it won't work. Never has."

The dwarf burst into tears.

Elf and goblin were gobsmacked by this unexpected
display. More than disconcerting, it was *loud*. Beings
who lived in boundless caverns deep in the earth had
no grasp of *indoor voices*. Roseberry and Nutmeg
clapped their hands over their ears and tried to reason
with the distraught Kurlian. They were compelled to
do this at the top of *their* lungs in order to make
themselves heard. The noise level in the elf's office
soon made Pandemonium sound like a Quaker
prayer meeting.

"WHAT THE BLAZING DOGWORT IS GOING
ON IN HERE?"

Roseberry's door flew open and a one-eyed ogre
terrible to behold stood wedged between the jambs,
his gnarled oaken club pounding the floor for order.
All the fungoid furniture crumbled. The pixies fled
their glowglobes *en masse,* leaving elf, dwarf, and goblin to crawl single-file between the ogre's legs, out of
the darkened office and into the corridor, where they
slumped in a row against the wall. The ogre eyed
them severely.

"Well?" he demanded in a more reasonable tone of
voice. It still sounded like a forklift goosing a dragon.

"I was just explaining the Whoopee Clause to the

new guy, Sigmoid," Roseberry said. "He over-reacted."

"The Whoopee Clause?" the ogre repeated. And to Kurlian's horror, *he* shuddered. "I remember when it was *my* turn." He shuddered again and began to bite his nails, spitting out clippings the size of shingles.

"What'd she make *you* do?" Nutmeg inquired.

Sigmoid screwed his lips up tight. "Won't tell."

"We'll tell if you will," Roseberry urged.

The ogre remained unmoved. "Can't say as I'm all that interested in hearing about the bedroom antics of elves."

"Same here," the goblin said, then he chortled. " 'Course's not like we've got *her* head for business. Clever old cow. Years ago she made some elves do the winky-dinky-doo in front of her while she took notes. Elves bein' elves, they didn't have nooooo problem turnin' it into a spectator sport—"

"There is no shame in performing the Dance of Life for the eyes of others," Roseberry said huffily.

"And *that*, kiddies, is how the witch invented the *Kama Sutra*," said the ogre. "One of our best-selling products in the Mortal realm."

Kurlian scratched his head. "I thought it *was* a Mortal creation."

"They'd like to believe that themselves, but just *look*. 'Basic' positions? Ha! As if Mortals could ever come up with *half* o' them greased weasel contortions. All the witch needed to turn a tidy profit for U.H.E. was a notebook, a sketchpad, and a couple of elves in heat!"

"Actually, there were five of us," Roseberry murmured. Seeing the shocked stares of the other three, he snapped out a defensive, "*What?* At least it got me out of the Whoopee Clause without having to bed the witch herself."

"She *allowed* an alternative?" Kurlian Bluechip felt a faint surge of hope. "Maybe she'll let me do the same."

"Could be." Sigmoid the ogre scratched his head.

"I've heard tell o' such things. There's even a sort o' legend in the union handbook as tells of how some day the witch will face a warrior maiden of great prowess who'll put paid to the Whoopee Clause forever. 'Course them's just legends and union talk. Can't put much faith in 'em."

"What do I care for legends?" Kurlian cried. "All I want to know is: Can I get around the Whoopee Clause?"

"Depends."

"On what?"

The ogre got a cunning look in his eye. "Hard to say. Hard to think, what with this parlous great thirst I got and the misery in me limbs from patrolling the halls."

Kurlian could tell whither the wind blew. "If there's somewhere we can all share a few tankards—*and* find me a way of escaping the Whoopee Clause—then the drinks are on me."

Shortly after, in the U.H.E. Underlings Cafeteria and Brewpub, the quartet of Seelie folk huddled over four pints of nut-brown October ale and earnestly discussed the dwarf's problem. Being the employee of longest standing, Roseberry spoke first:

"Such things as alternative service to the witch are rare, but not unheard of. I recall once, some centuries ago, the great dwarvish bard Jingli signed on the U.H.E. dotted line but fulfilled his contract through other means than playing hide-the-acorn with the witch."

Kurlian puffed out his chest with pride in his fellow dwarf. "No doubt he sang for her one of the great and stirring epics of our people, thus satisfying her."

"Sort of," said Roseberry. "As I heard it, his idea of foreplay was to start crooning one of those interminable dwarf doo-dahs and she cracked around Canto the Thirty-third. She released him from the Whoopee Clause if he'd just shut up. She'll never fall for *that* ploy again."

"Never?" Kurlian's recent hope died young. He

began to snivel, which was only a bit quieter than the racket he made when he went full-throttle weepers. The elf and the goblin covered their ears.

Sigmoid the ogre took direct action, picking up the dwarf by his belt and hanging the little fellow upside down, shaking him gently (for an ogre). "That'll do," he said.

"Put me down, or pay for the next round yourself!" the dwarf snapped.

The ogre complied, but stuck to his guns. "So you've got to bed the witch, wah, wah, wah. Think you're better'n the rest of us? Quitcher bellyachin'. Sooner you do it, sooner it's done."

"Sooner *I'm* done, you mean," said Kurlian. "This will kill me."

"Naaah. Worst it'll do is rough you up some, if she's in a playful mood." The ogre grinned.

"No," said Kurlian firmly. "This will *kill* me."

The way he said it caused all three of his colleagues, plus a nosybody mailroom gremlin just passing through the cafeteria, to take notice. Roseberry gave the gremlin a *move along, move along, smartly now!* glower, to no effect, then asked Kurlian, "What do you mean?"

"You *don't* know about the Dwarven Rule?" Elf, ogre, goblin, and gremlin all shook their heads. The dwarf took a deep breath: "It is written in scrolls as old as Time and older than Fate that no dwarf may come unto his chosen bride's bed if his body be sullied by fleshly dalliance."

"Oh, *I've* heard this one!" the gremlin broke in. He was a scruffy, snaggle-toothed specimen so wizened and malodorous that Kurlian wondered how desperate the witch must be if she'd demanded Whoopee Clause fulfillment from this repulsive creature. "Thought it was a joke. Stupid stuff, if you ask me."

"No one asked you, and it's no joke," the dwarf grumbled.

The gremlin ignored him. "*I* heard it don't matter a nit's nipple if you dwarfers do boinkies with everyone, everything, *and* my late Granny Zagroon after you're wed. But *before* marriage? Nothing. What's the point of *that*?"

"Quiet or I'll feed you to the automatic envelope-licking machine," the ogre told him. "Could be the dwarfs got a good reason."

"We do," said Kurlian. "It's the unicorns."

"Ah!" Roseberry brightened. "So it's true: You little fellows *do* have the unicorn market sewn up."

The dwarf bobbed his head. "Lock, stock, and virginity. Unicorns are a cash crop like no other. They feed themselves, never get sick, don't need guarding, sell for plenty in the Mortal realm, and the only maintenance they require is to live within spitting distance of a population that's one hundred per cent prenuptial virgin."

"Lucky for you they don't insist on *post*-nuptial virginity," the elf said.

"Unicorns don't *insist* on anything. They're fairly dumb, three steps below a golden retriever and four above an infomercial addict. Instinct drives 'em. If they catch a whiff of premarital please-and-thank-you, they leave the area *and* the authority of their former owners. According to our laws, any dwarvish tribe thus bereft of its unicorns has the right to hire a seer and an executioner, the former to discover the party or parties whose behavior caused the beasts' departure, the latter to—" He slashed a finger across his throat and made a *khhhhkkk!* sound.

"Couldn't you just build fences?" Roseberry asked.

"No fence can hold them," Kurlian countered. "And where's the wight with the carborundum balls to try stopping a full-steam-ahead unicorn migration?"

A cataract of tears poured from Sigmoid's eye. "Me great-great-grandad perished unto death in the big unicorn shift of '07," he said.

Kurlian tapped the side of his nose. "That was when King Vog's tribe lost their herds, all because his son Morgrim couldn't keep his lust in his *lederhosen*. It was Vog's fault, letting the lad live in that forest commune with six other dwarven twits and that Mortal slut. Exiled princess, my pickax! It didn't matter when the others took their turns with her, them already being married, but when young Morgrim had a go—" Kurlian clicked his tongue. "Bye-bye unicorns. Morgrim was the first one they trampled on their way over the border. Saved his dad the price of that seer/ executioner package. Vog's tribe never recovered economically. Had to rent themselves out as lawn ornaments. Only consolation was that the stampeding 'corns flattened Princess Mattressback, too."

Roseberry was confused. "So she *was* a princess?"

"Unproven," Kurlian sneered. "The only thing snow-white about *her* was the bottoms of her shoes, 'cause her feet were always waggling in the air."

"Hey, I *know* her," the elf exclaimed. "She worked over in Archetypes-for-Hire. I heard she married a prince on her summer vacation and lived happily ever after."

"Spin-wizards," the goblin informed him. "The witch brought 'em in on the case herself, once word got back. Wouldn't do was the stockholders to hear of scandal touching a U.H.E. employee. Bad for the corp'rate image."

"I chipped in on her wedding gift!" The elf looked fit to be tied.

"She worked here?" Kurlian was startled. "But— but the Whoopee Clause?"

"Oh, she fulfilled it. The witch is an Equal Opportunity Exploiter," Sigmoid the ogre said solemnly. "Which is one reason she heads the Team Bonding campout whenever we get enough new members in our all-sylph secretarial pool. Some o' them poor ladies is pulling pine needles out o' their wings for weeks after."

"Which is why *I'm* here now," said a fresh voice from the end of the table.

Elf and goblin, gremlin and ogre, all turned to see who had just barged in on a conversation already amoebic in its ability to draw in helpless passersby.

They saw a second dwarf, twin to Kurlian Bluechip in every detail.

"No one told me we had *two* new employees." Roseberry was miffed. "Mouse-puckey, now I'll have to go through the whole welcome-to-the-Whoopee-Clause folderol again."

"No, you won't," said the second dwarf. "I'm here to put an *end* to the Whoopee Clause once and for all." The newcomer hopped onto a vacant chair, leaned one elbow on the table, and added, "Who's a lady got to slay before someone buys her a drink in this dump?"

Kurlian clasped his beard. "Gurfrieda!" he exclaimed just before he toppled over in a dead faint.

He came back to his senses to find the ogre tenderly pouring a container of cafeteria lemonade over his face. He sat up in time to hear Roseberry inquire:

"—just *like* him?"

The second dwarf chuckled and took a long pull from her mug of ale. "Not *exactly* like him, but the differences are nothing *you'll* ever see, elf-boy."

"But the *beard's* a disguise, right?" The elf reached out one tentative hand, as if intent on giving the facial adornment in question the customary yank-test for authenticity.

Gurfrieda slapped his hand aside. "Touch it and die. Sloppily."

"Gur— Gurfrieda?" Kurlian asked, shaken. "D— darling? What— what— what—?"

"—am I doing here?" The dwarf-maiden smiled, foam clinging to her mustache. "What do you *think*?"

"Following 'er 'eart's one true love, she is," the gremlin said with a happy sigh. "Couldn't bear to be parted from 'im fer an instant." Sentimental tears slid from the creature's eyes. This set off the ogre again, and pretty soon he, the gremlin, and the goblin as well were all enjoying a good, romantic weep.

Gurfrieda spared them a look of unmitigated disgust, then gave Kurlian a hard thump on the head. "Yes, what *were* you thinking, coming *here* for employment?"

"But—but your father—your bride-price—U.H.E.

salaries—" He spread his hands. "I figured it was a good bet."

"Oh, a *great* bet, I'm sure," Gurfrieda mocked him. "For the witch! You couldn't do a little spade-work and find out *why* U.H.E. pays so well?"

"No one told me about the Whoopee Clause until after I signed on! And the contract changed itself! And—!"

"And you didn't think that a scam the witch has been pulling for *aeons* would be all over the Internet? *Nice* job-research skills, ninny." Gurfrieda spat in his beard and left the cafeteria.

Kurlian caught up with her by the vending machines just outside. The hour being inapt for any of the Seelie folk's sixteen official mealtimes, the place was deserted. The anguished dwarf flung himself after his sweetheart and latched onto one chunky leg. The elf, ogre, goblin, and proof-against-all-hints mailroom gremlin tagged along to watch.

"Forgive me, my love," Kurlian sobbed. "Your beauty robbed me of my wits; I was rendered stupid by desire! I could only think of amassing your bride-price as swiftly as might be!"

The dwarf-maid rounded ferociously on her suppliant suitor. "What's the big rush? We're *dwarves,* you moron! We're *immortal!* Well, barring unicorn stampedes. You've been a virgin for centuries. You couldn't wait a *little* longer to get some?"

Roseberry cleared his throat and attempted a diplomatic intervention. "Perhaps he was only thinking of *your* needs, ma'am."

"What needs?" Gurfrieda countered. "I got any needs, I go down to Madam Bunny's House of Commercial Affection and ask for the blue plate special."

The elf's eyebrows rose sharply. "Er, begging your pardon, ma'am, but doesn't something like that rather . . . perturb the unicorns?"

The female dwarf laughed loud and long. "Not likely! It's only virgins going astray that provokes 'em."

Roseberry's brows rose higher yet. "By this I take it to mean that you are not—?" He blushed like a common gnome.

"If I were, it'd be a grievous insult to the memories of my last six husbands, now wouldn't it, Twinkles?" Gurfrieda gave the elf a roguish look and a gratuitous pinch on the fundament that sent him leaping into Sigmoid's arms.

"Seasoned lass, ain't she?" Sigmoid remarked.

"With the experience of six husbands behind her," Roseberry muttered, slowly climbing back down to the floor. "At least that explains why our dwarvish friend is in such a hurry to accumulate his bride-price."

"Hotcha," agreed the gremlin.

"Which I'll never get now!" Kurlian howled his grief at the sorcery detector on the ceiling. "No way to leave this corporate prison unless I submit to the witch's lust, no way to submit to the witch's lust without causing the flight of our tribe's unicorns! Alas, alack, wurra-wurra, doggone it all to—!"

There was a soft *whunk* behind Kurlian's left ear. Grinning like a drunken hedgehog, he crossed his eyes, rolled them back in his head for safekeeping, and slumped to the corridor floor unconscious.

Gurfrieda repocketed a small, ladylike cosh and told the remaining males, "When menfolk start saying things like *wurra-wurra* and *doggone it*, they're not going to be any help at all. Best to tidy 'em aside till things are settled. You there—" She indicated Sigmoid the ogre. "You look capable. Find a well-ventilated, out-of-the-way closet and stick him in it.'

"Yes'm," said the ogre, hastening to obey.

"And don't forget where it is!" she shouted after him. "Now *you*—" She meant the goblin. "You're with Security?"

The goblin gave her a snappy salute. "Watchman First Class Nutmeg at your service, ma'am."

"And you *look* like a first class nutmeg, too. Excellent. Go back to your normal rounds and precisely twenty minutes from now, knock at the witch's office door."

"That's all? Just knock?"

Gurfrieda sighed. "*Can* you outthink moss? No, I don't want you to *just* knock. Knock *first*, for appearance's sake, then come right in. Please tell me that that big bunch of keys at your waist is for opening doors and not just to supply some deadweight when they want to drown you."

"A little from Column A and a little from Column B," Nutmeg admitted. His face sagged with regret. "Ma'am, I'd be glad t'oblige you, but as for knocking at the witch's door and then barging in . . . Ma'am, that's not my designated beat. It'd mean my job, and me nigh fully vested in the pension plan, and with stock options, and me aged parents to support, and me wife and squirmlings, and—"

The dwarf-woman flung him a bag of gold that hit him dead center in the brisket and slammed him into the wall. He weighed it by hand, bounded to his feet, and with a jolly, "Sod the stock options!" he was off and running.

Gurfrieda chuckled. "Like my fourth husband Dagmunt always said, the best keys are made of gold. And now—" she turned to Roseberry.

"You want *I* should do something, too, m'lady?" the gremlin asked, sidling up to Gurfrieda. His tone was unctuous enough to grease the axles of a thousand chariots.

"Yes, you can drop de— No, wait a minute." She stroked her beard in thought. "There *is* something you could do for me: Bring me an apple."

"Why d'you want an apple?" the gremlin asked. Gurfrieda's reply came couched in the form of another sack of gold, to which she first attached a live mouse as a bit of *lagniappe*. The gremlin popped the squeaking snack into its mouth and bounded back into the cafeteria, all cheerful cooperation.

"Was that really necessary?" Roseberry asked. He

looked tediously beautiful even with one hand cupped
over his mouth in a bout of elfin nausea.

"It got him out of the way, didn't it?" Gurfrieda
countered. "Now you can do your part untroubled by
that buttinski, if you move fast."

"And what *is* my part?"

"Taking me to the witch's office at once."

The dwarf-woman's resolute words had a strange
effect on Roseberry. With the dignity and elegance
that had made his people the target of countless cus-
tard pie attacks by less lordly Seeliefolk, he knelt before her. When he spoke, his words were freighted
with a degree of grandeur the elves reserved for the
most momentous circumstances.

"Madam," he declared. "Thou art, I trow, she
whose coming was foretold. Yea, in sooth thou needs
must be the great Liberator, the maiden warrior of
whom the old ones sing and the scribes do write in
the union handbook. I am thy humble servant."

Gurfrieda patted Roseberry on the shoulder.
"Honey, *humble* and *elf* go together like *friendly*
and *taxman*."

"But it is so!" Roseberry maintained. "As Sigmoid
told your betrothed, there is a prophetic text within
the pages of our union handbook that ordains the
coming of a warrior maiden who shall defeat the witch
at her own game and rescue all generations of U.H.E.
employees, present and future, from the hag's carnal
appetites."

As long as the elf was down on his knees, Gurfrieda
found it easy to throw one arm around his neck,
buddy-buddy, and calmly explain, "Look, Twinkles,
liberation prophecies are an orc's toenail a dozen
among subjugated populations. I think they're started
by the guys doing the subjugating. An underling who's
waiting to be saved by some heroic yo-yo on a white
horse is an underling who is *not* investigating his inde-
pendent options."

"We've tried other ways of winning our freedom
from the witch," the elf told her. "Once upon a time,

the leadership of the Brotherhood of Ogres, Orcs, Goblins, Elves, and Revenants staged a test-the-waters protest in the cafeteria over the quality of the Friday meatloaf." He sighed. "Shortly thereafter, the B.O.O.G.E.R. bigwigs vanished entirely and for a while after that we were served *much* bigger portions of meatloaf."

"You have my sympathies and most of my appetite for the next two weeks," Gurfrieda told him. "That still doesn't make me your magical maiden-warrior. Being married six times puts a little strain on a girl's maidenhood."

"Perhaps the prophecy refers to your purity of *purpose*," the elf offered. Waning hope shone pathetically in his eyes.

"Scratch an elf, find a spin-wizard." Gurfrieda grinned through her whiskers.

Roseberry sighed. "We're doomed."

Gurfrieda pinched his cheek lightly. "Don't put all your eggs in one prophecy, Twinkles: I'll face the witch. I admit that I came here just to pull Kurlian's chestnuts out of the fire, but when I see how that hag's broken the spirit of a fine-looking elf like you, it makes my dwarvish blood boil." She gave Roseberry another pinch on the cheek, only with a semantic difference.

The assaulted elf leaped to his feet, clapping his hands over the area of Gurfrieda's unasked attentions. "Madam!" he gasped. "And you about to be a married woman! Again. What *are* you thinking?"

"Twinkles, if you've gotta ask, it's gonna be *oodles* of fun explaining." Gurfrieda gave him a saucy wink just as the gremlin came bounding back, a shiny apple in his paws.

"Here you go!" he wheezed, eyes glittering with anticipation. "Whatcha gonna do with it, eh? Poison it an' give it to the witch? Poison's nice."

Gurfrieda said nothing. She merely accepted the apple with one hand, reached into her belt pouch with the other, and withdrew a small glass vial from which she poured three black drops—no more, no less—over the ripe fruit. The apple's rosy skin turned a peculiar shade of purple, then irised through a number of rapid cosmetic hue-shifts—purple to green to yellow to blue—before returning to an even more tempting shade of red than its original color. The dwarf studied the apple, gave a satisfied bob of her head, and tossed the vial to the gremlin.

"Oooh." The gremlin held it up to the light, tilting it to see the dregs slosh back and forth within. "'Kin I keep what's left?"

"Use it as you like," Gurfrieda told him graciously. The mailroom gremlin dashed away, cackling aloud his plans for vengeance against the ogre up in R&D who had absentmindedly done something unspeakable down the mail chute. When he was out of sight, Gurfrieda faced Roseberry: "Take me to her. Now."

Roseberry regarded the dwarf-woman with profound respect and a little pity. "She has spells that ward her office against all venoms," he said. "They cause the poison's powers to rebound against the would-be poisoner sevenfold. They also work on gifts of unwanted Christmas fruitcakes."

"I figured she'd have something like that," Gurfrieda said. "That's why I did *not* use poison."

"No?" The elf cocked his head. "You *were* a little cavalier about giving the leftovers to a gremlin. If it's not poison, then what is it?"

Gurfrieda waved the apple under the elf's nose. Roseberry inhaled the fruit's perfume, and before he could exhale he was smothering the dwarf-woman's face with passionate kisses. The effects wore off just as he was on the point of nibbling her mustache. "By the sacred Dance of Life!" he blurted, thrusting her away. "That's an aphrodisiac!"

"And a darn good one." Gurfrieda linked her arm through Roseberry's. "Now let's go see a witch about a contract clause."

*   *   *

Of course Sigmoid *did* forget where he'd stored Kurlian. It took Gurfrieda most of the afternoon to find her betrothed. She offered him a smile as he emerged, blinking in the light, a motherly "Don't fret any more, love; your troubles are over," and a kiss that was part tonsillectomy.

When he finally broke free of his fiancée's enthusiasm, Kurlian gasped, "My troubles are over? How—?"

"Feast your eyes, loverboy." With a flick of the wrist, Gurfrieda unfurled a copy of Kurlian's contract. Halfway down the parchment was a series of vicious slashes executed with what *looked* like red ink. Gurfrieda enjoyed the look of growing wonderment on Kurlian's face. It was almost a pity to put an end to it by telling him: "You and all employees of U.H.E., present and future, are no longer under any contractual obligation to the aforementioned U.H.E., its officers or executives, entailing coerced intimacy."

"Uh?"

Gurfrieda gave her glassy-eyed gallant a doting look. "Whoopee Clause go bye-bye."

"But how did you—?"

"You know how some folks say that all us dwarves look alike?" She sighed. "They really *can't* tell us apart."

"Oh," said Kurlian. And then: "*Oh!* Gurfrieda, you don't mean that you—? That she—? That you, third person plural, both actually—? Oh, *Gurfrieda!*"

"Oh, shut up," his fiancee growled. "There came a point in our . . . negotiations where the witch *had* to realize she'd made a mistake, but by that time it was too late: I'd taken steps to make sure she was powerless to exert even eleventh-hour self-restraint. Not that she actually *minded* following through with me . . . until *afterward.*" The little lady's mustache lifted ever so slightly at one corner.

"Afterward . . ." Kurlian repeated. "So you used your, er, newfound position of influence with the witch to thus, ahem, appeal to her more tender side, softening her heart toward her employees?"

Gurfrieda snorted. "For pity's sake, you sound sappy as a Mortal! You'll be talking about the redeeming power of the love of a good dwarf next!"

"Then what did—?"

Gurfrieda thrust one hand into the bosom of her tunic and withdrew a crinkly, crisply folded parchment which she handed to her swain. "What's this?" he asked, unfolding the document.

"My wedding gift to you, my love," Gurfrieda murmured, her whiskers tickling his ear. "A talisman of ultimate power."

Kurlian examined the parchment, baffled. "What talisman? This is a purchase order!"

Gurfrieda smirked. "Specifically, a purchase for every share of U.H.E. Preferred I could snap up. Our tribe is now one of this company's major stockholders and *I'm* our designated spokesdwarf. *Now* do you understand why she rescinded the Whoopee Clause when I showed her this . . . *afterward?*"

"Indeed I do, my dreadfully clever love. Despite the witch's power, she became your thrall the instant she realized you'd made her break the supreme rule, the rule each C.E.O.—witch or wizard, Seelie or Mortal, Harvard or Yale—*must* obey." Kurlian Bluechip doffed his cap and solemnly intoned: "Never diddle the stockholders."

Gurfrieda's right hand began to toy with the ends of Kurlian's beard. "Outsmarting witches always gets me in the mood," she purred, her left hand toying elsewhere.

"D—darling, we *can't*," he panted, feebly attempting to escape her clutches. "We *shouldn't*. Think of propriety! Think of my neck! Think of the *unicorns!*"

"Where do you think I got the money to buy up all those U.H.E. shares?" she replied. "I convinced our Tribal Council to sell off our unicorns before I came here. We'll be just as rich, and live simpler lives: Wall Street doesn't give a damn about virginity."

A radiant smile lit up Kurlian's face. "You mean—?"

"Shut up and kiss me, you little lug," said Gurfrieda, and hauled him back into the closet, shutting the door behind them.

THE KEEPER OF THE MORALS

by Dean Wesley Smith

I NURSED the scotch-rocks like it was the last drink I was ever going to have instead of just the first for the night, twirling the glass and the golden liquid on its paper napkin like a kid's toy. More than likely, it was going to be the drink I remembered most in a long line of drinks, followed by picking up some blonde—they were always blondes—and taking her back to my big house in my Porsche for some fast, sloppy sex and then uncomfortable good-byes.

Around me, the party atmosphere of "Danny's Crib Lounge," combined with the music from too many speakers, kept the noise level just under that of a jet taking off. I had been lucky tonight to find a place at the bar. Usually I ended up standing, drink in hand, pretending to actually talk to someone I mostly couldn't hear.

But tonight was special. That's what my six coworkers from the legal department had told me. I had closed negotiations on one of the company's biggest deals today, opening up a wildlife refuge for my company's oil rigs to go in and drill. Tomorrow, when the news got out, our stock would shoot up, the left-wing environmentalists would cry, I would get a bonus, and then I would go back to work on the next big deal.

But tonight I got to celebrate.

But I didn't feel like celebrating anything.

Thirty-six years old, and I had no idea how I had gotten here.

In this bar.

Doing the job I did.

None. Not a clue.

I used to be one of those liberals who would think of the now-me as the devil. I started off using my legal degree to fight to keep wildlife refuges closed up to companies like the one I now worked for. I took the job with my current employer thinking I could stop some of the company practices from within.

Yeah, right.

What the hell had happened to me?

That wasn't a question I asked myself that often these days. I usually just thought about the money, the stock options, and buying a bigger house, even though, alone, I rattled around in the one I had like a kid lost in a big, new school.

I had enough money, but I kept thinking I needed more.

Why?

A soft touch on my shoulder made me turn to my right and into the gaze of a beautiful woman with golden hair and large brown eyes.

My stomach twisted as she smiled a perfect smile showing off perfect teeth. I had barely sipped my first drink, and this woman looked fantastic.

My type. She fit it perfectly. In looks as well as everything else. Side-by-side, walking down the street, we would look like Ken and Barbie. The perfect American couple. Her features were almost as chiseled as mine.

Could I get any more superficial? There was more to women than just blonde hair and a beautiful face. I used to look past all that surface stuff, looking for a soulmate, but now, it seemed, I never did.

Just like I never really looked at what I did at work.

I felt like I knew her, then shook *that* thought away. I always felt like I knew every blonde I ended up with, but never did. Some day I'd have to get some counseling on that, figure out where in my past the blonde search started.

She leaned in real close and indicated she wanted to say something in my ear over the music and noise.

I turned my head just slightly

"James, Bob sent me," she said, her breath on my ear like what I imagined a whisper from an angel might feel like. "He thought you might need a little boost."

I turned to stare at her directly, then shouted into the music. "Bob? My boss?"

She nodded.

Bob, the short, fat bastard, had sent me a hooker. How crude was that? No matter how good-looking this woman was, I just wasn't interested. Even if she was bought and paid for already.

"Tell him thanks, but no thanks," I said into her perfectly formed ear. "I like to find my own dates."

She laughed, and the laugh seemed to cut through the noise like sharp scissors through tissue paper. "Not *that* kind of boost," she said, leaning in close again.

Her breath smelled of faint cloves mixed with vanilla.

"This kind of boost."

She touched me on the shoulder and I closed my eyes as her hand stroked my arm, filling me with the warmest sensation. Man, she could "boost" me any time she wanted.

Suddenly, all my doubts about what I had done were gone, my drive to get the bigger house was back, and my need to get laid by a beautiful blonde hit me like a sledgehammer.

I opened my eyes to thank her and suggest we go somewhere a little less noisy, but she was gone, vanished into the crowd like so much smoke.

"Well, not sure what old Bob was thinking," I said. "That was lame."

I downed the drink, ordered another, and turned on the bar stool to study the crowd, the memory of her already forgotten. I was looking for a companion for the night. After all, I had some celebrating to do.

I awoke to my alarm the next morning, my head fuzzy from all the scotch and my tongue feeling like I had run it through sawdust. The sheets on my massive bed still smelled of last night's conquest, a blonde with a chest twice the size of her IQ. She wore a perfume that after six drinks, had driven me nuts. But this morning, the remains of it smelled like an air freshener in a men's room urinal.

I vaguely remembered she had left at some point in the middle of the night, calling a cab and taking enough money from me to buy her her own cab. I didn't care, it was only money, and after yesterday's closing of the big drilling deal, I was going to be making a lot more of it.

By the time I was through my morning routine and powering toward work in my Porsche, the remains of the scotch hangover were gone and I was looking forward to all the praise I was going to get at work, not counting the bonus. There had better be a damn big bonus.

Then, like a cloud lifting, I remembered the encounter with the woman Bob had sent. My bonus better be a lot bigger than some strange blonde in a bar, making promises and then not even hanging around to follow through. If Bob paid her more than a few bucks, he was going to have to get his money back, that was for sure.

It took me a few more blocks to really put her face back in my mind. It was as if the scotch had erased it. I prided myself on never forgetting a name or a face. Then what she had said came back. She had promised a "boost." She had touched me, and my attitude had changed. Often just the touch of a woman did that to me. Or at least took my focus temporarily away from a problem.

But this time it had felt different, and there was just something about her I couldn't shake. That feeling that I knew her, that same feeling I had with every damn blonde-haired woman I met. That was part of it, sure. But there was more. Bob was going to do some explaining on this one.

As I expected, when I arrived in my office, on the seventh floor of the ten-story corporate headquarters, there was a message waiting with my secretary to join Bob in his office. Usually I beat him into work, sometimes by hours, but on days after closing big deals, I gave myself the freedom to just get there when I wanted to. After all, I deserved that luxury for one day. Tomorrow, I would be back working harder than anyone in the place, coming in earlier, staying later, working weekends. It was the only way to get ahead in this business, and I planned on getting very, very far ahead by the time I was done.

Bob was sitting in his big chair, feet up on his desk as I knocked and then entered his office. He was almost as wide as he was tall, and had a face like a troll stuck in the mud. I tried hard to never stand beside him in any function or picture. It would just make him look bad, and making a boss look bad was never a good career move, even though I was after his job. He was number one in the corporation's legal department; I was number two.

"Nice job on closing that deal yesterday," he said. "Stock is going through the roof, and the guys upstairs are taking hundreds of phone calls from every media outlet there is."

"Great," I said, smiling and sitting down across his desk from him. But it didn't feel that great. It was done, I had managed to pull it off, now it was time to move on, get to the next big deal. The fun was in the chase, not in the having.

It was that way with women as well.

And with my cars and houses. What I owned or had at the moment didn't mean anything. All that mattered was what I was trying to get.

"Bonus check coming your way this afternoon, approved from upstairs," Bob said, smiling a smile that turned his wrinkled face into a mass of sneers. I knew that smile. It was sincere, even though it didn't look it.

"Thanks," I said. "And if you paid that blonde you sent my way last night more than ten bucks, you got taken. She vanished without so much as a kiss good-bye."

He actually jerked, glanced at me, then looked away, as if I had surprised him by remembering her.

"No big deal," Bob said, shifting his gaze to some-thing in an open drawer beside his desk as he sat up.

I had hit a very sensitive topic for some reason. I knew Bob after the last two years, and I had made it my job to know his moods and actions. I had sur-prised him.

"Who was she?" I asked, pushing the topic. "She was sure a looker."

He shrugged, which I knew meant he was going to flat-out lie to me, or give me a half truth.

"Just someone I know from personnel," he said. "I just suggested she stop by and see how the celebrating was going."

"This someone have a name?" I asked.

He laughed and wagged a fat finger at me. "You know the rules on dating someone in the company."

I smiled. "You were the one that sent her, remember?"

"Not to screw your eyes out," Bob said, shaking his head and pretending to laugh. "Now, can we get to work and leave your personal life outside these walls? What little I already know about it scares hell out of me."

I dropped the subject, and Bob and I started in on the next project, working to get right-of-ways through some old family farms for a pipeline. But I had no idea of letting the chase of the blonde from personnel go that easily. When I got my teeth into something like this, I never let go until it was finished.

While Bob was off with the higher-ups having a two-drink, two-hour lunch, I told my secretary I was not to be disturbed, then used my company security clearance to access employee records on a secure screen on my computer.

Sometimes certain legal work required me to do just that, so no one would think what I was doing odd if they noticed at all. It didn't take much of a scan of the people who worked in personnel to tell me that part of Bob's story had, indeed, been a flat-out lie. But I didn't doubt she worked for the company. The question was in what department, and why hadn't I seen her before?

I used the fact that I hadn't seen her to eliminate a dozen different departments I worked in and around regularly, depending on the project. But that still left over five hundred personnel photos to go through.

It took me until two in the afternoon.

She wasn't there.

So who was she, and why had Bob been surprised I remembered her? She was clearly doing a favor of some sort for Bob. And the way Bob had acted, knowledge of her was not something Bob was willing to share.

I sat back, put my feet up on my desk, and covered my eyes, trying to sort out all the details like a giant legal puzzle.

I still believed she worked somewhere in the company. That was the way Bob lied, with half truths, or truths that left out real basic information.

And I believed now that she had been sent to give me something she called a "boost." More than likely some sort of drug or something on her hands. The fog about last night had now completely cleared and I had a very real memory of what her touch had done to me. If it was a drug, I didn't much like that idea at all. I took my share of alcohol, but drugs were not something I did, or ever wanted to do. Too damn scary, and too much chance of messing with my mind. I made my money with my mind. I ruin that, and it would be all over.

She had to work here somewhere, but where?

I looked up the official number of employees in the company from the records I had just gone through, then went into the payroll records and asked how many people were drawing official compensation.

Bingo.

The number was different by one.

So somewhere, this company had a secret employee, and I had no doubt that when I found that employee, it would be a beautiful blonde with wonderful brown eyes and a very scary touch.

I had very little time over the next three days to continue my search for my elusive Blonde Booster, as I was starting to call her. But then, on Saturday, Bob had decided to not come in, and I was left pretty much alone in the building. When I worked a Saturday or a Sunday, I was often one of only a very few in the big ten-story building. I always got a lot done and liked the quiet. Besides, except for drinking at night and searching for blondes to take home, I didn't have a hell of lot more to my life than work. Kind of sad when I thought about it, but I didn't much think about it that often.

This Saturday I liked the quiet for another reason. I had a quest.

Instead of going out last night, I had actually stayed at home with take-out Chinese food and studied floor plans of office layouts of the entire company building. There were only a few offices not clearly marked, and those would be my first targets.

I arrived at my office around ten, carrying a large mocha coffee and wearing jeans and a sweater. The old suit and tie were just not needed on a Saturday.

I took the floor plans out of my briefcase and spread them over my desk, studying them once again while I savored the wonderful flavor of my coffee. Somewhere in this building the Blonde Booster might have an office. If she did, I was going to find it. If she worked from home, then I'd next go into personnel records, working through the payroll until I found out where her checks went. Having high-level security clearance sure came in handy sometimes.

I was staring at the map when a soft voice said from the door, "Looking for me?"

I managed to somehow remained fairly contained, and didn't snort any coffee out of my nose, which, considering the surprise I felt, was a miracle.

"Actually, I was," I said.

She was more beautiful than I remembered. Long blonde hair flowed down over her shoulders, and her eyes were round, her smile real. She wore a baggy sweater and jeans with tennis shoes, but even that dressed down, nothing about her amazing body was really hidden.

She moved over to my desk, glanced down at the floor plans of the big structure, and then pointed with a fantastically perfect finger and short fingernail to one office that wasn't marked. "That's my office."

"That was going to be my second stop," I said. "Do you have a name?"

"Glenda," she said. "For now, just call me Glenda."

I pointed to a chair on the other side of my desk and then sat down as she did, keeping the desk between me and her. No way I wanted to get near that booster touch of hers again. Or at least not right away. I needed some answers first.

"I'm guessing from Bob's reaction that it's a surprise that I remembered you."

"Not really," she said, shrugging. "I can only do so much on the memory fogging aspects. But it really doesn't matter anymore, since I got the last of what you had at the bar the other night."

I didn't much like the sound of *that*, but she went on before I could ask what exactly I was now missing completely.

"Since I did," she said, holding my gaze, "you're going to be promoted upstairs next week, over Bob and into a VP position in management, and my presence here would have been told to you then anyway."

I had so many questions about all that she had said, I couldn't think of which one to ask first, so instead I just sipped my coffee and stared at her beautiful face. My goal was to be a vice president, then maybe even higher, but I sure hadn't expected it this soon, and not over the top of Bob.

I did a quick run-through of all the questions, then settled on starting with the most basic. "So, what's your official title here?"

"Keeper of the Morals," she said with as straight a face as I had ever seen.

"And your job description?" I asked, trying not to laugh at her.

She looked me right in the eye. "I extract and contain employee personal morals, mostly in the legal and management departments, so that they can work with the full interest of the corporation at heart."

"And just how do you do that?" I asked, remembering what I had been thinking about at the bar, how I had changed, how I had no idea how I had become the person I had become. That memory scared the hell out of me suddenly.

And made me angry at the same time. I didn't much like the idea of something being taken from me without my knowledge, especially under orders from Bob.

"Magic," she said. "Every major corporation has someone like me, a person of magic who can, for a fee, do as asked. And I have to admit, my fee is *very* high."

She smiled at that. She clearly enjoyed money as much as I did.

"I'll bet," I said, trying but failing to push away all the memories of what I used to think, how I used to feel about the job I now did.

"Remembering your morals, aren't you?" she asked, smiling at me.

"I have to admit I am. And you're starting to scare me, to be honest with you."

She laughed. "Take a deep breath and look at those memories, at how you used to be. You're going to be a vice president of this company, with a big office two more floors up. Do you really care about how you used to feel when you drove that Volkswagen and camped out at music concerts?"

I started to say that I did, then realized she was right. I didn't care. But I didn't care because she had taken that caring from me. She and Bob.

"What did you do to me?" I asked.

"The first day you were here at work, we met. Remember?"

I started to shake my head, then suddenly the memory of her shaking my hand and holding onto it that first day came flooding back. We had spent a wonderful lunch and afternoon together, talking, laughing, touching.

The memory of that fantastic day flooded back over me like a wet dream. "We went back to my place that night, didn't we?"

She nodded.

I remembered now that I felt like I had fallen in love with her in that one short day. How could I have forgotten that? It still felt like I was in love with her now that I remembered. No wonder I kept going home with blondes. I had been looking for Glenda all this time.

I shook my head. I hadn't felt this far off balance in years. I looked into those wonderful eyes and managed to get out my question again. "What *exactly* did you do to me?"

She shrugged. "I used my magic to take your morals, so you could be a better attorney for the company. That's all. Got the last of a vast supply the other night in the bar."

I wanted to shout at her, call her a common thief, but my legal mind just wasn't believing what she was saying. My memories of my actions, of how I used to feel and think, were clear. I used to care about something more than money and a bigger house.

But now that was all I cared about.

That thought hit me like a hammer to the skull, and

I knew, without a doubt, she had done just what she said she had done. She had taken all my caring away.

And the moment I accepted that, my mind snapped back to clear thinking, and I knew what I had to do.

"I seem to remember that afternoon and evening as being very special, at least to me. You do that with all the lawyers?"

She actually had the decency to blush. "No, only you. You were my first, and the only since. I've been just waiting until this day came, so I could again show myself to you."

I stood and moved around my desk, kneeling at the side of her chair and touching her wonderful soft skin. "You could still care about a man who has had his morals destroyed?"

"I'm pretty sure that not having morals doesn't mean you can't still love," she said, putting her other hand on mine and holding me to her. "And I didn't destroy them. They're just stored, just like all the others."

"You're not kidding, are you?"

"Not kidding," she said softly.

"And you can put them back into people?"

She nodded and said nothing.

I laughed and stood, moving away from her, pacing, thinking. I often did some of my best thinking while pacing. I was angry, in love, and scared to death about what had been done to me. I needed to get those thoughts sorted out so that my next action wouldn't be completely stupid.

All the time I paced she sat silently, watching me.

Finally, I knew I needed a little more information before I went any farther. I turned to her frowning and worried face. "How easily are these morals moved around and put into people?"

She held up what looked like a small fountain pen. "I have yours right in here. I promised myself I would give them back to you if you asked. That's how much I care about you."

That thought suddenly set me back.

"All my morals fit into a pen?" I asked, stunned. "Guess I didn't have that many, huh?"

"Highly compacted," she said. "You had an over-abundance of them, to be honest."

"Yeah, I remember that," I said, laughing. "But for the time being, put that away. I don't want to accidentally get them back just yet."

She now looked puzzled, then the pen vanished back into her baggy sweater somehow. Maybe later, if things went the way I was hoping, I'd get to inspect those pockets a little closer.

"One more question," I said. "Who ordered you to take those from me?"

"Bob," she said. "With approval of the president of the company."

I nodded. That was all I needed.

"I think I owe you a long, early lunch, don't you?" I said, smiling at Glenda. "You saved me a lot of searching around the building."

She still looked worried, but I had a hunch if this woman could really do what she said she had done, and liked money as much as I did, then we were going to be very, very happy for a time in the very near future.

I took her by the arm, and like a modern version of Ken and Barbie, dressed down, we headed to lunch.

I escorted Glenda to this fantastic, small restaurant where I knew we could talk for hours and not be disturbed. Over chicken slices and strong cups of mocha, we discovered we really liked each other. And that we both had the same goals, to be fantastically wealthy and powerful.

And I came to remember that even with my morals, I had wanted that same goal. Only I had planned on doing really good things with all the money once I got it.

I asked her why she just couldn't magic-up money and she said it didn't work that way. Her talents were more personal based, giving someone either good feelings or takings feelings from them. That's why the company had hired her to help them with the attorneys and management teams.

"Better than what a lot of my type do for money," she said, looking very alluringly at me.

"What's that?"

"Call girls, dating services," she said. "We can *really* make a man feel good."

"I've noticed that."

"I'm not doing anything," she said, laughing.

"I'm kind of wondering why not?"

"Yeah. Me, too," she said, smiling a smile at me that I would never forget.

With that, we moved to my house, with me breaking far too many speed limits along the way. We barely managed to get inside and to the bed before working as much magic on each other as we could do.

In the euphemistic sense, of course.

More directly, we had great sex. Better than great, actually. But I won't go there.

Finally, after who knows how long, we both lay there exhausted. And for the first time, I didn't want this blonde to leave. I wanted her to stay right beside me.

"So, what exactly can you do with my morals?"

Naked, lying there with her golden body facing me, she suddenly become very worried again. No doubt she thought I might ask for them back, and to be honest, I had thought about getting them back into me as quickly as possible. Not much thought, but the idea did sound right. They had been taken, I wanted them back, just like anything else I owned that was taken.

"You said you can put them back, right?"

She nodded.

"Can you put mine, or Bob's, or the president's, or some in general from the corporate supply into someone else?"

She now looked puzzled, then nodded. "I don't see why not."

"And even though what you give them is not their own morals, they would still work?"

"Sure. I'm sure it would be as if they got their own back."

I kissed her, then said, "How about we use that vast supply you have in storage to sabotage our company's rivals? Think we could do that?"

She blinked once, then twice, as if not really hearing me.

"You and me," I said, stroking the soft skin on her arm. "Working together. You get the morals into some of those decision makers in other companies, cripple them with good intentions and feelings for the underdogs, and I'll take advantage of the situation. Together, we can make a fortune and just keep on moving up in the company."

Again she blinked, then she moved into me with her full body and kissed me like I had never been kissed before. Clearly, she liked my idea. I had no doubt that a woman who could steal other's morals for corporate and personal gain would like it.

The rest of that afternoon and evening we did things sexually I had never done before, or thought possible. Amazing how the promise of a lot of money and a little lack of morals can motivate a person. And I'm sure there was some magic involved as well.

Six months later, I moved into my new corner office on the tenth floor, right next to Glenda's and two doors down from the president's office. Given a little time, that office could be mine as well if I wanted it. I didn't want it.

The view out my window was stunning, looking out over the city. I had gone through two levels of vice presidents since my move out of the legal department. My official title was now Executive Vice President in Charge of Corporate Acquisitions. And I had bought enough of the company stock that, if I wanted to, I could have a seat on the Board of Directors.

I didn't want that any more than I wanted to be

president. And besides, most of my stock was in special holding corporations very hard to trace back to me.

I just wanted to be rich. Fantastically rich. And I was almost there.

In my top drawer was the pen that held my morals, locked away safely. Glenda had told me how the pen inserter worked and let me keep them just to make sure they didn't get mixed up with all the other morals we were taking from the corporate morals pool.

Over the past six months, Glenda and I spent every night together in my big new mansion. Next month, we had decided, I was buying a yacht. All of it was in my name, of course.

I had taken care of dear old Bob quickly after moving upstairs. A little planted evidence and a double dose of morals from Glenda sent him scampering. The little bastard was working legal aide down in a shelter and living in a studio apartment after his wife had kicked him out. Served the bastard right for stealing from me.

Now, it was time to put the rest of my plan in motion. With one last look at the fantastic view from the office I had worked so hard to get to, I unlocked my drawer and took out the magic pen holding my morals, then tucked it safely in my pocket.

Then I quickly went over my resignation letter. It said what I needed it to say. I had moved nothing into my office that I wanted to keep. There was nothing about this job that I cared about. Nothing to pack. Having no morals could make you feel that way.

All I ever wanted was the chase, the hunt, the excitement of the search, keeping score with the money. I had been that way even before having my morals stolen.

Now, things were going to get really exciting.

After six months, I had convinced myself that I didn't much care about Glenda, either. After all, she was the one who took from me what was mine. There would be other blondes, I was sure. Granted, Glenda was damn fun in bed, but as she had told me that first afternoon, many witches were good in bed. It came with the magic.

Sally was almost as good as Glenda was. I had met Sally two weeks ago, when she joined Glenda and me for a little three-way afternoon fling. And with a little training from me on some of Glenda's special moves, Sally would be almost as good.

I dropped off my resignation letter with the president's secretary. Then dropped off my good-bye letter in Glenda's office. I told her that her things had already been moved out of my house and which storage unit she could find them in. Granted, it was a cold way to end a relationship, but what did she expect from someone who didn't care? She knew what she had gotten into with me. After all, she was the one who took all my caring and stored it in a magic pen.

On the way down to the main entrance, I stopped off in the basement and slipped a tiny, but very powerful device into the main air flow duct. It was a device that Glenda and I had come up with to use on other corporations. And it had worked wonderfully, spreading morals throughout a building in high doses, so high that often before I could schedule a corporate takeover, the company was dissolving into chaos.

This company, in a short time, would be experiencing the same thing. Glenda would be able to stop some of it if she wanted to, but not enough, and I doubted she would even try.

I had six more of the tiny morals bombs in my briefcase.

I made sure I was outside the building before the thing triggered and started giving back all the corporate executives and lawyers their morals. In very high doses.

The next morning I called my six different stock brokers and put in orders to short a large chunk of my corporate stock, buying options on some more and running puts. I had no doubt the stock was going down, and I was going to make a ton of money on the way down.

Six weeks later, I was richer than I had ever imagined as my former company stock hit bottom and was bought up by yet another rival. During those weeks, Glenda had tried to call me twice, but both times Sally answered the phone.

Sally said Glenda was crying, which meant that she, too, had been dosed. All I could do was shrug. What did Glenda expect, anyway? The sex had been good, she should let it go.

Yet I didn't tell Sally that I dreamed of Glenda every night, and imagined having sex with her when I was with Sally. I figured that given enough time, that would change. But so far it hadn't.

Ten months later, I had bought massive amounts of stock in six other companies, morals bombed them, and then got even richer as they crashed and I shorted the stock all the way down. I had become a morals terrorist, destroying companies by making them do the right things. I was sure my bleeding heart liberal self would be proud of me.

By this time, Sally was also a distant memory, just like I had hoped Glenda would become. Now I spent every night back at Danny's Crib, getting drunk and searching for that perfect woman. Blonde, of course.

None of them came up to Glenda, but I still searched.

Tonight seemed to be no different than any of the others, yet it was. I knew I was done for the moment, the big plan finished, the last stock sold. I was so rich, it seemed almost silly to keep going. But I knew I wanted more.

I swirled my scotch, letting the ice click against the side. I could feel it through the cold glass, but I couldn't hear the ice over the pounding of the loud music. I was sitting on the same bar stool that I had been on when Glenda had taken the last of my morals.

My world, it seemed, had come full circle. Now, finally tonight, over a year after that night, was as good as time as any to get who I really was back.

I took out the magic pen I had been carrying for the past month. It was time to retrieve what had been taken from me, to become a whole person again.

I was fantastically rich, I could use that money for some of the causes I supported before I took the corporate job. And the old me would be proud of the fact that I had brought seven greedy corporate giants to their knees. I was sure of that.

I took a quick drink of the scotch, sat the glass on the napkin, then without another thought, placed the pen against my skin on my palm and triggered it.

It was as if I had a bad cold that suddenly had cleared up. Everything I had done over the past years in my corporate job came flashing back to me like a movie in fast forward.

And then I suddenly realized how many people I had hurt along the way.

I could almost feel their pain.

Bob, Glenda, Sally, a hundred different blondes, and thousands of employees with families and jobs.

I had hurt them all.

And suddenly I knew that. And suddenly I cared.

"Oh, no, what have I done?" I shouted into the loud music.

And with that I broke down right there on the bar.

And I couldn't stop sobbing into my arm. The bartender finally had me escorted outside and I sat in my new Porsche in the parking lot, banging my hands on the steering wheel and shouting at nothing while I sobbed.

I just couldn't stop.

I had hurt so many people. I could almost feel all their pain, understand everything I had put them through. It was like waves washing over me. Every memory, every deed suddenly was real, had real people attached, had real consequences.

I had nothing to live for anymore.

I was the lowest of scum.

I had guns, lots of guns, back in my house. Just one bullet would end this, take these thoughts, these memories, these feelings away.

As I reached to start the car, Glenda climbed into the passenger seat. It took me a moment to realize who it was.

"I was wondering how long it would be before you took back your morals."

All I could do was sob that I was sorry. So sorry.

I had never felt so sorry for anything in my entire life. I had loved Glenda, had hurt her.

I didn't deserve to live.

"I know you are sorry," she said, her voice cutting through the massive waves of self-pity and sadness for what I had done.

Her hand touched me, that wonderful hand, and I suddenly started feeling calmer.

"I'll take about half," she said. "Then we can talk. Is that all right with you?"

All I could do was nod. At this point, I needed anything to make this pain go away.

She kept stroking my arm and I calmed down, got a part of my brain back, got some basic control of myself.

Finally, she stopped. I could feel all the remorse and sadness for my actions, but only as background thoughts. My brain was back.

I turned to stare at her. "You knew I would take my morals back?"

"Of course," she said. "From that first moment in your office. I had money in dummy corporations and shorted our company's stock just like you did as it went down. I got almost as rich as you did."

I sat there for a moment, my mouth opening and closing, realizing just how smart Glenda was, how she had played me just as I had played her.

"And the other corporations?" I asked. "You were following me, weren't you?"

"Of course," she said. "I love you, remember? But that didn't stop me from making even more money while you were doing what you were doing."

I could feel the guilt starting to come up again from what morals she had left in me. She could clearly see it as well.

"You need another little bit drained off?"

I nodded, and she touched me again, and like climbing a long staircase, I got closer to thinking even clearer, like coming out of a dark basement into the light of day.

"Thanks," I said. "I would have killed myself if you hadn't come along."

"I know," she said, her voice sad. "No person with as many morals as you had to start with could live with what you did over the last few years."

"So, after what I did to you, why did you save me?"

"Love," she said. And then she smiled that smile I had come to know so well. "And greed. We make a really great team."

"Yeah, but you'll never trust me again."

She laughed. "I didn't trust you the first time. Any more than you trusted me. But the sex was great. That's good enough to base a pretty good relationship on, don't you think?"

With that, she actually managed to make me laugh a little, which came out like a hiccup.

I turned in the car seat to face her. "Yeah, it was. I must admit, I've missed that. And I've missed you, every day. I was just so damn angry with you for taking something of mine."

"I know," she said. "But this time you wanted me to take them. And you can have them back any time you want."

I held up my hand. "No, let's just leave it at this level for the moment. Small enough to not control my thoughts, but not completely gone."

"That was the level I settled on for myself as well," she said.

I realized, right at that moment, staring into those

golden eyes and smiling face, that I never wanted to hurt her in any way again.

"I really do love you," I said.

"I know," she said. "I love you as well."

"So how come I didn't feel that when I had no morals?"

She shrugged. "I have a hunch that without morals, you don't care about anyone else but yourself. And love requires that caring to work for any length of time."

I nodded, deciding I'd just accept that for the moment and think about it later, when all the swirling emotions were a little more under control.

"So what next?" I asked.

She laughed. "Well, I'm blonde."

"Right on that," I said.

"And I have it on good authority you like picking up blondes in this bar here." She pointed to the front door of Danny's Crib.

"Right again," I said, smiling at her.

"So how about you take me back to that obscenely large mansion of yours and show me what tricks you've learned in bed over the last ten months."

"I'd love to," I said. "And you can show me what you've learned."

"Not a thing," she said. "I've just been waiting for you."

Again, I just sat there, my mouth opening and closing like a damn fish out of water. I stared at her, into those wonderful golden eyes, taking in that fantastic smile. And I let myself feel the love for her, the emotions of sadness at what I had done to her, and the fantastic feeling of happiness that she actually wanted me back, and had waited.

It seems we had a lot of real feelings to talk about.

But that could wait. Sex came first.

Lots and lots of sex.

She was a blonde, I had picked her up at Danny's Crib, just like all the others. But I had a feeling, an honest feeling, that this time, she would be the last blonde I ever picked up there.

And it was a feeling I liked.

COSMIC BALANCES INC.

by *Kristine Grayson*

THE computer spit out the information, then locked as a single piece of paper printed to the left of Grint. He closed his eyes, resisting the urge to bang his head against the screen.

Could anything else go wrong today?

He stood on his chair and peered over the fabric walls of his cubicle. As far as he could see, other minions were working their computers, taking notes, making life-and-death decisions, finishing their daily quotas.

He wasn't even halfway there, and it was already two-thirty in the afternoon.

His boss, a stunning, six-foot-tall woman who wore her red hair up (adding at least six inches to her height), emerged from her office. She started into the maze of cubicles, walking with purpose.

Grint ducked back inside his. He had no idea what his boss would do if she caught him staring at the other minions. She could do anything. Rumor had it that she was the one who had convinced Mata Hari to be a double agent.

Of course, other rumors stated that she had been Mata Hari in her previous life. Who knew? All he could be sure of was that she was tough, she was

222

mean, and she believed that minions should stay on the job until each day's work was done.

He sighed and sank into his chair. The desk still smelled of the coffee he'd spilled that morning, and the garbage can still carried the faint odor of the burrito he'd tried to eat last week when he decided to have lunch in and get work done. Of course, he had to get a burrito that had been improperly cooked, and he'd missed two days of work, and returned to find that no one had emptied his garbage can, which really was the worst of it. The fact that no one had picked up his assignments was irritating, but survivable.

Until now. He crossed his legs and grabbed the paper from the printer. The letters were faint. He was running out of toner on top of everything else. He had to squint to see the information—and when he finished reading, he wished he hadn't squinted at all.

What he had thought was that this one lost soul was, in fact, one lucky soul. The bastard—and the man had truly been a bastard in both senses of the word— had received a blessing just before he died, and somehow, it had negated all the times he'd been cursed.

At the moment, the lucky soul was standing outside the Pearly Gates in a line that extended halfway around the cloud. Grint had the rest of the day to make sure the lucky soul was truly supposed to pass through those gates. If Grint missed, he'd be fired.

He'd seen it before. Stazy, who'd had the cubicle next to him, had let a saintly woman who'd been cursed just as she stepped in front of a bus, slide into the fires of hell. It had taken two days, fifteen instant replays, and one innocent bystander interview to determine that what the automated Cosmic Balance Acceptance System had thought was a curse had really been a startled response.

In that instance, *God damn you!* accompanied by a shaking fist had meant *get out of the way* instead of *go to hell, you awful person.*

Accidents like that—not the bus part, but the misinterpretation of exclamations made in the heat of the moment part—happened all the time. It was up to the Cosmic Balance Examiner to resolve surprise issues in a timely manner, so that saintly women who'd unfortunately died under the wheels of a bus did not end up burning for eternity when they were supposed to sit in the coolness of the clouds.

The fact that the saintly woman had gone to hell for two days was a firing offense.

The fact that Grint's man was still in line gave him time to clear up the mess.

Grint ran a hand through his short-cropped black hair. Before he started on the case, he punched the speed dial on his phone, then put the receiver to his ear. He prayed for his answering machine, and, for once, his prayers were answered.

"Babe," he said after the beep. "Gotta work late. Might be on a few out-of-the-office reviews. I'm really behind from that burrito thing. I'll make it up to you this weekend. Promise."

Then, as he hung up, he realized he probably shouldn't have promised anything. If something went wrong, he might have to work the weekend. Then Sherry'd be really pissed.

She was already beginning to believe he had some action on the side.

He *wished* he had some action on the side. Then he wouldn't have to review other people's lives all the time. Then he could stress about deceiving his wife while spending time with his girlfriend or vice versa.

But he wasn't handsome enough or nice enough or interesting enough to have action on the side. Hell, he wasn't handsome enough or nice enough or interesting enough to have a wife. He'd lucked into Sherry because she was desperate to marry before the ole biological clock ticked down, and he didn't have the heart to explain to her that he couldn't father children.

He hadn't even told her he was no longer human. He was just a minion, trying to make certain the cosmic balance worked in each individual life.

He'd opted for minion status, way back when. Back when his own life had very little balance—cosmic or otherwise. He'd died without a requisite number of blessings or curses. He could have been reincarnated, trying again to live a life that someone noticed. Or he could stay in purgatory until a slot opened up. But he wasn't guaranteed a spot in heaven or in hell. He had to take what became available.

Or he could become a minion and, with diligent work and a standard annual review, he could earn his way to the Pearly Gates. Of course, if he got fired like Stazy, he'd have a one-way ticket to hell.

What the Cosmic Balance minion who'd informed him of these choices had failed to mention was that Grint would have something resembling a life outside his work. People—real, living, breathing people—could actually see him and interact with him, and cling to him desperately when they felt they needed a man (and any man would do).

He'd let Sherry believe that he could live a normal life with her, and that was probably bad, but she'd let him believe she was in love with him, and he hadn't found out otherwise until a month or two ago when she was talking to her mother about getting a loan for some kind of fertility treatments.

I thought we'd have a baby by now, Sherry'd said over coffee in their too-small dining room. Her mother had been clutching a cup and staring at the cheap pictures on the wall. *If I'd known that it would take us this long, I'd've married Larry instead.*

Larry. Grint had met Larry, and Larry was no prize. In fact, being placed in the same category as Larry was somehow offensive, even though Larry was the same kind of nebbish that Grint had been in his actual life.

Grint suspected he was even more of a nebbish now. At least he hadn't screwed up at his real life job. In those days, he'd been a night janitor for an office building. He'd taken a lot of pride in the way he kept each office—hell, each cubicle—so clean that it shined.

No such janitor here, not at night and certainly not in the day. If Grint had that job, he knew he'd have a stellar review at the end of each quarter.

But paperwork and computers and information tracking—he'd been lousy at that kind of thing when he'd been in school. And if he'd known he was signing on for that kind of work, he might actually have chosen purgatory, and taken his chances with the whole stupid lottery system.

Instead, he was stuck here, with this little piece of paper and someone else's confusing life. That someone else was named, unfortunately, Binky Innis, born out of wedlock, father unknown. His mother, Rosemary Innis, cursed the day Binky was born on the day Binky was born, and that brought officials from CBI into that squalid hospital room, just to make sure there was no misunderstanding. These were higher-level minions, the kind who could actually turn themselves invisible and be present at the moment of a cursing (or a blessing), unlike Grint who'd never been officially invisible in his life.

Birth day curses (and birth day blessings) were powerful and rare, which was why they required a CBI minion to witness the event (of course, the minion had to know it was coming—and Grint had been present at dozens of lunch room discussions about the ethics of allowing a birth day curse to even happen, given the negative impact it had on a young, fragile, and innocent life. CBI's mandate, of course, was noninvolvement, but still, lots of minions [many of whom were minions because of similar bad fortune that they'd tried to overcome] believed that every little soul needed a bit of t.l.c. in the beginning, and the fact that so many of them got none made for a terrible playing field.

(Once Grint had pointed out that the playing field might be terrible, but it was at least level [statistics showed that about .01 percent of all babies born received a birth day curse and about .01 percent of all babies born received a bona fide birth day blessing, maintaining the ever-precious cosmic balance] and for that bit of wisdom, he was ostracized for more than a week. He only got allowed back into the fold when he brought dark chocolate from home [and that had been an accident, too, since he'd been planning to give it to Sherry after a particularly devastating fight, and he didn't want to keep it in the hot car in the hot parking lot for an entire afternoon]. He got on everyone's good side, which meant that they promptly forgot him, and went back to their everyday business. Such was his life. Or his nonlife, as the case might be.)

So poor Binky Innis was the recipient of a birth day curse, and things didn't go much better from then on. Rosemary abandoned him when he turned two and his grandmother got him, thinking he would be the cute lovable child she never had, and she soon realized she still didn't have a cute lovable child. She didn't curse him—she was too nice a woman for that—but she bit her tongue so much trying to prevent herself from doing so that she had permanent teeth marks in its tip.

Teachers disliked him, but none of them cursed him. Other boys hated him, but none of them cursed him, either. They just beat him up. So he beat up any smaller kid he could find. And the smaller kids, mostly little girls (years younger than he was) started the second wave of curses.

The third wave came when Binky (who now called himself Bruiser, thinking the name had power [when it sounded, to Grint anyway, like a name someone would give his dog. Come to think of it, so did Binky. No wonder the guy ended up so messed up]) started hanging out in bars. Since he received his full height at 14, and since he lived in a community that cared more for bar revenue than the legalities of drinking ages, his barroom days began in his fifteenth year and continued until a few moments before he died.

In Grint's review of the file, he could find no blessing at all. None, not a one, and no reason why dear old Binky/Bruiser found himself outside the Pearly

Gates where, the big screen at the end of the cubicle row showed, he was currently badmouthing the Boy Scout (a real Boy Scout, who'd died trying to get some kind of merit badge) in line ahead of him. Apparently, Binky/Bruiser had a sense that he needed to cut the line and get inside those gates fast, where no one could touch him—at least for a few days while this all got straightened out.

That whole idea scared the crap out of Grint. A little old lady mistakenly burning in the fires of hell simply suffered. A mean-spirited curse-hound like Binky/Bruiser could do a lot of damage behind the Pearly Gates. In other words, if B/B got inside heaven, everyone else would suffer.

Including Grint.

So he had to discover what caused the snafu.

And at the moment, he didn't have a clue.

The lunchroom was closed by the time he finally took a break for dinner. He wasn't the only one standing outside the cafeteria looking just a little lost. At least half a dozen other minions had gathered there as well, all of them working late on difficult cases, all of them terrified for their own futures.

Except for some woman misnamed Charity. It soon became clear that she was the night shift supervisor, there to guarantee that none of the minions banded together or changed assignments. It was her job, Grint eventually realized, to make certain the minions couldn't do things the easy way.

She wouldn't even allow them to share a pizza. She made them order individual pizzas, and then she made them wait near the front for the poor pizza delivery guy to show up.

Grint took his pepperoni and cheese back to the cubicle, even though the smell of rotted burrito and stale coffee made him queasy. He tucked one napkin under his chin, another in the middle button of his cheap white shirt, and a third in the NASCAR belt buckle that Sherry had given him, even though he'd never watched a day of NASCAR in his nonlife (or in his real life for that matter).

He ate and studied and couldn't find a single blessing anyone had bestowed on B/B, not even an accidental blessing that missed its intended target and landed on B/B instead.

Grint was about to call in Charity to see if these were the kind of circumstances that warranted help, when he saw the toast.

He'd been rerunning the last few moments of B/B's life, watching them on a small screen next to his computer. He'd looked at these last few moments half a dozen times already, always concentrating on B/B, who was hunched over the bar, drinking some green beer, and looking green himself. B/B was feeling the nausea that, in some men, came just before a heart attack.

Grint already knew the sequence of events: B/B would suck on that beer, ask for another, reach into the jar of pickled eggs, pull one out, and fall over backward, sending the egg flying over his head and into the face of a nearby patron who, predictably, cursed. That curse might've been an epithet, but it might've been heartfelt, too.

Whatever it was, it wasn't enough to get B/B away from those Pearly Gates. Grint had already checked. A mild *goddammit to hell* might've been referring to the egg, might've been referring to B/B, or might've simply been the patron's standard exclamation when something surprising happened.

Grint didn't have to do the bystander interview because rerunning the scene (and querying the higher ups at CBI) did not result in B/B being sent into the fires. So, something else had happened.

Something big.

Something powerful.

Something that guaranteed B/B a place in that line, a place so firm that his new harassment of the Red Cross Aid Worker two people ahead of the Boy Scout didn't automatically send him to purgatory.

In frustration, Grint tossed a pizza crust at the rerun screen, and it had hit the zoom-out function. And that's when he saw a little woman, no bigger than Grint himself, climb on top of the bar, a mug of beer in hand.

She was dressed all in green—kelly green, which looked good on her. Even the jaunty Robin-Hoodish cap looked good—or it would have if she hadn't had a matching green feather, a feather that drooped behind her skull and looked vaguely like a question mark that had fallen against the side of her head. Her eyes were as green as her clothes, and her hair, underneath that strange cap, was a startling black given how very pale her skin was.

She held up a mug of green beer and tapped a green fingernail on it for quiet.

Grint turned up the sound. He didn't like how this was going.

She actually got the bar to quiet down. Not a soul spoke. They all looked up at her, and her green-tights-encased legs.

"In my country," she said with a real Irish brogue, "we give blessings on saints' days. Let me give you one and please, to accept it, take a sip of your beer when I'm through."

Grint groaned. The people around the bar held up their mugs in anticipation.

The little woman extended her mug, and said in a loud voice, "Blessed be everyone in this room. And may you be in heaven a half an hour before the Devil knows you're dead!"

"Hear, hear!" someone shouted, and then everyone in the bar drank in unison.

Grint zoomed in and reran the event. Sure enough, it had been B/B who had shouted "hear, hear" and then he'd taken a drink. That last fateful drink. Only a few seconds later he had taken the pickled egg, then fallen over with a heart attack.

Only a few seconds later.

Grint felt as green as B/B's beer. The pizza threatened to come back up. He grabbed the sheet of paper with all of B/B's statistics and there it was, so plain he shouldn't've missed it the first time around:

Binky Innis aka Bruiser aka that Mean SOB had died in the last few hours of March 17.

St. Patrick's Day.

Grint's hands were shaking. He took the image of the woman, froze the frame and printed the image. Then he put the image in his scanner (for reasons he didn't understand, his rerun imager and his computer were not networked), and scanned it into his computer.

Then he ran the face recognition software, asking for a special concentration on leprechauns.

She showed up after only fifteen seconds—a full facial shot without the hat. Her name was Erinna Gobra. Her eyes were that green and amazingly large, even in the DMV photo (although Grint wasn't sure why a leprechaun needed a driver's license). Her hair really was that black, and her skin that pale. She had thick red lips and a hint of mischief around the eyes.

Triple threat: A real blessing, accepted, on a saint's day, from someone who spoke for the saint. On St. Patrick's Day, a leprechaun's curse damned, and a leprechaun's blessing blessed fivefold.

But, according to the computer calculations, a fivefold blessing still shouldn't have negated all those curses that B/B had received (and deserved!) throughout his weasly little life.

Grint's hands were shaking. He got up and went to the Pearly Gate's streaming video that fed into the wallscreen near the door, and looked once again for B/B. There he was, pulling on the pigtail of a little girl who'd leaped in front of a truck to save an old man she didn't know. The little girl was sobbing—not because she was dead, but because B/B was tormenting her.

The line had gotten very short. Grint's time was almost up.

And he still didn't know what to do. B/B shouldn't

be in that line, and yet there he was, shouting obsceni-
ties at the Mother Teresa clone a few yards behind
him.

Grint stomped back to his own desk. He studied the
leprechaun's photo, then asked the system for more
information on her.

She was a known troublemaker, out to break the
CBI system. The CBI system was a sign of corporate
greed, she'd said on more than one occasion, reducing
the human equation to a series of numbers that had
little meaning when someone found himself face-to-
face with his destiny.

She had given that blessing deliberately to a room
full of drunks, because she knew someone had probably (sincerely) cursed them recently. She was trying to
negate previous curses, and she went from place to
place doing so—in and out of prisons, touching the
heads of serial killers and child molesters, blessing
them as if they had souls; going to hospitals and cursing newborns, just to throw the system out of whack
(most of those birth day curses had been caught and
negated, thank heavens); and doing crowd-pleasing
blessings on important holidays, like Christmas, Yom
Kippur, Ramadan, and of course, her personal favorite, St. Patrick's Day.

She'd been flagged, though. If Grint had had more
time, he would have found her and been able to negate the blessing or at least reduce its power.

But even with the flagging, he'd missed her, and he
shouldn't have.

The computer had frozen at the moment of B/B's
death, right?

Right?

Grint grabbed his paper, and looked at it again.
Then scratched his head and frowned.

He was bad at dates. He'd always been bad at dates
and times. He'd even been bad at them when he was
(theoretically) alive. He didn't celebrate many holidays, and even if he had celebrated a few, Sherry

wouldn't have let him go out last night because it was a drinker's holiday.

Last night.

St. Patrick's Day.

First of all, this should've been someone else's case. And secondly, this was March 18th. The day *after*. Hell, he'd gotten the download the afternoon after.

And that was wrong.

He was about to run through the file again when a chill ran through him.

That brogue echoed in his imagination: *May you be in heaven a half an hour before the Devil knows you're dead.*

B/B hadn't gotten to heaven yet. He was just in line. The Devil wouldn't be involved until later in the day—and Grint didn't want to see that temper tantrum.

He'd seen St. Peter get mad at Stazy for the elderly lady thing. That was bad enough. But the Devil was known for his temper. St. Peter was known for being . . . well . . . temperate.

Grint's stomach rolled. He was about to punch the button for his supervisor when a puff of green smoke appeared in the remaining pieces of pizza. Erinna Gobra, the leprechaun, stood on top of a piece of pepperoni. She raised her arms and the piece of pepperoni flew toward Grint as if it were a magic carpet.

The pepperoni landed on his shoulder, staining his white shirt with tomato sauce.

"Oh, crap," he said, and flicked her off. He'd worked all evening to prevent a stain, and there she was, the unwanted leprechaun, ruining everything from his day to his clothing.

Erinna tumbled backward and landed in the cheese. She got up, dusted herself off, and grinned. But the grin had a malevolent edge.

"I don't think we're starting off on the right foot," she said in that brogue. Only it sounded fake since she was so small and her voice so tiny.

"I'll say." Grint had dipped one of the napkins in water, and was dabbing at the tomatoey spot on his shoulder.

"You could've killed me," Erinna said.

"And then where would you've ended up, hmmm?" he asked. "Someone at CBI would be balancing your blessings and curses, and if you keep pushing me, I'm going to curse you with all my middle-management anger and power."

"Oooooo," she said, stepping out of the cheese onto the pizza box. "Such threats."

"Or I'll just squash you." He picked up the nearest keyboard and raised it.

She snapped her fingers and grew to cat-size, sitting on the edge of his desk. Her legs looked fine even at one-tenth power.

"You wouldn't want to do that," she said with that malevolent smile.

"What do you have against us, anyway?" he asked.

"You?" she said. "I have nothing against you. I don't like CBI."

Neither did he, but he couldn't say that. He had a hunch he was on review at this job already.

"CBI and its ilk are so impersonal," she said. "In my day, blessings and curses were the province of magical beings."

"They still are," he said.

"The magical beings who were in charge of their own patch of woods. Or bit of river, or whatever plot of land they'd been assigned."

He was making the stain worse, so he quit dabbing at it. "That was a long time ago."

"Not that long," she said. "And it was a better system."

He shrugged. "I can't do anything about it."

"I know." She wrapped her hands around her knee. "All you can do is write me up. And I'll keep messing up your systems, until—"

Systems! She was talking to him so that the clock would tick down, and B/B would be in heaven, and that half hour was critical. If B/B was in heaven for a half hour, he was more-or-less grandfathered in, and it would take an act of the Demon/Angel Board to toss him out.

"Excuse me," Grint said, and sprinted away from his cubicle. He was running for the night supervisor. As he hurried, he realized that a pizza box was coming at him at full clip. Erinna was riding it, just like she had that piece of pepperoni.

He waited until she was close, and then he knocked her out of the air.

Then he dove into the supervisor's office, slammed the door closed, and stood there, plucking nervously at the napkin still tucked into his NASCAR belt, while he explained the twisted circumstances that had gotten a nasty piece of work like Binky Innis that close to the Pearly Gates.

"Good work, Mr. Grint," Charity said when he finished explaining. She pressed a few buttons on her system. Behind her, a screen lit up and, as he watched, the line near the Gates appeared. B/B was only three people from St. Peter when a hole in the cloud appeared, and B/B fell back to Earth.

"Isn't he going to hell?" Grint asked.

"We have to reset a few systems," Charity said. "That's one powerful blessing your friend created."

"She's not my friend," Grint said.

"Then why is she sitting on your shoulder?"

He looked. She was sitting in the tomato stain. He resisted the urge to flick her off.

"Get down!" he snapped.

Erinna grinned at him. Those green eyes twinkled in a way that made him nervous. Sherry could probably sense the flirtation from miles away.

"We've been looking for you, Ms. Gobra," Charity said. "You realize that you'll have to serve fifteen years in CBI's review wing just to make up for this one offense."

"You wouldn't," Erinna said.

"We have to. You know the rules."

"I hate the rules," she said. Then she raised her hand and disappeared in a puff of green smoke.

The smoke smelled faintly of mint. Grint coughed, and waved it away. "I could've caught her," he said.

"I know," Charity said.

"Why didn't you let me?"

She grinned. "Do you realize how automated this system would be without people like her?"

"You mean you let her mess up as a check on the system?" Grint felt anger build. He'd wasted an entire afternoon and one favorite shirt because of this woman.

"Her and some of her little friends," Charity said. "Be grateful, Mr. Grint. Without people like her, you wouldn't have a job at all."

He almost said he didn't want the stupid job. Almost. And then he remembered his other choices.

Besides, someone had just noticed him. A leprechaun had spilled tomato sauce on him and used him in her nefarious plan. Nothing that exciting had ever happened to him before.

He cleared his throat, and resisted the urge to wipe at the stain again. "You're going to take care of B/B?"

"I will," Charity said. "And congratulations."

"Huh?" Grint said.

"You've been promoted." She didn't sound particularly pleased about it. "You've been reassigned to the Little People Division. Leprechauns, nymphs, nyads, brownies, and anything else that's tiny and angry at their loss of personal power now falls under your purview."

"But I don't know anything about these creatures," he said. "I was surprised to learn that demons existed."

Not to mention minions and angels and God Himself. But Grint knew better than to say that. He'd said it once, and nearly got bounced to hell just for having the temerity to say what was on his mind.

"And look how well you've coped," Charity said. "Now that you've discovered how wonderful and manipulative the little beasts are, you can start working on stopping them. Unless you like all that computer work . . . ?"

She said that last as if she knew he hated it. Could she read his thoughts?

He shook that idea out of his mind. There would be nothing worse than a night supervisor who knew what all her little minions were thinking.

"I'll take it," he said, wondering how working in an area he'd never heard of with creatures he hadn't believed in was in any real way a promotion. "You know, though, I'd be willing to settle for just cleaning the offices."

Charity crossed her arms. "Settle. Settle's a word we don't like around here, Mr. Grint."

"I meant—"

"I know what you meant," she said. "And let me remind you that this is a corporation. We follow the Peter Principle here."

"Yes, ma'am," he said, stumbling out of the office. He was tired and he wanted to go home and he wasn't sure how he'd make it through the promotion. Did he have to finish the work from his previous job? He was too scared to ask.

He made it all the way back to his messy desk when he realized that she hadn't said St. Peter's Principle. He actually had to tap into the Internet for it. The Peter Principle: "In a hierarchy, every employee tends to rise to his level of incompetence." Well, he was already at his own level of incompetence. He supposed he had just moved into a whole new realm.

He'd finally gotten his wish. He'd been noticed.

And he wondered if that meant someone had cursed him. Hadn't Sherry said to him just the other day, *Be careful what you wish for?*

Hadn't she?

Or had he said it to her?

He supposed he could look it up on his rerun screen. But he didn't.

Instead he started in on the files that had built up while he'd been saving heaven from Binky Innis.

Grint wouldn't be coming home tonight, either. He supposed that would be the last straw for Sherry. And that clinched it. Someone had cursed him . . .

. . . and he was getting everything he wished for, and finding, just like the old saying said, that none of it was what he really wanted.

THEOBROMA

by Diane Duane

THE bells, the *bells:* the sound of them brought him very slowly out of a dream, and he cursed under his breath as he woke up, because he knew it was one of those dreams he was never going to be able to recover no matter how he tried. Ken cursed harder as he rolled over and realized that "the bells" were nothing more than the "real ring" ringtone he'd downloaded for the phone last week. He was bored with it already. *And how bored is everybody else?* he thought, as he levered himself more or less upright and fumbled around on the dressing table, wincing at the sunlight streaming in through the bedroom window and trying to find the PDA-phone without opening his eyes a millimeter wider than he had to.

There was a thump as it fell onto the rug by the bed: he'd left the "vibrate" setting on at the club last night, and now the thing had walked itself off the table. Ken started to bend over to pick it up, and then the throbbing in his head warned him that bending over right now was *not* a good idea.

Ooh, too many Caipirinhas, he thought. *And when am I going to learn that* any *Caipirinhas is too many for me?* Meanwhile, the phone lay there on the rug, ringing away.

Ken moaned. "Will you just come *here*, please?" he said in the Speech.

The phone leaped into his hand. *Because you ask nicely . . .* it said.

"I always ask nicely," Ken muttered, fumbling for the right button. "Hello?"

"You need to get your butt down here," Malesha's voice said.

"*What??* Are you kidding? You said today was an off day for me!"

"That was before today turned into the nightmare it's presently becoming," Malesha said.

The fact that she sounded perfectly calm did nothing for Ken's temper. Malesha *always* sounded that way, even if the roof was falling in (which had happened last week) or Earth was being invaded by giant alien talking squid (the week before). It was infuriating. "This is *not* fair to me!" Ken said, swinging his legs out from under the covers, as he already knew what the end result of this conversation was going to be.

" 'Fair,' " Malesha said, "and our career choice—" —that being the code word used in the office for the practice of wizardry when there were nonwizards around "—are usually mutually exclusive, as you know. Your client's going to be here in eleven minutes. *You* be here in ten."

"Oh, come on—!" Ken said. But it was too late. She'd hung up on him.

He scowled at the phone.

Not my *fault,* it said. *Don't shoot the messenger!*

"I could be tempted," Ken said, and tried to sit up straight. Then he put the phone down in a hurry and put his head in his hands. "Oooooh . . ."

Better take an aspirin, the phone said.

"You are a *personal digital assistant*," Ken said, straightening up again to find out how it felt. It felt awful. Nonetheless, he stood up, and only wobbled once. "*Not* a paramedic! Unfortunately. Because that's what I need."

Self-pity looks bad on you, the phone said as Ken staggered into the bathroom.

"My *face* looks bad on me," Ken muttered, glancing just once at the mirror, and away again, in a hurry. "Just shut up and let me get on with pulling together the shattered fragments of my life."

The phone remained mercifully silent. Ken turned on the shower and waited for the water to come up to heat, while his thoughts ran in small tight circles and his brain tried to get itself going. *She was really pretty last night. What was her name? Angela?* Something with an A.

Steam started to rise. Ken started rooting around for his razor, which as usual was hiding at the bottom of a basket of men's grooming products. Then he straightened up again, leaving it where it was, as "ten minutes" meant designer stubble again this morning. "What was her name?" Ken said to the phone as he pushed the shower curtain aside and got into the tub.

Who?

"You know perfectly well who. The brunette, last night. The one in that little red—you know, the dress thing—" Though it hadn't exactly been a dress. It definitely *had* been little. "You know, with the real high—"

It's hard to be sure. There were so many *ladies you were drooling over last night.*

"Oh, great," Ken muttered, "first you're an EMT, and now you're my mother. Give it a rest."

Six minutes now . . .

"Come on, what was her name?"

If she was so hot, you'll remember yourself. Myself, I think she deserves better.

"*I* deserve better than your value judgments," Ken muttered, squeezing his eyes shut and pushing his face up into the stream of theoretically hot water. "I'm going to trade you in for a number two pencil and a notepad."

You kidding? Not even the Powers that Be can read your *handwriting.*

Ken fumbled for the soap in silence, considering
that this was probably true. "What's it about?" he
said, finding the soap and getting busy with it.

"It" what?

"Whatever Mal's calling about."

Chocolate, the PDA said.

Ken's eyes flew open, regardless of the water and
the hour of the morning. "You interest me strangely."

Heh, said the PDA.

"What *about* chocolate?"

Please! Not while you're washing there.

And not another word would the PDA say on the
subject, not even when Ken was out of the shower
and dried and dressed and running down the stairs
from his little studio apartment. He never bothered
with the elevator on the way out to work in the morning: not even a wizard would willingly deal with getting stuck in the elevator this time of day. There were
just too many possible complications, and though most
people wouldn't normally notice wizardry even if you
did it right under their noses, there was no point in
taking unnecessary chances.

Meanwhile, he was happy enough to let the PDA
play out its little drama: first of all because no one
was any too sure about Manual sentience issues in
these new portable formats—they were all still in
beta—and besides, the walk from Ken's place was
short, and the peace and quiet gave him a few extra
minutes to enjoy his coffee on the way to work. He
swung into the Korean place on the corner, and Kim
the counter guy had his coffee ready as usual. Ken
put down his buck on the counter, picked it up, and
was out the door again, slurping the bitter coffee
through the patented scald-yourself-regardless top and
speedwalking westward toward the corner of Forty-
eighth and Park.

He paused there at the Waldorf's northwest corner
in the hazy spring sunshine to wait for the light along
with eight or ten other people, his gaze resting half-
consciously on the scarlet and chrome-yellow tulips in

the median. His place might be hardly more than the size of a walk-in closet, but it was perfect for a city wizard who preferred a short commute: three minutes' walk from the nearest Food Emporium, five minutes from the office, and ten minutes' walk from the worldgates at Grand Central. The light changed, and he charged across in company with the office ladies in sneakers and the suits with their little razor-thin briefcases, meanwhile hunting for that babe's name. She had been hot, indeed, *well* beyond hot. Brunette: Ken preferred them—anyone willingly bucking the blonde trend these days was worth investigating. *Didn't begin with an A,* he thought. *It was a C. Celeste— Celine—*

First letter, the PDA said. *Sounds like—*

Ken opened his mouth, then (saved again by reflex) fumbled in his jacket pocket for the phone's mike/ earpiece, stuck it in his ear. "Don't taunt me," he said to the dead earpiece. "It's cruel, and it speeds up entropy."

The PDA snickered. Ken grinned. Mobile phones made this particular aspect of wizardry so much easier: you could "talk to yourself" all you liked in the streets, these days, and no one could tell telepathy from telephony. *"Begins with a C,"* the PDA had said. *How often has* that *been true lately?*

"I'm batting at least .150."

But not in any league that matters. Two minutes, the PDA said.

Ken broke into a trot again. *Even if I'm not dead on time, I can at least look like I'm out of breath—* But he was already close enough that he was going to have a hard time getting that breathless. Even from here he could see the sign over the brownstone's cellar door: HIGHRISE EMPLOYMENT. He had never been able to find out to his satisfaction where the blame for the terrible joke lay: Malesha and Tik took turns blaming each other, leaving Ken to suspect that it was both of them.

He thumped down the stairs and paused to look in

through the little barred window before opening the
door; their quarters were tight, and there was almost
always someone standing right where you would
whack the door right into the small of their back. But
he could see only one person inside this morning: an
attractive brunette lady, wearing a charcoal-gray
skirtsuit, leaning on the counter that separated the
office proper from the "front of house."

Ken opened the door carefully, slipped in
sideways—the space between the door and the
counter was limited—and smiled at the brunette, up-
grading her from "attractive" to "extremely attractive," despite her worried expression. At the sound of
the door shutting, out of the back office popped Tik.
Tikram was one of those people who looked as though
he should have been a star in some obscure
Bollywood-movie romance: tall, slender, dark, with
close-cropped hair, handsome aquiline features and
deep liquid eyes. He could have been called pretty if
he weren't so aggressively muscled: it had occurred to
Ken that the two factors possibly had something to do
with one another.

"Ah, the token native arrives," Tik said under his
breath, and took the half-finished coffee out of Ken's
hand. "You still drinking this stuff? You astound me."
He took a slug himself, and as he finished, whispered,
"Just in time. She's on the poke this morning."

On cue, Malesha came out of their tiny back room
with an armful of files, looking as usual like a cranky
Nefertiti, with her tight, beaded cornrows up in an
Hérmès scarf. The blazer and pants suit, unusual for
a woman whose normal fashion modes were native
African or tweaked punkette, suggested that Malesha
had something high-tension scheduled for the morning. So did the residue of some recent wizardry hanging about her, which Ken could practically smell as
that kind of lightning scent that was unique to her.

"I've got an appointment uptown," she said to Ken,
reaching over the counter to push the files into his
hands. "And this lady has a problem . . ."

So did everybody who walked in their door. The question was always, was it going to be a problem better handled with an employment database and the Internet, or with wizardry?—because other wizards all over the metropolitan area referred problem interventions over here, but always under cover of the kind of help that you would normally expect to get at a more normal employment agency. Ken juggled the files into the crook of his left elbow and put out a hand for the lady to shake. "Ken Moorman," he said. "How can we help you?"

"Miz Cruzeiros here has had an unexpected vacancy in her business," Malesha said, "and she needs to fill it in a hurry. I'm sorry to make you tell the story twice," she said, smiling winningly at Ms. Cruzeiros, "but sometimes in this weather our staff have difficulty making it *in* on time. Ken, before you get started, can I have two seconds . . . ?"

She steered Ken away for a moment and lowered her head by his. "I think something may be missing from her kitchen," she said. "Check it out and let me know if I'm right."

He had a feeling she would be: Malesha was an unusually accurate seer, even by wizardly standards. "And you're not going to beat me up for being late?"

"I'll do that later," she said. "First things first. Get busy."

Ken turned back to Ms. Cruzeiros, smiled at her, and nodded toward the one little desk on the "client" side of the counter, the sum total of their public space. "Please, sit down," he said, making his way to the other side of the desk and putting the files out of harm's way. *This is what you get,* he thought, *for letting yourself be snookered into agency work. You could have gone it alone, practiced quietly between jobs and slept late whenever you liked. But no, you had to let your local Advisory talk you into this multiple-wizard gig. "It'll be good for you,"* he said. *"It'll be a challenge." Yeah, well, it's time I called him and said, Carl,* mostly *what it'll be is a big fat pain in the—*

"I'm sorry," Ms. Cruzeiros said, looking around her a little dubiously and not sitting down. "When I told my lawyer that I needed to find an agency temp for my staff, I thought he understood that I meant a *catering* agency temp—"

"We handle catering," Ken said, putting the papers down to one side and pulling the computer's keyboard over. Starting to use a computer as if you actually had something useful stored in it was, he'd found, a good way to calm the antsier clients down, the ones who were sold on postmodern furniture and floor-to-ceiling windows as signs of a successful business. "We're extremely well connected: I placed a sous-chef at Termagant & Co. just last week. Please sit down and let me know how we can help you."

Ms. Cruzeiros put her eyebrows up at that: T&C was the hottest restaurant in town right now, having lasted in that position for more than the usual three days. *But then maybe a restaurant where you go expecting to have the staff yell at you was always going to do well in this town,* Ken thought. *Can't wait for these "themed" places to go away . . .*

"Well," Ms. Cruzeiros said. "We—I run a chocolate store down in the Village. Theobroma—maybe you've heard of it?"

It was Ken's turn to put the eyebrows up. "Who hasn't? Best chocolate south of Union Square. A friend of mine gave me some of the lemon cream eggs last Easter. They were dynamite."

Ms. Cruzeiros nodded, somehow looking more tired than pleased at the compliment. "Thanks. Unfortunately I've lost my chocolatier at short notice. I need to find another."

Ken nodded, opening up the in-house jobseeker database to see if they had anybody suitable on it. "Is this going to be a long-term placement," he said, "or are you just looking for someone to hold the space until your employee returns?"

For a moment there was no answer. Ken looked up from his typing and saw that Ms. Cruzeiros was blushing furiously. And fury did indeed seem to be the cause: her face had gone both grim and strangely tragic in the space of about a second. It looked to Ken as if she was struggling with some uncomfortable decision. Finally she said, "Long-term."

"All right," Ken said, turning his attention back to his typing, and thinking, *Oh, boy, here we go: there was personal stuff going on* . . . A screenful of names came up—a mixed bag of bakers, patissiers, and other allied trades. "There are some possibilities here," he said. "People who've done chocolate work as well as general patisserie. How does that sound?"

"I don't know," Ms. Cruzeiros said, and now looked more tragic than furious. "I never really assumed I'd be in this kind of situation: I didn't think I'd ever have to replace R— my chocolatier. He was so perfect for the job that I'd completely let the issue go out of my mind . . ."

"Maybe," Ken said, "if you'd let me come down to your establishment and have a look around, I'll be able to get a better handle on what's actually needed."

Ms. Cruzeiros looked surprised by that. "Would you do that? I mean, I appreciate it, it's very kind of you if you have the time, but I mean, isn't it a little unusual—?"

"Not at all," Ken said. "If it helps us get the placement right for you, it's time well spent." He looked up as Malesha came out from the back room with yet another pile of files, which she handed to Tik. "Boss," he said, knowing perfectly well what the answer was going to be, "can I be spared for an assessment run?"

"Sure," Malesha said, "no problem. Tikram will hold the fort till you're free again. Call in when you're done."

Ken nodded and got up. *I think something's missing in her kitchen*, Malesha had said. *Meaning something besides the chocolatier— So what* else *is missing . . . ?*

He pulled the courier bag he used as a briefcase out of the bottom desk drawer and ushered Ms. Cruzeiros out. There was an empty yellow cab just coming

down the street toward them as they stepped up onto
the sidewalk—that was Tik's doing; of the three of
them, Tik had the best relationship with the wizardries
that affected the mechanical world, and empty taxis
would hunt him down in blizzards or the pouring rain.
Ken pulled the cab's door open, saw Ms. Cruzeiros
comfortably seated, then went around to the other
side and got in.

"Eighth and Jane," she said to the cabbie, as Ken
pulled his door closed. The cab took off with a lurch.
"We're a very small business," Ms. Cruzeiros said,
putting her own bag down between her feet as she
belted herself in. "And though we have a loyal following, in this market we don't dare do anything that's
going to endanger that." She ran one hand through
her hair, looking fretful. "Even if I had a new chocolatier on site this afternoon, it'd still take him or her
days to get broken in. And in this weather . . ."

"Is the weather a problem?" Ken said.

"For chocolate?" She laughed, sounding rueful.
"Weather's nearly always a problem if you're not
careful. If it's too hot, the chocolate won't temper cor-
rectly: if it's too cold, it seizes: if it's too humid, it
blooms . . . There are a hundred things that can go
wrong. And making chocolate in Manhattan is like
trying to do organic chemistry in a subway tunnel.
We're the only ones still doing it here. Everybody else
is out in Queens or up in Westchester somewhere, in
big climate-controlled factories . . ."

Ken got out his PDA and started scribbling hastily
on the handwriting-recognition part of its screen. It
would have taken much closer observation than Ms.
Cruzeiros was giving him at the moment for her to see
that he was writing, not in one of the PDA-proprietary
shorthand styles, but in the device-friendly form of the
wizardly Speech. Most of what he was going to need
to know about this situation he wouldn't find out until
he got down to where the trouble was, but in the
meantime the notes he took would all feed into what-

ever wizardry he found himself having to do. *Something missing,* Ken thought, while she talked on about cramped quarters and brownouts and landlord troubles, and on all of these he made notes. Then, *Make me a list,* he wrote in the Speech, *of everything you need for a successful chocolate shop.*

His writing vanished. *Going to be a long list . . .* said the PDA, the characters scrawling themselves across the little screen.

Better get started, then, Ken wrote.

The screen blanked. Ken tucked the PDA away. "I'm sorry," Ms. Cruzeiros said as the cab turned onto Fifth Avenue and headed downtown. "I'm kind of in ear-bending mode today . . ."

"Ms. Cruzeiros, please don't worry about it," Ken said. "It sounds like you've got reason to be."

"Ana, please," she said then.

"Ana. I'm Ken. I take it this vacancy came up rather suddenly."

"It did," she said. For a moment her mouth set into that unhappy, grim look again. Then she sighed. "I suppose I really should have seen it coming," Ana said. "But sometimes you just get taken by surprise—"

She went quiet again. Ken went back to "making notes." "How many square feet in your production area?" he asked.

She told him. It was small for any kind of business: *close quarters,* Ken thought. *Probably the kind of place where tempers have no trouble flaring when you're caught between commerce and art, with sugar on top.*

"Well," he said, "I'll look around, take some measurements, do some imaging of the workspace. The images can go up on our Web site if you like—it always helps with recruitment. Then make some calls. We could possibly have some people down here to talk to you this afternoon—"

"That would be great," Ana said as the cab pulled over on one side of Eighth Avenue, just shy of Jane Street. But as she got out and looked over at her premises, Ken got the feeling that it wasn't "great" at all: that this suddenly empty position was the last thing Ana wanted to fill.

She looked around her strangely, like someone trying to avoid having to make a damaging admission. Then she gave up. "I hate to say it," she said, "but we really do need to get someone in here in a hurry, because though I've been working with my chocolatier for maybe four years now, I haven't been able to get *anything* right in here since he left. Local conditions have been perfect for chocolate these past couple of days. I thought I could manage. But—" She shook her head. "It seizes, it blooms, it burns, it melts at the wrong speed: everything that can go wrong with chocolate has been going wrong. I find that, far from being able to cope, I'm actually completely incompetent."

And I thought she looked angry before, Ken thought. *I was mistaken* . . . This was one of those people who was harder on herself than on anyone around her. "Let's have a look around," he said.

The sign over the shopfront said THEOBROMA, in black on white, in a spidery font of the century before—and the sign was that old, too. Ancient green shades were pulled down over the windows on either side of the door, and inside the door itself. Ana unlocked the door and went in, not lifting the shade or flipping the CLOSED sign over. Ken went in behind her, gazing around at the beautiful old nineteenth-century tiles on the walls and the floor, all black and white, and the hammered-tin ceiling. The left side of the store was one long glass case full of beautiful chocolates, light, dark, shiny, cocoa'd, all in their little paper nests. The aroma was ravishing. "This was the last batch Rodrigo made before he left," she said. "The last decent batch we've got . . ."

The anxiety in her voice was painful. "Would whoever you hired be doing counter work as well?" Ken said.

"Absolutely," Ana said. "I'd love to be able to afford separate counter staff as well, but our profit margins are a little too close to the break-even line . . ."

She went toward the back of the store area, and Ken followed her. Through a bead-curtained door was more white tile, this time less decorative. The walls and floor gleamed with them, and around the edges of the room were huge slabs of white marble and many bizarre-looking machines. Ken wandered over to one of them, like a huge pot with a water jacket around it, and some kind of stirring mechanism inside.

"Tempering vat," Ana said. "The fountain wrap keeps the chocolate at a steady temperature after it's melted. The one over there with the big rollers in the drum, that's a conching machine. It rolls the melted chocolate around until the edges are worn off the cocoa crystals. That's how you get that really smooth mouthfeel on the best chocolate. . . ."

The description joined with the pervasive fragrance of the place to make his stomach growl. "This is a terrible place to be before lunch," Ken muttered, holding the PDA up to each wall in turn, ostensibly to take wireless measurements of the space.

"I guess it is, if you're not used to it," Ana said. "It's been a long time since I noticed . . ." She smiled, a sad smile, shaking her head. "When I first started helping my mom, ten years ago, before she died, I couldn't stay out of the stock. Afterward, I didn't have the time or the inclination to indulge myself. It's easy when you're working under someone who's known the ropes for half her life . . . harder when you don't have her around anymore and you're trying to find your own way. There were a lot of stumbles before Rodrigo came along and helped me get a handle on things. It's going to be strange working without him. . . ."

Ken lowered the PDA and scribbled on it. *Got what you need?*

Working, boss.

The screen went blank except for the familiar little turning-hourglass icon as the Manual went to work on an analysis of the surrounding space. "What kind of hours are you looking for from whoever applies for the position?" Ken said. "Full time? Part time?"

"Officially, all the hours God sends," Ana said, "but I guess it wouldn't be smart to put that in the ad." She went over to the conching machine, looked down into it. "That's the trouble with this work. It takes . . . commitment—"

She broke off again, and Ken hardly needed to be a wizard to hear that she wasn't talking about chocolate-making right then. He glanced down at the PDA's screen; as he did, it started to fill up with the graceful curving characters of the Speech, showing him the list that the PDA had been compiling for him. Ken tapped at it, bringing up for comparison the list of needful things that it had compiled on the way down in the cab. And the two lists tallied very closely together indeed . . .

. . . with one exception.

The missing object was indicated by a long string of characters in the Speech. Ken nearly whistled out loud as he read the description and started to understand its ramification. . . . *positive interventional effects usually relationship-based—affinity and effectiveness increases with duration of relationship and location, but is easily derailed by local physical or emotional disruption* . . . He nodded to himself. *I get it now,* Ken thought. *Wow, she really* does *have a problem.*

Ana had drifted up behind him and was looking curiously at the PDA. "Your handwriting's worse than mine," she said, seeing nothing but the indecipherable scribble the PDA showed any nonwizard who looked at it while it was in Manual mode. "Didn't think that was possible. You get WiFi on that?"

"Uh, yeah, when the conditions are right," Ken said. *Which is always* . . . "Just checking the home database here . . ."

But Ken was doing more than that. Every wizard has a specialty, whether it's the one that seems to come naturally when first practicing the Art as a child, or one taken up later in life to better match his or her outlook as an adult. Ken was now beginning to exercise his own specialty, listening hard to everything around him, listening to life—and he was hearing plenty of it. But the one kind of life he was listening for was not in his immediate range.

Not here. We're going to have to do a longer-range search. At least it won't have gone too far—

"All right," Ken said at last. "Ana, can I make a suggestion?"

"Sure."

"I don't think it's another chocolatier you need. What you need is to get your old one back."

That grim look attached itself to her face again. "I think that's going to be impossible," she said.

"I wouldn't bet on that just yet," Ken said.

The grimness started to go angry now. "Oh, really! And how would you know—"

"Just bear with me for a few moments while I explain," Ken said. "How long has the business been running now? I mean, including your parents, and theirs . . . from the very beginning?"

"A hundred and ten years," she said. "They came over from Spain."

Ken nodded. "Correct me if I'm wrong," he said, bending over to look under one of the cupboards, "but some of them were in chocolate even earlier than that? I think that was on the flyer that came with the cream eggs."

"That's true," Ana said. "The family was in confectionery right back into the 1600s."

"Around the time the Spanish brought chocolate back with them from the New World," Ken said. "Along with, I strongly suspect, some things that went with chocolate."

She looked at him a little strangely. "Chilies? For those you want the Mexican place down the street."

Ken shook his head. "Something a little different," he said. He bent over to look under the big conching machine.

"What are you looking for, roaches?" Ana sounded

indignant. "We're very careful here. We don't have roaches!"

"On the contrary," Ken said. "You *are* very careful, and as a result, you have very careful roaches. *Guys?*" he said in the Speech, and whistled.

Ana went ashen and stood absolutely still as about a hundred roaches came flowing out from under the baseboards, all together, gathered into a little group, and looked up at her and Ken.

"See," Ken said, getting down on one knee and putting down a finger to one of them, which promptly climbed up on it and sat there waving its antennae, "they know you're so careful about cleaning up and never leaving sweet things around because you really hate having to kill anything. So they're careful to stay well out of sight inside the walls, and never show any sign that'll make you have to call the exterminators. However—" he cocked an ear at the roach sitting on his finger, "—they *do* like to hide in your wall space when the Chinese place around the corner has gotten so filthy in the back that the Board of Health guys descend on them. Then, when the coast is clear, they go back. They hate the cooks over there, because most of the time they ignore the roaches completely, except when the City's about to show up. You, however, are consistent. Roaches like consistency."

Ana was standing there with her mouth open. Finally, she found presence of mind enough to close it. "Horse whisperers I knew about," she said. "*Roach* whisperers . . . ? Only in New York."

Ken resisted the urge to roll his eyes. He'd been called worse things. "I wouldn't define my role that narrowly," he said, and let the roach on his finger back down onto the floor. "Let's just say I'm a student of the art of conversation. I listen to anything that has something to say to me. Mostly animals, though I do inorganics occasionally, just to keep my hand in." He looked down at the roaches. *"Okay, guys and gals,"* he said, *"back to business now. And leave those wires alone."*

Ana watched the roaches vanish under the baseboards again, and swallowed. "And here I thought you
were in personnel," she said.

"I am!" Ken said. "They're personnel. Just not
human personnel."

"Oh, yeah," Ana said. "Who do they work for?"

"Life," Ken said, and went over to the sink to wash
his hands. "The same as you and me. They do it the
way they were built to. We do it —" He pulled a
paper towel, dried his hands, and chucked it in a
nearby trash container. "Differently. And some of us
do it *very* differently. Which is what I'm getting to
here." He looked around the candymaking kitchen
one last time. "Because, taking everything together—
the nature of your business, your reputation, the way
the place looks, and the history of your company—
something is definitely missing."

"What?"

"Your xocolotl."

"My zoco*what?*"

"Lotl. The creature that's been living in this building, maybe in this kitchen, for the past hundred years.
The one that helps make your chocolate come out
right even when the conditions are all against you."
She was staring at him openmouthed, but this was no
time to let her get her disbelief going again. "I have
a feeling your mother probably knew about it. Maybe
she meant to tell you and just never got around to it.
And after that— You didn't think it was *just* luck
that's pulled you through, all those times when things
should really have gone wrong, did you?"

She frowned. "Excuse me! I thought skill might
have had *something* to do with it—"

"Of course it does. That's the only reason a xocolotl
would ever have chosen to stay with you. They're intimately associated with chocolate culture . . . have been
since human beings discovered it, and them."

Ana looked understandably confused. "There are
lots of animals associated with human food production," Ken said. "You wouldn't be surprised to see a

horse or an ox plowing, would you? Or a dog herding sheep? This is like that. It's not quite a symbiotic relationship. But some creatures just seem to be particularly well suited for some kinds of business, or just one kind. You've heard about those moths so specifically evolved that they can drink from only one kind of flower—and the flower's come to depend on them in turn? There are similarities here. There are other animals that do jobs nearly as specialized. And still others that don't so much *do* anything . . . but their presence, or absence, is felt. They're catalysts, in a way. In the xocolotl's case, its presence has a subtle effect on your ingredients, the surroundings in which they're kept . . . the people who work with them."

"Oh, come on," Ana said after a moment. "It sounds like one of those fake sciences, like astrology! Mysterious vague influences—"

"Like gravity wells?" Ken said. "Same principle. Some things bend space-time out of shape in strange ways. And gravity's weak, in the great scheme of things. Some things are *much* better at warping space. How many times have you gone looking for your house keys lately and not been able to find them?"

Ana suddenly looked rather thoughtful.

"This is what we're after," Ken said. "At least to start with." He showed her the PDA.

The screen was showing an image of something like an iguana, but mottled in ivory and chocolate-brown, in patterns that were vaguely reminiscent of a Gila monster's. "You haven't seen anything like that around here?"

Ana shook her head. "I think I'd remember."

"It's been here, though . . . and for quite a long time. I can feel it. However, it left suddenly a few days ago."

Ana blushed again, once more looking furious. "Whatever happens with Rodrigo," Ken said, "you're going to have to find the xocolotl and bring it home. It's lived here a long time; it's repaid you for its security with at least some of your success. But it also doesn't know any other way of life, and it won't last long out on the streets. Once it's back here, things will start to go right again."

She just looked at him for several seconds.

Uh-oh, the PDA said.

Then Ana let out a breath. "Who am I to doubt a man who can talk to roaches?" she said.

"If I were anyone else," Ken said, "I might have mistaken that for irony. Do you have something you can change into? This isn't going to be the kind of work you want to do in Manolos."

She caught his glance at her shoes, and grinned. "Wait here," Ana said, and vanished through a side door and up a flight of stairs. A few minutes later she came down in sneakers and jeans and a T-shirt. "Where are we going?"

"Not far," Ken said as they went out, and Ana locked the door behind them. "No more than a four-block radius."

"Who'd have thought the Twilight Zone was so nearby," Ana muttered as they headed down the street.

It took nearly an hour and easily a couple of miles of walking for Ken to get anything out of the PDA but repetitions of *Cooler . . . a little warmer . . . no, cooler again.* The problem was partly the xocolotl's relatively slow metabolism, and partly the location where it had chosen to lose itself, the multitude of surrounding life signs tended to drown its own signature out. But three blocks away from Theobroma, the PDA suddenly said, *One block south. One block west.*

"Does it see it?" Ana said, looking over Ken's shoulder.

"Not clearly, but we're close," he said. "Your xoco must have been really put out to go this far."

Ana said nothing for a moment. "This is so weird," she said. "Magical lizards hiding in people's kitchens. Some kind of chocolate elemental—"

"It might be too much to call them magical. And elementals are usually a little more, uh, confronta-tional."

"But where does the xoco come from? Is it some kind of alien?"

"I don't think so," Ken said as they crossed the last street onto the block they were heading for. "But there's an alien connection to the chocolate. Do you believe in UFOs?"

Ana stared at him, completely flummoxed. "I have no idea. I haven't given it much thought."

"But you know a lot of other people do."

"Well, sure."

"But doesn't it seem a little strange when you think of it?" He glanced down at the PDA and turned to his left down the block. "Here we are right out at the edge of our galaxy: a nothing-special little star system out by itself. Why would aliens be coming all the way out here to see us?"

She gave Ken a rather cockeyed look. "You're going to tell me, I suspect."

"Oh, never *tell*," Ken said. "Suggest, though. I'm going to suggest that we are the only source of something worth coming thousands of light-years out of your way for. Cocoa beans . . ."

Ana burst out laughing. "You are completely nuts!"

"Possibly," Ken said. "But you're the one with the store called 'Theobroma'. Food of the Gods, huh? Well, what if the Great Space Gods that some people carry on about only came here for the chocolate? There's your question for the day." He stopped by a wire-fence doorway, slipping the PDA into his pocket. He didn't need its help now. "What's back there?"

She peered through the grating. "A convenience store. No, wait, there's a bakery there, too: the back door's down at the end of the alley." Ana shook the gate slightly, frustrated. "No use, it's locked."

"Not for long," Ken said. He bent down as if to look through the keyhole. *"Buddy,"* he whispered in the Speech, *"do me a favor here, will you? We're on a mission of mercy."*

The lock's bolt threw itself. Ken pushed the gate

open very softly, trying to keep it from creaking, and
held it open for Ana: she slipped through, staring at
him again. "How did you do that?"

"I asked nicely," Ken said.

"Magic!" Ana said.

"Same thing," Ken said. "Ssh! Come on."

They made their way down the alley, past the piled-
up trash outside the back of the convenience store.
"Smell that?"

"Wish I didn't," Ana said.

"No argument. But I don't mean the garbage.
There's something else here . . ."

Her eyes got wider as she sniffed. "*Cocoa* . . . ?"

"Your xoco's been down here," Ken said. "Come
on."

They went on past the steel back door of the convenience store, farther down the alley. More garbage—
"You're kidding about the UFOs, though, right?"

"You're just not going to take me seriously, are
you?" Ken shook his head, smiling slightly. The smile
was only partly for her: inside his head he could feel
what they'd been looking for, that slow, dark, bitter-
sweet tone of mind. "We're getting close now. Just
follow my lead—"

He paused in front of the last steel door in the alley,
knocked. After a moment bolts were thrown, and the
door opened a crack.

To the face that looked out, Ken simply held up the
PDA, knowing that its Manual function was causing it
to display itself as whatever ID would be most useful
in this situation. "Can we come in?"

The door opened. As he tucked the PDA away,
Ken snuck a peek and saw that it was pretending to
be a New York City Health Department ID. He re-
pressed a grin as the head baker came to meet them.
He was a large, florid Italian gentleman of the kind
usually depicted in standup signs outside pizzerias, the
only difference being that he was wearing a gauze-
backed black-and-white-checked food service cap, and
whites that were even whiter in places with flour.

"You guys were in here three days ago, and we had
a clean bill of health. What now?"

"We're looking for lizards," Ken said.

"Lizards?"

"There are some loose in the neighborhood," Ken
said. "They're fond of food service environments like
this—nice warm places with quiet spots to hide.
Mostly brown, about a foot long, look like iguanas.
Won't take more than a few minutes to check the
place. Do you mind?"

He was ready to drop into the Speech for extra
persuasiveness, if he had to, but there was no need.
What the PDA looked like was already enough to do
the job. "Quiet!" the boss snorted, for across the room
a gigantic kneading machine was roaring away and
making enough noise for a cement mixer.

"Thanks," Ken said, and made his way in, with Ana
close behind him. The staff got out of their way, looking at them with wary interest.

Ken held still for a moment, listening hard, and finally found what he was looking for; then he checked
the cupboards down the side of one wall, first, before
opening the middle one and seeing, as if surprised, the
patterned shape back in the shadows. *"I'm here to
take you home, fella,"* he said.

I don't know you. You go 'way and leave me be,
said the xocolotl.

He looked over his shoulder. "Ana?"

She came over, got down beside him, looked into
the cupboard curiously. "Is that—"

Ken nodded. The short-spined iguana head turned,
and one eye regarded Ana, chameleonlike, from several angles, one after another.

I missed you, it said.

Her eyes went wide. "I heard that!"

"It's not unusual," Ken said, "once you believe
you can."

Let's go back, the xocolotl said. *The chocolate here
is bad.*

"See that? No problem at all," Ken said. "Here,

stick him in here and we'll take him home." He held
out the courier bag.

"Do they bite?" Ana said.

"If he bites *you*," Ken said, "I'd be astonished."

Carefully, Ana reached in and picked up the xocolotl. The bakery staff, standing at a safe distance to
watch, made impressed noises as Ana brought him
out. "Not poisonous, huh?" said the head baker.

Ken stood up. "Not to her, anyway," he said.

Ana slipped the xocolotl into the bag. Ken caught
another glimpse of that roving eye, which finally fixed
on Ana again. *No more fighting,* it said.

She looked at Ken with a slightly stricken expression. "How do I explain—" she whispered.

He shook his head. "One thing at a time," Ken
said. He helped her up. Behind them, the head baker
was nodding in the resigned manner of a man who's
glad that he's not to be cited for having a concealed
lizard on the premises. "Thanks, good-bye. You want
a cake to take with you? No? Okay, good-bye—"

The door slammed behind them. "Why didn't you
want the cake?" Ken said, amused.

"Because he's right about one thing," Ana said as
they made their way back down to the alley gate.

"Oh?"

"The chocolate there *is* bad."

As they walked up in front of Theobroma again,
Ana suddenly stopped, looking at the door. The
shades were down inside the windows, still, but Ken
could see the one inside the door moving, as if someone had closed that door hastily, or brushed against it.

"Oh, no," Ana said softly. "Not another break-in! We
had one last month! And in the middle of the day—"

"No," Ken said, "somehow I don't think so." *But
just in case*— he said to the PDA.

I've got three defensive spells ready, the PDA said.
Normal shield, high-yield shield, and ramrod—

Set up number two, Ken said, *for two people and a
lizard. Ready?*

Go.

Ken went to the door, softly spoke the lock open, looked over his shoulder at Ana. She nodded.

They went in.

There was no one in the front of the store. But in the back, in the kitchen, someone was moving around.

Ana went past Ken into the kitchen so quickly that he couldn't stop her—could only follow, in a hurry, getting ready to use that shield if need be. But in the doorway he stopped, still a few feet behind Ana.

In the middle of the kitchen stood a large, broad-shouldered man possessing the kind of dark and improbably good looks that normally left Ken feeling annoyed, as their presence usually meant that some pretty lady he'd been hitting on was going to waltz out the door with their owner. But in this case, the guy looked both infuriated and embarrassed, much defusing the initial effect of his rampant handsomeness.

"I'm sorry," he said. "I'm sorry. I had to come back. There was something I had to take care of, something missing—"

"Could it possibly," Ana said, "have been this?"

She had dropped the courier bag, and was holding out the xocolotl.

Rodrigo stared. *"Where did you find him?"*

"Under a proofing cabinet, down in Richter's," she said. "He was upset."

Rodrigo stared at her. "But how could you tell that he—I mean, he can't—"

"I called in a consultant," Ana said. "Not the kind I thought I was getting, I can tell you that . . ."

Rodrigo stared at Ken.

"I am on errantry," Ken said, "and I greet you."

Rodrigo's mouth dropped open. "You know the words!"

Now it was Ana's turn to stare. "What words?"

"The words the old *brujo* spoke to me when I told him I was looking for a place in this strange city where a xocolotl lived, there had to be one place at least, and he said, Search all these places till you find the one where someone smiles at you—"

Ana was staring at Rodrigo. "Whoa, whoa, time out, you were dating me for my *lizard?*"

"No, of course not, but you were here, too, and when we started to work together, and I got to know you, I—"

"And we worked so closely together all that time, and you never told me about the xocolotl! We got so close, and—"

"I couldn't tell you! *How* could I tell you?"

"You said you could tell me *anything*! Everything!"

"But not this! This is crazy! This is *magic*! How could I tell you, you would have thought I was—"

"Never mind, where did you go, why did you just go storming off like that, where have you *been*—"

"Nowhere, without you, nowhere, I—"

Suddenly the xocolotl had been deposited on one of the nearby spreading slabs, and the two were very much together in the middle of the room. Ken turned away, scribbling at the PDA. The voices behind him fell silent.

Tell me when it's safe to turn around.

You mean you're not *listening, Mister I Can Hear Everything?*

Ken blushed. *No. So you just keep an eye on things.*

The clinch broke. "I am so, so sorry. I didn't mean any of those things I said."

"Oh, neither did I! I'm so sorry, too."

"I panicked, that was all. I didn't know what to say—"

"I panicked, too. That was why I ran, and I—"

"And I— Yes. That's all: yes."

"Oh, I am so glad. So glad—"

It was once again turning into the kind of conversation that left you feeling that you needed a scorecard, not to mention a comfortable sofa and a six-pack. "Excuse me!" Ken said.

They both looked at him.

"I take it," Ken said to Rodrigo, "that that's the end of this particular work stoppage on your part?"

"It will never happen again," Rodrigo said fervently.

"And I take it," Ken said to Ana, "that you're willing to take him back on?"

She smiled slowly, turned back to Rodrigo. "Permanently," she said.

The xocolotl, ignored, climbed slowly down from the spreading slab and vanished under the pedestal of the tempering bath. From inside the wall, Ken heard a faint insectile cheer.

"Then my work here is done," Ken said. And the two embracing figures in the back kitchen never even noticed as Ken eased his way out the locked front door, whispered the lock shut again behind him, and went to find the inevitable cab that would be waiting to take him back uptown.

"No sale, boss," he said as he walked in the door twenty minutes later.

"No?" Malesha came out of the back, pulling her scarf off and shaking the cornrowed braids down with an expression of weary relief. She plunked herself down in her chair. "You had to do an intervention, though . . . ?"

"One of your big flashy spells, I bet," Tik said, leaning over the counter and disposing of the last of a hamburger from the bar-and-grill up the street. "Probably met the Lone Power in single combat and kicked His sorry butt right down to the Bowery."

Ken dumped his bag by his desk, shook his head. "Nope. Talked a couple of locks open, did some remote sensing, faked my way into a bakery. Oh, and found a lost xocolotl."

He expected some kind of response at that, but got nothing. "And what about the thing that was missing?" Malesha said.

Ken's eyes went wide. He stared at Malesha in a moment's panic that he had missed something. "You

mean there was something missing *besides* the
xocolotl?"

"Only the loooooove, baby," Malesha said, and put
her feet up on the counter. "Nothing but the
looooove. . . ."

Tik guffawed. Ken just looked at her as she beck-
oned to her coffee cup, and it sailed across the room
to her.

"I bow, Leesh," he said. "I bow to the master."
And he turned back to his desk before she could see
the grin—because she was right, as usual.

And the bells . . . those, too, turned out to be nothing but an echo of what was to come. Three months
later he was standing outside the Cathedral of St. John
the Divine, helping about five hundred other people
throw rice at Ana and Rodrigo.

And the wedding cake was chocolate.

CHOCOLATE ALCHEMY

by Lisa Silverthorne

TUCKED in an obscure corner of Pike's Market, Starling Chocolates stood in shadow beneath the Public Market sign. Seattle smelled of brine, a hint of sweetness in the gray morning air as Orriana Starling pressed her finger to the door's old brass lock. Sorceresses had no real need for locks, but they kept people honest. The purple wood door, carved with griffins and mermaids, creaked open and she stepped inside.

The handful of business cards and envelopes, slipped through the door's mail slot and scattered like rune stones across the floor, sent a cold chill through her stomach. They'd found her again.

"Lights," she said in a soft voice, and the small space lit with harsh fluorescent light. "Softer, please."

The lights responded by giving her little storefront a soft shimmery glow, illuminating the corporate logos on some of the envelopes which filled her with dread. Sooner or later, the corporate executives always found her little shop, "tempting" her with franchise offers and buyouts. She sighed. Even though she'd gotten attached to Seattle with its deep teal waterfront and white-capped mountain, she'd have to move again.

Orriana stepped over the pile of mail, willing the envelopes and cards into smoke that drifted up toward the ceiling and curled around the ceiling fan. She walked across the black-and-white tiles to the Victorian display cases that sat in the center of the room. The scent of freshly poured chocolate warmed the air. She stepped behind the counter and glanced into the pristine kitchen where she pretended to make her chocolate. It hadn't been used for the eight years she'd owned the shop.

Conjuring chocolate was big business in the magical—and human—circles she traveled. She'd collected chocolate memories from the Aztecs to the Swiss, creating chocolate from every moment in history. Mundane and magical adored her chocolates.

She clapped her hands, and faeries flitted through the room like illuminated butterflies, ready to restock the chocolates she conjured. Those gossamer wings held the magical light, casting an otherworldly glow through the store as the faeries nestled among plants, figurines, and cobalt glass jars.

In front of the window were four round tables. Orriana imagined fresh Gerbera daisies on each table, and they appeared one by one in glass bowls. A faerie with pale mint hair fluttered past Orriana, tugging at Orriana's blonde hair.

"Don't you have chocolate to stock, Peri?" Orriana asked with a smile as the faerie giggled, flitting toward a mermaid statue on the shelf.

Peri turned over the open sign, then flitted past the wooden tables. She hovered behind the counter as Orriana slid open the nearest case to check stock. Three shelves held pastel dishes heaped with truffles and turtles in a variety of dark and milk chocolates. Standard mundane fare. But her magical offerings were her favorite. Among her best sellers were chocolate travel squares, moment truffles, and regret turtles. One bite of the milk chocolate travel squares propelled the connoisseur to the French Riviera or Christmas in New York. Renaissance Italy. A taste of the marketplace, a sweet hint of its music, the rich chocolate painting a Tuscan blue sky and creamy marble.

She had a square for every region, every time in

the world, including a "no place like home" square.
Milk, dark, or white, depending on who ate them. Moment truffles brought back the most wondrous moments of life to be savored bite by dark chocolate bite,
a soft chocolate ganache to fade the memory and finish with warm mellow flavor. Regret turtles took the
crunch of toasted pecans and the hard edge of a difficult memory—a moment wished to be taken back—
and softened it with buttery caramel and delicate
milk chocolate.

Orriana had eaten a lot of regret turtles this past
year, so much of her magical life coming back to haunt
her. She'd moved the shop four times, changed the
name in every location, hoping to cut herself off from
these corporate intrusions. Sooner or later, though,
they found her again. But she refused to give up her
passion—her chocolate shop.

Every time that bell above the door chimed, a part
of her cringed, fearing the parade of suits would saun-
ter through that door, professing the deal of a lifetime
and demanding she give up her independence to wor-
ship at the corporate altar.

As if.

The bell above the door trembled, and Orriana's
gaze darted toward it, her heart hammering her throat.

A man walked in, looking a little lost, a little unsure
of himself. His dark hair was thick and wavy, and he
wore an expensive olive suit, cream shirt, polished
shoes, and silk tie. Orriana sighed. Corporate from
every angle.

"May I help you?" she asked, fiddling with the
sheer lavender cuffs of her blouse.

Who was it this time? Jenson Brothers, Limited?
The Pyramid Group? Maubry Enterprises? They'd all
been trying to buy out her little shop for years, wanting to process and package her chocolates for their
own huge profits. Without her magic, the magic that
brought this chocolate into being, she wished them
great success.

But his smile was different from the others. He

glanced around the little shop and his brown eyes mirrored his warm smile as he took in the smells and magical ambiance that was Starlings. A hint of recognition touched his kind brown eyes. He had no idea what he saw was magic, but he felt something, smelled something more than money. Most of the mundanes missed that little spark.

"May I help you?" she repeated, leaning on the counter with her elbows.

"This place," he said, his gaze meeting hers with an intensity that unsettled her. "I had no idea." He turned in a slow circle, his gaze on the figurines, the lights, the daisies, and finally the display case of chocolates. His eyes widened. "I've never seen anything like this."

Neither had she. A mundane with a clue. A sense of something grander than himself. But quite nice to look at, she had to admit.

"Thanks," said Orriana. "Everyone loves chocolate."

He dropped down on his haunches, studying the bowls of truffles with wide eyes. Some chocolates were hand-painted, others dusted with lacy powdered sugars. When he looked up, his gaze met hers again, a steamy expression that warmed her as he rose.

He was quite attractive—for a corporate type.

"You've got to be Orriana Starling," he said, his voice soft and quiet. Dreamy, she decided. She liked dreamy.

He extended his hand. Orriana reached out and shook it, noting the brightening of the lights in the room and the twitter of the faeries as she drew her hand back. What were they giggling about?

"That's me," Orriana answered. "And you are?"

He stared at her, unblinking for several moments. "Oh," he said, looking away to slide a leather card case out of his pocket. She frowned when he handed her a crisp white business card.

"Doug Ackerfield. I—I'm with Maubry Enterprises."

Orriana leaned against the counter, smiling as Mr. Ackerfield read his own business card. Couldn't remember his own name. Good, the wards she'd set at the door were still working, keeping the corporate intrusions out of her business.

"I'm here to follow up on an offer my company recently made to you, to franchise Starling Chocolates across the—"

Orriana held up her hand. "As I already told Mr. Maubry's lawyers, I'm not interested in a franchise or any sort of marketing opportunities, Mr. Ackerfield."

"Why not?" he asked, holding out his hands. "This place would be a runaway hit across the country. You could make millions! Don't you recognize its growth potential?"

Or the trouble it would cause her? Going national with her conjured chocolate meant revealing her magic to the world. Something she could never do. Besides, she thought with a smile, she could make millions right now, with a flick of her fingers.

Time to send Mr. Ackerfield on his way.

Orriana reached into the case and picked up a butter-yellow dish of truffles, each painted with a pale yellow M on top. One moment truffle for Mr. Ackerfield.

Using tongs, she picked up a truffle with an orange M and held it out to Johnny Corporate, wishing she'd grabbed a regret turtle instead. He seemed like a nice enough guy, and so attractive, but moment truffles had a way of distracting people. And, right now, Mr. Ackerfield needed to be distracted from this franchise nonsense.

"Here's a chocolate on the house," she said. "Maybe this will help you better understand my product's unique, uh—properties?"

He cupped his hand, a black Movado watch around his wrist, and Orriana laid the truffle in his palm.

"Thank you," he said as he picked up the truffle and pressed it to his mouth.

He took a bite and closed his eyes. Orriana held

back a chuckle as she watched the pleasant memory roll across his face, lines and tautness relaxing with every shift of his jaw. The last two executives from Maubry Enterprises had left in a daze after one of those chocolates, forgetting all about why they'd even come. She didn't dare roll out the memory-smudging caramels. Too early for those, she thought with a grin, watching Mr. Ackerfield lost in some cherished memory.

At last, his eyes rolled open, and he stared at her a moment. With reverence. He reached across the counter and laid his hand against hers, and the heat burned through her.

"I'm not sure what's in these chocolates," he said in a quiet, raspy voice. "Would you have coffee with me tonight? To—to talk about the chocolates, I mean. And the franchise opportunity."

Orriana felt a force drawing her to this man, and before she could stop herself, she answered yes. No! That should have been an emphatic no. What was the matter with her?

He grinned, laugh lines curving across his cheeks. "See you tonight. At six, right? That's what time you close?"

Orriana nodded and watched the poor man shuffle out of the store, still a little dazed, his feet practically floating.

"You gave him the wrong truffle," a soprano voice replied, hovering against her ear.

She turned toward Peri, the mint-haired faerie hovering beside her, arms crossed and that smug Fey look on her face.

"What do you mean? It was a moment truffle."

The little faerie shook her head and pointed toward the case. "You gave him a love wish truffle."

Orriana's eyes narrowed, a cold feeling growing in the pit of her stomach. "No, I didn't. It was a moment truffle."

Peri thrust her hands to her hips, shaking her head slowly as she flitted into the case and landed beside the yellow bowl. She pointed at two truffles with orange Ms painted on them.

"See? M for moment truffle." Orriana crossed her arms, summoning her best smug look.

Again, Peri shook her head. She reached toward the truffle and turned it upside down. "No. Yellows are moment truffles. This one's orange, so it's a W. For love wish truffle—remember? You set up the crazy letters and colors, not me."

Orriana cringed. Oh, no—what had she done? Love wish truffles made the diner fall in love with the first person they saw. She never put love wish truffles into the case. How had they gotten there? What would she do now? She'd meant to make Mr. Ackerfield go away, not fall in love with her.

"How did those get into the case? I made them as an experiment."

Peri shrugged. "You said to stock all the chocolates, so we did."

"Me and my big mouth." Sighing, Orriana plucked the love wish truffles out of the case and placed them in a paper bag.

"Reverse it," said Peri as she flitted out of the case, turning circles in the air. "Give him a breakup butter cream."

Orriana groaned. Breakup butter creams weren't exactly items she stocked in her case either (like love wish truffles). It wouldn't do to randomly break up people's relationships any more than it would to get perfect strangers to fall in love. She had a few hours before closing. Plenty of time to conjure a tray of breakup butter creams for Mr. Ackerfield.

Orriana called in a friend to run the counter while she conjured recipes and magic by the old hearth beyond the kitchen, determined to counteract the love potion she'd let loose on poor Mr. Ackerfield.

Every time the bell rang with its soft distant chime, her concentration faded a little. The store smelled warm with cocoa butter and steamy milk as she conjured the hot chocolate mixture, warmed with a white-gold magical flame. Sugar sweetened the air as she materialized a copper pot. It sat on the old hearth bricks, glistening with silky chocolate as she whispered every love spell counteractant she remembered. She poured rose water and unrequited maiden tears into the pot, casting doubts and her own images of the perfect man into the mixture, stirring it with a heavy heart and a wooden spoon.

After a time, a pale halo clung to the mixture. Even as she stirred it, Orriana felt sad, felt a loss as the mixture darkened. She poured the chocolate into a mold of roses to flow over the harmless balls of butter cream filling. A sprinkle of magic not to melt the centers. After they cooled, she'd dust them with powdered faerie sugar through a maiden's lace veil. At least leave the poor man a whisper of hope.

When she finally looked at the clock on the wall, it was nearly six. Mr. Ackerfield would be here soon, for coffee and a breakup butter cream.

"Orriana?"

Her friend Maddie walked through the kitchen and stood beside the old fireplace, thick red curls crowning her head. Maddie knew some of her secrets. The faeries even listened to her, once in a while.

"What's up?" Orriana asked, a bridal veil in her hand.

She draped it over the tray of butter creams that hovered in the air and dusted sparkles of sugar through the veil.

"There's a Doug Ackerfield here for you."

Orriana smiled.

"I'll be right there."

"He's really cute," Maddie whispered.

Orriana waved her off and continued sifting sugar. Sure, mundanes were cute, but they weren't the kind of creature sorceresses went into business with—especially the business of magic. They were either greedy or terrified by it.

When the breakup butter creams were finished, Orriana snapped her fingers and sent the veil away. Grabbing a small red plate, she set two butter creams on it and carried it out front, through the spotless kitchen.

Doug Ackerfield stood there in a gray windbreaker, distressed blue polo shirt, loafers, and jeans, those brown eyes smoldering, a hint of chocolate at the corner of his mouth. He held out a bouquet of flowers to her: pink roses, sunflowers, foxglove, purple statice, and Gerbera daisies. She felt a twinge in her chest at his smile and those flowers—her breath caught.

He took a step toward her as she walked out from behind the counter.

"These are for you," he said, holding out the flowers.

Orriana set the plate on the nearest table and took the flowers. That's when she saw the two Tully's coffee cups on the table.

"Thank you, they're beautiful."

She reached out and squeezed his hand. Immediately cringing. What was she doing? She was supposed to get rid of him. Not encourage him. Poor mundane. Touched by magic and didn't even know it. Like being hypnotized at a party—one clap and he acted like a chicken. Besides, she wouldn't give up her shop over a nice smile and some flowers.

He motioned toward the coffee. "I got a couple of mochas," he said and sat down.

Orriana turned the open sign to closed as Maddie opened the door to leave. She shook her head. This guy was probably supposed to get a franchise agreement signed, not moon over a sorceress and some mochas.

"Call me later," said Maddie with a wink and a nod toward the table. "I gave him a couple more chocolate samples."

"Go home, troublemaker," said Orriana, shooing her outside.

She turned toward the door, whispered "lock," and

called up a glass vase before sitting down across from
Mr. Ackerfield. He had the warmest brown eyes she'd
ever seen. For a mundane. She set the flowers on the
table and picked up her coffee cup. He wiped his
mouth with a napkin and sipped his coffee.

"So, Mr. Ackerfield," Orriana said with a smile.
"What would you like to know about my chocolates?"

She took a sip of hot coffee as he stared at her a
moment longer.

"Please, call me Doug."

He turned the red plate around, studying the butter
creams. "How do you do it?" he asked and finally
looked up at her again. "I've tasted Godiva, Valrhona,
and Scharffen Berger, but they pale by comparison.
There's something . . . wondrous about these
chocolates."

"Listen, Mr. Ackerfield—"

"Doug," he said and laid his coffee-warm hand on
hers, the faint scent of his spicy cologne mixing with
the scent of chocolate and coffee. He leaned toward
her. "These chocolates are almost as wondrous as
you."

Before she could stop him, his lips touched hers,
tasting warm with mocha, and for a moment, she let
down her guard, let go of the wards she kept in place
against the mundancs she'd always tried to avoid.
They lived a different life, wanted different things—
at least she'd thought so until now.

No, she couldn't do this. Besides, it wasn't real.
She'd forced the love wish on him. For an instant,
she'd hexed herself into believing it, too. That this
strange attraction she'd felt was real. It was hollow.

She pulled back from him, a hand to her mouth,
staring into his fever-bright eyes. His face reddened.

"I'm sorry," he said, his gaze falling to the table. "I
shouldn't have done that. My apologies."

Orriana sighed. After all, he had come to talk about
franchises. Sooner or later, all mundanes went back
to the subject of money.

"It's all right," said Orriana. Time to end this before it got messy. She slid the red plate toward him. "Have a butter cream. It's a new product."

He glanced at the plate again, hesitated, and then picked up a chocolate.

"I'd intended to talk to you about franchises," he said. "But, honestly—I don't see any way we can capture the essence of Starling Chocolates. It's got a magic to it that I don't understand."

Orriana's mouth fell open. "What do you mean?"

He lifted the butter cream toward his mouth, but stopped.

"These can't be packaged," he said, holding the chocolate up to the light. He shook his head. "They're one of a kind."

What? She stared at him in surprise. A mundane turning down money?

"We can't standardize these chocolates," he said with a sigh. "Maubry's crazy to even try it." He lifted the chocolate toward his mouth. "And I won't turn these works of art into fast food."

Orriana reached out and stayed his hand. "You won't?"

He shook his head, his gaze haunting as he stared into her eyes. And she felt lost there a moment, somewhere between mundanes and magic.

"Can't," he said in a half-whisper. "How could we capture the best moments of someone's life and suspend them in chocolate to melt on my tongue? And then package it?"

He lifted the butter cream to his mouth again.

"Wait," she said, a hand on his, holding back the chocolate. He couldn't eat this now. She wouldn't let him.

He frowned. "Why?"

But staring at him, those bright eyes, the laugh lines curving around his cheeks, she knew it was all fake. She was fooling herself with her own magic. In a few days, when the love wish wore off, he'd be back spouting franchise opportunities like the rest of them. Her chest tightened. No, she had to give him the butter cream.

"Never mind," she said, trying to mask her regret. "Go ahead and try it."

Doug lifted it to his mouth, but stopped. "I'd love to see how you make these."

Her eyes widened. Was he here to steal recipe secrets, too?

"I couldn't—"

"I'm not after your secrets, Orriana." He set the chocolate on the plate, and Orriana felt her body tense. Why wasn't he eating the chocolate? "I just . . ." He sighed, staring down at his hands. "I just want to get to know you better. And this place that's clearly your passion."

He'd feel much better after eating the butter cream. She wouldn't, but he would.

She nodded toward the plate. "Eat your chocolate, and I'll show you how I make these butter creams."

Grinning, he picked up the chocolate, at last pressing it to his lips. Orriana cringed as he took a bite of the butter cream. She rose from the chair and moved toward the counter. When she turned around, he was on his knees, looking pale and shaky.

"Doug?" she called.

When he didn't respond, she hurried over to him, a hand on his arm.

"Doug? Are you all right?"

Never had she seen such a forlorn look on a mundane's face before. He looked up at her through glassy eyes.

"I'm not sure," he replied.

Orriana helped him to his feet and sat him back in the chair. Above them, faeries flitted across the ceiling in soft shimmers.

"Man, I'm seeing stars," he muttered, then turned his gaze to Orriana. "Why am I here?"

She winced, remembering that warm coffee kiss

he'd left on her lips, and for a moment, she'd thought she could stay here in Seattle with her little shop and something she hadn't known in a very long time.

"Oh, I remember," he said and reached into his jacket pocket.

He laid a folded packet of papers on the table.

"Maubry is prepared to offer you a substantial deal on Starling Chocolates, to open shops across the country. In malls and other upscale shopping centers."

Orriana snatched up the papers and thrust them back at him. "As I said before, I'm not interested, Mr. Ackerfield. We're closed now. Please leave."

Still looking confused, he rose from the chair and moved toward the door. Orriana flicked her index finger at the door, unlocking it. He opened the door and stood staring around the room with its shimmers of faerie lights.

"Have a good night, Orriana," he replied, a hint of sadness in his tone.

"Good-bye, Mr. Ackerfield."

He walked out into the twilight, and Orriana felt the sting of moisture in her eyes. There had been so many possibilities in him, so many moments in that kiss. Wrought by her own magic, but it was as phony as the corporations pretending to do her a favor. It was time to leave. Find another quiet corner of the world. She'd done it before.

"You're making a mistake," Peri whispered as she flitted past Orriana's head, turning circles in the air.

"I'll say," Orriana snapped. "Whose dumb idea was it to employ nosy faeries?"

Peri twittered, her laugh like wind chimes. "You're just angry because you know I'm right."

Orriana propped her hands on her hips, glaring at Peri who hovered just out of her reach. "I got rid of him like the others, but he won't be the last. It's time to leave now."

"What if he is the last?"

Peri's words cut through her.

"It's not the corporations you're running from, is it?"

Was she right? Orriana laid her hand against her mouth, remembering her almost electric attraction to Doug. That kiss had done more than any magic she could have conjured. Was she more afraid of Doug than of Maubry Enterprises?

"But it wasn't real," she said to Peri as the little faerie circled her head. "It was a love wish truffle. You saw the effect the breakup butter cream had. It wasn't real."

"Prove it," said Peri, turning a few more circles. She raced toward the ceiling, scattering magical smoke in her wake. Remnants of the morning's junk mail that she'd incinerated.

The coils of smoke undulated around Orriana's head. Prove it? What if that meant betraying her magic to the mundanes? Was Doug worth that risk?

She walked over to the display case and reached into the butter-yellow bowl of truffles. Picking up a moment truffle, she bit into the rich chocolate.

Warm lips. Scent of cedar and coffee. The touch of his hand against her cheek washed over her in soothing waves. She let the memory tremble through her a moment before she signed a release symbol in the air. The moment faded.

"Told you," Peri singsonged as she swept past Orriana's face. "Your memory was of him, wasn't it?"

Glaring at the smart-mouthed faerie, Orriana snatched a regret truffle out of the case. She had no regrets and she'd prove it.

She bit into the chocolate, and the caramel was bitter against her tongue, the pecans hard against her mouth as the image of Doug walking out the door played over and over.

Was Peri right? Would she regret this moment?

Orriana reached out to the smoky coils that streamed around her, those diffused essences of business cards and franchise opportunities swirling around her. Doug's card was in there somewhere. She ran her fingers through the smoke, the regret aching in her bones. Maybe Peri was right?

She whispered his name into the smoke, her breath scattering the smoke. A last test. If he heard her voice, then maybe he'd understand about her magic and the chocolate.

The seconds fled past as she waited, hoping that Doug had heard her call to him. Her regret was a bright flame roiling at the memory of those warm brown eyes, that cedar coffee smell. Peri's frantic dance through the room made her pulse race, the flame growing hotter with "what ifs" and "should have beens" until Orriana couldn't stand anymore.

"Enough," she snapped, signing a gleaming release symbol in the air with her forefinger. The aching regret faded.

"Told you," Peri repeated with a giggle.

"I'm not selling out my magic!" Orriana shouted, shooing Peri away from her. "Not for Doug or anyone!"

The bell on the door chimed, and the door creaked open.

Orriana froze. Doug Ackerfield stood in the doorway, a lost look on his face.

"Magic?" he asked, his eyes wide. "Real magic?"

"What are you doing here?"

He stared at her a moment, his hair a little windblown, those brown eyes glassy.

"I was three blocks away when I heard you call my name. Was it part of this magic?"

Orriana nodded. "All of it's magic."

His mouth fell open as he watched Peri soar around his head and leap away.

"You see her?" Orriana asked.

He nodded.

"How? Mundanes don't see the magical world."

He took a step toward her, laying a hand on her arm. "But you're wrong. We may not recognize what we see, but we do see things. And taste them. So the chocolates are magic?"

"Every one."

"What was in the butter cream? The one you insisted I eat?"

Orriana sighed, her gaze falling to the floor. "I accidentally gave you a love wish truffle, so I had to undo that. With a breakup butter cream. It was easier than the truth."

He smiled, cupping her chin and she shivered at his warmth, wishing things could be different.

"So the spell's been broken, right?"

Orriana nodded and Doug stepped closer.

"But it doesn't change anything," she said with a sigh. "I have to leave now. Now that you know about the magic."

He shook his head as he pulled the cell phone out of his pocket. With his thumb, he tapped out some numbers and put the phone against his ear.

"Craig, this is Doug. Yeah, I'm at the shop right now."

"No!" Orriana cried and lunged for the phone, but he stepped out of her reach, pacing toward the display case.

"Turns out the recipes weren't original after all," he said, grinning at Orriana as he stepped behind the counter. "Yeah, can you believe it? Said she imports the chocolates from some shop down in Guatemala."

Doug stepped into the kitchen and Orriana followed. He peered into the spotless sink and at the pristine stove then turned to her, smiling. "Trust me, I've seen the kitchen. She's never even fired up the stove. Right, I'll call around first thing tomorrow, see if I can locate the importer. Tear up the papers? Will do. See you tomorrow, Craig."

He closed the phone and dropped it back in his coat pocket. Orriana grabbed hold of his arm. He slid the papers out of his pocket and tore them in half. He tossed them into the air.

"You just threw away a multimillion-dollar deal."

He slid his arms around her waist, shrugging as bits of paper landed like confetti on the floor. "There's always another deal. But real magic . . . that's something to protect."

"That takes care of your company. But what about the others?"

"I'll spread the story around, make sure you aren't bothered anymore by what'd you call us—mundanes?"

Orriana nodded.

"When I'm done, no more corporations will bother us."

"Us?" she asked with a smile.

He nodded. "Even mundanes want to believe in magic. Some even have a little of our own."

"What magic?" she asked.

He leaned toward her. "I'm still here. And I didn't give you any love wish truffles," he said. "Now, I want to talk about a different kind of franchise. Just you and me."

"I'm listening," she said.

He pressed his mouth against hers, and she closed her eyes as the static charge rushed through her. He was right. Maybe the mundanes did have their own magic. She'd certainly fallen for it.

Orriana slid her arms around his neck and kissed him back. It was the one mundane thing better than chocolate.

NO REST FOR THE WICKED

by Michael A. Stackpole

THERE were lots of reasons I hated Johnny Dawes. The way he slapped my back as he entered Club Flesh was fast moving up on the list. It hurt. He always caught me on the scar from the bullet that had shattered my left shoulder blade.

It was easy for him to hit me there. He'd been the one who pumped that bullet into me. That one, and a couple more.

That shooting thing, that was pretty high up on the list, too.

The same question always came with the backslap. It bugged the hell out of me.

"No one's killed you yet, Molloy?"

"No one's that good."

I always gave him the same answer. It bugged the hell out of him.

He stared at me with cold, dark eyes. I'd heard it said he'd once killed with a glance. I almost let myself believe it. His gaze did send a chill through me, but the club's dark, stuffy heat warmed me again fast.

He broke off the stare and smiled at the bartender. "The Dom, Eddie, please."

"Sure thing, Mr. Dawes. Up in VIP, right?"

"Perfect." Dawes purred the word, and Eddie's face brightened. That tone, that smile; Dawes was feeling generous. He expressed it with C-notes, and they came in showers. That made everyone around Club Flesh happy—servers, dancers, even the other bouncers.

Hell, me, too. I was no Boy Scout. I took my cut. I always used it to buy myself the biggest, bloodiest steak I could find.

It reminded me of what I'd looked like after he shot me.

Eddie gave me a glance and shook his head. "I don't know why you don't like him, Trick. Guys like that don't have to be generous."

I nodded. Dawes was the sort of sugar daddy all girls dreamed of. Tall, slender, dark and handsome, a flashy dresser without resorting to cheap jewelry, he could have stepped off a fashion-show runway in Milan or New York. The touch of gray at his temples made him more distinguished. Even the banded collars and slender black chokers he wore, with that big ruby brooch at his throat, made him look sinister—and lots of girls squealed over that.

"It ain't that he dresses better than you, is it?"

"Nope, Eddie, it ain't that." I turned away from the bar, hoping Eddie wouldn't continue. He already knew all the reasons I hated Dawes—the shooting, being framed for a crime that got me busted from the force, Chrystale, all that. Just none of them worked for him. He kept trying to find the *real* reason.

Eddie jammed the bottle of champagne into the ice bucket with a wet crunch. "It's a *talent*-thing, right?"

"Prolly." Like anyone else who couldn't use magick, for Eddie, the mysteries of life became explained by magick. Since the vast majority of people had no talent, they flat didn't believe it existed or were very afraid of it. Sometimes both—which is why televangelists flourish still. Those of us with *talent* could spot it in others.

Sometimes the result felt like poison ivy on the soul. With Dawes and me, it was leprosy.

And other times it was like falling in love. Which made it all the worse when you weren't.

Music shifted, began to pound. I knew the song well. I thought of it as *her* song. It defined her. I'd be sleeping, hear it faintly through a wall, and she'd creep into my dreams. A woman on the street humming it would seem that much prettier. I'd ridden elevators playing a Muzak version well past my floor, chuckling that private way you do after leaving a sweaty night with your lover.

Chrystale. She took center stage wearing a white gown slit to the hip. White stockings clung to her long, slender legs. Golden hair cascaded to the small of her back, rising as she spun, exposing her bare spine. My fingers tingled, caressed with distant memories. Her blue eyes flashed, warm, challenging; her smile daring the men in the club to approach her. A proffered dollar might get a laugh. Five, a hug. More would get dreams, and more might make them come true.

Fat wallets bulimically vomited money. Patrons would remember the night as enchanting. They couldn't help but. All the dancers at Club Flesh had *talent*. It was part of the business. Most were minor *glamor* girls. A few were *sirens*.

Chrystale was a full-blown *enchantress*. With a whisper and a caress she could make any man believe he was the most desirable man in the world. He'd keep believing it as long as he paid. The lucky ones might even believe it a little bit longer.

Chrystale had talent, tons of it, but *talent* alone isn't enough. Magick isn't the simple flash-bang crap Hollywood tosses on the screen. If you're gonna use it, you have to find your trigger—the thing that frees your magick to work.

She'd found it: music. Any music would do, fast, slow, didn't matter. But when it was a song she connected with, that was something special. She could put a smile on the faces at Mount Rushmore.

In addition to your trigger, you had to figure out your channel. For most of us it was something simple—earth, air, fire, water, that kind of thing. Some joked that Chrystale's channel was wood. If it had been, she'd have been doing erotic puppet shows with marionettes. Instead she pulled customers' strings.

Her channel was more esoteric. It was rare. Emotion, seduction, love, maybe. Even someone with talent couldn't be sure what his channel was. If you found out, you never told anyone. It could make you vulnerable.

Lastly, you had to handle the power. Most talents were barely practical. A guy with chili peppers as a trigger and fire as a channel might need to down a bushel basket before he could light a cigarette. To get that right, he'd have to practice a lot, too. Most folks didn't have the smarts or patience to put it all together.

But there were exceptions. Chrystale had learned to handle the power early in her life. I'd heard dozens of stories. She needed it to handle a perverted uncle. Maybe she was sold as a slave to some emir. Why she learned doesn't matter. Even sitting far from the stage, I could feel it—and I was the last person she wanted to be attracting. I just caught the overflow from what she was using on the knot of bikers stage front.

Her overflow was what made me miss the itch at first. I should have picked up on him the second the guy walked in. Massive and built, he wore tan jeans and a jacket. The denim jacket had the same club colors the others wore. That should have told me something right there. Most gangs don't allow variant uniforms.

This guy was all variant. He had his blond hair in a Mohawk. He had a hard look on his face. Every guy who came in thinking he was going to score some pussy tried to look tough. Quick on, though, they smile, hopeful against hopeless. But this guy, rigor mortis had set in on his face.

The itch came when he started for Chrystale. The guy might tip. He might not. One thing was for sure. He *was* going to cause trouble.

"Eddie, set me up, quick."

The urgency in my voice widened his eyes. "Sure, Trick. You want the six or the twelve?"

"Knappogue Castle, the fifty."

"The fifty? Jesus, Trick, that's a Cee a glass. Are you sure? I have to get the keys."

"Shit." I didn't have time to argue. I reached over and grabbed the bottle of twelve-year-old Tullamore Dew. I popped the spout off and took a hard pull. The whiskey burned down my throat. Another swallow, then I set the bottle down and wiped my mouth on my sleeve. Sliding off the barstool, I cut around past VIP. I approached the stage from opposite the guy. For just a second I could feel Dawes behind me, his eyes boring into me.

I shot a glance in his direction, but his stare got eclipsed. Brittnee, a new hire, barely a *glamor* girl, had plunked herself in his lap. She wanted him because he was dangerous. *Not as dangerous as Chrystale. Watch your back, little girl.* Dawes was a cold-blooded killer, but Chrystale did it with green-eyed fury.

I locked back onto Mr. Mohawk. Getting closer, the itch dug in with claws. He felt it, too. It tore him away from looking at Chrystale. That took some powerful magic. His face hardened, and his hands knotted. He felt he was up to it.

Barely a dozen feet apart, our *talents* ran up against each other. I saw him through magic. It wasn't the sort of picture I wanted to be seeing. Most guys would be leopard-spotted with weaknesses. Pick one. Bang. They're gone.

This guy glowed gold like a knight in armor. That usually meant his channel was fire. That intense a glow and he was triggered to the gills.

Light coalesced in the palm of his right hand. It grew into a knife about a foot long. He gave me a hard stare and growled. "You really don't want the kind of trouble I am."

Blue plasma pooled in my palm. I opened my hand and it shot up to eye-level, like water from a fountain.

Mr. Mohawk laughed. His knife grew. "Mine's bigger."

I shrugged. "It ain't the size of the ship, but the motion of the ocean . . ." The blue light pulsed again, rising, falling, up and down, swelling and shrinking. It got a little warm—the temperature of beer that's been left out too long, left out until it becomes flat and sour. Stale. Stale beer, just rocking in your stomach, rocking with the motion of a boat on the ocean. A small boat rising and falling with the swells, the endless swells that slosh the warm stale beer around . . .

Mr. Mohawk jackknifed forward and vomited all over one of his buddies. His golden glow gone, he landed on his knees, then plopped face-forward in a puddle of vomit. His body convulsed. A bit more beer jetted from him. He slackened.

Problem solved.

Such was Chrystale's hold on her audience that the biker wearing Mohawk's last six-pack barely knew he was wet. Anyone who had seen the man go down wouldn't remember anything but his standing, turning gray, and puking. They'd not remember me or the confrontation.

No magick, no fight, nothing to haunt nightmares.

In fact, if it weren't for the screaming, chances were they'd *only* remember Chrystale. The scream slashed into Chrystale's music. Discord killed her magic. Brittnee hit notes no human throat should ever produce. She created sounds no one could have turned into beauty.

I spun. Brittnee, hands clawed and covering her bare breasts, had slid from Johnny Dawes' lap. Blood drenched her. Her eyes were stark in a glistening, fluid mask. Another gush of blood choked off her scream.

Johnny had slumped back on the couch. His head lolled to the side. The problem was that his head lolled two *feet* to the side. His heart pumped gushers of blood to drip down the wall.

Eddie appeared at my side. "Oh, shit!"

"You can put the Dom back in the cooler, Eddie."

"I guess." He shook his head. "I better call the cops, huh?"

"Yeah, they'll be all over this. And, Eddie, the fifty . . . Find the goddamned keys."

"Gotcha, Trick. I'm pouring two." He smiled. "I ain't sure what it does for you, but I know what it will do for me. After seeing that, though, I don't think it will be enough."

You're not supposed to speak ill of the dead. I was in a mood to scream it. I wasn't sad Dawes was dead. I liked it.

What I didn't like was feeling cheated. He tried to kill me. He got me busted from the force. He stole my woman. He then offered me a job. He was the only one who would in this town.

I took it to eat, sure. But I also wanted to be close to him. Close enough to kill him some day.

"Looks like it just wasn't his day."

I glanced up. Detective Winston Prout stood there, his face all mashed up like someone was trying to juice it for disgust. He wore white from head to toe, including a straw skimmer of the kind that died in the big Depression before last. It should have stayed dead. Even his shoulder holster was white. He would've owned a white pistol, too, but gunpowder does stain.

He also had no talent. I'm not referring to magick, either. Fact that he caught this case meant two things. Top brass didn't give a crap about who did it. They liked Bennie Saint for it, and that's who Prout would give them. Unless, of course, he found a way to toss me into the mix.

"Dawes had better days."

"Won't anymore, just like you, Molloy."

The guys from the meat wagon pulled the stretcher out of VIP One. Where they put his head under the sheet made it look like he'd died of elephantiasis. Fitting. Guys always said he had balls the size of watermelons.

"Detective, you have something to ask me? You know we're not going to discuss the 'good old days.' "

"Look, Molloy, I was in Internal Affairs, and your case fell to me. Now I'm in Homicide and caught this. You dirty in this one, too?"

Just for a second I glanced at him through magick. Looked like he had black measles. One hit. One poke. So tempting. *So very tempting.*

I let it go. "Here's the deal. I woulda been happy to slag Dawes. I was hoping to get evidence that he framed me. He was worth more to me alive than dead."

Prout scratched a note into his PDA. "He was seeing Chrystale Malvin, right? Stole her from you?"

"Refreshing your memory?"

"Hey, you know I have to ask."

"Yeah." I looked past him at where Chrystale was huddled under a blanket, face streaked with mascara. A policewoman, a uniform, was talking to her. I don't think Chrystale was hearing much, though. She just clutched a cup of coffee. I was hoping Eddie spiked it good.

I studied Prout's face. Good little churchgoer like he hated being in Club Flesh. It repelled him. And it attracted him. He'd be dreaming about it for a long time. And praying about it for longer.

"Chrystale and me, long over. She'd gone to him. Alpha male gets all the pussy, right?"

Prout flinched. "Who else has a motive? Bennie Saint? Mrs. Dawes? The girl he was doing when he died?"

"Bennie, sure? They split the profits from the rackets. Easier to divide by one, you know?" I leaned back against the bar and spread my arms out. "Britnee? No chance. She thought she could replace Chrystale. Not the first. Wouldn't have been the last."

"Did Chrystale think she was being replaced?"

"You asked her, so you know." I shook my head. "I didn't see anything like that."

Prout smiled venomously. "And you were watching, right, pick her up on the rebound."

"Yeah, that's me. I work in a club with a hundred women prancing through here half naked, and I have one-itis for a stripper? I've had more women than you've had wet dreams. Next question."

"Was Mrs. Dawes the jealous type?"

"Don't know her. You'll have to ask her." I shrugged again. "I'll tell you this. If she was and she did this, she's been damned patient."

Prout nodded, then lowered his voice and moved closer. "I think this was talent related. You *feel* anything?"

"Hey, Prout, I ain't freaking Gandalf. The coroner has some forensic *talent*. Ask her." I leaned forward, too, lowered my voice. "What did him?"

"Choker he was wearing sawed right through his neck."

I sat back, surprise all over my face. If it was magick, if it involved an enchanted device, that was highly specialized talent. If there was a hitter running around with that sort of ability . . . I ran a finger around to loosen my collar.

"You got something for me, Molloy?"

"Jesus, don't talk to me like I'm your favorite snitch."

"It's against the law to withhold evidence."

"No? Really? I wish they'd covered that at the academy."

"You should have paid attention at the academy. They covered bribery." Prout snorted. "Oh, yeah, you majored in it."

I wanted to kick him in the nuts hard enough that they'd nail his hat to the ceiling. I let that urge go, too. Not sure why. I guess it was because I figured he didn't have any balls.

I sighed, just exhausted. "I come up with anything, I'll let you know."

He made a note of that, then gave me a nod. Dismissive. I would have kicked him for that, but he moved on.

I levered myself away from the bar and crossed over to where Chystale was sitting. I nodded to the uniform. Friendly. She returned it and backed away a bit. I sat and pulled a chair closer.

Chrystale didn't even look at me. "Don't start, Trick."

"Don't start what?"

"Anything. Not now. You can't think that this . . . that Johnny's dying . . . that it changes anything between us."

"Hey, I know you're the one that broke my heart. I'm still looking for pieces. But I also know you were the one who came to intensive care. You were there. You snuck me whiskey. Doctors think it was a miracle."

"It was Tully Twelve." She swiped fingers over her cheeks, smearing them black. "It was that bitch, Britnee. She stole my perfume and doused herself. She said it would make Johnny fall for her."

"Think that's her trigger?"

Chrystale shook her head. "I don't care." She looked over at me, her eyes still beautiful despite the silence. "Did you know I was quitting? Two months. Johnny and I were going to go away."

"Don't, Chrystale."

"Don't what?"

My eyes narrowed. "Remember what you said to me that first time? When we were laying there all tangled in the sheets? You told me, 'Never fall in love with a stripper because, at some point, we'll lie to you.' You never did to me. Don't start now."

She snorted, then sniffed and snagged a tissue from the box between her feet. "You're an idiot. I lied to you from the start. I lied when I told you I loved you, and I kept on lying. Then Johnny came along. He was better."

Her words came cold and gushed into my guts. The

whiskey should have been warm in my belly, but it froze over. Ice needles skewered my stomach. I would have puked, but they kept everything caged in down there.

I gave myself a second, and the obvious question came out. "What did you lie to him about?"

"You don't want to know."

"I do."

"I told him you were a better lover than you ever were." She looked at me. "Why are you making me do this to you? Just go away."

"Not going to happen, Chrystale. A friend needs my help."

"Don't you get it? I was never really your friend."

"Okay, so I owe you a debt. I want to repay it. Is that a problem?"

She thought for a moment, then just kind of wilted. "Take me home."

I went to work on Prout, and he questioned Chrystale a second time. I didn't listen. I guess he got all the same answers because he released her. She wandered into the dressing room and changed. Out of her heels, wearing baggy sweats and a baseball cap, you'd never have known who she was.

I tucked her into my car. "You have to give me directions."

She looked at me. Her expression said "Don't even try to tell me you don't know where I live," but then she shook her head. "Can't go there. Too many memories. Take me to your place."

I did as commanded and tucked her into my bed. I closed the door and sat on the couch thinking. That's a dangerous thing for a man with a belly full of whiskey who can work magick. I opened my hand, and the blue plasma gathered. It flowed into a simulacrum of Chrystale. She stood in my palm and then, matching the music running through my head, she began to dance.

I would have kept watching well past dawn, but my

phone rang. The ringtone made Chrystale go all spastic. I closed my hand, then answered the phone. "Trick. Make me happy."

She did. Cate Chase, the county coroner, shared my hatred of Johnny Dawes. He'd given her some of the toughest cases she'd ever seen. Not a single conviction, either. Having him on her table was enough to make her millennium.

She confirmed what Prout had said. The choker had garroted him cleanly. "Magick, no doubt. Interesting enchantment, too. Can you come down here? You got to see this."

"Is he still stretched out on the slab?"

"Big as life." She laughed. "Well, a head shy of that, really."

Cate Chase was one of those women that frustrate their mothers. "You'd be so pretty, dear, if you lost a few pounds. You have such nice bone structure." It was true of Cate, but the bone structure fitted a linebacker, not a ballerina.

No complaints.

Toe shoes and pirouettes weren't much use slicing and dicing corpses.

For a linebacker, she was hot. Two months in a gym, some roadwork, and she'd have pulled long green at Club Flesh. Guys always have that amazon fantasy. Red hair, creamy skin that never saw the sun, she'd have been a star. She even had talent, but being able to analyze stomach contents with magick has limited value on the stage.

"Good to see you, Trick."

"You, too, Cate." I looked around. "This won't get you in trouble, right?"

"Naw. Anyone complains, Johnny's head shows up in their bed." She waved me over to a table where she'd set up one of those Styrofoam wig stands. She took the choker out of a plastic bag and slipped it around the neck on the stand. She tightened it up, then centered the ruby.

"This was on the outside of his shirt, right?" She grabbed a square bottle of cologne. "He wore *Warlock* by Michael Kors. Hundred bucks a fluid ounce, but just a dab will do you."

She spritzed it over the neck and choker. I caught the scent in the back draft. Citrus, some flowers, some spice I recognized from Singh's House of Curry. I didn't like it, but Johnny hadn't worn it for me.

Cate picked up a rounded bottle. "Now, this is . . ."

"*Possession.*"

She looked at me with new eyes. "Side of you I don't know?"

"I do fetch-and-carry work. I've made runs to the store."

"Okay. So one of the girls there wears this. She must do well. Pricier than *Warlock.*" Cate extended the perfume bottle as if it were bug spray and pumped it once. The perfume puffed out, a thin, musky cloud that drifted down slowly.

Crack! The choker contracted, popping the head off the wig stand. It flipped up and bounced down, rolling to a rest two feet away. Just like Johnny's head.

I went to reach for the choker and the ruby brooch, but Cate slapped my hand away. "You'll lose a finger."

"Looked like the brooch had a spring-loaded reel in it."

"It would have if some tinker were putting it together. This was definitely talent." She poked a pencil down behind the brooch and lifted the choker. "The magick got triggered when the two scents mixed. The girl had some *Possession* on her wrist and slipped her hands around his neck. The magic tightened the fibers in the fabric, and Mr. Dawes lost his head."

I scratched at my jaw. "Pretty sophisticated stuff, that magic."

Cate laughed at me. "Are you kidding? Hello? Didn't you used to be a detective?"

"What am I missing?"

"This magick is dirt common." She smiled. "You're

wearing jeans. What the hell do you think 'shrink to
fit' means?"

I blinked. "Magick does that?"

"Yep. Shrink, stretch, dry cleaners do it all the
time."

"No kidding? How about the perfume trigger?"

"Takes some learning, but it's not an unknown
skill." Her smile broadened. "Turns out that many
folks in the laundry business use something similar for
getting out stains."

I raised an eyebrow. "So there's a dry cleaner-
hitman out there?"

"Stranger things, my friend . . ." She frowned and
pointed at my chirping phone.

I checked Caller ID. "Stranger things indeed. I better take this."

"Who is it? Prout?"

I shook my head. "Nope. The grieving widow. I
wonder what she wants."

I should have cleaned up before I went to visit Mrs.
Dawes, but I didn't want to go back to my place and
disturb Chrystale. I'd never been to Dawes' house, but
I knew where it was. Everyone did. Up in Union
Heights. Not the biggest house, not the highest on the
hill, but real nice. Could have fit my apartment in the
pool house and Club Flesh in the garage.

A little Latina answered the door and conducted
me into a book-lined study. Books had been bought
by the yard by some decorator. The dark brown of
leather spines and shelves contrasted with the pastel
lime on the walls and carpet. Massive room, lots of
windows looking out over the city. At noon it was
light, airy. At night, the view would be spectacular.

Same could be said of the widow. Brunette, olive
skin, shorter than Chrystale, but with many of the
same curves. She dressed well, really well. Her heels
weren't platforms. Her skirt matched the gray jacket
on a chair. The ivory blouse had the collar up, but
enough buttons had been undone that I could see a

little lace and a lot of cleavage. Full lips and large brown eyes in a strong face. When she smiled, it looked genuine.

Even though she showed far less flesh than most of the young girls coming to the club, I found her hot. Dawes had been a fool. I'd known that all along. Now I just knew how much of a fool.

"Thank you for coming, Mr. Molloy."

"You can call me Trick."

She glanced down, heavy lashes hiding her eyes. "I abhor nicknames. Patrick would be your given name?"

I nodded.

"I am Altair. My father built this house. Vincent Battielle."

"I know. He was the local Godfather." I raised a hand. "Don't get your Irish up. I know he did good things with some of his money. When Johnny hooked up with you, your father split the business between him and Bennie Saint, then retired to Tucson. Johnny wasn't as good as your father."

"I know."

"Why'd you stay with him? You had to know he was sticking it to anything with two X chromosomes."

A little fire played in her eyes, but I didn't get the itch. "Love can be emotional and physical. I didn't care what he did with his body. His heart was my concern. That's all I care to say on that matter."

"Okay, then why call me?"

Altair waved me to one of those stick-and-cloth chairs older than the country. I sat easy, waiting for it to crack. She seated herself in its mate. She did a better job of it.

"I understand you believe my husband had you framed and thrown off the force. He falsified information that you had taken bribes."

"You're well informed."

"It might be that within his papers, there is some form of evidence—exculpatory evidence—that would exonerate you. I would offer you a trade. That evidence for your services."

"What kind of services?"

"You still have ties to the police. They are stone-walling my lawyers, but we both know they will be considering me a prime suspect. I want to know what they know."

My eyes narrowed. "Do you have some exposure here?"

"Let us imagine that I came to believe my husband's affections were wandering away in more than just the physical realm." She kept her voice strong, and studied her nails the way a cat inspects its claws. "Let us further imagine I might have discussed with an individual if there was a way to work an enchantment on one of his chokers to have it tighten slightly—slightly, mind you, nothing more—under certain circumstances."

"That's a lot more imagination than I got." I leaned forward, ignoring the chair's protest. "Did you talk to someone about that? The cleaners who do your stuff?"

Altair shook her head. "I've given you enough to see why I have concerns. Do we have a bargain or not?"

I stood. "Look, lady, I don't know if you whacked your husband or not. I don't care. If you did, I'd shake your hand, kiss your ass, whatever you wanted. But if I do what you want, and you *did* kill him, then the cops will haul me in with you as an accessory after the fact, for conspiracy and any other charges they want to make up. Did you do for Johnny Dawes or not?"

"No."

"But you did talk to someone about the choker."

"Yes."

"Who?"

She looked up at me, her face set, eyes watching for my reaction. "Bennie Saint."

She wanted reaction? She got reaction.

I sat down. Hard. The chair held. "Bennie Saint?"

A bunch of things clicked together in my head. "You thought you could mention this idea to him, show him Johnny was vulnerable. You give him a shot at killing his rival. Was that enough, or did your physical affections wander, too?"

"Do you want the information I have, Mr. Molloy, or not?"

"I don't really know."

"That's a stupid answer."

"No, it's not. See, I have to figure something." I watched her for a reaction. "I have to figure if you were innocent, if you did what you did knowing what you were doing, or if you did it figuring to have your husband killed and have Bennie fingered for it. They go away, and daddy's little girl gets the business. That's it, isn't it? It's all business for you?"

"That answer is well above your pay grade, Mr. Molloy." She smiled primly. "The question is are you and I going to do business?"

The short answer was yes. Over the next week it got to feeling like I was almost back on the force. It was like it had been before. I'd be out, sniffing around, meeting guys at coffee shops, donut stands, diners, even the club. Some guys would talk, others would just glare. It split along the lines of who thought I'd been framed and not. More in the not camp, but I'd known that.

I even shadowed the shadowers. I went to the Dawes funeral, dressed up in my best suit. Chrystale helped me tie the tie. I went, watched for folks. Big Bennie Saint was front row with the mourners. If Altair had gotten physical with him, she was either in love or really dedicated. I'd heard Bennie once found a princess enchanted into a frog, but when he went to kiss her, she croaked that she didn't date outside her species.

Prout showed up, both at the church and when they slid Johnny into the Battielle Mausoleum. He had guys taking pictures and writing down license numbers. I got some good shots of him, too. The nose picking one will be useful, I'm sure.

For all that work, though, I heard nothing. I knew Altair would keep me on a string until someone fell for the crime. Prout and his bosses were pushing for Bennie to go. Had I been in Prout's shoes, I'd have coached a confidential informant into being an eyewitness. It wasn't like Saint was a Saint, after all.

Best part of that ten days was Chrystale. She was still torn up. Torn up real bad. Strippers might lie to you, but mobsters, they die on you. One *is* worse than the other. I felt for her, I really did.

She got all apologetic about kicking me out of my own bed, but she didn't offer to share. She did clean up some. She would have done laundry, but she couldn't understand why I insisted on buying new shirts instead of washing the old. She cooked. She always could cook. She even made me a couple of the things I remembered from before.

We were sitting on the couch, soft music playing. She looked at me. "I probably should be going, Trick."

"You don't have to." I wanted to reach out and just pull her to me, just to hold her. Nothing more, really. But I didn't. "You can stay as long as you want."

"No, I can't, Trick." She picked up the remote and killed the pod. "Look at me now, without the music."

"What? You weren't magicking me."

"But I could have. I wanted to." She'd pulled her hair back into a ponytail and tied it with a red scrunchy. "It's my nature, Trick. I want people to see the best of me, and that means they see through magick."

I took one of her hands in mine. "No, baby, that's not it. You don't have to use magick with me. You just have to be yourself."

"But that's who I am, Trick. I'm Chrystale. I play with your heart, then I break it. That's all I'm good for."

"No, it's not."

"Then it's all I'm good *at*." She pointed the remote at the pod again. "Do you want me to start it? Do you want me to wrap you up in music, in me? I'll squeeze you tighter than that choker. You'll forget everything. Who you are, what we've done, you'll remember none of it. Is that what you want?"

"No. I don't want that." I shook my head, then reached out for the remote. She let me take it. "All I want is to know why you feel you have to go."

She glanced down, and falling tears dappled her gray sweats. "I have to go because if I don't, I'm never going to want to leave."

She left later that night. I helped her pack. She said she'd bring the duffel bag back to me. She lied. We both knew it, but it was a lie I could live with. When the door closed behind her, I retreated to my bedroom. I dove into the bed and wrapped myself up in sheets that smelled of *Possession* and Chrystale.

And I slept.

I didn't get to sleep as long as I wanted. Half asleep I answered the phone. Cate's voice, not Chrystale's. Images in my dream shifted, going places I didn't want to. That brought me fully awake.

"Fourth and Main. You'll want to get down here, Trick."

I pictured the intersection. I ruled out the two chain coffeehouses and the bodega. "Solomon Meier, tailor?"

"Someone will be sewing him a shroud."

"I'll be down in a heartbeat."

"Don't be in a hurry. He isn't."

I'd only met Meier once, and I'd felt the itch. A body we figured Dawes had killed had been clutching an ivory button. I made the rounds, looking for anyone who could identify it or might be asked to replace it. Meier said he didn't know it, but would get in touch if someone wanted it replaced. The boys in organized

crime later told me they had a file on him. He specialized in fitting suits to make shoulder holsters invisible.

Cate found me, gave me a visitor tag and led me
to the alley behind the shop. The body lay crumpled
beside a dumpster. "When I saw him before, Cate, his
head was a lot more round."

"Tire irons will create some havoc." She pointed.
"The murderer waited behind the dumpster, clubbed
him good, even stepped in his brains as he was leaving.
Size thirteen, nice shoes. We'll match them easy."

"Size thirteen. Big boy. Bennie Saint's size."

"Prout's off trying to locate Saint to check for an
alibi."

I glanced down at the mortal remains of Solomon
Meier one last time, then Cate's aides shooed the
house flies from his face and started tucking him into
a body bag. "He looks a little stiff. How long?"

"Killed four hours ago, give or take."

Prout came trotting over with a triumphant grin that
even my presence couldn't erase. "Just got a call from
the Dawes house. Half hour ago, gunshots. Murder-
suicide, the widow and Bennie Saint. He did her,
then himself."

Cate shook her head. "How does that make any
sense?"

I connected the dots for them. I didn't tell them I'd
talked to the widow. I just speculated. Cate remained
skeptical. Prout listened like he was at a revival
meeting.

Then he decided to give his testimony. "It all fits.
Meier did the magick, probably tried for a payoff to
keep his mouth shut. Bennie goes to the widow to tell
her they have a complication, but that he's taken care
of it. She tells him he's an idiot, she doesn't love him,
and he's going down. He kills her, then himself."

I frowned. "Why kill himself?"

"Remorse. He killed the woman he loved."

I laughed. "A gangster like Saint showing remorse?
No one will believe that."

I was wrong on that count, of course. The brass

believed it. So did the press. We'd gotten the trifecta inside two weeks. The local Syndicate had been decapitated. Made for great headlines. Changed nothing on the street.

I asked around. The cops who went through all the papers at the Dawes' house never found any evidence I'd been framed. Most of them were sympathetic. Prout wasn't smart enough to find it and stash it. It had to have been someone else.

If it ever existed.

Life continued, 'cept Chrystale left Club Flesh. Or she never came back. I didn't know what happened to her. I tried not to care. It was tough.

I almost made it.

Then, about a week after she'd left, a bottle of Knappogue Castle, the fifty-year-old stuff, arrived at my apartment. There was a note attached. "I'll love you until the day I die. ~C"

He came out of the darkness slowly. He walked as if without a concern in the world. "Come to pay your last respects?"

I took another pull from the half-empty bottle, then set it down. "I came to piss on your grave. Nobody was home."

"Did she tell you, or did you figure it out?"

"I got it. Cops never found the files your wife offered me to clear my name." I shrugged. "You're the only person who gained by having those files vanish."

"Well done, Molloy." Johnny Dawes laughed, but it didn't come out right. Happens when you had your head stitched back on by a tailor. "You have no idea what you're tangling with, whereas I know *you* inside and out."

I gathered the magick and looked at him through it. He became a man of onyx. Blackness meant weakness. Not here. It armored him, made him stronger.

I sheathed myself in blue and let plasma dance and play in each palm.

He laughed at me. "Water is your channel."

"Chrystale told you that?"

"That, and more. Everything. Whiskey is your trigger. You're powerful, but not powerful enough."

Dawes' head snapped up and tracked right to left. His eyes became a deeper dark. Black beams swept out. Something squealed above me. Wings flapping spasmodically, a bat slammed into the mausoleum.

It fell to the ground, dead.

I got it as he turned his gaze on me. Didn't know what his trigger was. Champagne maybe? Didn't matter. His channel, though. Death.

And he was *strong*.

Black beams crushed me against the mausoleum. I hit my head. Stars exploded before my eyes. My magick faltered. My shield evaporated. Pain ripped through me. Three spots. The three entry wounds.

They'd been reopened. Blood started leaking. Bone cracked. Pieces of my shoulder blade ground in my back.

He released me. I slid to the ground. Blood glistened on the mausoleum facade.

He chuckled. It wasn't right at all and sent a chill through me. "Now you know, water boy. I'll finish what I started."

"Give it your best shot."

"I don't need to." He glanced at me again. He focused on my left arm. Muscles shrank. Fingernails got longer and brittle. Bones twisted with arthritis and liver spots dotted my flesh.

I invoked a shield and cut off his gaze. He pushed, I fought back. He relented. The shield closed around my arm like a cast, then slowly evaporated.

"Nice healing trick. Now I understand how you survived in the hospital. It really is immaterial, however. Death is a higher order than water."

I reached back and pulled myself to my feet. "If you're so strong, why use a gun on me, the tire iron on Meier?"

"You, I wanted you to hurt bad. Meier, I could have made it look like natural causes, but," he shrugged, "a clumsy murder made getting rid of Bennie and Altair simple. They stroked with a glance, and gunshots scrambled the evidence. So easy."

"I won't be easy."

"But you'll die anyway." He stared hard at me, but I was ready this time. I raised a shield on my left arm, mostly blue, with shimmers of white worked through it. I didn't block, I deflected. My shoulder screamed under the pressure, but I just needed a little time.

I gestured with my right hand. The blue plasma launched at him like a bullet. It hit him in the chest. Splattered like blue paint, then the droplets sank into the inky armor. Dawes shook, he shuddered and danced back a step.

He dropped his gaze. Not his guard.

"What did you do?"

I hugged my arm to my belly. "It's not water."

"What?"

"My channel isn't water." I nodded at the whiskey bottle. "Whiskey. Comes from some Gaelic something. Means water of life. My channel, it's life."

Dawes straightened up. "Idiot. I'm dead. I have become my channel. You're not strong enough to affect me."

He hit me again, jamming the shield back against me. He pushed, pushed hard. I hit the mausoleum hard. The shield pressed in. My chest tightened. Pain grew. A rib popped, two. His black beams gnawed at my shield. I tried to reinforce it. I couldn't.

He got through. Molten agonies geysered through my chest. Felt like stomach acid had gushed into my guts. Everything was on fire. My world began to close in. Darkness. Like before. Like when I'd been shot.

Then he screamed. It didn't sound right either, but that was good. He staggered back, blinked. Looked at me plainly, his armor gone. "What did you do?"

I coughed wetly. "Couldn't affect you. Just them."

He began to claw at his own flesh. He tried to get at them, to kill them. He tried to kill them all, but he couldn't. There were just too many.

Once, back before I was booted from the force, Cate promised me a good time. She took me to a place upstate called the Body Farm. On a secluded site forensic guys let bodies rot so they could see how it happened. Cate told me that inside of a week, maggots could consume sixty percent of a body's mass.

That little pulse of life I'd hit him with woke them up. They hatched. They were hungry. They worked fast. Dawes' flesh writhed as they moved beneath it. He clawed at his cheek. Flesh came away in his hand. Ivory maggots squirmed, dropping from face and fingers. One ate its way through his hand.

Dawes started dancing like a man on fire. He beat at invisible flames until his hands flew apart in a rain of bones. Then his gut began to expand, shredding clothes Solomon Meier had tailored. The bacteria in his guts merrily reproduced, releasing enough gas that he plumped right up. Pressure built, blew out at his left hip, dropping him.

He tried to stare at me again. An eyeball rolled from his head.

I stepped on it, felt it pop, then slid to the ground myself.

I grabbed the bottle of whiskey and raised it in a salute. "To your health."

She was waiting for me by the time I limped home. I understood the message with the bottle. It was what Dawes had said to her. He thought he was being clever, the way he used her. Then she learned the truth.

And she lied to him about me. She let me kill him for her.

Chrystale stepped from the shadows. Somewhere music played. Her music. She looked at me. Smiled.

"I love you, Trick."

I took her hand.

Sometimes you just want to believe the lie.

ABOUT THE AUTHORS

Editor **Loren L. Coleman** is a longtime novelist with over twenty books published, including the trilogy that recently relaunched the Conan novel line. He also edits for an online fiction site, BattleCorps.com, and is currently working with Adventure Boys, Inc. to develop a brand-new fiction property for young boys. *Wizards, Inc.* is his first anthology. Loren lives in Washington State with his wife and three children, two Siamese cats, and a neurotic border collie. He holds a black belt in traditional Taekwon Do, coaches youth sports, and is currently relearning the piano. He has also logged far too many hours on Xbox 360 playing Call of Duty 2 and Oblivion.

Orson Scott Card is the author of the novels *Ender's Game*, *Ender's Shadow*, and *Speaker for the Dead*, which are widely read by adults and younger readers, and are increasingly used in schools. Besides these and other science fiction novels, Card writes contemporary fantasy (*Magic Street*, *Enchantment*, *Lost Boys*), biblical novels (*Stone Tables*, *Rachel and Leah*), the American frontier fantasy series *The Tales of Alvin Maker* (beginning with Seventh Son), poetry (*An Open Book*), and many plays and scripts. He was born in Washington and grew up in California, Arizona, and

Utah. He served at a mission for the LDS Church in Brazil in the early 1970s. Besides his writing, he teaches occasional classes and workshops and directs plays. He recently began a long-term position as a professor of writing and literature at Southern Virginia University. Card currently lives in Greensboro, North Carolina, with his wife, Kristine Allen Card, and their youngest child, Zina Margaret.

Steve Perry was born and raised in the Deep South and has lived in Louisiana, California, Washington, and Oregon. Before turning to full-time freelance writing, Perry held a variety of jobs, including: swimming instructor and lifeguard; toy assembler; hotel gift shop and car rental clerk; aluminum salesman; martial arts instructor; private detective; Licensed Practical Nurse and Certified Physician's Assistant. Perry has sold dozens of stories to magazines and anthologies, as well as novels, animated teleplays, nonfiction articles, reviews, and essays, along with a couple of unproduced movie scripts. For the past several years he has concentrated on books, and is currently working on his fifty-seventh novel.

Phaedra Weldon lives and writes in Georgia. After a third-place win in the first volume of *Star Trek Strange New Worlds* anthology, Phaedra wrote other Star Trek pieces including an S.C.E. novella as well as fiction and source for the Classic BattleTech universe. She has placed several short stories in various anthologies, and is looking forward to the publication of her first novel about an astral-projecting investigator.

Mike Resnick is the winner of five Hugo Awards, a Nebula, and other major awards from the USA, France, Japan, Croatia, Spain, and Poland, and currently stands fourth on the all-time list of award winners (according to Locus). He is the author of more than fifty novels, fourteen collections, 175 short stories, and two screenplays, as well as the editor of more than forty anthologies. His work has been translated into twenty-two languages.

Annie Reed is an award-winning writer whose short fiction has appeared in *Ellery Queen Mystery Magazine*, three volumes of *Strange New Worlds*, and several DAW anthologies, including *Time After Time, Hags, Sirens, and Other Bad Girls of Fantasy*, and *Cosmic Cocktails*. She lives in Northern Nevada with her husband, daughter, and a varying number of high-maintenance cats. In addition to science fiction, she writes mystery, romance, and women's fiction

Over the past twenty-five years, **Nina Kiriki Hoffman** has sold novels, juvenile and media tie-in books, short story collections, and more than 200 short stories. Her works have been finalists for the Nebula, World Fantasy, Mythopoeic, Sturgeon, and Endeavour awards. Her first novel, *The Tread that Binds The Bones*, won a Stoker Award. Nina works at a bookstore, does production work for the *Magazine of Fantasy & Science Fiction*, and teaches short story writing through her local community college. She lives in Eugene, Oregon, with several cats, a mannequin, and many strange toys. Nina's newest young adult novel is *Spirits that Walk in Shadow*.

Jay Lake lives in Portland, Oregon, with his books and two inept cats, where he works on numerous writing and editing projects, including the World Fantasy Award-nominated *Polyphony* anthology series. His most current works are *Trial of Flowers* and *Mainspring*. Jay is the winner of the 2004 John W. Campbell Award for Best New Writer, and a multiple nominee for the Hugo and World Fantasy Awards.

Kristine Kathryn Rusch is a Hugo award-winning writer who was, once upon a time, a Hugo award-winning editor. She has published fiction in almost every genre under a variety of names. Her latest science fiction novel is *Buried Deep*. Her novella, "Diving into the Wreck," won Europe's most prestigious fiction award last year and this year won the *Asimov's* Reader's Choice Award. For more information, go to her web site at www.kristinekathrynrusch.com.

Laura Anne Gilman is the author of the popular Retrievers series, which includes *Staying Dead, Curse the Dark, Bring it On, Burning Bridges* and the forthcoming *Found in Darkness* (2008). She is also the author of the Grail Quest trilogy, and over twenty-five stories published in such magazines as *Realms of Fantasy, Amazing Stories, Dreams of Decadence, ChiZine,* and *Flesh & Blood,* and the anthologies *ReVisions, Powers of Detection I* and *II, Did You Say Chicks?,* and *Polyphony 6,* among many others. You can reach her via e-mail at wren-sergei@comcast.net or online at http:// suricattus.livejournal.com/.

Esther M. Friesner has published over thirty novels and over 150 short stories including Nebula Award winners "Death and the Librarian" and "A Birthday." She is at present best known for the *Chicks in Chainmail* anthology series she created and edited, the most recent being *Turn the Other Chick.* Her latest works include *Temping Fate* and *Nobody's Princess.* She lives in Connecticut with her family and assorted cats.

Dean Wesley Smith is the best-selling author of over eighty novels and a hundred short stories. His most recent two novels are *The Hunted,* a thriller written with Fred Stoeker, and *All Eve's Hallows,* a fantasy novel. He lives on the Oregon Coast with his wife, writer Kristine Kathryn Rusch, and five cats.

Kristine Grayson, who has been called "reigning Queen of paranormal romance," has published six funny paranormal romance novels. The most recent is *Totally Spellbound.* Her most recent short story, "The Last Vampire," appeared in *Time after Time,* published by DAW. She stays away from corporate environments, preferring to remain at home with her husband and their six cats.

Along with four cats and numerous seriously overworked computers, **Diane Duane** and her husband, Peter Morwood, live in a pastoral townland set in the foothills of the Wicklow Mountains. Diane enjoys travel, and she and Peter travel in Europe as much as possible. In her spare time, Diane collects recipes and cookbooks, gardens (weeding, mostly), studies German and Italian, listens to shortwave and satellite radio, and dabbles in astronomy, computer graphics, iaido, image processing, amateur cartography, desktop publishing, and fractals. She is trying to learn how to make more spare time.

Lisa Silverthorne has published over fifty short stories. She dreams about becoming a novelist and writes to discover the magic in ordinary things. Her first short fiction collection, *The Sound of Angels*, is now available. You can visit Lisa's web site at: http://www.drewes.org/

Michael A. Stackpole is an award-winning author and game designer, best known for his *New York Times* best-selling *Star Wars* novels. He believes firmly in research being vital for getting stories right. In this case, it involved a lot of study of the magical powers of Irish whiskey. His web site is www.stormwolf.com.

MERCEDES LACKEY

Reserved for the Cat

The *Elemental Masters* Series

In 1910, in an alternate Paris, Ninette Dupond, a penniless young dancer, recently dismissed from the Paris Opera, thinks she has gone mad when she finds herself in a conversation with a skinny tomcat. However, Ninette is desperate—and hungry—enough to try anything. She follows the cat's advice and travels to Blackpool, England, where she is to impersonate a famous Russian ballerina and dance, not in the opera, but in the finest of Blackpool's music halls. With her natural talent for dancing, and her magic for enthralling an audience, it looks as if Ninette will gain the fame and fortune the cat has promised. But the real Nina Tchereslavsky is not as far away as St. Petersburg...and she's not as human as she appears...

978-0-7564-0362-1

And don't miss the first four books of
The Elemental Masters:

The Serpent's Shadow	0-7564-0061-9
The Gates of Sleep	0-7564-0101-1
Phoenix and Ashes	0-7564-0272-7
The Wizard of London	0-7564-0363-4

To Order Call: 1-800-788-6262
www.dawbooks.com

DAW 23